Pra

"Molly Campbel
charming novel. It was such a pleasure to get lost in this world, and in Campbell's capable hands."
– Julie Klam, *New York Times* bestselling author of *The Stars in Our Eyes*

"*Crossing the Street* is a compelling story about all the different people in our lives who become family. Campbell draws us into her characters with heart and humor and with a unique voice that will stay with me for a long time. I can't wait to read her other books!"
– Camille Di Maio, author of *The Memory of Us* and *Before the Rain Falls*

"I am crazy about Molly Campbell's writing. Her characters are funny and real. Her storytelling is fresh and poignant. She breaks the rules and looks fabulous doing so. *Crossing the Street* is a surprising and unpredictable, thoroughly enjoyable read!"
– Amy Impellizzeri, award-winning author of *Lemongrass Hope* and *Secrets of Worry Dolls*

"A humorous coming-of-age story where secrets of the past collide with the present and family bonds are stretched to the limits of forgiveness. Quirky, hopeful, and wonderfully original."
—Beth Hoffman, *New York Times* bestselling author of *Saving CeeCee Honeycutt* on *Keep the Ends Loose*

"Miranda Heath, the earnest fifteen-year-old narrator of *Keep the Ends Loose*, has voice for days and a genius for description. Her casually brilliant observations about her family – which is both completely screwy and entirely real – will keep you in the edge of your seat. Miranda's creator, Molly Campbell has a true humorist's touch, light and occasionally scathing, but filled with compassion all the while."
—Robin Black, author of *Life Drawing, A Novel*

The World Came to Us

The World Came to Us

Molly D. Campbell

This is a work of fiction. Names, characters, places, and incidents either are the product of the author's imagination or are used fictitiously. Any resemblance to actual events, locales, organizations, or persons living or dead is entirely coincidental and beyond the intent of either the author or the publisher.

The Story Plant
Studio Digital CT, LLC
P.O. Box 4331
Stamford, CT 06907

Story Plant Paperback ISBN-13: 978-1-61188-281-0
Fiction Studio Books E-book ISBN: 978-1-945839-34-4

Visit our website at www.TheStoryPlant.com

First Story Plant paperback printing: October 2019

Printed in the United States of America

To my beautiful daughters

Chapter One

Π

"Mom. You can't become a recluse all by yourself." She stood in the doorway, her mouth a round "O" of surprise.

"Tommy, what are you doing here? And why didn't you come in the back door?"

"I didn't want to scare you. But you are scaring me right now. You look awful."

She stood her ground, not budging an inch from the threshold. I noticed the hollows of her cheeks and the greasy hair. Her stylish spikes looked as if they hadn't been shampooed in weeks. She wore pajamas. It was three o'clock in the afternoon.

"How do you know I am a 'recluse,' as you call it?"

"Mom. You have neighbors. Mrs. Cullen has called me three times to tell me she hasn't seen you outside in weeks. And we both know she is the neighborhood watchdog. And your brother. Rob says you won't let him in the house."

The funeral was a month ago. Attended only by close friends, the way Mommy had wanted it. In the small chapel at the Unitarian church, I had to concentrate very hard to hear the words that were spoken, the remembrances, and the songs that were sung. My entire chest felt as if a cannon ball had smashed it. It hurt to breathe. I have almost no memory of the reception that followed, the food, or the people who hugged us hard and cried, too. It is just a wash of color and noise in my head. The only clear picture of that whole afternoon is when Mom, Rob, and I each placed our mementos in the casket with Mommy. Rob gently placed a sprig of lavender on her collar. I put in the Teddy bear that Mommy gave me for my eighth birthday, and Mom laid her stethoscope across Mommy's shoulder in the casket before they closed it.

Sam Poole, my Mommy. The one who brushed my hair without ever pulling harshly at a snarl. The one who could always make me giggle at knock-knock jokes. The maker of my most favorite spaghetti casserole with black olives. The reader of countless bedtime books. She defended me from Howie Prescott, the meanest, ugliest bully at Framington Elementary. When I told her and Mom that Howie said he was going to kill me someday, Mommy called his mother and reminded the horrible woman that if Howie laid a finger on me, Mommy, as a veterinarian, would gladly neuter little Howie. Mommy. My dear Mommy died of cancer, Mom in bed with her, stroking her hair, and me sitting so close, holding her brittle hand.

Mom stood, still leaning against the doorway, her hand on the doorknob, barring my way. I set my duffel down on the front steps and put my hands on either side of her face, smoothing the pallid cheeks, feeling the bones of her skull under my fingers.

She put her hands over mine and her tears rolled over our fingers. "Tommy, you look as desolate as I feel."

She stepped aside, and I leaned down and grabbed my bag. I followed her into the hallway. I shut the door behind us. There wasn't much natural light; Mom had all the blinds downstairs closed. The desk in the front hall was covered with unopened mail. The stairway was cluttered with shoes, books, clothing, and wadded up Kleenex. It smelled like dust and coffee grounds. "You are holing up in here, Mom. I haven't taken five steps into this house, and already I am in shock."

What a pair we were. I, a thirty-year old adult career person, unable to cope with the death of one of my parents, wallowing in despair in my apartment in Columbus. My dearest remaining parent, isolating herself at home for a month after her wife's death, living in darkness and existing on coffee and tears. Evidently, she thought I was holding up just great, and I thought she was learning how to be a widow successfully, and both of us were lying to each other. *Ridiculous.*

"Why did you come home? I am coping." She rubbed her temples, and I saw that her fingernails had a fine line of dirt underneath. I caught a whiff of perspiration.

As I followed her into the living room, I could see the vertebrae of her back clearly through the jersey pajama top. We sat side by side on the sofa. The coffee table was covered in a layer of dust.

"Mom. You are not *coping.* This is not healthy. You are wasting away, all alone here."

"I am alone, and I *need* to be here by myself. I can't go anywhere or do anything just now." She looked at me, and the sadness radiated from her eyes, the droop of her cheeks, her shoulders, and her unwashed body. She let a drop fall from her nostril onto her chest. "I cannot go out. I need time."

I looked around at the dust covered table in front of us containing a bowl full of unopened mail that I assumed to be sympathy cards, at the blinds that were tightly drawn against the outside world, and at the once vivacious Meg Poole, now a sorrowful wisp beside me. There was a framed photo of Mommy on the mantel, taken on the last day she was able to stand by herself; on the day her staff at the vet clinic gave her a *Thanks for Everything* party. In it, she props herself in front of the building, one hand on Mom's shoulders, her wonderful employees surrounding her, holding her up with fake happy smiles. She looks right at the camera, eyebrows raised, as if she thinks this is a silly, sentimental sort of display. But there is obvious pain behind her show of strength. Her smile is forced. Her eyes are too bright.

BAM!

All of my bravery, every bit of it, detached itself from my body and flew off into the ether, and I reached out and stroked Mom's matted hair. She groped for me, and we both dissolved into ugly sobs. We rocked in one another's arms, Mom patting me gently on the small of my back with feathery little strokes.

"Mom," I gurgled. "I am staying *here*."

Π

Meg Poole is an unpredictable woman. She cut all her hair off into short spikes when I was born, because "she didn't want to fool with all that curling iron crap." She had a tattoo of a rainbow on her wrist, long before either tattoos or rainbows were in fashion. She raised me with her partner Sam, just the three of us against the world, long before the Ohio Supreme Court allowed the two of them to get married in 2015. She and Sam were brave. They faced things head-on, and taught me to do the same. This decision to become a hermit just didn't fit into our worldview. Mom was financially secure, because Sam had the foresight to sell her veterinary practice as soon as her cancer was diagnosed. So Mom had the wherewithal to stay home, and that made it even harder for me to argue with her crazy decision to do it.

Π

It was the following morning after my surprise visit. After we cried ourselves dry, we had spent the rest of the evening arguing about our situation, which we couldn't resolve. I had managed to get Mom to eat some soup and crackers, take a shower, and go to bed with clean sheets. After she retired, I did some mega-dusting, tidying up, and dish-washing. Windows and blinds were opened to the August breezes, what little there were. I left the AC on. At that moment, utility bills were not important. The house seemed to breathe a sigh of relief. I know I did.

Both of us were pale and wan in the morning sunlight streaming in through the bay window above the sink. It warmed my forehead and glinted off Mom's wedding ring. We sat at the kitchen table, coffee in front of us, continuing our discussion of the afternoon previous.

Hand on forehead, swiping at her spikes, Mom was still not defeated. "Tommy. You have a job, for God's sake. You cannot stay here. You have to go back to Columbus."

"I don't have to at all. Two reasons: First off, I despise my job. I hate managing other people's stupid social media accounts. It is the most worthless occupation on the planet. I don't care if "Author Sheila Morgan" has twenty or twenty thousand Twitter followers. And my email box is always overflowing with stupid requests for me to set up "Facebook live chats" and Skype interviews. I hate my self-centered clients. They all want to make millions, but want me to do all the work. They all want to *go viral,* for heaven's sake. And second, I can do this stupid job from anywhere. I am so good at it, that if I decide not to quit altogether, Killer Bee Media will be happy to let me do the job here. Columbus is not an issue. Do you want more coffee?"

Π

She massaged her scalp one last time and put her chin in her palm. I noticed all the wrinkles around her eyes. They hadn't been there back on Memorial Day. That was such a wonderful holiday. Mommy closed her clinic for two days, I came home with my dog, and we had a cookout with steamed lobster and corn on the cob. Mom's face was clear, her black eyes popped, and she radiated energy. *How had she shriveled so fast?* Mommy had been dead for only a month.

"Nope. No more coffee."

"Look, kiddo." Mommy called Mom "kiddo." I went for broke. "I am as stubborn as you are. If you are going to hole up, I am going to hole up. Here. In this cozy house where we have been so happy, since I was born. We will stay here together and heal together. Got it, sister?"

She tilted her head back and closed her eyes in resignation. Straightening her legs under the table, dropping her arms at her side, she went limp, head resting on the back of her chair. "Tommy, if you are going to be mulish about this, I am just too sick and tired to argue. We will 'hole up,' as you call it, together. For as long as I need to stay here, I will. And I guess I am stuck with you here as well."

I snapped my fingers. Mom opened her eyes.

"Ground rules. We have to set up ground rules. But I can tell you *right now* – the overreaching rule – YOU ARE NOT STAYING HERE 'AS LONG AS YOU WANT TO.' I give you ONE YEAR, Mom. ONE YEAR. Tomorrow I am going to Columbus to pack, and I will be back on Saturday. Saturday is," I wrestled my iPhone out of my pocket, "August 27, 2016. You have until August 27, 2017 to remain sequestered here. With me. On that date, we open the door and rejoin civilization. One year. Got it?"

She reached out her hand. I took it, and we shook in agreement. "Agreed. No more ground ruling until later. But now, Tommy, I need to lie down and cry myself to sleep. I couldn't sleep last night, and I am exhausted. So I am going back to bed."

As I watched my dear parent shuffle out of the kitchen, my heart swelled with victory. Then the realization that I had just agreed to become a hermit for an *entire year* hit me with the force of ten fire hoses, and I nearly lost consciousness.

Chapter Two

П

I had purchased a legal pad and some markers at Staples during Mom's nap, and when I returned, I tried to take one myself. Instead of napping, I wept, the tears rolling into my nose, producing massive nasal discharge, staining my cheeks, and turning my eyes into bloodshot holes.

If you cry a lot, your eyelids swell up so that you look either like a battered prizefighter or an allergy sufferer. I struggled out of bed and stumped into the bathroom. I peered at myself in the medicine cabinet mirror. Slits for eyes. Black hair tangled up in fuzzy mats, grayish skin, the "stay all day" lipstick from yesterday still a burgundy stain around the edges of my lips. A pimple seemed to be erupting on my left cheek. I splashed some cold water on my face, brushed my teeth, and gave up on the rest of me.

I smelled frying bologna. I grinned in spite of myself. Mom was making my favorite: fried bologna sandwiches. Probably there was chicken noodle soup on the stove.

There was only one place set at the square white table that Mommy had found at the Antique Mall on the way to Columbus. I rubbed the gold edge of my placemat and glared at Mom. "Thank you for this." I pointed at my mug of soup and sandwich. "You have to eat something, too. I can see your backbone through your T-shirt. No ground rules until you eat at least one piece of toast, or a slice of bologna."

Mom turned from the window, coffee mug in hand, and glared back at me. "Before you start in on me, let me just say that *you* look like something Herkie dragged in. You have very little credibility here. And by the way, I am not hungry."

Herkie is my adorable rescue pit bull. More about her later.

I spread some mustard on my sandwich, took a bite, and chewed, thinking of an appropriate response. Nothing came to me, so I took a few sips of the soup, which Mom had topped with freshly snipped parsley. Still nothing. I finished one half of my sandwich, the crispy lunchmeat and mustard still as delightful as I remembered. So fortifying.

I glanced at the sideboard that Mommy had also found—at a garage sale down the street. She had hired two high school boys to carry it home. She refinished it, lined the shelves with gold striped shelf paper, and arranged cookbooks, vases, stoneware crocks, a white soup tureen in the shape of a turtle, and various other decorative items on the shelves. Mommy was a nester, and as a result of her talents, this kitchen, this house, and our lives were cozy and comfortable. I loved my parents so much, and now one of them was missing. I had to keep the other one going, so help me. "Mom. Speaking of ground rules,you have to eat. Enough to stay healthy. You may not wither into nothingness and just fade away. MOM."

She stuck out her tongue at me, but accepted my other sandwich half. I pushed my placemat across the table and motioned for her to sit down. "While you are eating that, I'll go get the legal pad and Sharpie I bought for this very purpose, and we can begin."

I labeled the top of the page GROUND RULES FOR RECLUSES. Mom came up with the first one.

WE CAN'T LEAVE THE HOUSE DURING THE DAY. NIGHT TIME IS OK.

"Why night time?" I figured recluses wouldn't go outside at all.

Mom looked at me as if I were a complete dummy. "Tommy, we can't stay in the house every minute for a year. We aren't prisoners. We are withdrawing from civilization temporarily. To heal. Well, I need to heal. I don't know what you need to do. As a matter of fact, I don't think you should even do this. I am the one who needs time to be alone. You are too young for this." Her eyes widened, and she smacked the table with the palms of both hands. "Tommy, you need to go back to Columbus. You can't do this. We can't do this. What kind of a mother am I that I would even consider letting you move back here, even for a few weeks?" A tear formed in her right eye and slowly escaped down her cheek. She rubbed it off.

I closed my eyes and resisted the urge to put my forehead on the table. "Columbus is overrated. I hate my stupid little dank apartment. The bathroom smells like a men's locker room on humid days. I have enough money saved so that I can quit my job. However, as I said, I can work remotely from anywhere. I could use alone time, too."

Mom raised one eyebrow. "Why do you need alone time, Thomasina?"

I do not love my name. I am named Thomasina after my Uncle, who also happens to be my biological father: Robert Thomas Carruthers. Long story short: Uncle Rob, Meghan Carruthers' beloved brother, was the sperm donor. Samantha Poole was the one who gave birth to me. We are all biologically related. But I adore my Uncle Rob, and so I sort of like the fact that I carry a part of him around with me. I only wish his middle name were Paul. I like the name Paula. But I digress.

"Mom. I need to grieve. But more importantly, you need me now."

Mom held out a hand: *halt.* "Tommy, a year is a long time. You are a young woman. You can't put your life on hold like that. What if the person of your dreams is living in Columbus? If you move away, you might miss him. Or her." (Mom always needs to leave the door open. She knows I am heterosexual, but just in case-God bless my mom).

"Ha! But what if he lives here?"

Mom smirked. "You won't meet him. Because *you won't be leaving the house!*"

"OK, you have a point." My head was starting to ache. "To quote you a few seconds ago, I am young. I have time to meet Mr. Right, OK? And presently, that is not a priority." I waved the legal pad at her. "Back on task, OK?"

I went back and put a number 1 beside the first rule. I then put a 2 on the paper and held it up in front of my face. "Ideas?"

Mom picked at the cuticle on her thumb. Her head jerked toward the refrigerator. "What about stuff like groceries? Will we have to go to the store at night? And the pharmacy? Are they open at night? What about if we have to go to the doctor or the dentist? Or the post office?" Her forehead squinched with alarm.

"No worries. Grocery stores deliver, as does the pharmacy. If one of us has to go to the doctor or dentist, we will temporarily suspend the ground rules." I put 'except for emergencies' in parentheses after rule 1. I had another thought. It put another little rip in my heart. "And of course, we can go visit Mommy's grave any day, any time. That doesn't count."

Mom's shoulders dropped a mile. Her hand went to her eyes, and she held it over them for a few more seconds than I would have liked. I cleared my throat. "Second rule?"

Mom let go of her eyes, shot me a watered-down smile, scratched her neck, took a sip of coffee, and stared off into the distance. I drummed my fingers on the table. Mom shook her head. "This might be impossible. What about gardening? We can't let the yard go to ruination. What would people think?"

"Well, considering that they will already be 'thinking' we are weird for suddenly becoming hermits, the fact that we may have to hire somebody to do yard work and gardening will be secondary, don't you think? Hey, are you getting cold feet?"

She straightened her spine and humphed. "Of course not. But we have to think this through. Cover all the bases. For instance, what will you do with Herkie? She will need to go on walks."

Speaking of Herkie. Herkimer Tallulah Poole is my adorable pit bull. I discovered her on PetFinder.com when I was idly trolling for pets one evening. The minute I saw her brown face, dissected right down the middle with a white stripe, I fell in love. She was rescued from a shady situation by a pittie rescue in Herkimer, New York. Thus the name. She is my soul mate. "We have a fenced in backyard. She can do her business there during the day. I will walk her at night. And the backyard. We can go out there with Herkie and scoop poop in the day. Mom. RULE TWO."

"OK, OK." She rubbed her temples. I noticed the age spots on her hands. *When did those crop up?* At 55, she shouldn't have those. I looked down at my own hands. Dry, ragged fingernails from biting, but no age spots. I wondered if a year at home might bring them on. I sighed.

Mom held up two fingers, holding them together, then separating them like a peace salute. "We need to be sure that we aren't together too much. You will be working from home." She poked me for emphasis. "So let's say that for at least, I don't know, four to five hours a day we should be separate?"

"But what will you do for five hours?" I thought that was a reasonable question.

Mom bristled. "Do you think I am some sort of passive invalid? For heaven's sake! I have paperwork, first of all." Since Mommy had sold her practice, there were still loose ends with the estate. "Then there is the Internet, housework, cooking, *because you can't make anything besides peanut butter and jelly,* books, and I might learn to crochet. There are instructional videos on YouTube."

Mom's Internet prowess was news to me. But of course, I haven't lived at home since I went away to Ohio State University at aged 18. Mommy's practice had a web page. She spent time at home answering her emails. Mom and Mommy shared a laptop. I had FaceTimed with them weekly. Of course Mom knew about stuff like YouTube. I gave myself a mental slap upside the head. "Right. Of course. I apologize."

I wrote SEPARATE TIME DURING THE DAY under Rule 2.

"Rule 3?"

Mom started clearing up the brunch things, wiping crumbs off the table and loading our dishes into the dishwasher. Something buzzed from the vicinity of the back door where we hung our coats. Scuttling over to the coatrack, she rooted around in her ancient red corduroy barn coat, extracted her cell, and looked at the screen. "A text from Rob. I'll answer it later—it's not important." Suddenly, she clutched the phone to her chest. "OH. What about everybody? We aren't cutting everybody out of our lives, are we?"

"Don't panic. That will be Rule 3." I wrote PEOPLE CAN COME OVER HERE; WE JUST AREN'T GOING OUT. "Rob can come over any time. So can anybody else we want to see. We are cloistering ourselves, but we aren't going into solitary confinement. We have to stay sane during all of this." The gravity of what we were embarking on hit me once again like a blow to the head, and I tried to take a cleansing breath. My chest seemed unwilling to expand. "Are you certain about this, Mom? We can stop this right now, you know."

Hands shaking slightly, Mom wiped the screen of her cell phone with the fingers of one hand. She scuffed over and lowered her skinny back end onto her chair. Setting her phone face down on the table, she covered it with both hands reverently. "No, honey." She reached over and stroked my bangs. Her touch was gentle and soul smoothing. "This is a necessary thing for me. I am crushed and mangled inside, and I need to surround myself with my house, my memories of Sam, and my grief. It scares me, yes, and I have to admit that I wonder if I will be able to last it out. But Tommy, I also need to figure out how I am going to carry on into the future. I have to come up with a plan for my life. And that is going to take time, because I haven't got a clue. I am totally alone now."

Mom and Mommy had always been isolated in a world where marriage meant a man and a woman. Yes, things got better when gay marriage became legal in Ohio and being lesbian somehow became much more "preferable" to being transgender or non-binary, and people started to become hysterical about bathrooms. But being a gay couple has never been mainstream. Especially in the very small city of Framington. But Mom and Mommy managed to make our family seem safe and normal for me, at least in the confines of our house. The outside world was a bit dicier. We were our own little island of female in a world dominated by heterosexuality. But now we were two thirds of a whole. And we were both raw and bleeding. Unmoored. Mom seemed utterly lost without Mommy.

I looked out the window into the backyard. There used to be a swing set out there that Rob put up for me. I used to swing so high that Mommy would run out of the kitchen screeching, "For God's sake, Tommy, *stop pumping! You might just fly off that swing into the stratosphere!"* Mom would follow after her, put a hand on Mommy's shoulder and say, "Easy, Sam. Just notice how tight her grip is. Tommy will never fly off into space. *You won't fly away, will you, Tommy?*

Nope. I am going to stay right here. For now.

"We need to move on to Rule 4."

Mom stood up and looked down at her legs, shaking out first one, and then another. "Exercise. We need to get it. Since we aren't going to the gym or tennis. Jane Fonda tapes?"

I snorted. "Mom. YouTube is today. Jane Fonda is a hundred years ago. But yes, we can do exercise along with yogis, personal trainers, kick boxers, or whomever you choose. We can do it in the family room, and Herkie will do it with us" (Herkie is an extremely imitative individual. She is a natural at *downward facing dog*). We can order Fitbits and count our steps. So. Rule 4 is EXERCISE INDOORS.

She picked up a sponge and grabbed the plate off the table. Pivoting to the sink, she squeezed a drop of Dawn onto the sponge and began to swipe at the plate. As she rubbed, way longer than the few crumbs on it required, she began to sway back and forth, humming Mommy's favorite song, *Here Comes the Sun.* My heart swelled with a tiny hope that Mom was smiling to herself with a good memory. But she swung towards me and dropped the plate on the linoleum, tears wetting her cheeks. The plate shattered right along with my heart.

Chapter Three

Π

Columbus. The Big Apple of Ohio. Home of Ohio State, Jeni's ice cream, and my humble apartment. My best friend, Suzanne, had been keeping Herkie for me. I swung by her place to pick up my dog.

"Really? No shit? You are gonna be a *hermit?*" Suzanne's mouth hung open. "Why are you letting your mom do this? And why can't you just go visit her on weekends, for God's sake?" Suzanne Lampley is a realist.

I paced in a circle around the perimeter of Suze's square, glass-topped coffee table, Herkie at my heels, wagging and panting with excitement at seeing me after that agonizing, two-day separation. "Because Mom looks like death, and one death in the family is enough. I have to take care of her."

Suze shook her head, her freckles blurring, her green eyes blazing. "*You* look like death, you fool! You think locking yourself away for, what, a fucking *year,* will accomplish anything?"

I reached down and picked up a pinecone off the table. Suze and I collect them on long walks. If we lived on the coast instead of the Midwest, I suppose we would collect seashells. I turned the cone over in my hand, its sharp pointy edges poking my palm like little pins. "This is not a time for me to think about myself." I set the pinecone down, but it rolled off the table onto the carpet, where Herkie tried to bite it. I bent down to take it away from Herk before it poked her tongue. When I straightened up, I saw stars. "Actually, I will accomplish something. I am going to spend one year in introspection and reflection. In addition to making sure Mom doesn't do anything drastic to herself. So there. And *you* can come visit on weekends."

Suze stood and hiked up her pj pants. Her pink tank top had what looked like ketchup stains on it. She looked around at her cluttered living room, books and magazines piled up in corners, a full laundry basket by the door, and she started to laugh. "Sure, sure—I can give up a few weekends. My weekends are reserved for housecleaning," she gestured around the room like a game show model, "but you can see how that has been going for me."

When I was about to leave with Herkie, her dog food, dishes, and leash, Suze stopped me with a tight hug. "You promise you will keep in touch?"

"I promise. FaceTime. Text messages. Actual phone calls, for God's sake."

Suze held me at arm's length. I felt her fingers press into the muscles of my shoulders. "And promise me you will stay sane."

I cleared my throat. "Not sure I can, but that will be at the top of my to-do list."

Suze waved until Herkie and I drove out of sight.

π

It didn't take me long to pack up. I am the furthest thing from a hoarder imaginable. I filled two suitcases with clothes, one cardboard box with books, and another with Herkie's bowls, leashes, blanket, and toys. I decided to leave her hairy and tattered dog bed in the dumpster behind my apartment. A new home demanded a new, fluffy bed, which

I would get at the PetMart on the way out of town. Herkie loved to go in there with me because all the workers fawned all over her, and she got treats galore.

I stood in the middle of my soon-to-be-former apartment. The television was there when I arrived three years ago, and the snowy picture was not worth the haul. I would leave it for the next unfortunate tenant. The tea colored walls had cracks. I had hung a few posters around, but none of them were even framed, just dry mounted. The one of frozen Niagara Falls had a bent edge. There was a hole in the sky above the falls where I had accidentally poked it with a pencil while having an argument on the phone with my ex-boyfriend, Ryan. He called me a commitment-phobe, and I lashed out at Niagara. I pulled that one off the wall and into a trash bag.

I turned in a circle. Miro's *Dog Barking at the Moon* was nearly intact, and I took it down reverently. It would look good in my room at home. I laid it aside to take with us.

Herkie padded over to the poster and sniffed it. Her soft brown eyes looked at me questioningly. She seemed concerned at all of the upheaval. "Herk, dearie." I leaned down and kissed her beefy head. "You will love it in Framington. It is a big house, with nice old floors you can slide on. Mom won't mind. There is a big backyard with lots of room to run around. But best of all, *get this:* you won't have to be alone at home during the day any more!" I fluffed her ears. "Nope! Because your grandma and I will be home ALL THE TIME with you!" As I said this, I felt a little sick, but I feigned enthusiasm for both our sakes. "Herkie, we can do this! Mom can't be completely alone. Heck, the two of us are alone, aren't we, girl? So being back in Framington with grandma will be a bonus for us, won't it?"

There wasn't much else. I slept on a futon; I would not take that dingy bedding with me. It went into the trash as well. The futon would stay behind. I felt a twinge of guilt about leaving so much detritus behind, but then again, my landlord, Edith Snell, had whiskers, a very nasty attitude, and she had never done me any favors. Herkie and I scudded over to the kitchen. I had nothing much there to take—I ate mostly on paper plates. I took my favorite and only mug off the shelf, its rim chipped, but the white and yellow stripes still bright. No coffee pot, no pots and pans. My God, my life here had been meager.

I sat down in front of Herkie, cross-legged. She plopped down beside me and put her head in my lap. I stroked her and closed my eyes, trying to imagine what the coming hermit year might be like. On the one hand, I imagined the relief of working at home, without having to share a cubicle at Killer Bee Media with Malcolm Rogers, who picked his nose. I sighed with pleasure. I looked around at my dismal, empty apartment – compared and contrasted mentally with the beautiful, cozy, and well appointed home I was returning to – it would be like opening a new book. A fresh start. But then I thought about how stir-crazy I got whenever I had the flu and had to stay at home for longer than 48 hours. The boredom. The claustrophobic feeling. The twitchiness in my legs. That feeling of being imprisoned. *What was I thinking?* I rested my forehead against Herk's, listening to her adorable panting. I was jolted by the brilliance of an idea.

"Herk, my girl. You know, it won't be that bad. We *are* going to go out of the house. We have to, for our own sanity, right?" My wondrous dog lifted her head off my lap and cocked it at me, and I had a surge of optimism. "We'll just turn night into day, like the people who work third shift. We'll be out and about, but just in the night. It's in the ground rules that nighttime is not off limits. Hell, we can stay out for hours if we want to, because we'll be safe." Herk cocked her head in the other direction. "Because of *you,* Herkie. Nobody will dare try to confront us because you are a pittie! You are like a suit of armor, get it?"

Π

Mom was waiting for us at the front door as we drove up. I had texted her. She stood framed in the wide doorway, the shadows of the front hall behind her, a forced-looking smile, having made a real effort in the clothing department: teal and silver paisley leggings, a floaty sort of lemon yellow blouse, and bright white Keds. She waved enthusiastically, but did not budge from the doorway. I silently vowed to fatten her up over the coming months.

I opened the driver's side door and stepped out, Herkie nearly crushing me as she barreled past me and out of the car, careening towards my mother. "Mom! We haven't started yet! Come help me with my stuff."

Herkie bounded up, nearly knocking her down with fervent bumps and licks. Mom bent over and put both hands on either side of Herkie's muzzle, murmuring to her. Herk settled right down, sitting on the pavement, her tail thumping. Mom kissed her snout and looked up at me. "I think this one and I will get along just fine."

We carried in my suitcases and boxes. I stood in the front hall, surrounded by the sights and smells of growing up. The chintz wallpaper that extended all the way up the stairs, blue and maroon flowers and tendrils. Mom hated it; Mommy said it was "vintage." The dark, waxy hardwood floors, where roller-skating was verboten, but I did it anyway when nobody was home. The scratches and streaks were still evident—*who did I think I was kidding?* The faint odor of . . . what was it? Dust? The souls of those who lived there before we moved in? Furniture wax? Whatever it was, it was the smell of home. Herkie ran upstairs and right back down, wagging, excited. Mom stood behind me, silent. I turned and caught the look on her face right before she smiled at me: the shadow of apprehension in her eyes, the frown lines around her mouth.

I looked at my watch. "OK. Let's synchronize. It is high noon in four minutes. We have four more minutes of freedom. Then the year of staying IN begins."

Mom clapped her hands, grabbed me by the wrist, and pulled me outside. She whistled for Herkie, and for four minutes, we ran around the front yard, whooping and turning in circles. It was both exhilarating and sad. After we caught our breath and Herkie urinated in the mulch under the boxwood hedge, we walked inside, hand-in-hand, and gently shut the door behind us.

Chapter Four

Π

Mom stood at the counter, covered with flour, peering down at the cookbook, also covered with flour, on the kitchen counter. She was massaging pie dough. "It says here not to 'handle' the dough too much, or it will get tough. But the damn stuff won't hold together. So how do I mash it back together without handling it?" She rubbed a swath of flour across her forehead.

Rob was coming over. Our first guest. We were both so excited; as the first three days at home were so uneventful, we both nearly quit. However, Meg Poole is a very determined individual, and she texted me from the basement, where she was unloading laundry. The text was pithy: *We need Rob over here; we are both so sad it may just kill us. Invited him for dinner.*

A family like ours has so many layers that the complications are inevitable, confusion is rampant, and both frustration and anger float just under the surface. My "Uncle" Rob is one of those. He has held my hand while leading me into the scary woods at my first Girl Scout Campout. He has cheered while running along side my bike as I veered wildly towards the curb, yelling encouragement. He got us both pogo sticks on my tenth birthday. We bounced until I wet my pants from laughing. He is a bright light. But there are lines at the corners of his eyes that make him look older than his age, and when he laughs, sometimes he dissolves into tears.

I took Rob to school on career day, where he told the fourth grade class that being a firefighter was very dangerous and exciting, and all the kids loved his speech. (By the way, Rob is a lawyer. What a piece of work.) Rob loomed large in my life, all right. He came over to the house every Christmas Eve dressed as Santa. He played Monopoly with me for hours. And the year I turned sixteen, Rob bought me a used Volkswagen, and I cried. That night, I told Mommy I wished I had a father like Rob, and that was the night I found out he *was* my father. Artificial insemination.

I remember the way my insides roiled when I learned who my father was. Of course, there was a big chunk of my "unconscious" that had sort of figured that out already. Uncle Rob was so kind, so beloved, so involved. His love seeped deep into my pores. But there were countless days when I observed kids my age with their dads and wondered what it would be like to just *have one*. To casually link hands with him and walk down the street. To be able to refer to someone as "Dad." I remember feeling envy and resentment towards "regular families." But I began to tamp all of that down, as a survival strategy.

Certainly, this new knowledge explained the pain I often saw in Rob's eyes when he said goodbye, and the silence between Mom and Mommy when one more Father's Day passed without celebration. I was afraid to ask either of them why. I guess I didn't want to know the answer.

It was an unspoken rule. Rob was not the "Dad." He was beloved, a part of the pack, included in all the stuff that meant "family." But he wasn't Daddy. The pattern had been established. I didn't let myself dwell on my own yearning for a father. All those little pangs of regret were just squished down until they were too small to pay much attention to. Sort of like having a paper cut: you know it is there, it hurts like a bitch sometimes, but you ignore it, because it is, after all, *a tiny thing* in the overall scope of life.

This all sounds like it was easy to do. I had a father, but not a dad. Rob was the "Uncle." Just move along, folks. But it haunted me, and I am sure that it caused Rob to suffer. But we have all heard about how the psyche manages to trick us into going along, plodding from day to day, walling off the things that don't make sense, the traumas, the confusion.

I still have moments when my heart seems to drip pain; my head swims from the reality of being Tommy Poole. I think of my friend Suzanne, whose father and mother held hands as they walked down the street. Mom and Mommy were afraid to do that in Framington. We were The Three Musketeers, Mom, Mommy, and I.

Three Musketeers. I bit my lip. My heartbeat lost its rhythm for a few beats. I slammed the door on a memory. *Don't go there, Tommy.* It was Mom and Mommy. The ideal lesbian couple. The women who followed all the conventions, for Rob's reputation, my protection, and for Framington. They were just lesbians. But in all other respects, "a regular couple."

I watched Mom wrestle with the pie dough, her lips drawn into a straight line. She wielded the rolling pin like a weapon. "How thin should the crust be? About a quarter inch?" She smacked the dough with the rolling pin, thinning it down by force.

"Mom. That pie will be as tough as nails. You are beating it to death."

She turned and pointed the rolling pin at me, a fine mist of flour particles drifting off it to the floor. "It will be fine with ice cream. I will put a lot of blueberry filling in it—there won't be that much crust. And you know Rob. My brother will eat anything."

π

The pot roast was delicious. Mom makes gravy that I would just as soon eat out of a bowl with a soup spoon. The three of us sat in the dining room, candles flickering, hardly filling the long, shiny oak table. My plate was empty, Rob was finishing up his second helpings, but Mom sat, her gravy congealing on her beef.

"Meg. Eat something, for God's sake." Rob swiped a piece of bread in the remainder of the gravy on his plate. "Mourning is one thing. Starving is another."

At seven o'clock in August, it is still light outside. I watched kids skateboarding down the driveway of the Morris' house across the street. They screamed directions at one another: "Go down on one foot this time! No! Come HERE!" They had no idea how free they were. I looked down at my plate, pushed around a pea until it fell off the edge. I set my fork down and looked over at my mom. "Rob is right. Nutrition is essential."

Mom waved a hand at us, as if we were annoying bugs buzzing around her. She raised her wine glass and took a huge sip. "There is sugar in wine. And antioxidants or something. It can help stave off heart disease."

Rob snorted. "It can do that. It can also turn you into an alcoholic." He shook his head. "Meg. Tommy. Why are you doing this?"

Mom pushed her plate away and crossed her hands on the table. It looked to me as if her nose was runny. I dug around in my pocket and handed her a wrinkled Kleenex. She looked at it for a moment, then set it beside her plate. She wiped her nose with her napkin and remained silent, looking out of the room towards the living room, as if there were a person in there. I turned my head and looked through the hall, half expecting to see Mommy sitting on the sofa, reading the newspaper.

Rob stood, collecting his plate, pointing to Mom's. "No, I am finished." I grabbed my plate and hers, and followed Rob into the kitchen. I scraped Mom's dinner into the garbage, rinsed her plate, and loaded it into the dishwasher. Rob handed me the other two plates, and I loaded those, avoiding his eyes. I reached for a sponge to wipe the counters, but Rob took my arm gently and led me over to the kitchen table. "Sit."

I sat. I twitched in the chair. I glanced around, looking for an out, but there was none. Rob stuck out his index finger and aimed it at me. "What is this whole hermit thing about, Tommy?"

It was the question to end all questions, as far as I was concerned. I hadn't totally thought this thing through. "As far as Mom is concerned? I think she feels so alone without Mommy..."

"So the thing to do when you feel alone is to cut yourself off from the world? This is logical?" Rob's cheeks began to redden. "And you are doing this with her? Two women, just hiding away for a year? For God's sake, Tommy!"

I bristled. "As you say, cutting yourself off from the world is crazy. This is true. So I am not letting her do that! I am staying here with her. And Herkie. She isn't alone." I didn't sound all that convincing, even to myself.

"Why so long? I could see a month or something. But a year is ridiculous." Rob's forehead wrinkled up like an accordion.

"So maybe it won't take a year. But Rob—she wanted to do this for longer! I had to cut it off at a year. Rob. Mommy is gone. We are both so empty inside." I stood up and walked over to the kitchen door and opened it a crack. Mom still sat at the table, looking off into the distance, her face in her hands. I wasn't even sure she knew we had left the dining room.

"I get it. I miss Sam, too. She was my sister-in-law, after all. We have lost a piece of ourselves. But Tommy, you shouldn't be shutting yourself away, too. This is crazy." He circled his temple with his index finger, shaking his head and frowning.

"Here is what I think." I leaned against the doorframe. "I think Mom needs time to sort herself. And I think that in the back of my mind, I have always wanted to retreat to some sort of haven. To find out just what I am made of—can I be a thinker? Can I learn how to craft things, or paint? Maybe write poetry?"

Rob scoffed. "This isn't Walden."

"But that is just the thing! It *is* a haven—this house is the place where all my happiest memories are! Mom is here! Who knows what we will learn and do in this year? People go on sabbatical all the time. This is ours. Can you understand *that?* If you think of it as just an interesting and exploratory interlude in our lives? And, Rob, you will be here a lot, too. This could be a terrific opportunity for you, as well!" By this point, I am certain that my eyes resembled those children in the Keane paintings; I was pouring it on so thick.

Rob shrugged, but he smiled. "OK. An interesting interlude. That already sounds poetic. But seriously, Tommy. This is a crazy thing you are doing. You need to ask yourself why you are so willing to give up an entire year of your life to this. It just doesn't make sense on the surface. Leaving your life and all your friends to hole up here."

The edge of the door cut into my spine. I straightened up. "Here's the thing, Rob. I don't have many friends. I have a *scarcity* of friends. And the ones I have don't understand me. Hell, *I don't understand me.* I am low on the self-awareness scale. Near the bottom. You may have a point, there. And I am confused. About love. About relationships. About how people stay together, and what drives them apart. I have so much on my mind. I need this alone time for my own head."

Rob took a step towards me, arms out. I let him hug me for a split second, until every single corpuscle and fiber inside me said *get off this subject before it suffocates you.* I pulled away from Rob and pasted on a smile. "Pie. We need pie."

I took the pie out of the cupboard. Despite all the heavy-handedness with the rolling pin, it looked crisp and delicious. "Rob. Mom made this for you. Her first attempt. See? Already the sabbatical is yielding results! Get out the ice cream and a scoop."

I stuck three forks and a knife in Rob's back pocket, grabbed three bowls and balanced the pie on them, and we returned to the dining room. Mom started as if waking from a dream. We served the pie. It was mediocre, but Rob ate two pieces.

The doorbell rang just as we were urging Mom to take "just three bites" of pie. Herkie growled, like the perfect watchdog that she is. I raced to the door, grabbed her by the collar and handed her off to Rob, who stood behind me with Herk, just in case we had polite robbers.

I opened the door to a stout, red-faced man. He was balding; there were a few wiry white hairs escaping from his coal-black toupee. He wore a crisply ironed white sport shirt, khaki trousers, and brown and white saddle shoes. He was brandishing a walking stick, apparently getting ready to beat down the door with it.

"Hello. Can I help you?" Herkie growled again. Rob took a step back. I noticed that this man's fingernails were buffed to a high shine as he brandished the walking stick at me.

Again, I tried to be polite by asking, "Can I help you, sir?"

He snarled. He really did. "That is a pit bull! One of those fighting dogs! They are vicious! We can't have dogs like that in this neighborhood!" He banged his cane on the pavement.

The man looked vaguely familiar to me. "Who are you, mister? You can stop banging." I stuck my foot under his stick and knocked it out from under him.

"Percy Warner, from next door. That is a vicious dog!" He righted his stick and glared at me.

Mom suddenly appeared behind Rob and pushed him and Herkie aside. She put her arm around my shoulders and leaned out to the pig-man, smiling. "Hello, Percy. You remember my daughter, Tommy. She has come to live with me awhile. And this is her darling dog, Herkie, who has never had a fight with anyone in her life, dear."

Percy Warner made a fist and shook it in our faces. "Listen to it growling! It is vicious! All those dogs should be put down! They kill babies!" His face was so red, it was purple. There were disgusting flecks of spittle on his lips. I thought he might have a stroke right there on our rainbow welcome mat.

Mom reached out and patted his fist. "Oh, Percy, calm down. Herkie is growling because you are shouting at us. She senses you as a threat. Any dog worth her salt would do that. You need to take your bluster and go home. Herkie is never out but in the backyard, which as you know, has a six-foot iron fence around its entirety. She will take her walks late at night, on a leash, after you and the neighbors are safely in bed. She will not be eating you or any babies at any time. Now for heaven's sake, Percy, go home and have a shot of whiskey to calm your nerves." She gave him a steely smile and shut the door emphatically. As it shut on his face, we heard him splutter about Herkie sticking her face through the bars of the fence and biting him. My mother, bless her, flicked up a middle finger at the door.

Rob and I gave her a round of applause, and Herkie sat down and thumped her tail. She is a good dog. She's never been to dog school, but she has a heart of gold. Who is the good girl? She knows *she is.*

Mom took a slight bow and then snapped her fingers. "I stocked up on dog treats for occasions just like this. Come on, everybody—actually, I think Herkie deserves a treat from each of us!"

As Herkie crunched on her treats, I asked, "I kind of remember that piggish guy, Percy. But I don't remember much about him. Didn't he have a family? I don't recall any run-ins from when I lived here. What is up with him, anyway? What turned him into such a menace?"

"Oh, life did. Divorce. I think he is estranged from his family. He has gradually, over the years, become more and more ornery."

Rob clucked. "Yup. That guy. It wasn't so bad when he was working—he wasn't home that much. Retirement can sour people. What did he do for a living, again, Meg?"

Mom rolled her eyes at Rob. "He is a retired florist. Rob, you know him via all his stupid lawsuits. He was a Framington City Commissioner for years."

Rob smacked his forehead. "Of course. He used to get on the local news for various frivolous lawsuits. I remember one in particular, in which he sued to have St. Paul's Episcopal stop ringing their bells on Sundays because it 'disturbed the peace.' Jesus."

I sprang to attention. "What if he sues US about Herkie?" My heart nearly pounded out of my chest.

Rob cleared his throat. "He can't sue you for having a dog, Tommy. There is no breed-specific legislation in this town. Herkie is just another dog."

I looked over at Mom, whose expression was a mixture of anger with a little worry thrown in, her forehead wrinkled and her lips in a thin line. It did not inspire confidence. I began to pace around the kitchen, clasping and unclasping my fists. On my third lap, I stubbed my toe on the kitchen table leg and howled in pain. Herkie trotted to my side and jumped up on me, her claws making red welts on my thighs. I didn't correct her, despite the infraction. I leaned over and kissed her on the head before sinking onto the kitchen floor to inspect my toe to see if it was broken. Herkie licked my toes.

Mom put the dog biscuits back in the cupboard and sat down beside me and Herkie, motioning for Rob to do the same. "Here is the thing, family. We are fine. We are here together. We are staying *in.* Herkie will go out in the yard when Percy is not out in his—we can control that. And Tommy, when you walk her in the neighborhood at night, nothing will happen. And if it does, we have Rob to represent us." Mom held out her hands to us, and the three of us joined hands like some sort of prayer circle.

Rob chortled. "Shall we all chant or something?"

Mom let go of our hands. "Don't be ridiculous." She scrambled to her feet, as Rob looked over at me with raised eyebrows. I grimaced.

Rob got up and held out a hand to help me up. Herkie got in between Rob's legs and almost tipped us both over. Rob shrugged. "Yup. You can call on me, all right. I am the frivolous lawsuit king." He put an arm around his sister and kissed her on the cheek, and gave me a high five. Then he picked up his car keys off the counter and headed for the back door. As he shut the screen behind him, he howled like a wolf. He shut the gate to the driveway with a loud bang for emphasis.

"Hush, you rabble-rouser!" Mom laughed as she locked both the screen and the kitchen door.

When I finally went upstairs that night, I patted the bed, and Herkie jumped up beside me and slurped my cheek. I patted her head and shut my eyes, letting the events since Mommy's death swim around behind my eyes. I thought about my life in Columbus, sparse as it was. The conversation with Rob throbbed in my brain.

I rummaged around in my bedside table, shoving aside paper clips, rubber bands, Chapstick, stubby pencils, and other detritus. I found a Post-it pad and a pencil that had a decent point, and I wrote *LOVE. WHAT THE HELL IS IT?* on the Post-it.

Herkie watched me with interest as I got off the bed, walked to the mirror above my dresser, and pasted the note on the top right corner. I stood, looking at the question.

Herkie grinned, as only pit bulls can. I scuffed back to the bed, lay down beside her, and she flopped over, her head on my abdomen. I felt some of her drool seep into my T-shirt and cool my abdomen. The tension in my muscles let up a bit, and my breathing became more even. The power of the canine. I stroked her head and pondered the Post-it.

Chapter Five

Π

Things settled down pretty quickly into a predictable routine. I got up at about eight every morning to let Herkie into the backyard to do her business, keeping an eagle eye out for Percy Warner. Then, I sat in front of my computer, making my clients shine on social media until lunch. Mom made us lunch, usually a sandwich and some fruit—all the while complaining about the quality of the produce that our local grocery store, AllFoods, delivered.

Mom waited for the mail, so she could chat with Ralph, the letter carrier, whom I am sure was very surprised at all of the sudden attention.

Most afternoons, she retired to her room for a couple of hours after that, and as I sat again at my computer, I began to notice the rhythms of the house: the way the sun moved from the front of the house to the back as the day wore on. The same creaking tread on the stairs that told me that Herkie was going up to join Mom—that same creak that gave me away the Christmas when I was six and tried to sneak downstairs in the wee hours to see if Santa had come. The ticking of the clock on the living room mantel that echoed all the way upstairs. The hum of the fridge. The house enveloped me in that familiar warmth and security of childhood. This was so uplifting, this house. My shoulders relaxed—they dropped about two inches as I took in the sights and sounds around me. Home. My God, I wanted to go back in time—play Scrabble with Mommy after dinner, eat sugary snacks, collect comic books, and resume taking naps.

After working enough for the day, I would sit in the soft, tan corduroy wing chair by the bay window in the living room and look out the window. People watching.

"Herk, see that lady watering her geraniums across the street? She always wears that same faded blue apron with the red polka dots on it. She looks sad, don't you think? She must be mourning the loss of her little son. His name was probably Jimmy. He probably died after he rode his sled down their front hill one winter, right into the path of an oncoming car. It would have been so tragic. I bet he would have a gravestone in the cemetery near Mommy's, but his mother can't bring herself to visit it because she is overcome with guilt that she wasn't out there watching him sled that day. She was inside, in bed with the meter reader. So this woman, her name is probably Rita, has never stopped blaming herself."

Herkie always listened intently to my stories about the citizens of the neighborhood.

"And so, after the funeral, Rita just started to hate herself. Her husband, call him Howard, felt he was to blame for Jimmy's death as well because he was always working and never made time to do things like sled with his son. Howard became depressed. He committed suicide. Isn't that terrible, Herkie?"

Herkie would look solemn.

"So now there Rita is. Just watering her plants, and feeling desolate every day. Jesus, Herkie! I have got to stop this!"

After times like that, I would pour myself a Coke and wonder if Mom and I were going to make it.

Π

The first time I took Herkie for a midnight walk, the night was cool, but the early September pavements were still warm, so I could walk barefoot down the sidewalk beside her. There was just a slight lift of a breeze around us, and the streetlights looked like little moons at the end of every block.

The world is transformed at night. I was so accustomed to my daytime world, the clanging and zooming. But out here, in the deep hours, everything had ground to a beautiful, dark and shadowy halt. Almost silent, but there were muffled sounds of birds rustling in the trees. A swoosh of a car once in awhile, headlights illuminating us briefly, then gliding on. We walked past houses with just a few lights on upstairs.

"What do you suppose is going on in that house, Herk?" I pointed to the faint light in the window of a stately looking colonial. "Is someone reading in bed? Or maybe they are having sex? Herkie, don't blush."

We walked on, past houses completely dark, and then we approached a porch where someone sat on the steps, the glow of a cigarette poking holes in the shadows. As we drew abreast of the porch, a husky female voice called out to us. "Is that a pit bull? Is he friendly? I love dogs."

We stopped and looked up at the house. It was a girl, not a woman. I could tell by the way she suddenly stood, her outline slender and her movements quick. She began to run down her porch steps towards us, without even waiting for my reply as to the tameness of my dog.

"Hi. I'm Dana." She bent down to Herkie, murmuring endearments, and stroking Herkie's ears. Herkie, naturally, was in heaven. Her tail wagged in circles as she licked this girl's outstretched hand.

What an odd kid. She looked, in the light of the street lamp, to be about fourteen or fifteen. Her skin looked like bleached linen, white and a little ghostly. Her hair was very black, straight as skewers, and cut just below her ears. I wasn't sure in the light, but it looked purple in places. She was dressed all in black. I thought she was wearing a dress, but when she straightened up to look at me, I realized it was just a long, loose T-shirt with some sort of symbol on it.

Her face was both dead and alive. That white skin was corpse-like, but her eyes were blue-green, rimmed with black kohl, and they blazed out at me with such intensity I nearly stepped backwards. Then she grinned at me, and her smile disarmed me completely. She had dimples, for heaven's sake.

"Hello. I am Tommy, and you are right, this is a pit bull. Her name is Herkie. I think she just fell in love with you."

This Dana child laughed. She puffed on her cigarette one more time, and then threw the butt into the street. "I sit out here all the time, but I have never seen you walking. Are you new here?"

"No, actually I grew up here. My Mom lives three blocks over. I am staying with her for awhile."

"How come you are walking around at this time of night?"

She was apparently as blunt as she was unusual looking. "Because it is gorgeous out here now. No heat. No traffic. No noise."

She looked at me as if that was the stupidest thing anyone had ever said. "First of all, this neighborhood doesn't have traffic any time. It is a suburb. Second, it is September, and it isn't that hot during the day any more. Third, this neighborhood is as dull as dirt—there is *never* any noise." Her smile challenged me.

"Are you always this, uh, direct?" I chose not to say *rude*.

She laughed. "Yeah. I don't mince words. Small talk sucks. And this isn't some sort of cocktail party. It is nearly one in the morning, and you are standing in front of my house, a complete stranger with a dog, all of a sudden. I told you. I sit out here all the time, and I have never seen you before. So there must be a story."

Jesus H. Christ. Who was this kid? "I am walking this time of night, if you must know, because I don't leave the house during daylight hours, OK?"

Her eyes got big, and she grabbed my forearm, her nails digging into my skin. "My God, are you agoraphobic?'

"Of course not. Agoraphobics don't go out of their houses *at any time*. No. I am, if you must know, a recluse." I smiled, but removed her hand from my arm politely.

"Shut UP!" Dana sat down on the bottom step of the stairs leading down from her porch. "You have to tell me the whole story. Come on. Sit!"

This kid was unreal. Herkie sat immediately. I had no choice but to sit also. "Look. I don't know you."

"But you should. I am extremely interesting." Her nose was pierced with a tiny, silver ring, as was her left eyebrow. There were heavy rings on both of her thumbs. There was a tight, blue-black choker wound around her neck that looked to me like razor wire. Oh. A tattoo. Very interesting, indeed.

I didn't know exactly how to thumbnail my story, but I gave it a try. "I am a recluse, as is my mother, because we are both mourning the death of my other mother, who died recently of cancer. We did not expect her to die so suddenly. My mom was overcome by Sam's death. Sam is my other mom. Mom and I need to reboot, and we need to do it alone. We are alone. We want to be alone for now."

She leaned in to scrutinize my face. I leaned away—this kid was too intense. "Wait. You can be alone without being hermits? What is with the not leaving in daylight thing about? Sounds like you are zombies."

I sighed. This wasn't going to be easy. This Dana person was too damn smart. "I can't explain it, because it is kind of weird. But my mom declared she wasn't going to leave the house for a year. I had no choice but to come home and stay with her, because I thought she might do something terrible. I am hermit-ing with her to make sure she is OK, and that she recovers from Mommy's death."

Dana nodded. "So you are being crazy together? You and 'Mom' because 'Mommy' died?"

"You are very astute. That is it."

She leaned back against the step and looked up at the sky. "Lots of stars out there tonight. Are you going to be walking about this time every night? Because I will be here waiting for you. I think we should be friends."

Chapter Six

Π

"Mom. Did you know that Emily Dickinson loved to bake?" This time it was bread. Her back was to me, but I could see her slapping and banging a football-sized lump of dough on the counter.

She gave it another thump and turned to me. "Me and Emily are like this." She crossed her floury fingers. "This is really a great way to get out your anger. I am beating *the holy hell* out of this dough."

I had to laugh. "One thing, though. I am sure Emily would tell you that beating the holy hell out of dough will result in very, how shall I say this, 'battle weary' bread?"

As I joined her at the counter to examine the dough, which looked completely defeated and slightly rubbery, I reached out with my index finger and gave it a poke. "Mom, this thing deserves a military burial."

Mom rubbed her temples and sneezed from the flour that wafted into her nose. We both began to laugh, and Mom picked up the dough. I opened the cupboard under the sink for the trash can, and Mom ceremoniously dumped the dough into it, as I saluted.

"Do you want some coffee? Let me wash my hands and I'll pour us some."

"Sure, Emily." I sat down at the kitchen table. The sun shone in on Mom's ropey forearms as she reached for the coffee pot. She poured us two generous mugs of Starbucks

Italian Roast, and set them on the table. She opened the fridge to pull out the milk, and once again, I was shocked by how thin she was. "Mom. You have got to perfect this baking thing, before you wither away completely. You need carbs, stat!"

"I know. But my throat seems to close when I eat. And I just don't have an appetite."

"Do you want to order some Ensure with the next grocery delivery? Liquid nutrition?"

She shrugged and took a sip of her coffee. As if it were a eureka moment, she shot me a look and added a large slug of milk to the mug and downed a huge sip. "There. Liquid nutrition plus an infusion of caffeine. I can do this myself. No Ensure."

"Maybe we could start looking up recipes online. We could make dinner together in the evenings. Stuff that is gourmet-ish. You know, so delectable that we cannot resist, and then we will both get fat? We can subscribe to those dinner boxes!" I reached over and added some extra milk to my coffee, too.

Mom pursed her lips. As she stared into her coffee, I could see that she was struggling with her thoughts. The wheels were turning. "Tommy, I wonder why they came up with the term 'gay' for homosexuality because so much of it is the furthest thing from gaiety." She sniffed and rubbed her eye, and I noticed the trembling of her fingers.

"I am not sure, but I think Gertrude Stein had something to do with the term." I surprised myself by remembering that.

Mom shook her head. "Oh, well. That explains it. Gertrude and Alice B. always looked so joyful." She put her hands flat on the table and watched them tremble. "I am a wretched gay person at this moment. Look at my hands; I am shaking like an old woman. Sam and I had an uphill battle our whole married life, and now she is gone, and I am alone, completely empty. Gaiety!" Her eyes glittered with tears.

"First of all, stop it with the 'alone' business. I am right here in front of you. In lockstep with you for a year, for heaven's sake!"

I must have startled her. She looked up from studying her hands suddenly, as if just noticing that I was across the table from her. As her eyes focused on me, just one tear escaped; she let it run down her cheek.

"Tell me the story again about how you and Mommy met." This was a family favorite. I hoped it would help her to remember it right then.

Mom heaved a sigh and reached over and patted my hand. "Your motive is obvious. But OK." She took a sip of coffee and began. "It was a hundred years ago, seems like. I was just starting out as a real estate salesperson for Framington Realty. I really wanted to score a big commission, as I had been working for them for three months and had sold nothing."

I smiled. "Yes. You were in a panic. Go on."

"I got a message that there was a vet looking for a house. My first thought was some soldier, probably with PTSD, looking for a place. I got ready to meet this Sam Poole in the office, and I wondered what he would be like, and if he would have any flashbacks when I showed him houses—what if something in the backyard reminded him of battle? There was a trench behind the first house I was going to show him, because of big plumbing repairs, and I was worried it might set him off.

"I was so engrossed in thinking about all of this that I didn't notice that a woman was standing in my office doorway. When she cleared her throat and I looked at her, I thought she was the most interesting looking person I had ever seen. She had bright, white hair tied in a ponytail! And orange glasses! And she was young!"

I nodded. The best part was coming. "And?"

"Well, she was very tall. She was wearing these green rubber boots up to her knees, and they were all muddy. They didn't go *at all* with her corduroy slacks and the black turtleneck. And she was wearing a strand of pearls! I couldn't wrap my head around her, but I just knew that this was a significant thing, this meeting. This was a person that was going to be important to me.

"I said something like 'Can I help you?' and she said that yes, she was Sam Poole. Every thought in my head scrambled, and then I started to laugh so hard. She looked confused until I explained the fact that I thought she was a soldier. Then *she* looked confused."

"Right—until you showed her the phone memo; that said 'vet,' right?"

"Right. Then Sam told me she was a veterinarian. And the boots made sense. She worked on horses back then."

I poked her hand. "Mom. The best part. Come on!"

She grinned. "OK. The best part. Sam reached out to shake my hand and I stood up to take it and knocked my nameplate off my desk. We both tried to catch it and ended up bumping heads. I saw stars. And I knew she was the one. Because of the stars."

My moms weren't star-crossed lovers. They were star-studded.

Π

That night was overcast, and there weren't any stars. I have to admit I sort of rushed Herkie the first few blocks, pulling at her leash every time she stopped to sniff a tree trunk or fallen leaf. As we neared the porch where we had met that unusual force of a girl, she stood and called out, "Hi, pit bull! Hi, Thomas!"

Herkie strained at the leash towards her, and it slipped right through my fingers. Herk cantered up to meet her, and this Dana phenomenon somehow managed to hoist Herkie up into her arms, all wriggling 55 pounds of her, and hug and kiss her a few times before releasing her with a groan. "This is a delicious pit bull dog! What is her name again? Hanky?"

As Herkie continued to writhe around Dana's ankles with much saliva and adoration, I managed to get hold of her leash and attempt to calm her down. "Sit, HERKIE, sit!"

Dana, rubbing a spot on her bumblebee striped leggings where Herk had probably speared her with a claw, laughed. "HERKIE. I am so sorry to forget her name. But Herkie is a *weird* name."

We began to walk toward the end of the block. "She is a rescue dog from Herkimer, New York. So her name is Herkimer."

"Got it. Still weird. If I had a dog, I would name him Saylor."

"Why?"

She stooped to pet Herkie on the rump. "Sabine and Saylor? Eloise's dolls? Haven't you read that book a thousand times?"

We were stopped on the curb, waiting for a car to pass in the darkness. Dana waved to the driver, who honked in return. "That's my neighbor, Mr. Ellis. I think he may be a pervert, but I am giving him the benefit of the doubt. Anyway, I have always wanted a dog and a cat. I would name the cat Sabine and the dog Saylor. Total literary allusion."

I had no reply. I was still processing both the perceived pervert and the literary allusion, so when Dana began to cross the street, Herkie and I remained rooted to our spot on the curb.

"Are you walking this animal, or not?" She stood on the opposite curb, her arms crossed against her chest. She waved us forward. "Come, Herkie!" Herkie jumped forward, pulling me along.

We started up the next block, Dana at quite a brisk pace. I put my hand on her arm to slow her down a bit. "OK. Here's the thing. Dana. If we are going to walk together (and I pulled a bit harder on her arm), first off, we have to slow down, because I am not an athlete. And second, I don't know anything about you, or you me. So we need to share backstories, don't you think?"

She laughed. Husky and raspy, like a rake through leaves. "OK. But we need to sit down. I can't give you the full benefit of my history if I can't look you in the face."

So when we got to the next street light, we sat down on the grassy front bank of a brick ranch house with lights shining out of a picture window. Dana smoothed her stick-straight hair and tucked a lock behind her ear, and she began. "Hi. My name is Dana Stryker. The spelling is important, because it is not S-T-R-I-K-E-R, it's S-T-R-Y-K-E-R. I am a foster child. I live with Trudy Owens. She is the best foster parent that I have experienced. I have been in ten foster homes. Some worse than others. Trudy wants to adopt me, but I don't want to be adopted."

"Wow."

"I know. I won't go into those other situations, because I have blotted them from my memory, and nobody needs to know about them." She bit at the corner of her thumbnail. "So do you want to hear about my parents?"

"Sure. Yes."

"My mom and dad died when I was two. My mother's name was Merle Evans. My father's name was Anthony Stryker. They were married, of course. I was their only child. My mother had the most beautiful auburn hair, and she smiled. She always smiled. Merle was only five feet tall, but somehow she seemed much taller, at least that is the way I imagine her. Anthony was six foot one, and he had a bald head and brown eyes that crinkled at the edges, you know, like when he grinned? I know this from the photos that I have of them. I have three photos. I wish there were more."

I stroked Herkie and nodded.

"Anthony was a cop, and Merle was a housewife. We lived in a little brown house with green shutters. I don't really remember it, but it's in one of the photos. In that one, we are all three standing in front of the house and laughing at something—it may have been at the photographer, but I think it was just because we must have laughed all the time."

At that, I had to breathe for a second to get a grip on my heart, which seemed to want to escape out of my chest cavity. I stroked my diaphragm. Dana looked at me with raised eyebrows, but kept right on talking.

"Anyway, I had a couple of years with two parents who adored me, a Teddy bear, lots of friends, and sunbeams, you know what I mean? Then, when I was two, they were driving down the highway after a night on the town, and they were hit head-on by a drunk driver and killed."

I gasped. "Oh, Dana. I am so sorry."

Dana ran her hand over the grass, head bowed. She didn't speak for what seemed like five minutes, but it couldn't have been that long. She raised her head suddenly. "For your information, I am not crying." Her cheeks were damp.

I was at a loss for words, because I was nearly in tears right along with her.

She motioned for us to get up and start walking again. "Yeah. So there weren't any close relatives. Merle had an aunt who was persuaded to take me in." Dana paused. Her eyes squinted closed. Then she opened them, and held out her left arm to me under the streetlight and pointed to a row of scars starting at the wrist and running up to her shoulder. Little, circular, angry scars. "Dear Aunt Ellen smoked."

My God. That statement was so shocking I nearly choked to death on my own saliva.

"Long story short, my kindergarten teacher noticed, and I was removed from sweet Aunt Ellen and started the rounds of foster homes. One good one, the rest not. But I ended up here, and Trudy is a peach, and so here I am. Backstory complete."

I nearly let go of Herkie, but managed to grip her leash with my now clammy fist. "Oh, Dana."

She rubbed the scars on her arm, scowling at them. "I was going to get a tattoo to cover them up. You know, like a winding reptile up to my shoulders, with the scars as part of his scales. Trudy said it would be OK. But I decided that I need to remember them, the scars. It's important."

"Why?" I wouldn't want to remember abuse.

"Because then I am taking myself out of it. Leaving all the others behind. They don't deserve that. We have to remember who we are and be strong. It's hard to explain, really. I am part of an army."

I had no idea what she meant. I watched as she smiled a hard smile then began to bite her thumbnail. She spit a piece of cuticle into her hand and studied it. "People like me—we have to band together."

"You stand up for one another? How many of you are there? My God, Dana, there can't be that many. In the world, yes, but here in little bitty Framington?"

Dana gave me an incredulous look. "There are all kinds of abuse, dummy. Haven't you ever seen a person smack a kid in the grocery aisle? Heard of leaving a three-year-old home alone? You are aware of the word 'bully,' right? Ever heard of Michael Vick?" She leaned down and stroked Herkie's muzzle. "I could go on and on. Jesus, Thomas, wake *up.*"

I wanted to put my arms around her and tell her it was OK. But I watched Dana stand, flex her arms—first one, then the other—her muscles strong and hard beneath the scars. She stood and strode off down the street, beckoning me and Herk to follow. I realized that this was a girl who seemed impervious to pity, or sympathy, or things like hugging. I imagined her wearing armor, sitting astride a huge, white steed.

Dana slowed down to wait for me to catch up. When I reached her, she turned her head to look at me, and her eyes glistened in the moonlight. She reached for my arm and wrapped her hand in mine. The image of her as Joan of Arc dissolved. I squeezed her hand, and she squeezed back. "The Eloise book. It was my mom's. She signed her name in it. It's probably my most prized possession."

We walked into the shadows.

Chapter Seven

Π

I heard her up in the attic, thumping around. Seven a.m. Good God. I wrestled the sweaty sheet off myself and sat up, listening. I knew it wasn't a raccoon, because they are nocturnal, and they don't yell "HELL AND DAMNATION!" after a particularly loud thud. I sighed, thrust my feet into my slippers, and padded out into the hall.

The door to the attic was open, and as I looked up the dusty stairs, I saw two sets of footprints—one human, the other canine. I yelled up into the eaves. "What are you two doing up there?"

Herkie appeared at the top of the stairs, her face wreathed in cobwebs, tail wagging with gusto. She yipped at me with that characteristic pit bull grin. Mom called down for me to "Come up here; I want to show you something!"

I sneezed twice as I went up the stairs. Herkie had stirred up the dust. I leaned down to wipe the cobwebs off her snout, and they stuck to my hand with that yucky insistence that webs have, and I swiped my hands on my pajamas, trying to dislodge the mess. I gave up and followed Herk to where my mom sat on an old army footlocker (must have been Grandpa's; neither of my parents were in the service), a gritty cardboard box on her knees.

"I am starting a project to clean out all this dreck from the attic. I don't want you to have to go through all this stuff after I die. And I just dropped a box on my foot."

I tensed. "This is a great way to start the day. Are you planning to leave this mortal coil any time soon?"

She shot me a disgusted look. "Tommy, of course not. But with Sam gone, I have come to realize that I am not getting any younger, and this is my responsibility. And what better time to do this than during our year of solitude?"

That did seem logical. "Move over, Mom. Let me see what you are looking at."

The box was filled with photos. Some Polaroids, and also the kind in the slick envelopes that you used to have to go to the drug store to get developed, back in the olden days before all our images of life were right there on an app in our cell phones. Mom's fingertips were black from the attic dirt that sifted down continually from the tarry eaves of our hundred-year-old house. Everything in the attic was covered in a fine, gritty residue.

"Look! This is one from the Easter when you were three! You hunted for one egg, ate some jelly beans, and wanted to call it a day. Oh, look at Sam in this! That was the year she got contact lenses. Look at how she is squinting. They absolutely ravaged her eyes. She was in pain all the time, and it killed her to be outside in the light. Those lasted for what, six months? And Rob has bunny ears on." In the photo, I stood in the backyard, a coat over my pajamas (Easter in Ohio is not a tropical affair), holding a large Easter basket. My hair was in what Mommy called a "practical" hairstyle—short, with bangs cut in a precise slash across my forehead. I frowned at the camera, probably because Mom was urging me to say "cheese." Sure enough, Rob stood behind Mommy and me, wearing the huge bunny ears and a goofy grin. He held two fingers behind Mommy's head, making bunny ears for her. I pressed the picture to my heart. Mom gently removed it from my hands to show me another one.

"This must have been a first day of school picture. What were you, in first grade?"

I remembered that day. In the photo, I stood in front of the white garage door, wearing a chartreuse T-shirt, and a denim skirt that I wore nearly every day that year because it had a ladybug embroidered on the pocket. Pigeon-toed, in the blue Keds with bright yellow shoelaces. My brand new navy blue Land's End backpack with my initials, TCP, embroidered on it. Thomasina Carruthers Poole. You couldn't have your actual name on anything, because then a kidnapper could call you by name. Really. "That was my first day of first grade, Mom. Remember? You were going to let me walk to school by myself, but Mommy said that was out of the question, and she had Nancy Frederick from next door walk me every day? Nancy was so nice. I wonder what ever happened to her?"

"Oh, they moved to Cincinnati. I have no idea." She didn't seem to be paying attention. She stared at the next picture from the pile, a dreamy look on her face. She stroked the surface of the photo, as if she could caress the woman in it. I leaned in to see. It was a picture of Mommy holding a little scruffy, white dog. He seemed to be struggling to get out of her arms; his back feet were blurred from the motion. Mommy smiled, determined, all her teeth showing. She looked so young.

"When was this? We have never had a dog. Mommy said she saw enough animals at work. How old was she in this picture? She looks like a kid."

Mom stroked the photo one more time and turned to me, her eyes bright. "This was the summer we moved into our first apartment. That was Bruno. Somebody brought him in to Sam's clinic. They found him wandering by the side of the road. He was just a puppy. We had him for seven years, until he developed mast cell cancer that spread very quickly. He died in our arms. Sam had to give him the shot to stop his heart." Mom wiped her eye with a dirty finger. It left a smudge under her eye like a bruise. "Sam couldn't bear to have another pet. Between losing dear Bruno and dealing with sickness and euthanasia at work, she just couldn't let herself get that attached to a pet of her own again."

My heart lurched. Mom seemed so happy to have Herkie with us. I looked at Herkie, covered in dust, sitting happily at our feet, the white spots on her fur dingy, a dead stinkbug on her shoulder. "Mom. This is something we should do together. I want to hear all your stories. I want to look at all of these pictures. And whatever is in these other boxes."

She nodded, sniffed, and then sneezed, alarming Herkie, who jumped up and put a paw on Mom's thigh in concern. Mom rubbed her nose on her sleeve, and then gathered up the loose photos and returned them to the box. "Yes. We should make albums. Otherwise, these will just turn into dust, and we won't have any memories to share in the future. With grandchildren." She poked me in the midsection.

"Good idea. I will order some albums from Amazon, and we can do this in the evenings when we aren't watching one of your Masterpiece Theatre shows."

We sorted through a few more piles of photos, Mom making comments like "You look like such a string bean in this; that was during your 'awkward stage,'" and "Oh, here we are standing in front of the Christmas tree! What was that—when you were in third grade? You wanted a pony, so Sam got you an aquarium with a seahorse. That died immediately."

Photo after photo. At the park. Birthday parties. The summer we all went to the beach. Grade school assemblies. Dance recitals. As we sorted through the images of our family's life, remarking on our evolution, with me getting ever older and Mom and Mommy aging as well, wrinkles and graying hair showing in the photos as they stood beside me, smiling at one another, it suddenly occurred to me that the photographer had to have been Rob, all these years. Rob documenting our lives, standing nearly always just outside the frame.

I held a photo of myself at around the age of ten or eleven. I had just gotten braces, and in the photo, Mom and Mommy are laughing, their arms across one another's shoulders as I scowled at the camera, refusing to bare my teeth, my hands behind my back. I remembered vividly that afternoon in the fall, leaves swirling through the air, the three of us standing on the front walk. I had goose bumps from the chilly air, a terrible adolescent attitude, which Mom and Mommy tried valiantly to ignore. Rob took what I thought were more than enough shots, and I wrested away from my mothers and turned on them. "Do we have document every single moment? Outside? In front of the entire population of Framington? Me and my gay parents? This is bullshit!" I ran inside and slammed the door behind me. Neither Mom nor Mommy followed. But I heard Rob's heavy steps on the stairs, and he knocked on my bedroom door. Of course, he came in.

He sat on the side of my bed and looked at his hands. His dark hair fell down over his forehead, and I thought he might be crying. He reached out and put a hand on my ankle, patted it with his gentle fingers, and without looking at me, said "Your mothers have always done absolutely everything they could to give you a safe and happy life." His pats became a bit rougher as he said, "You know they haven't had an easy time. How many of your friends have two mothers? Have you ever considered the way people around here look at them? Talk about them? Or are you just focused on how people treat *you?* Tommy, you aren't the only one in this equation."

Mom cleared her throat, bringing me back to the moment. I fingered the photo taken right before that adolescent outburst. Mom is smiling, but only barely. Mommy's eyes are wide; she probably senses the anger in the set of my shoulders under her arm. I look like I am ready to explode, my hands balled into fists. I handed the photo to Mom.

She studied it again, rubbing the image with her thumb. "Do you remember when this was taken? You look so angry. Must have been the precursor of teenage angst. You had a rough time, growing up as our child. I always wished I could help you with your anxiety. You were such a worrier."

My throat tightened. I looked down at the box, filled with all those tiny pieces of paper covered with images of me, Mom, and Mommy, now fading and curling at the edges. "Yes. The three of us. You, Mommy, and me. Can I have one of these?" Mom nodded. I slipped one of the photos into the back pocket of my jeans.

We rummaged through the box, pulling out more decks of photos. Mom, a dreamy look on her face, sorted through them, putting aside one here and there.

"Mom, what is it like to be in a marriage? Is it hard to stay together for so many years?"

I was holding a photo of Mom and Mommy, along with the four friends that they were closest to for as long as I can remember: Alice Jones, who was a Borzoi breeder whose dogs all became patients of Mommy's; Leah Nash, who went to college with Mommy; Sukie Barnett, my God Parent, who died of cancer when I was in college, and Penny Suarez, who Mom still called on the phone at least once a month. They were on a picnic somewhere, all of them wearing silly hats, arms around one another's shoulders, grinning at the camera. I wondered who took the picture.

Mom ran a hand through her hair. "Why do you ask? That's a strange question, out of the blue like that."

I held out the picture and showed it to her. "Where was this taken?"

She took it, tapping it with her finger. She peered closely at it. "Oh, I think that was soon after you were born.

You were so colicky! We got a baby sitter and went out into the woods to frolic—we needed the break. My God. Look how young we all were."

"What ever happened to Leah Nash?"

She looked up at me, her eyes narrowed. She handed the photo back. A few seconds passed before she answered. "She moved to Chicago in 1990."

I pushed the photo back into her hand. "She came to the funeral. But not to the gathering afterward. How come?"

Mom dropped the picture into the box and picked up another handful of shots. "Tommy, I have no idea. We were all good friends, but time goes on, and people grow apart. She was more Sam's friend than mine. Maybe she just came to pay her respects, but didn't feel like horning in on our family's mourning. It was nice of her to come. I had no expectations that she would stick around after the funeral. It doesn't matter." She began to sort through the photos in her hand. "Oh, Tommy. Look at this one—you were wearing jelly shoes! Remember those?"

That afternoon, after I set up a Twitter chat for a client who was touting her startup cosmetics company, I shut down my computer with a loud click. I picked up my cell and looked at my home screen. A photo of our house. Large, gray stucco, with a pointed peak, white trim, surrounded by boxwood hedge, a lion head brass knocker on the door. A big house, but such a small world. I opened my drawer, took out the Post-it pad, a pencil, and wrote another notation:

SECRETS

I stuck that under the first Post-it on my mirror and went downstairs for a break. I needed some caffeine to clear my head.

Chapter Eight

П

As soon as I clipped her leash to her collar, Herkie trotted out the front door, sniffed the night air, her nails clicking on the pavement. We reached the end of our front walk, and she took a hard right, pulling me in the direction of Dana's house. Herk never wavered. As far as she was concerned, we no longer took midnight walks—we went over to Dana's house.

As Halloween approached, things turned nippy in Framington. The few remaining leaves still attached to branches shone russet and gold in the streetlights, and we scuffed through the mountains of the ones piled at the curb, waiting for the city to remove them. Herkie loved to rumble through the piles. I hoped nobody was watching from their windows as we walked by.

Dana stood at the bottom of her front steps, her cigarette signaling us from a block away. Herkie strained at her leash, but I was training her in delayed gratification, so I told her to "sit" and "stay." However, as I was a terrible dog trainer, Herkie often pretended not to know what I was talking about. She didn't sit, and I had to brace the leash with both hands to keep her from galloping toward Dana.

I called out to Dana, "You can go ahead and call her!"

Dana yodeled, "Come pit bull!" and I released Herk, who took off like the proverbial bat leaving hell. I caught up with them as Dana smacked kisses all over Herkie's happy nose.

"This pit bull is the very best dog the world has to offer." Dana squatted in front of Herk, closing her eyes as the best dog ever licked her eyes.

I sat down on the steps. "I know. She doesn't have a mean bone. And yet, our asshat neighbor thinks she is lethal, and he shakes his fist at her from inside his back window whenever I let her out to do her business in our *totally-fenced-in-with-a-six foot-iron-fence backyard.*"

Dana smirked. "Maybe you can train her to attack on command, and then she can kill him."

"That is not remotely funny. I am afraid he is going to call the police on her. I have to be very careful."

Dana stood up, stretched her hands over her head, fists clenched, the cigarette hanging from the side of her mouth. "I'll put him on my list."

"What are you talking about?"

Dana looked down at me, took a final drag on her cigarette, then crushed it under her studded Dr. Martens boot. Then she sat beside me and patted my knee. "I keep track of things. Score. Things need to be even." Dana closed one eye and nodded slowly. Under the dim light of the autumn moon, her hair looked even purpler than it had before. Her barbed-wire tattoo twisted as she turned to me and pointed, her fist in the shape of a gun. "Nobody's alone out there."

"What are you talking about, kiddo? Lots of people are alone. I am alone. Well, my mom and I are alone. It was our choice. And there are plenty of people who are alone, not by choice. That is just factual."

Dana spread her arms in front of her and wiggled her fingers, as if warming up for something. "Thomas. You are just like the majority of people. You think you are operating in a vacuum. You just don't notice that there are people, other people. And they are watching you. Noticing things."

I leaned back on my elbows, feeling the concrete press into my flesh. "So? I realize people notice things. I notice things, too. What is your point?"

Dana smiled at me. Her teeth gleamed in the moonlight like a row of Chiclets. Her front left tooth was chipped. It gave her a look of vulnerability. "Hey, do you want to meet Trudy? She has been wondering about you."

So she changed the subject. Dana stood, brushed the backs of her thighs with her hands, and motioned for Herk and me to follow her. We climbed the steps to the dark oak door of her bungalow. Dana opened it with a creak, and motioned us in with a flourish. "Hey, Mother Figure! We have guests!"

It was a typical foyer: Hardwood floors stained a golden brown. A little side table against the left wall, lamp lit, a dish with keys. An oval braided rug: burgundy, brown, and gold—straight out of L. L. Bean. Walls the color of weak tea. Living room on right, dining on left. Stairs in front of us. Coming down the stairs was what at first I thought was a woman wearing some sort of Halloween mask, one side normal, and the other a thickened, red web of scars.

She was short. Not as short as a little person, but she looked like she might fit in my pocket. Maybe five feet tall. In the hand that wasn't gripping the banister was a book. She was wearing a blue terry robe over pajamas—no surprise, as it was after midnight. As soon as she caught sight of Herkie, her "mask" altered, and the area of her mouth gaped in a wide grin. "Oh, this is the famous pit bull!" Despite the wreck of her face, her voice was as soft as a lullaby.

I tried to gather my wits about me. As she got closer, I could see that this was a woman who had suffered a massive burn. The scars wreathed her smile; one in particular had nearly obliterated her top lip. I gasped, then instantly regretted it. I put my hand over my mouth, and then snatched it away. I was mortified at myself. So I stuck out my hand like some sort of politician, grabbing Trudy's and shaking it violently.

"Oh, so nice to meet you. So nice. Oh, yes. I am Tommy Poole, your daughter's friend. We met one night a few weeks ago as I was walking my dog," I pointed to Herkie, whose head was under this strange woman's hand. "I see that both you and your daughter are dog whisperers." Blathering.

"Oh, yeah. Trude, this is Thomas. And pit bull, otherwise known as Herkie. Thomas, this is my foster mom, Trudy Owens."

Trudy beamed at us. Her blue eyes were the color of swimming pools, surrounded by dark lashes. She must have covered them when whatever it was burned her, because they were unscathed, beautiful. As soon as I looked into them, I sort of forgot about the scars. I realized that I was still grasping her hand, and I dropped it. Awkward was the word for my entire performance so far, but Trudy Owens didn't seem to notice it.

"The benefits of being night owls—wonderful new friends! Would you like to come in and have some iced tea? Chamomile?"

I nodded, not trusting myself to speak further. We filed into the cozy living room, where two coffee-colored sofas flanked the stone fireplace. Rust velvet throw pillows. Another braided rug, this one navy and gray with rusty flecks. Craftsman touches everywhere, including leaded glass windows on either side of the mantel with Gingko leaves embedded in the glass. I loved it.

As soon as Trudy left to get the tea, Dana whispered, "She pulled a pot of soup off the stove onto herself when she was a toddler. No such thing as plastic surgeons in PikeTon, Kentucky back then. Well, not for poor people."

"I am sorry, Dana."

"Don't be. She deals with it. But growing up wasn't easy. You know the drill. Bullies, name-calling, loneliness.

Here's the thing, Thomas: she survived. And guess how she did it?" Dana's eyes narrowed, her brow drawn into two straight lines. "She had a friend. One person. Who looked out for her."

Trudy scuffed in, carrying a small tray with two tumblers of iced chamomile. Not my favorite tea, but I accepted one and took a large sip. Ugh.

"Mother Figure, I was just telling Thomas about you. You know, the accident. Have to get that out of the way immediately, right?"

Trudy offered the tea to Dana, then placed the empty tray on the coffee table and lowered herself onto the sofa opposite us, carefully arranging the blue terry cloth to cover her lap. As she smoothed the sash of her robe, I saw that her left hand was also scarred. I tried not to stare.

Trudy looked into my eyes and smiled, lifting her robe to expose the scar on her forearm. "Yes. We have to address the elephant in the room every time. Then we can get over that and just talk. Be friends." She lowered the sleeve and continued, "I suffered this burn from boiling water when I was three. My mother had her back turned in the kitchen. The rest is history. Oh, I nearly forgot!" She reached into the pocket of her robe and pulled out a Ritz cracker. "Can Herkie have a treat? I am afraid I don't have any actual dog biscuits."

Herkie accepted the cracker and crunched it with great relish. "Herkie loves everything. Thank you." I grabbed her by the collar before she jumped into Trudy's lap. "What is the magic that you two possess with dogs? Herkie likes people, but I have never seen her fall in love with anybody the way she has with the two of you!"

Dana shrugged, but Trudy answered. "An underdog recognizes an underdog. Right, kiddo?" She exchanged looks with her daughter. "It takes one to know one."

I squirmed a little in my seat, and took another sip of tea. I wiggled my toes inside my sneakers and bit the inside of my cheek. I glanced at my wrist, but damn, I didn't wear a watch. "You know what? It is getting late, and Herkie hasn't even pooped yet. I better get out there and let her do her business. It was so nice to meet you, Trudy. No, Dana—you stay here with your mom. Herkie and I need to get going."

Dana walked us to the door. "Jesus, Thomas. You got white as a sheet in there. Are you scared of my foster mom's face? Just like everybody else? That is ironic, since you are so obviously a member of our tribe." She couldn't shut the door behind us fast enough.

I managed to get as far as the end of the block before I had to stop, sit down on the curb, and try to sort through all the thoughts surging inside my head. Dana called me a member of her tribe. Outliers. *Was I one of those?* I thought about my first encounter with stereotyping. First grade. Playground at recess. A chant, lead by Lisa Freed: "Tommy's moms are queers! Tommy's moms are queers!" Mrs. Damron heard it and shushed Lisa, but as she dragged her away, Lisa stuck out her tongue at me and laughed.

Oh my God. The father/daughter picnic that year. When Donnie Grange whispered that "You can't go, because you only have mothers. Your family is a bunch of weirdos."

I hadn't thought about that in years. Dana called me on it. I sat there, breathing through my mouth and leaning against my dog until I could gather my wits about me. Mom. Mommy. Others.

It was a long walk home.

Π

"Mom, do you know Trudy Owens?" It was cooler now, so we could be up in the attic in the evenings now. So far, we had sorted through a dozen boxes of stuff, some of it going to Goodwill. I kept Mommy's Ohio State sweatshirt. It was at least one size too small, but I didn't care. Mom sat in an old, ratty lawn chair missing at least three rows of netting. She was going through Christmas ornaments.

"You made this construction paper Santa in first grade." She put it to her nose and sniffed it.

"Come on. How can you tell just from looking and sniffing it that I made it in first grade?"

"Because it says so," she turned it over, "right here on the back, in your spidery handwriting: 'Tommy Poole, grade one.' Trudy Owens? Sure. She is the Grocery Manager at AllFoods. Wonderful woman. Such a tragedy about the burns."

I sorted through the rest of the box of clothing. Nothing worth saving. I wondered once again how all this stuff got stored in the attic in the first place. I looked up as Mom ooohed over another ornament.

"This one was the year Sam and I took you skiing in Aspen. You hated it, and whined the entire time, and we ended up coming home early. What a tyrant you were at 13. We bought this ornament to remember that awful trip." She twirled the little ski sweater, pine green with a red stripe. I remembered that trip. I got my period, a huge pimple on the tip of my nose, and on my first trip down a hill, I fell and sprained my wrist.

"If you recall, they didn't have feminine hygiene products in the ski lift restroom, and you suggested I buy a pair of socks in the gift shop and stuff them in my underwear. And my wrist that swelled to three times its normal size? Me? A tyrant? How about you two—so obsessed with 'making family memories' that you ignored my medical emergencies?" We both laughed. Mom put the sweater back in the box of ornaments.

"Tommy, do you think we should put up the tree this year? With it just being the two of us?" She sighed and blew the air through her lips loud enough to bring Herkie up the stairs at a trot, alarmed.

"Of course we should. Rob will come. And maybe I will invite my new night friend." I reached down to chuck Herk under her chin. "The one Herkie runs to see every single time we go out for our moonlight walks. Dana. I just mentioned her foster mom, Trudy. You said you know her."

Mom did that foldy thing where you tuck the corners of a cardboard box so that they intertwine. I have never mastered that skill. She raised her eyebrows at me and my sweet doggo. "You never mentioned that you have a 'night friend.' Oh, yes! I knew that Trudy was a foster parent. I think she has had quite a few kids over the years. So this Dana is living with her? What is she like? Is she a nice little girl?"

I snorted. "Let's see. Where do I begin?" I rolled my eyes. "First off, she isn't little. She is nearly sixteen, she has tattoos, she smokes, she calls me 'Thomas,' Herkie 'pit bull,' and Trudy 'Mother Figure.' She is as tough as nails, and she could probably take on a street gang with one hand tied behind her back and turn them all into choirboys, if you catch my drift. Yeah. She's a nice little girl."

Mom put a hand over her mouth, shocked, I was sure. "But she's your *friend?*"

"I know, right? But Mom, here's the thing: Herkie fell in love with her at first sight. You know how Mommy always said that dogs have infallible judgment when it comes to humans? And this kid scared me at first with her ferocity, but she grew on me. Smart as the proverbial whip, and underneath her razor wire tattoo, I think she is actually quite vulnerable." An image of Dana giving me the bum's rush the night before came to mind. "Well, sorta vulnerable."

"How long has she been with Trudy?"

I shook my head. "I don't know. Maybe a year? Apparently, Dana has had a history of abuse. She told me she had been with a number of foster families that she won't discuss. Oh, Mom, I am so embarrassed. I met Trudy last night. I couldn't disguise my shock at her appearance, and I am sure it was a complete insult to her. Dana was happy to see me go. What a jerk I am!"

"Well, I am sure that Trudy is used to people's reactions by now. Don't be too hard on yourself. Dana might have prepared you for seeing her mom. That was rude of her not to, don't you think? Rude to both you and Trudy?" She pressed her lips together.

I paused to let that sink in. "Maybe that was a test. Maybe Dana set me up to see if I am a true blue person, and I obviously failed the test. Or do you think she just doesn't see Trudy's real face when she looks at her? She just sees Trudy? Maybe she assumed that I would see the real Trudy, too?" I put my face in my grubby hands and shook my head, inhaling the dust. I sneezed. Mom rooted around in her pocket and handed me a wadded Kleenex. I swiped at my nose with it, and then blew. Herkie jumped.

Mom licked her finger, reached over, and wiped a smut from under my eye. "I can't make any sort of determination about this kid's character without meeting her. I think you may be right about her, though—any friend of Herkie's is a friend of ours. And since we are 'shut-ins,'" she cocked an eyebrow ironically, "why don't you ask her to come over? I could bake something."

I held out my hands in protest. "Mom. We have established that you are *most decidedly not* Emily Dickinson. No baking! But it's a good idea. I will ask her to come over to meet you, since I met her 'mom.' Should I call her a 'mom,' since she is a foster parent? Maybe I will just stick with calling her Trudy..."

By the time I had finished that little soliloquy, Mom and Herkie were on their way downstairs, probably to look up some muffin recipes.

Chapter Nine

Π

Cabin fever. The dictionary defines it as a type of hysteria that results from spending too much time indoors. Irritability. Feelings of frustration. Boredom. Nowhere in the definitions do you find mentioned enlightenment, introspection, or Henry David Thoreau. I checked at least three different online dictionaries, but nope. Mom and I had certainly lapsed into a rhythm. She did more housework than necessary while I worked on my computer, making social media stars out of my annoying clients. Then, in the afternoons, she napped.

This was her "my time." Mom coined the phrase for the hours during the day when she lay down on her duvet in the master bedroom to dream of idyllic days in the past with Sam while I bounced from wall to wall in the rest of the house.

At first, being home all day was so refreshing. No pressure from annoying coworkers, horning into my cubicle with YouTube videos on their phones, "so hilarious." No meager packed lunches. No stupid meetings in which the moderator had never heard of the word *agenda.* No Spanx under business suits. But that was day one of hermitude. Pretty soon, I had memorized the repeating pattern on the wallpaper in the dining room (four ivy leaves, one berry, four ivy leaves, three berries, *a bird,* four ivy leaves—you know where this is going), counted the steps on the front and back stairways (twenty and twenty two), noted that there were seven dead flies in between the storm windows and the screens in my bedroom, and ascertained that we have four half-used bottles of Worcestershire sauce in the pantry.

I tried keeping a journal, and that was a bust. The first three entries were:

Monday. Still hot. We have been hermits for a week.

Friday. Hot. It is four days later. I wish I were a poet.

Thursday. Forget this.

So this year was going to be a colossal challenge. As I sat in the sunroom, looking out at the backyard, I wished I could just run out there. It wasn't off limits, but we only went out there for dog business. Wait. Maybe run out there naked, singing *Joy to the World* (the bullfrog one, not the Christmas carol) at the top of my lungs. Just as I was picturing that, and almost feeling the breezes rushing against my nudity, I caught a movement out of the corner of my eye. Something bright red.

I turned and looked over at Percy Warner's garden. There he stood, fat and sassy in a red sweat shirt, toupee riding a little low on his forehead, potbelly bulging, surveying his kingdom. He squinted his piggy eyes, hand over his forehead, gazing through the fence at *our* yard. Suddenly, he straightened up, seemed to gasp, and then ran as fast as his stubby legs could carry him over to the edge of the iron fence dividing our yards. He pulled a cell phone from his pocket and held it to his ear.

I knew what to expect next. Our landline rang.

"Hello?"

It sounded like he had a tracheotomy, he was gasping so loudly. "SHIT. There is dog shit right here! It is on THE PROPERTY LINE. I want this dog shit out of my yard IMMEDIATELY, or I will call the city!" More gasping and rasping.

Rage. It filled my lungs, my heart, and my brain. If I had a gun at that moment, I would have aimed it right through the picture window at the center of that red sweatshirt and pulled the trigger. Instead, I pushed the button and 'hung up' on him. I waited for my breathing to slow down.

Damn. The lawn service must not be getting all of it. I didn't blame them; I would try to overlook as much dog poop as possible if I were a gardener. But I would have to do something to calm Percy down. I looked at the receiver in my hand and regretted hanging up like that. Rudeness begets God knows what else. *What should I do? Flowers? No. Way too much an admission of guilt. Cookies? A good idea, but we wouldn't be able to deliver them.* I put the receiver down in the cradle and started walking aimlessly.

I paced the perimeter of the downstairs. Sunroom, hall, into the dining room, through the kitchen, then back out into the hall, through the living room, into the sunroom. I picked up speed, hoping to burn off a few calories while walking and brainstorming. Suddenly, I was joined by a concerned Herkie, who must have been worried that someone may have decided to chase me.

Herk and I marched on, my thoughts twirling. *This guy hates my dog. But lots of people are scared of pits. Their unfair reputation. What can I do to make him realize that you* (I leaned down to grab her snout and kiss it) *are a moosh? How can I get through to this guy?*

My cell beeped. Caller ID said *Suzanne Lampley.* Hooray for friends. I pulled it out of the waistband of my leggings.

"Hello, Suze. You can't imagine how much I want to talk to you this very instant!"

She "ahem-ed" at her end. "Is this a crisis? I am not prepared to deal with a crisis right now. I am calling from my car. I am actually on my way over to spend the weekend with you! Isn't this a thrill? We can discuss your crisis and solve every single world problem as soon as I get there."

I did three modified jumping jacks, one-armed, holding my cell to my ear. Herk jumped right along with me. My heart pounded. "This is the best news, ever! The walls are closing in over here, I have an evil pig for a neighbor, and I need to tell you about this kid I met who is a combination gangbanger/philosopher. And so many other things. So many. How soon will you be here?"

"Tommy, deep breaths. I should arrive in about an hour and a half. Change the sheets in the guest room. I refuse to sleep among Oreo crumbs like the last time I was there. Gotta go—the cops ticket you if they see you on a cell phone. Bye!"

I grabbed Herkie's front paws, and we did a little jig in the hall. Then I raced up the stairs, Herkie nearly tripping me up as she leaped at my legs. "Mom! Mom! Wake up! We can have a PAR-TAY this weekend!"

Π

Herkie and I posted ourselves at the front window, scanning every car that came down the street. I straightened up with every swoosh of tires, but was disappointed. Then suddenly, the sight for sore eyes roared toward us. A lime green VW, vintage, of course, with an orange daisy painted smack dab in the center of the front hood. I let out a cheer, and Herkie wagged, despite not having one canine idea what was going to happen.

I ran to the front door and threw it open as the dazzling car pulled into the driveway. I nearly ran out to hug Suze, but I remembered the rules and pulled my leg back inside the threshold. Suze flung her door open and stood, carroty curls shining in the sun. She slammed the door shut and held out her arms. Herkie ran into them. "Hi, honey!" She bent down and encircled Herk's thick neck in a hug, then straightened and shot me a squinty look. "Why are you frozen to the spot? HUGS, Tommy!"

I remained rooted, despite every single nerve in my person telling me to rush out there. "Hermit rules! Come in here this minute!"

Suze put her hands on her hips and rolled her eyes skyward. "Crap! I have to carry all this shit in myself?" She opened the hood of her vintage VW. It was loaded. "I have here an entire cooler full of Jeni's ice cream, a bag of bull penises for Herkie (!), five board games, including Trivial Pursuit and Jenga, some potpourri and bubble bath for your Mom, a giant-size barrel of pretzels, and of course, clothes. AND BEER. I have to bring this all in myself?"

I looked around for witnesses, and seeing none, I skipped out to Suze's car. We hugged the breath out of one another's lungs, Herkie restrained herself from knocking us down with enthusiasm, and we carted Suze's things inside. It took three trips, my God.

I hated shutting the front door. As it clicked closed, the brightness of the sun suddenly diminished, along with the happy thrum of my soul. But as we lugged the cooler of Jeni's into the kitchen, Suze's laugh reverberated against the walls, and I cheered right up again. Suze humped into the hall and staggered back into the kitchen with a second cooler. The beer.

Mom heard the hubbub. She burst into the kitchen and enveloped us both with a hug. "Oh, Suzanne! You are just the right thing! This is going to be such a fun-filled weekend!"

I studied the crinkles around Mom's eyes. I had never heard a person use the term "fun-filled" in actual life. Mom's cheeks were flushed, her eyes sparkled, and she rubbed us both on our backs. Rubbed and patted. Smiled, rubbed and patted. She dropped her arms and stepped back. "Oh, what's this?"

Suze opened the first cooler. "Jeni's! Brown Butter Almond Brittle. Coffee with Cream and Sugar. Of course,

Middle West Whiskey and Pecan. Salted Peanut Butter with Chocolate Flecks. Have I forgotten something?"

I shrieked. "I WANT TO START ON THE PEANUT BUTTER RIGHT NOW!"

Mom grabbed me by the back of my shirt. "Calm down, tiger! We have to have a smorgasbord for dessert tonight. Rob is coming. We can call out for pizza delivery. I have salad makings. But dessert will be the climax. Tommy, we need to make room in the freezer."

As I shoved bags of peas, Lean Cuisines, and veggie burgers out of the way to make room, Mom and Suze lugged the rest of her stuff upstairs. They murmured and laughed as I shoved the icy treats into the freezer; I could hear their footsteps above me. The sounds of *people* in the house. I shut the freezer door and leaned against the fridge, reveling in the noise.

Suze thundered down the steps and entered the kitchen with the bag of penises. "I thought at least one of us here might enjoy these." She giggled and opened the bag, taking out a long, thick stick. She waved it around like a magic wand, before summoning my dog. "Herkie, come! Oh, my God, no pun intended!" Herkie sniffed the treat, then gently took it in her teeth and carried it out of the kitchen.

"Those are actual bull penises? Come on."

She held up the bag and read the label. "Made from 100% grass-fed beef pizzle. I asked the guy at the pet food store what pizzle was, and he said 'beef dicks.' So yes. These are the real deal, and the guy said they are the very best treats. You can interpret that any way you would like." Suze pulled out another stick and held it in front of her pelvis suggestively. "We might get some use out of these?" She began to do an Elvis Presley bump.

I grabbed the stick from her, dropped it into the bag, and shoved the bag into the cupboard under the sink. I whirled around and rubbed my greasy fingers on my leggings. "Let me just say that if I ever even consider these as adult entertainment, you can shoot me. Enough about bull dicks. Should we have one of your beers?"

"Of course!" Suze looked around for the other cooler—the one that had the Coors.

Cradling our cool bottles, we sat down on the polished wood floor against the kitchen cupboards, our legs straight out in front of us. I swallowed nearly half of my beer in one pull, the delicious bitterness bubbling down into my stomach. Suze shot me a look.

"You are drinking like a pro, kid. Are you sure this shut-in thing is a good idea?"

I looked down the neck of my bottle and noted the remaining brew. I felt a little prick of alarm, then remembered that the only stuff I had been imbibing lately was caffeinated. "First off, this is the first alcohol I have had since I came home. Honest." I gave Suze the Girl Scout salute. "Second, of *course* this 'shut-in thing' is a lousy idea. But it wasn't my idea, and I cannot leave Mom here to stew alone."

Suze made a wry face. "She seems fine to me. Normal."

I twirled the bottle between my palms. I noticed that a corner of the label was beginning to peel, and I picked at it, working as if my life depended on it. "She *is* normal. A normal, grieving, bleeding-on-the-inside woman. Suzanne, Mom is deceptively chipper. But she is hollow. She doesn't eat right. You saw how thin she is. She has started biting her nails. She has nightmares. If she were here by herself, I am not sure what would happen. So I have to stay with her. She is all I have."

Silence surrounded us. I continued to pick at the Coors label. The beer got warm. I took a sip and set the bottle down beside me; I didn't want the rest. I studied the cuticles on my thumbs.

Suze scrambled to her feet. "Well then. Let's just have us a rip-roaring weekend of fun." And with that, she pulled me to my feet into a hug, kicking over my bottle of beer. It made a foamy puddle on the floor. My darling dog padded into the kitchen and lapped it up.

Suze laughed. "Yes, you darling pit bull! You know how to get the party started!"

I hefted the beer cooler onto the counter, Suze opened the fridge door with a flourish, and we deposited the beer onto the shelves, reserving another two bottles for ourselves.

"And Tommy. If you don't get anchovies on at least half of one of the pizzas, I will put that photo of you with your pants around your ankles on Facebook."

Chapter Ten

Π

Rob brought vodka and tonic with a bag of limes. Mom was thrilled, because in her words, "Beer gives me gas."

Pizza is a kitchen food. We lit a couple of candles, Mom put paper towels and plates out, and we sat, drinking vodka, beer, and eating pepperoni with extra cheese.

Suze, who eats her pizza folded, and never gets any sauce on her shirt as a result, looked around at the three of us and observed, "This is a huge house. Meg, you have three sets of French doors! It isn't exactly Downton Abbey around here, but with a sunroom, five bedrooms, a finished basement and your foyer—which is the size of my apartment—is staying inside all of the time sort of charming? Like you are in your own totally carefree environment? Not like Miss Havisham—you two aren't nutcases or anything."

"Suzy, it *is* a large place. Sam and I picked it out, hoping we would fill it with a big family and lots of noise. That didn't work out. We only had the one (she crinkled her eyes at me in such a loving look I nearly cried) child, but Tommy made us so happy that we didn't mind that she was our only." Mom looked around the kitchen, as if hoping that Sam would be somewhere in the background. She drew her bottom lip in and bit it.

A piece of pizza lodged in my throat, and I started coughing. Mom clapped me on the back and kept on talking.

"It has always been a haven. So yes, I guess part of this is my withdrawing, in this place where I—*we*—(Mom tilted her head in my direction) feel safe."

Something pinged behind my eyes. I blinked hard. "Mom. You make our lives sound like some sort of fairy tale. My God."

Rob set his pepperoni on the side of his plate, smoothed out his paper towel and blew his nose loudly. "Tommy?"

Mom drew her eyebrows together and frowned at me. She rubbed her thumb over her wrist. "You are right, honey. No family is perfect."

She continued to look straight into my eyes, until I had to look away. "Yes, we were not mainstream. Of course it wasn't all sweetness and light. That goes without saying. But we had friends, and we had good times. Our circle was very limited, but there was a small gay community, and we embraced it. Framington was tolerant *enough*. So we lived here, did our work outside, and pretty much kept to our circle of friends and our little family. We stepped outside of the circle rarely, to march for gay rights in Columbus, and to support the LGBTQ community here. So when I lost Sam, despite the support of my friends, there was emptiness. I just can't go back out there and fight without her. Not yet."

Suze looked alarmed that she had somehow touched on all of this. "Oh, Meg, I didn't mean to make you explain yourself. I am sorry if you think I was making light of your situation." Suze spoke and shredded her paper towel into bits simultaneously.

Rob cut in. "Suze, it's OK."

I looked at Rob, his brow drawn up with concern. My father. Just thinking of Rob as the man whose sperm made me human was unnerving. Rob was my 'uncle,' my best friend and supporter as I grew up, my male role model, and the big brother I didn't have. The word 'Dad' had never entered my vernacular. It was always in my mind, however. Dearest Rob.

Mom continued. "Suzy, someday, I hope you find someone whom you love as much as I did Sam. And I hope you have a lifetime together. It is only when you know that kind of love that you can understand how much of a mortal wound it is when your partner dies."

Suze put her head down on the table and banged it twice. "I am such an idiot."

Mom got up and leaned over Suze, enveloping her in a hug. "No, honey. You are just honest and true. That's all."

Rob stood and began to gather up the pizza detritus. I rose to help him, running my hand over Suze's shoulders as I passed. Mom waved us off. "Let Suzy and me be alone for a few minutes. We'll clean up. You two go watch television or something."

Π

The news was on, but the commentators might as well have been speaking Greek, for all I could tell. Rob sat in Sam's worn, tobacco-brown leather recliner, straight up, not reclining an inch. I sat cross-legged on the floor in front of him – stiff, awkward, hesitant.

Rob looked down at me and a smile flickered, and then disappeared. He picked at the crease in his armrest, then he just let go. "I love you, Tommy. You know that. But I could never be your 'dad.' It just wasn't in the cards..."

"I know. Open secret." I looked around for my dog. I needed emotional backup. But Herkie was in the kitchen, probably eating her weight in pizza crust. "Rob, I grew up just fine. Nobody at school bullied me. Some kids in fifth grade started saying that I had 'Lesbo Moms,' and the school shut that down big time, so that ended as fast as it began. I was called 'Butch' a few times—no biggie. And Mommy coached our soccer team from sixth grade to ninth, so all the girls loved her." I looked up at Rob. He stared at the television screen, reached for the remote, and muted it. My lips felt so very dry, all of a sudden. "It was me. I was the one who wished for a mom and a dad, not two moms." My eyes burned.

"When they told me who my biological father was, I couldn't even take it in, you know? I was both thrilled and resentful. I wanted to have you as my dad. But of course, I knew that wasn't possible. We couldn't live together like Goldilocks and her three bears. And that made me even more angry. Why didn't they just have some random sperm donor? Why did it have to be this ungodly parental combination? And then it became obvious that we couldn't even talk about it. It was a forbidden subject."

Rob leaned forward and put a hand on his heart. "So that is why you are here. To try to make sense of your life so far. Sam is gone, and you are trying to fill in all the blanks. Honey, I understand. But be so careful. Your mom is not very strong."

I scrambled up onto my knees and put my hands on the arms of the recliner. "Haven't you felt resentment? You aren't married. You don't have any children you can claim as your own. You are fifty years old, Rob! You have been denying your feelings about this all your adult life. You aren't torn as well?"

He took my hands, clasped them in his, and then pushed me gently back down onto the floor. His eyes drooped. I waited for him to collect himself. "Meg, my sister is," he ran a hand through his hair, obviously casting around for words, "for want of a better term, the light of my life. Our parents always sensed that Meg was 'different,' and they tormented her with their attempts to make her conform. They made it very clear that she was some sort of a degenerate, and Gram and Gramps basically shut her off emotionally. Meg was treated cruelly by our parents from early on. When she 'came out,' they never spoke to her again. She was a junior in college. They informed her that the door was locked to her from that moment on. So she lived with me after that. Can you picture it, Tommy? Christmases in my little grubby apartment, the two of us? Meg cooking a turkey breast in my toaster oven?" Rob shook his head. "It was the two of us, until Meg made enough money in real estate to get her own grubby apartment." He looked down at me with those kind, deep eyes. "You know this; you never had a relationship with your grandparents on Meg's side. It was Meg and me against them, against the world."

He paused. It was starting to get dark outside. A shadow fell across his face, muting the gleam in his eyes and turning his hair into a dark whorl against the back of the recliner. "You see, Tommy, Meg so wanted for Sam to have their own child. And the only way for that to happen was for me to be the donor. You understand, don't you? "You are Meg and Sam's daughter. Real family. You are not adopted, or from a surrogate. You are your mothers' flesh and blood. I had to do that for them."

"But why did they suppress all this? Wasn't that so cruel to you? And to me? To keep me in the dark about all of it for so long, and just pretend to be our own little nuclear family of three? And their 'circle of friends.' Didn't they realize they were taking something important away from you and me?" My guts twisted. All of the uncertainty, resentment, and pain that I had pushed down bubbled up into an acidic broth. I rubbed my stomach and chest, trying to soothe myself before something inside me ruptured.

Rob must have sensed that I was about to come apart at the seams. He slid out of the recliner and sat beside me on the floor. He put his arms around me, and I let my head rest on his shoulder. I could feel the pulse in his wrist throb where it touched my cheek.

"Tommy. It happened the way it had to happen. Honey, this is *real life.* Real. Life."

"Real life. It is way too complicated. Rob, that picture Mom just painted in there. It's idealized. Things weren't cut and dried, us and them. Right?"

"Honey, we all carry around a picture of 'reality,' even if it's skewed."

"So everybody has their own version, I guess." There was a prickling in my lungs. "Layers and layers of stuff; life is such an amalgam of emotions. People. Truths. Things never revealed."

He raised his brows and grunted. We sat there, in silence, for what seemed like an hour. The only sounds were laughter coming from the kitchen, along with the occasional yip from Herkie. Cupboard doors opening and closing. The surge of the dishwasher. The light went on in the hall, and we heard footsteps and the tick, tick of Herkie's nails on the hardwood, coming toward us. Rob clambered to his feet and turned on a lamp. The sudden brightness made me squint.

"What have you two been doing, sitting here in the dark?" Mom stopped so suddenly in the doorway that Suze walked right into her, nearly losing her balance.

Rob unmuted the television. "We were sharing truths. Nothing earthshaking. You know, the kind of discussions hermits have."

As Suze righted herself and Herkie trotted into the room and grabbed a bull penis, I looked at my mother, her smile broad, but her eyes betraying a slight cast of worry. I waved my arms like a good game show host. "Come in, you two. The news is almost over. Jeopardy is on deck! I challenge everybody to a Jeopardy contest. The winner gets to eat an entire pint of ice cream all by *myself!*"

I think I pulled that off. Mom and Suze settled onto the sofa, Herk gnawed happily on her bully stick, and Rob shot me a look of gratitude. I squeezed his hand as I left the room. "I am going to get some Tums. Anybody want anything before Trebek starts querying?"

I shut myself in the downstairs bath, opened the medicine cabinet, and chewed those Tums as if my life depended on it. I washed them down with a swallow of water from the tap, ran a hand through my hair, and looked myself in the eye in the mirror. I jabbed a finger at my image and whispered, "Suck it up, Tommy. Just suck it *the hell up."*

As I got ready for dog-walking that night, I stood in front of my bedroom mirror and ran my finger over the Post-it note. I whispered the question to myself for the zillionth time: *Why am I doing this?* Grief? Guilt about how I had treated my moms? I rested my head against the mirror, letting the cool glass penetrate my forehead.

Chapter Eleven

Π

"I have pizza tummy." Suze rubbed her belly, which I have to admit was actually bulging. I looked down at mine, protruding under my fleece hoodie.

"I always have pizza tummy."

Suze snorted. Herkie pulled in front of us, the fall air giving her even more energy than her usual impatience to get to Dana's house. I yanked on her prong collar and began to prepare Suze for Dana. "She is very bold. Just saying. She might insult you right off the bat. Or who knows, she might just consider you a kindred spirit. But whatever happens, do *not* get defensive, because she will eat you for lunch."

Suze skidded to a stop. She held out her arm to halt our progress, and Herk sat abruptly with a whimper of protest. "Who is this kid, and why does she seem to have super powers? Is her real name Katniss?"

The breeze picked up Suze's curls and swirled them around her face, obscuring her eyes. She swiped them away and glared at me. Herk jerked at the end of the leash. "Stay, Herk, for Pete's sake!" I wrapped her leash around a lamppost and motioned for Suze to sit on the low stonewall surrounding the Epstein's front yard. "She is incredibly fascinating to me, because she is the absolute antithesis of any sort of teen girl I have ever known. She was abused as a child. She has spent the majority of her life as a foster child. I think that her survival so far has depended on her ability to swallow all that down. Instead of shrinking into herself the way I imagine bullied people must do, she has done the opposite."

Suze snorted. "Yep. Katniss. But why the attachment?"

I looked over at Herkie, who was busy licking her genitals. "First off, she is a dog whisperer. Herkie fell for her the moment Dana touched her ears. Second, she is frighteningly smart. And finally, I think I might be able to help her—you know, smooth off some of the rough edges."

Suze chuckled. "Right. Because you only see her in the middle of the night, you have never seen her among others, you have no idea who her friends are or *if* she has any friends, and you think you have great influence over others, holed up as you are inside your house with your mother." She rolled her eyes.

She had me there. I couldn't think of an apt response, so I patted the grass and said nothing.

"It's getting a little chilly sitting here. Let's not postpone this any longer." Suze stood up and swiped the grass off her rear. She reached out a hand to help me up, and Herk stood up, tail wagging, straining in the direction of Dana's house. I untangled her leash and we got moving.

Dana stood in the middle of the sidewalk, arms akimbo, her legs spread as if bracing for a confrontation. She wore a red bandanna around her forehead, black lipstick that made her dark eyes look even more oceanic and deep. Her black hoodie was unzipped, revealing a blood red T-shirt underneath. Overall, she looked like a modern gypsy gang member, though I have no actual one-on-one experience with real life gang members.

When she saw us, she dropped to one knee and held out her arms, and I let go of the leash. Herkie ran into her arms, and they hugged, Herkie covering Dana's face with dog slobbery licks.

"Dana. I want you to meet Suzanne, my best girlfriend. She is staying with us for the weekend." Dana used her upper arm to dry off her face, scrambled to her feet and stepped over my dog. She thrust out her hand and she and Suze shook. I believe Suze winced at the power of Dana's grip, but I can't be totally sure. Suze can be inscrutable.

"You look like a grown-up elf." Dana pointed to Suze's spirals of red hair. "Ginger and freckles. Did the kids tease you about that when you were in school?"

Suze looked stunned. The power of Dana's directness manifested. She put a hand to her head as if just at that moment discovering that her hair was curly. "Well, now that you mention it, for awhile in third grade, my nickname was 'Red.' But once I got into middle school, no. Not really..."

Dana held out a hand to stop her. "Sorry. That was sort of an insult. I pick up on things. You look like a person with a lot of confidence. Not like Thomas. She's not exactly a warrior, like me, but we are attracted to people who need us; it's just the way things work."

Suze kept patting her head as if in a trance. Dana motioned to Herk with a downward wave of her hand, and Herk curled up at her feet. Sidebar: Herk and I have never worked on obedience, and hand motions? No way. Uncanny. She then waved her hand at us. "You might as well sit down. The ground isn't too cold. It's easier to have a conversation this way." We sat.

"So you and Thomas are besties? Did you go to school together?"

Suze shook her head. "No. We met in Columbus at a bar. We had mutual friends, and at the time, my boyfriend was dating Tommy's roommate. So we kept running into each other, and we became friends."

"So what did Thomas do to save you?"

My mouth felt dry, all of a sudden. Suze's eyes got round. Herk snored.

"What do you mean, did she save me? I was never in danger or anything. We are just friends. We have the same sense of humor. We both love barbecue. Sappy movies. You know, that sort of thing." Suze put her hand on her throat and massaged it as if trying to swallow something that she didn't chew well enough.

Dana looked at me with a blunt, disconcerting gaze. "So, Thomas, you never stepped in to help your elfin friend out of trouble?"

I blinked rapidly. How could Dana see into our heads? Good, God, the child was preternatural. It took me a few seconds to answer. I cleared my throat. "Actually, there was that one time." I looked over at Suze, whose eyes had glazed over. "We were at a party, the kind where you know maybe just that one person who invited you."

Suze gasped and nodded.

"Anyway, I was the designated driver, so I was drinking Coke. Suze and Audrey, our other good friend, were wasted. Audrey came up to me and asked where Suze had gone. I hadn't noticed that she had left. I went out into the backyard to see if she had gone out by the pool for some fresh air, and I saw her sprawled on a lounge chair with this asshole guy on top of her, pulling up her top. I ran up and hit him on the head with my Coke bottle, and he fell off her. Audrey and I managed to get her into the car and home. So, yup, I guess I saved her once."

Suze regained her self and shuddered. "I try not to think about that. But it was a close call. I preach to my students about keeping their wits about them. Never set a drink down at a party and then pick it up again and drink from it. That sort of thing. These days, anything can happen. But I guess you know that, Dana."

Dana grinned. "So you are a teacher? What grade? I bet your students like you."

"I am not sure that is true! Yes. I teach English at Edgar High School in Columbus. All three grades."

Dana narrowed her eyes. "White? Suburban? Like here? Cliques, lockdown drills, mean girls, and teacher's pets?"

Suze puffed up her cheeks and released the air with a pop. "Wow. You cut right through the bullshit, don't you? Has anybody told you that you are an old soul?" Suze arched her eyebrows.

Dana smiled but didn't let up. "You didn't answer the question."

Suze straightened up and looked up and down the block at the houses. "Yup. Bexley is like Framington, only bigger."

Dana pulled her legs up onto the wall and wrapped her arms around them. She didn't look at either of us as she said, "Hey, Thomas. How much do you want to bet that Suze is the kind of teacher who lets her students keep their phones in class and has a swear jar?"

Suze looked as if lightning had just struck her. "How did you know about the swear jar? My God! Are you a witch or something?"

Dana chuckled. "Of course not. Every teacher has a swear jar. I have said *fuck* so many times in class; I think I have funded one entire year of meals at the Methodist Ministries homeless shelter. What is your charity? Let me guess...Samaritan's Purse? No wait—the ACLU?"

Suze leaned over and bumped Dana on the arm. "Ha! Gotcha there! No. I donate to the United Way."

Dana looked aghast. "But they spend so much money on administrative costs! You should choose a particular charity and donate directly! Everybody knows that!"

I stood up. "It is getting very late, and Herkie is getting absolutely no exercise. Plus," I held up the empty poop bag, "she hasn't done her business. Are you going to walk along with us tonight, Dana?"

Dana put her legs down and banged her heels against the wall, one at a time. "Nope. Not tonight. I have sixteen minutes of homework left to do, and you two will want to talk about how weird I am, so I will just go in." She blew a kiss to Herk. "Goodnight, pit bull. See you tomorrow night. Goodnight,

Thomas." She stood and turned to run up her steps, and as she did, she said "Nice to meet you, upper middle class white suburban teacher!" over her shoulder.

We walked on in silence for a while. Herk blessed us with a large poop. I tried not to step on any cracks, and Suze seemed a bit dazed. We crossed the street and turned left to walk down the hill to my house, where the only lights still on were in my bedroom.

"Jesus. That girl will either end up in prison or as the first female President."

I nodded, and we followed Herkie up the driveway and onto the back porch, where the light over the door cast shadows that looked like huge spiders.

Π

"So what's it like, having all the time in the world?" Suze asked me.

We were draped across the guest room bed, covered in Triscuit crumbs and pepperoni slices, looking at Facebook on our phones and giggling at all the stupid selfies.

"Well, not too bad, if you don't mind cabin fever. We have time to make recipes that call for things like capers and brown butter, I am all caught up on classic literature, and I now can go upstairs backwards forty times without getting cramps."

Suze put the final slice of pepperoni on the final Triscuit, munched, and looked at me seriously. "Is it worth it, all this 'seclusion,' just for your Mom?"

I rolled over and stared at the crack in the ceiling that looked slightly like Abraham Lincoln. "First off, I still work, you know. Second, Mom needs supervision, or she won't eat, she bites her fingernails to the quick, and she mourns."

Suze rolled over and stared at Abe, too. "You don't look that great, yourself. You only go out at night, so you are as pale as a ghost. Your best friend is a dog." Suze rolled her eyes. "OK, I guess that's an unintended truism." She waved her arm dismissively. "You consort with weird children at midnight, and you have a grudge against your elderly neighbor, and you plan to keep this up for months. This is nuts, Tommy."

"Do you envy me?" I looked at Suze and punched her arm. "You, who has to go to work and stare at Peter Hardison, who has pimples the size of St. Louis, and who has a crush on you and comes into your room after school for 'help?' Or those teachers' meetings where your principal has never once stuck to the agenda?"

She rolled her head back and forth. "Of course I envy you. But if I quit my job and moved in here, you wouldn't be recluses any more. This would become a halfway house for disgruntled and grieving women." She put a finger on the tip of her nose. "But what if I did quit my job and move in? Would that be cool?" She smiled a tiny, smug smile. "Because I have actually been approached to become the education coordinator for the emerging online curriculum for high schools statewide. I could do that job anywhere. You are not the only tech guru around, you know."

I sat up so quickly that the Triscuit box flew off the bed and onto the floor along with the empty pepperoni bag. *"SUZE! Could you really just switch around your job, bring your laptop and your Oxford Compendium of Great Literature or whatever it's called and move in with us?"*

Suze jolted upwards as if blitzed by a bolt of lightning. She wiped the crumbs from her shirtfront, picked a stray bit of pepperoni out of her hair, grinned, and held up her phone. "Let me just accept the position."

And the rest is hermit history.

Chapter Twelve

Π

Chilly day. Leaves starting to turn beautiful shades of red and orange; the ginkgo tree in Percy Warner's tree lawn is showering what look like golden coins all over the tree lawn in front of our houses. There is a gentle, cool (I assume, because I am always inside) breeze blowing. Mom is sipping tea, an empty photo album on her lap, photos of her, Sam, and me in piles all around her on the sofa.

"Tell me how on earth Suzanne arranged to come live here so fast?" She set her mug on the coffee table and smoothed a particularly faded photo of Sam holding a squalling toddler me on her lap.

Suze and her minimal belongings were arriving on Friday, in three days time. Mom and I had spent the previous day vacuuming, Febreezing, and otherwise getting ready, despite my protestations that Suze would not care if there were dust balls under the bed because she would just be adding to them, anyway. I took the photo from Mom and looked at me and Mommy in the photo. I sighed and gave it back to Mom for her album. "The universe was in alignment. Suze had like a hundred days of vacation unused, they wanted her to be the Online Education Coordinator, they absolutely love her and when she said yes, they nearly fell over themselves arranging for a long-term sub for the rest of the year and offering her the job. Suze is a force to be reckoned with, and they need someone like that to make things happen online. She even got a raise."

Mom leaned back on the cushions and fiddled with the collar of her turtleneck, pulling it up further on her neck. None of her clothes fit her any more. I hoped that having Suze around would perk up Mom's appetite. She was diminishing with each passing week.

"Tommy, should we make her follow the guidelines? Or will she feel like she is imprisoned?" Mom rubbed her collarbones and frowned.

"We talked about it. She wants to be in solidarity with us; that is why she is coming. I told her that she is an 'honorary' recluse and that if she feels the need to get outside, she can. Also, she says she will be our pipeline to the outside world if we need one. You know, in case of emergency."

Mom looked at me with an ironic smile. "If there is an emergency, you and I can go out, you know. For heaven's sake. What kind of 'emergency' would there be that would require a surrogate to leave the house for us? If there is a fire or if one of us has a heart attack, we can't send her out there in our stead!"

"You have me there. Are you really fine with having Suze join us? I can tell her not to come."

Mom waved her hands in front of her chest. "No, no! I think this will be a good thing for us—a breath of 'fresh air,' so to speak."

"So three won't be a crowd?"

Mom gently closed the album in her lap and set it on the table. She began decking up the remaining photos and tapping them into neat stacks, arranging them in neat piles next to the album. I noticed all the new creases around her eyes and the deepening frown lines around her mouth. She finished arranging the photos and wiped imaginary dust particles from her meager thighs. "No. You need something to distract you from my misery."

For a moment, my heart seemed to stop beating. I wished I had a magic wand that I could wave to stir up all the sorrow in the air of this house, blow open the windows, and send it out in a rush. I wanted the year to be over, our hearts to sing, and Herkie to have nine puppies. I wanted Mom to be fat and me to be skinny. I wanted to grab her hand, step over the threshold, and grin at the sun. I wanted to wipe my own mental slate clean.

Instead, I reached over and took my mother's hand, lifted it to my cheek, and held it there. "Mom. This misery isn't only yours." I moved her hand to my chest. "Feel that? It's my heart barely beating. It wants to stop altogether sometimes. But I won't let it. And I won't let yours stop, either."

Mom leaned against me, and we sat for a few seconds, her hand warm over my heart. Then she started to chuckle. "My Lord, Tommy. Let's just hope we don't drive Suzanne crazy, with all of our overflowing emotions and things."

I thought of Suze and her suggestion that we set up a Grindr profile for Mom. I giggled. "Mom. She is already crazy. By comparison, you and I are just slightly unbalanced!"

Π

Mom, Suze and I sat around the kitchen table. Mom riffled through her *Joy of Cooking*. Suze had her phone out, scrolling through recipes on the Food Network. I had the old recipe box. "Oh, look!" I held out a ragged, stained index card. "This is Grandma Poole's recipe for creamed chicken! It was so delish over biscuits. Should we make that?"

Suze licked her lips. "I am drooling. Sounds like a winner. Meg?"

Mom shut *Joy* with a decided bang. "I agree. It is delicious, and these days, we can use frozen biscuits. Although why I suggest that is a mystery, because I have all the time in the world to make scratch ones. And we can have salad and Suze, you can make your famous brownies."

Suze's famous brownies come from a mix, by the way, but she adds two entire Hershey bars to the mix.

"So tonight, when we walk Herk, I will ask Dana. I am sure she and her mom will be thrilled to come over." I put the recipe on the center of the table. "But don't order the groceries yet. Let's wait and see what they say."

Suze stood and went to the window over the sink and peered out. She knocked on the glass and waved. "There's old asshat. Hi, Mr. Warner!" She turned to us and giggled. "Might as well pretend to be neighborly. She turned back and waved a bit more enthusiastically. "He sees me. Think he might at least smile? Nope. The old shit."

Mom hissed at Suze, "Get away from the window! He knows you aren't sincere! Don't make things any worse."

"Wait right here. I am going to say 'hi' and see what he does. *The don't-go-outside rules* don't apply to me." She strode to the back door and threw it open. "Wish me luck, girlies."

Mom and I pushed our chairs out from the table, creamed chicken and biscuits forgotten. We squeezed next to one another at the back door and watched.

Suze ran over to the iron fence and held out her hand to Percy. I held my breath. He did not approach her, and words were exchanged. Suze put both hands on the fence and pushed her face between the bars. Whatever she said made Mr. Warner take a few steps backward. Then he made a fist at her, turned his back and rushed into his house in what looked like a full-on huff.

Suze hurried back to the door and waved at us wildly as she yelled, "That is one salty old man! I introduced myself as a friend of the family and said I was staying here for a while. He asked me if I had a dog, and I said not at the moment, but I was going to get four dogs at the shelter to keep Herkie company. *Joking!* I even laughed. He didn't get it. He threatened to call the city manager and tell them we were hoarding animals. Jesus."

Mom sagged into a chair. "Oh, Suzanne. You may have been joking, but this isn't good. That man is capable of anything. Really, I worry that he might put out poison or something. If only he could get to know what a sweet dog Herkie is." Mom sighed. Then she pointed a finger at Suze and me. "And don't you even THINK of getting any more dogs, for heaven's sake!"

Suze leaned against the counter, her face pale, every freckle standing out like polka dots. "Of course not, Meg. I am so sorry. I was joking, and I thought that might be a way to break through to that guy. My God."

I laughed. "But we could *foster* a dog, right?"

Mom put her head down on the table and moaned.

Chapter Thirteen

П

Candles flickered. The pale yellow linen tablecloth had not one wrinkle – I had ironed the bejesus out of it. Napkins in silver napkin rings. A centerpiece of orange and white gerbera daisies, delivered that afternoon.

Mom sat at the head of the table, a cheerful smile below worried eyes. Trudy and Dana sat on either side of her, Trudy with hair swept over the scarred side of her face, her fingers rubbing the condensation from her water glass, her eyes on Dana.

Not a lot of conversation, other than the few comments about the weather and how many trick-or-treaters everyone had. Dana asked if we had kept Herkie on a leash to keep her from devouring either the candy or licking the little beggars to death. Then conversation stalled. You could cut the awkwardness with the proverbial knife.

Dana, ramrod straight, looked back at her foster mother, her mouth set, an inscrutable look on her face. Suze and I stared at one another over our plates of creamy chicken. I cleared my throat and looked down at Rob, who sat at the other end of the table, his mouth full, his cheeks flushed.

I tried to create a small cavity in the awkwardness. "This recipe for creamed chicken is from my grandmother. She was a fantastic cook. She could make tough old birds taste divine. Of course, this is a modern-day chicken, so it never had a chance to get tough." Mom paused and wiped her mouth with her napkin, probably picturing Grandma Poole, the sturdy woman who worked on a farm growing up. She probably slaughtered hundreds of tough, old chickens in her day.

Mom licked her lips and continued. "I am not sure we did her justice, but I think it is pretty good."

I took a sip of water, which went down the wrong way. Dana reached over to pound me on the back. I coughed into my napkin, eyes streaming. Before she could jump up to perform the Heimlich, I grabbed Dana's arm to keep her in her seat.

Rob stood. "Are you sure you are all right?"

I nodded, wiping my entire face with my napkin and coughing one more time. I motioned for Rob to sit, and he thudded back into his chair. There was a brief silence, as everyone waited for me to recover. Then Dana laughed. "This is how nervous we make people. Trudy's face and my tattoos. Eating dinner with us is life-threatening."

Trudy made a shushing noise, but Dana continued. "Actually, though, once you get used to us, it's usually OK. We are pretty normal, despite (she pointed to her neck and Trudy's face) you know, *appearances.*" She continued to pat me on the back as I took a few deep breaths. "Mrs. Poole, I think this chicken is the best. I bet it was organic, free-range, without hormones, right?"

Suze burst out laughing. "Of course! And each chicken was hand-raised on a farm where the farmer's wife named them all and cried like a baby when she had to kill them."

Rob joined in. "Yes. We are having Matilda and Gretchen this evening."

Trudy looked down at her plate and smiled. "Gretchen is particularly delicious."

The rest of the evening was an absolute blast. Mom told Dana and Trudy to 'call me Meg, for heaven's sake,' and Rob and Trudy discovered that they had two mutual friends. Dana and Suze each ate three brownies. Mom brought out the Trivial Pursuit game, and we discovered that Trudy was an expert on baseball, and Rob knew that Giovanni Boccaccio wrote The Decameron. Everyone stayed late, and Rob, Suze and I (with Herkie, of course) walked Dana and Trudy home.

Small talk. The weather—crisp. The coming winter—snowy or not? Then conversation took a turn. Rob asked Trudy how she liked working at the store. "Are people nice to you?" He cleared his throat. "I'm sorry. Awful thing to ask."

"No. It's an understandable question. The answer is complicated. Yes, people are, of course, *nice.* But it is that insincere, awkward nice. People are polite, but you know, they don't really want to *see* me. So I am invisible to them. They look through me when they have to talk with me directly. So yes. People aren't mean or rude. They just deny that I exist."

"Huh. We kind of know that feeling, don't we, Tommy?" Rob kicked a rock into the street. "Our family. Weird. My sister's gay marriage. Nobody actually said anything to any of us openly. But we knew there were whispers all over town."

"Yeah. Alone. We were alone. Just our little gay family in a town full of straight ones. Alone with the two dozen other gay families in Framington. But Rob, you are politely lying. People said stuff to us—well, to me—plenty of times. The nickname 'Butch' comes to mind." I tugged on Herkie's leash.

Suze humphed. "I don't have anything in my life to compare with what you are saying. But in my opinion, nobody is ever really alone."

Dana laughed. "Oh hi, Pollyanna! We need somebody like you at our school. So the bullies and mean girls will all see the light and be nicer to all of us weirdos."

We were all in a line at the curb, waiting for two cars to pass us so we could walk across. Suze looked at Dana and smiled. "I AM at your school. I am at every school in the state. I coordinate online education, and I am in touch with every single teacher and principal. If there is bullying going on, I need to know about it. I can help."

Dana broke into a fit of hysterical laughter and set out into a run. "Lions, tigers, and bullies, OH MY!" Waving her arms over her head, she raced to the end of the next block. Then she turned and shouted back to us, her black hair glinting in the glow of the street light, almost as if sparks were flying out of her head. "Thanksgiving! Can we do it just like tonight? But with turkey? A great big one named Ethel?" And then she laughed so hard she nearly fell down.

Π

"The barking was so loud we could hardly hear ourselves think. There were so damn many dogs there. I knew that a little puppy would be too much, and Dana agreed. No house training. So when we saw this one, we knew she was the one," Suze said with a huge grin.

Dana held the leash attached to a gangly, meatball-faced, smiling, eight-month-old pit bull puppy. "She's a blue."

"Blue? She looks gray." I reached out and petted her on the head. She wagged her tail furiously.

We stood in the front hall in a little circle around the 'blue' dog. She was short and stocky, more like a bulldog than a Pit, in my view. She had a white patch over her left eye, and the rest of her was all gray. Except for the white tip of her tail. Honest to God, she was *grinning.*

Mom knelt down, and the pup licked her face. Mom giggled. "Oh, my gosh, she is an angel. How do dogs like this end up in shelters?"

Dana shook her head. "Backyard breeders. Dog fighting wannabes. It sucks. And when the dogs won't cooperate, or when they get caught, the dogs end up in shelters."

Suze agreed. "So I am fostering this one until she gets adopted. I am to take her to various places on weekends that feature adoptable dogs. A flagrant violation of house rules, but it can't be helped."

Mom stood up. "Not so fast. We have to bring Herkie in from the yard and introduce them. Herkie has to like this dog, or she can't stay with us."

Dana said, "Wait. It has to be on neutral ground. That's what they said at the shelter. Herkie might get territorial. Let me take the puppy outside. Suze, you put Herk on the leash and bring her out front. We can introduce them on the sidewalk and see what happens."

"Here's a thought." I pointed to next door. "In front of Mr. Warner's house. Very neutral. And if we are lucky, he will be looking out of his front window."

Mom and I watched from the living room window as Dana and the puppy bounced around on the sidewalk. As soon as Suze and Herkie stepped out the front door, Herkie looking very big and very muscular all of a sudden, the puppy spied them. She began to wag in ecstasy, her entire body in motion. She strained at the leash and pulled Dana towards Suze and Herk.

I held my breath to see what Herkie would do. She stiffened, her hackles up. Standing very still, she let the pup circle her and sniff. When the pup put her nose under Herk's tail, Herk whirled around, and I thought that the puppy was going to die right there on the spot.

Mom gasped. My heart raced. Then Herkie began to wag her tail, and she dropped down on her front paws, rear in the air, to challenge the puppy to play. They began to wrestle, leashes tangling, Suze and Dana struggling to maintain control. The puppy yipped, and when Herkie barked back, she jumped straight up into the air. Suze and Dana gave up and let go of the leashes. Herkie and the puppy fell rolling to the ground, and we could hear the girls' laughs as the two dogs rolled, woofed, and bonked one another all over the front yard.

"I will have to order another dog bed on Amazon," Mom said.

"Brace yourself for a phone call from Percy," I replied.

"And who knew there were such things as *blue* pit bulls?" Mom hurried to open the front door to let the dogs in. They dashed into the dining room, into the kitchen, and back out into the front hall, trailing leashes behind them. Dana and Suze were out of breath from trying to restrain them. They disappeared again.

Suze held up her arms to the ceiling. "What hath God wrought?" She giggled. Mom shook her head.

It was thrilling. More action in my life than ever. And Mom and I were 'in seclusion.' I had to laugh along with Suze. "Wait. This is sheer craziness. We are supposed to be *shutting out the world.*"

Dana looked at the three of us as the dogs made another clattering dash through the front hall, leashes slithering behind them. "It doesn't work that way. If you try to shut out the world, the world just comes to you."

Chapter Fourteen

Π

November nights were what I called damn cold. Suze called them "brisk." The dogs loved them. Walks became more of a beeline from our house to Dana's, with the dogs forging the way. We had ordered pinch collars on Amazon, which helped keep them from dragging us. Sort of.

Suze yanked back on Saylor's collar. Yes, Dana had prevailed on the name. "I swear, this puppy has the strength of ten men." She yanked again, and this time, Saylor responded by slackening off to a slow trot.

I zipped my fleece all the way up. "Do you think it is going to snow before Thanksgiving?" I looked up at the grayish sky. "The moon is behind all those clouds, and the sky has that snowy look about it."

Suze planted her feet and gave another yank on Saylor's collar. "Slow down, you cur! What? Snow? It might. So then we'll have to go inside to warm up with Trudy and Dana before we go back home. Fine with me. Trudy always has treats."

We heard a shout before we saw her. "PITBULLS!"

I didn't bother to try to restrain Herkie; I just let go of the leash. She took off at a gallop. "Let go of Saylor! She'll pull you down!"

Suze released her lead, and Saylor leaped after Herk. Dana loomed in front of us, her yellow scarf and red leggings flying.

The dogs met up with Dana, who stopped suddenly and held up one hand. Both dogs sat. Instantly.

"What the hell?" Suze gasped.

"She's an animal whisperer. She has powers beyond human." I waved at Dana. "Hi, kiddo!"

The dogs remained rooted to the spot. When we caught up with them, Dana handed us each a leash. "You two need to watch some YouTube videos on dog training. These beasts need some discipline."

"You think?" I patted Herkie's head, but she had eyes for only Dana at that moment. "You are better than YouTube. Maybe we could pay you to come over on the weekends and work with us. Lord knows we need all the help we can get."

Suze nodded her head with enthusiasm. "Yes!"

Dana knelt down and looked the girls in the eyes. "Saylor. Herks. We need to whip these women into shape!" She moved the palm of her hand towards the ground, and both dogs lay down. Dana frowned up at us. "I'll do it. Because nobody likes an unruly pit bull."

Dana stood, but the dogs remained recumbent at the end of our leashes. She put an arm around each of our shoulders and clucked. The dogs stood, and Dana gave Suze and me a little shove forward. We walked down the street towards Dana's bungalow, the dogs walking as sedately as little old ladies out for a stroll.

"So when do we start the training sessions?" Suze asked. "We need to start as asap as possible, as one of my more brilliant students said!"

Dana skipped backwards in front of the four of us, grinning. Her laugh nearly tripped her up. "Tomorrow is Saturday—is that asap enough?"

"YES!" Suze and I answered in unison.

"Hurry up! I am freezing! I am going to start wearing earmuffs." I put my hands over my ears. "And Trudy better have at least some Oreos tonight."

We followed the dogs through the grainy moonlight down the block. As we trooped up the stairs to the house, we saw Trudy standing in the glow of the front window, her hands over her eyes, peering out. As soon as she saw us, she waved.

When Trudy opened the door, we all wagged our tails.

Π

"So how is school?" Suze wiped Oreo crumbs from her cheek.

"The usual. Either boring or in a state of crisis."

Dana took a sip of her cocoa, licked her top lip, and went on. "Acne, hormones, bullies, and boredom."

Suze frowned. "That's a pretty jaded view. Isn't there anything good about it? I am sure you have friends."

Dana put her mug down. No comment.

Trudy smiled, but it didn't look convincing to me. "Hon, tell them about your friends."

"Well, first of all, I don't have 'friends.' Friends like on TV or in the movies—you know, the girls you giggle with and text all the time about your boyfriends. The ones you shop for prom dresses with and have sleepovers. I don't want any of that shit." She leaned back in her chair. "I hang out with a few people. But it doesn't go much beyond that."

Trudy leaned forward. The unscarred side of her face flushed as the scarred side paled. "Dana. You started to tell me about a girl named Jill in your math class. She transferred here from another school. Could she be a friend?" There was a hopeful note in Trudy's voice.

Dana put both feet up on the coffee table. She ticked her fingers against the side of her mug. "Jill is an aspirational."

"What is that?" Suze asked.

"You know. Every school has them. They're the ones who can't live with themselves the way they are. They're losers who would give anything to get in with a group with power."

"Are you an aspirational?" I asked.

"Ha! Nope. That is why I find girls like Jill so interesting. I like to keep track of them—see how they operate. They are dangerous, so it makes sense to know them."

I blinked a few times, trying to digest this. "So you hang out with the aspirationals?"

Dana shook her head. "No. I have a bunch of loser friends, too. You know, the ones with braces and brilliant minds. The invisibles. The Mark Zuckerbergs of the future. Oh, and there are the creatives. The ones who will end up in art museums or at the Oscars."

Suze scowled. "Ugh. So where do you fit in?"

Dana snorted. "I don't." It came out tough. But I saw the shift in Dana's eyes as soon as she said it. The way she looked away from Suze, the shield dropping away for just a split second before she gathered herself up again. "Fitting in is overrated."

Trudy put a hand over her scars. "People like us are always just on the periphery, you know. We don't try to fit in."

Suddenly, memories of high school basketball games, cafeteria lines, and school bus rides floated into my head. The humiliation of "Butch," despite pretending to myself that *sticks and stones will break your bones,* etc. Sitting by myself. Finding the word LESBO written on the outside of my locker. I rubbed my eyes.

Suze kept pressing. "Dana, is there anybody you like? Anybody you have fun with?"

Dana took a deep breath and let it out. She looked over at Trudy and her eyes softened. "Not really. High school is not fun. Everybody is having sex, posting nude photos on

Snapchat, ruining reputations, feeling insecure, and forming cliques. So no." Dana bit her bottom lip.

Suze raised her eyebrows, but before she could blurt out another question, I stood up. "Hey. Guys. We have an important dog training session tomorrow, and I am sure that you and I are going to need all our strength to learn how to be alpha dogs. So we should get going, Suze."

She got the message. We thanked Trudy for the cocoa and cookies, gathered up our wayward pups, and headed for the door. As it closed behind us, Dana said, "You two will never be alphas. But you can certainly learn from one."

On the way home, Suze and I held hands and pulled back on the dogs, who seemed to surge with power. "Are you a little scared of Dana?" Suze panted.

"What do you think?" I squeezed Suze's hand twice—our secret code for friendship.

"I think she could breathe fire."

"Maybe. But I think she knows how to cry, too. This girl needs us in her life."

We clasped our hands just a little bit tighter and walked the rest of the way home in silence.

Π

The basement is unfinished, the footprint of the house, and perfect for dog training. Saylor and Herkie had never been down there, and they spent a good five minutes nosing around the cobwebs in the corners and rolling in the dust before joining the three of us in the center of the space.

Dana, looking fierce in jeans with many holes, a Kreator sweatshirt, black high top sneakers, and blood red nail polish, looked at us seriously. "First off, I am not a dog trainer. But I have watched every episode of *Pit Bulls and Parolees.* Second, one of my fosters had two dogs, and I watched her train them. So I know what I am doing."

She reached down and unzipped the backpack she brought and pulled out two short leashes, each one about two feet long. "They already know 'sit' and 'down.' So the main thing you need to teach these two nerds is how to walk politely without pulling you. This is easy, but it takes consistency and a lot of repetition. So down here is a great place to do this—no distractions."

Dana made a kissing noise, and both dogs raced over to her, twirling and wagging like demons. We watched, wide-eyed, as she did that downward hand motion. Both dogs sat. She clipped a leash on each dog.

"Wait. We need to learn that!" Suze poked me on the side.

"Yeah! My God, how do you do that?" I took a step toward the dogs.

"Halt!" Dana held out her hand. I stopped. These hand signals worked, apparently, on both humans and dogs.

"The sitting command is easy. I'll show you. But you two need to pay attention here. Walking a pit bull is not like strolling around with, say, a goofy Labrador retriever. Nobody is scared shitless of Labs. Pitties have a bad rep, as you know. So they have to be completely under your control. We are going to start with these short leashes so that you and the dogs will be close. They should always be on your left. Head right at your knee—the 'heel' position." Dana handed Saylor's leash to Suze and Herkie's to me.

"The thing is to keep them at 'heel' first. Give the command, then start walking. The MINUTE the dog starts to pull out in front of your knee, TURN AROUND and walk in the other direction. Now GO."

"Heel." We both started walking. Immediately, Saylor pulled out in front. I stopped, confused. Suze realized what she was supposed to do and dragged Saylor around to walk in the opposite direction, with Saylor way out front.

"STOP." We did. Confused. This wasn't easy at all.

"The key is to be thinking a few steps ahead of the dog. What you will end up doing is whirling around every few steps. Don't forget to repeat the 'heel' command every time you turn. If you do this consistently, they will soon understand that they can't move out in front of you. And for God's sake, relax! You two are so stiff and stressed that the dogs know it. Try again."

After what seemed like ten years of whirling and heeling, the dogs were walking right along beside us, Suze and I were drenched in sweat, and Dana was grinning. "See? It works. The true test will be when you take them out tonight. Especially since they always want to streak over to my house. So tonight, take a totally different route, and use the short leashes. If you stay alert and keep this up, they should do great. Lesson over."

We unclasped the leashes. Saylor made a mad dash for the stairs. Herkie followed, scrambling to keep up. They scrabbled up the stairs as if escaping from a fire. "Well, that says it all. I don't blame them. I am exhausted and need a shower." Suze tromped wearily up the stairs.

"Do you want a Coke or something?" I opened the fridge and pulled out three icy bottles. I handed them around, and we slumped into the chairs. Suze took a long sip and then put her face down on the table. Dana laughed.

"What else do we need to learn?" I asked.

"You can get by with just this and teaching them to 'stay' on command. Really, guys, it's all about having the belief in yourselves that you are in charge. Dogs sense that stuff. They are no different than humans. They fall in line. But the majority of people who have dogs let them control the situation, and that is why so many dogs are rude and act like beasts."

I took another gulp of Coke and thought about the people at my office. Rude, boorish, and all in my face. "Geez,

Dana. There should be training classes like this for people. My God."

Suze lifted her head and cackled. "Absolutely!"

Dana looked cheerful. She stood and held up her empty Coke bottle. "You do recycling?"

I pointed to the cupboard doors beneath the sink. "The left waste can under there."

Dana deposited her bottle, shut the cupboard doors, and wiped her hands on her jeans. "Good session, you guys. But from the looks of you, you need naps. Old people have to get their rest." And with a benevolent smile, she patted us on our heads and left.

We didn't take naps. For heaven's sake, we were 30-year-old women! Mom served a delicious dinner of pork chops with caramelized onions, green beans and applesauce, which she also made from scratch—no Mott's around here.

I lost consciousness right after the fifth bite. Suze made it all the way to the cookies and cream Graeter's before she started to lapse into a coma.

"Good heavens, girls!" Mom rapped her knuckles on the table, rousing me. I had applesauce in my nostril. Suze stood, her knee joints creaking.

"Dana seems to have worked you and the dogs to a frazzle. They haven't come down out of their dog beds for dinner! Go on upstairs. You are no use to me here!" She snapped her dish towel at our asses as we left the kitchen.

At the top of the stairs, Suze gave me a hug. "Goodnight, Tommy." She started to shuffle toward her room, but turned back toward me.

"Hey. I am having some intuition here." She waved her arms towards the ceiling. "Our little bitty world here may be about to expand."

I nodded, although I think I was already nearly asleep on my feet. "Expand . . . explode. Who knows?"

Suze shrugged. "I think it rhymes with *Shmayna.*"

"Good night."

Funny. After I rubbed some Begay over my sore calves, brushed my teeth, and sank underneath the covers, all I could see, floating in front of my face, was Dana. Mom, Suze, Rob, Trudy, the dogs and I were all following behind her. On our way to someplace. We stayed right by her left flank...

Chapter Fifteen

Π

Not many people inhabit the night world. The day world is where most of us live, racing about in broad daylight, juggling our stresses like circus performers. We need briefcases, laptops, sunscreen, appropriate clothing, smiles on our faces, and words. Lots of words. We tell, we exclaim, we whisper, and we comment. All day long.

The night world is different. Words aren't necessary. Sounds surround those of us who venture out in the night, and all we have to do is listen. Interpret. Whistles of faraway trains bring nostalgia. Dogs howl back and forth like wolves. Some birds sing at night. There are owls in my neighborhood that hoot as I walk by with Herkie. Cars swoosh in the distance. When we walk in the darkness, we don't expect to encounter anyone, and except for Dana, we don't. Suze, Herkie, Saylor, Dana and I slip into the night world and let it cocoon us. Sometimes we don't even converse. We let the night world envelop us, and we think separate thoughts.

I never knew about the night world before Mommy died. I wonder how many of my fellow citizens of the dark joined it as I did, out of grief, sorrow, or disillusionment. Who is in these cars that glide past us as we walk? Where are they going? To work? The hospital? Or are they just driving, passing the time that weighs heavily on them after sunset? Who is the woman whose silhouette fills the second story window, backlit dimly, in the immense Colonial house at the corner of Lemon Street? She seems to be waiting for us to pass every evening. I wonder if she is lonely. I wave, and once or twice it seems as if she might be waving back. Maybe she doesn't really see us below. Maybe she is lost in her own night world. I wonder if she has any friends. If she has family somewhere in that big house. Who does she talk to in the daytime? Does she go out? Maybe she is a recluse, too. I try to imagine who she is, and what her family might be like. Maybe she has grown children who visit her on holidays. A son and a daughter, who have, perhaps, four children between them. Maybe they are two boys and two girls, and they don't really get along. Cousins who fight whenever they are together. The girls are in third and fifth grade, and the boys are in second and seventh, and they get on one another's nerves. Bickering. Holiday meals are to be endured, not enjoyed. I look back at her window as we pass, but the woman has disappeared. I wave once more at the window, just in case.

My thoughts shift to my own family. Thanksgiving is next week. Mom is having obsessive thoughts about linens, locating the 'good' gravy boat, whether or not she should ask Rob to bring anything, "He's a terrible cook," if Trudy and Dana like canned cranberry or freshly made sauce, and if a fourteen pound turkey will be big enough. I wonder what it would be like if Mommy were still here. I wish she were. I have so many things I wish I could talk to her about. Conversations that we should have had, but that I was way too scared to begin.

As we strolled, the dogs at our side (leash pulling a thing of the past), Dana heaved a sigh and broke our silence.

"I am so damn sick of school right now, I could barf."

Suze, jolted to attention, stumbled into me, and we both jostled to look over at Dana. She stopped to bend down and pick a blade of grass to chew on. The dogs sat down suddenly to sniff at the patch of grass she tore. We all came to an awkward halt.

"What is going on at school, kiddo?" I asked, also putting a stalk of grass in between my teeth.

"Sit down. A long story." Dana planted herself on the stoop of a house whose pavement lights provided shadowy illumination. We sat. Saylor and Herk lay in the cool grass, immediately relaxed, tongues lolling.

"I got caught out. My defenses were down."

Suze tensed up; her shoulders rose a few inches. She frowned. "What happened?"

Dana spit the grass into her palm and stared at it. "The usual shit. Cruelty rules."

Suze leaned towards Dana and put a hand on Dana's knee. Dana shifted backwards on the step as she removed Suze's hand. "Nothing unusual. Jill Bolton has officially become accepted into *the ranks*, is all."

"So what happened?" I asked.

"Jill apparently used me as a way in. She sent around a text inviting me and two other 'unfortunates' to Starbucks after school yesterday, for coffee and *moral support.* The text said that Ashley Craft had started some sort of rumor about her and she wanted to talk to us about it."

I nodded. "And?"

"I was the only one stupid enough to show up. I got there just in time to meet Jill, Ashley, and Ashley's minions on the way out. They surrounded me, put their arms around me, and one of them *accidentally* spilled her coffee all over me as the others videoed the whole thing. Posted everywhere and to everyone with the caption *Dana the wannabe – so SAD. As if she could be one of us.*"

"Oh, shit!" I looked at Dana, whose face was set, her eyes blank. "What did you do?"

Dana's face remained blank. "Nothing."

We sat for a few seconds in silence, the dogs' breathing punctuating the air. I felt sick, suddenly. Suze grabbed a handful of brownish grass and wadded it into a ball, carefully. She dropped it onto the pavement in front of her and stepped on it. Then she smoothed her hands on her jeans. "When are you going to respond?"

Dana smiled and pointed her finger at Suze. "You know stuff about high school, don't you? About how things work? Ha!" She jabbed the air with her finger almost as if shooting a gun. "I will respond when a response is necessary. Not just yet."

I was so confused. "But didn't this hurt you? What are you talking about *when a response is necessary?* Who are you? Some kind of Superhero? I don't get this."

Dana scratched the top of her head with her 'trigger' finger. "Nope. Not a Superhero. It hurt me, of course. It was a shock. Embarrassing and humiliating, just as they wanted. But I have been embarrassed and humiliated a lot before. You get used to it. You learn what to do with it, once you get over the initial pain of it all. And I was stupid to go to meet them. My savior side took control. So I deserved what I got." Dana licked her lips and stared into space. She didn't look like a warrior just then. She gritted her teeth and clenched her jaw, as if trying to get ready for a slap in the face. For just a fleeting second, she looked defenseless. But then she caught herself and her face took on its usual bravado.

Suze let out a huge sigh and put her arm around Dana's shoulders. "Please don't be a vigilante, Dana. Be careful. These days, what with social media and smartphones, lives can be ruined so fast."

Dana stood up, brushing Suze's hand away. "You *do* know stuff about high school, don't you? You truly do. Hey, I can't make any promises."

Dana leaned down and put a hand on each dog's tummy as they lay in the grass. "So long pit bulls. Have good dreams about kibble tonight, OK?" Then she stood and turned to walk home, her head held high, her shoulders straight. After a few steps, she turned and looked back at us, lifting her hand in a tiny wave. Then she resumed walking. We watched her until she disappeared around a corner.

I leaned against my friend, our heads touching. Suze took my hand and squeezed it. "We won't worry about her, OK?"

"OK."

We were both lying; I knew that.

Π

Thanksgiving in Ohio is a toss-up, weather wise. It can snow. It can rain, or the sun might shine and encourage everyone who hasn't taken a vow to stay inside to take a nice long walk to work off all of the turkey. Today was one of those brilliant, shiny November days. Warners abounded, passing our windows, wearing brightly colored fleeces, sunglasses, and smiles. Three o'clock in the afternoon, and the neighborhood was out and about, enjoying the caloric respite.

We needed to work off our dinner, as well. The meal was of legendary proportions: Mom's turkey melted in our mouths, the gravy was divine, and Trudy can make a mean green bean casserole. Suze and I had slaved over the dressing, but I think I put in too much sage. Nobody commented, but only Rob took seconds on that. There were the creamed onions that were Mommy's recipe. The mashed potatoes were just a tad lumpy. Mom seemed mortified about that. However, the pies were flaky (delivered from the bakery), and Dana had two pieces. Saylor and Herkie begged the entire time, and Mom cautioned us, "If you give them one more bite under the table, there will be diarrhea to deal with, and I am not going to volunteer for that."

We were all jolly during the meal, trying to ignore that this was the first major holiday with Sam Poole not a part of it. Rob laughed a little too hard at Suze's jokes. Mom wore too much blush. Despite that, she looked pale. I sighed so many times; Rob finally kicked me underneath the table. I felt a sense of relief when it was finally over.

Trudy, Dana, Suze and I offered to clean up, so that Mom and Rob could be alone in the living room. They wandered off together, arms entwined. "They need to talk, probably," I whispered.

The four of us began clearing the table and ferrying the mess into the kitchen. "Good silver—hand washed, right?" Trudy asked, holding up a greasy fork.

Suze's head shot up. She looked guilty. "I put all of it in the basket." She pulled out the bottom rack of the dishwasher. "Is that a no-no?"

"I think it's OK, as long as you don't mix silver and stainless. But let's just wash it all by hand. I don't mind." I took the basket out and emptied it into the sink full of sudsy water.

I ran a sponge over each knife, fork and spoon, Suze dunked them in the rinse water, and set them on the counter. Dana dried them and handed them to Trudy, who put them back carefully into the silver chest. We worked in companionable silence for a while. When the silver was clean, we moved on to the pots and pans.

Trudy handed me the roasting pan to scrub. As I took it from her, she frowned. "How are the three of you faring? You have been staying here now going on four months. Isn't it wearing on you? She tilted her head towards the window over the sink, where we could see into the Flints' backyard. Their grandchildren were playing tag, dashing around and shrieking like demons. "Don't you want to get outside?"

Suze threw her dishtowel over her shoulder and squeezed herself beside us to look at the kids playing. "We get out. You know that. Just not during the day."

I immersed the roaster in the hot water and squeezed more Dawn on top. "This needs to soak." I wiped my hands on my apron and leaned against the sink to peer at the kids more closely. They were playing Freeze Tag. "Yes. Trudy, yes. I want to go outside every day. But a promise is a promise."

Dana pulled out a chair and sat at the table, leaning it backwards. She looked up at us, clustered around the window over the sink. "I could use some inside time, myself, Thomas. Hiding from life."

The three of us turned in unison to look at Dana, balancing on the back legs of her chair, studying the cuticle of her index finger as if it held the key to the universe.

"What would you need to hide from, honey?" Trudy moved to put her hands on Dana's shoulders. Dana shrugged them off and wrapped her thumb around her fingers to make a fist, which she held to her chest. "Everybody knows high school sucks. There is just way too much crap going on all the time. But nothing. I don't need to hide from anything in particular. Just life in general. Sometimes." She wrung a rueful smile out at us. "Nothing. It's nothing. I just envy you guys over here, behind the walls of this house sometimes, that's all."

I sat down opposite her at the table. "Is it that thing about what's her name, Jill? The power hungry aspirational?"

Dana rolled her eyes.

Trudy and Suze sat down as well, the dishes momentarily forgotten.

Dana leaned forward, her chair thudding upright. "It's the daily battle. You know. What do you adults always tell us to do—just put one foot in front of the other?" Dana waved a hand at me and Suze. "But you guys over here are on, what do you call it? Sabbatical? From all of that stuff out there?" She pointed at the window. "To answer your question, yeah. It's the outside world. It's the Jill thing. The Jill thing, the every other girl who is popular thing, the nerds of the world thing, the social media thing, the academic pressure thing, the foster kid thing, the growing UP thing. It's every *thing.* And I, unlike my parental unit, here," Dana gestured at Trudy, "envy you." Then she buried her face in her palms, elbows on the table.

My face flushed. I thought about my own high school years. Figuring out who I was as the child of lesbians. The shame and embarrassment. The hormonal storm. The problems that seemed life shattering. Then I thought about Mom, an adult, unable to face the world, and Suze and me, hiding from it with her. "Oh, Dana."

Just then, Mom walked in to the kitchen. She took in the entire scene: the three women surrounding the anguished teen. The tension and concern in the air. Mom, who still grieved. Mom, who daily begged me and Suze to go back to work and leave her here by herself. Mom.

"The hell with the house rules today. Let's all go sit on the back steps and get some fresh air. We need it, don't we? Dana, you and Trudy aren't bound by any rules." Mom turned and yelled into the vicinity of the living room. "ROB! ROB, COME IN HERE! BRING COATS!"

Rob hustled in, his arms laden. "Robby, take the dogs, Trudy and Dana out in the back for some exercise! Come on!"

The dogs loved it. How long had it been since they had been outside in the brightness with three people to throw tennis balls for them? They were used to the all-too-brief potty breaks, with just enough human company to get their "business" accomplished. This was new and novel. They play-growled when Dana tried to take the balls from them, then barked when she wrested them away, to throw them again. Rob and Trudy got winded pretty quickly, but not Dana. She chased those pit bulls tirelessly. Girl and dogs ran until they could chase those balls no longer. Suze, Mom and I let the sun shine on our faces as we sat on the steps and smiled until our cheeks ached. And from his patio, we didn't notice that Percy Warner was watching it all.

Chapter Sixteen

Π

Social media takes on a whole new importance when you are living the life of a shut-in. Suze and I were lying on my bed, scrolling through Instagram (me), and Twitter (Suze) by the light of my Lego Superwoman bedside lamp, a relic from my childhood, when Mom strolled in.

"What are you two doing? You are going to go blind staring into those screens. The blue light is so bad for your brainwaves."

I turned my iPhone screen over and sat up, blinking. "Blue light? What on earth do you know about blue light? What the hell is it?" I rubbed my eyes. They felt sort of blue, come to think of it.

Suze sat up and scootched over, so Mom could lie on the bed beside us. "Tommy, for God's sake—everybody knows about how the blue light emanating from screens wreaks all sorts of havoc on brainwaves. For one, you can't sleep. This is why you and I are raring to walk the canines at midnight every night. We are infected with blue light, and our brains are *wired.*"

Mom nodded. "Of course, everyone also knows that social media is addicting. But really, since we have started this homebound experience, I have found great solace on Facebook. I have joined a grief group. It's a private group. For widows and widowers." She swiped at a stray spike that looked more like a cowlick. She seemed to be growing out her hair, I noticed.

"Really, Mom? That's great."

"It's gay. The group."

I had to laugh. "Seems a little contradictory. Get it? *Gay? Grieving?*"

Mom punched me in my side. It hurt. "That is a very poor attempt at humor. You know what gay means—it hasn't meant 'happy' for eons. The group is full of really nice people. Rod just lost his partner of forty years, Sydney. Rod is a dentist. I think he lives in New York State somewhere. And there is Brent, who has a penthouse; he posts pictures of it. He is grieving for his cat, but there are all kinds of grief, you know."

Suze stifled a cackle. Unsuccessfully. "It sounds nice. I am in a book club on Facebook. It's pretty boring. I would rather be in your gay grief group."

"Two things. You aren't gay, and you aren't grieving. Otherwise, it could be a good match." I hit Suze with a pillow. "Tell us more about it, Mom."

She sighed. "Well, there are three hundred members, but not all of them talk. You know—lurkers."

Oh my God, Mom is slinging social media lingo said a voice in my head. "Yeah? Go on."

"Most of us have lost spouses or partners. We talk about the horrible emptiness, the time on our hands. I have told them that I don't want to leave the house, but I am not an agoraphobic."

I rolled my eyes. "No. That would be another Facebook group."

Suze pinched my thigh. "Shut *up*, Tommy. Go on, Meg."

Mom pinched my other thigh. "I have met a lot of really terrific people. There is Sheila, who came out five years ago and found the love of her life. They were only together one year before Edie died. Then there is Marjory, whose partner (they never got married), Corrine died after they had lived together for twenty years. Corrine had cancer. Marjory had a leg amputated. Diabetes. She doesn't get out much without Corrine, so she understands how it is for me."

"Wow. I had no idea you were on Facebook, Mom. Here, I am going to "friend" you." I picked up my phone, but Mom grabbed it out of my hand.

"No! It's private, my Facebook! I don't want my daughter snooping around on my page! And I certainly don't want to know what you are doing on there."

I tried to grab my phone back, but Mom was too fast for me. She tossed it to Suze, and for a good minute, we had a game of *Keepaway* going on. But I snatched my phone out of the air, triumphant. I punched MEG POOLE into the search bar. Nothing. Then I snapped my fingers and typed in MEGHAN CARRUTHERS POOLE. Everybody uses their full name on Facebook. Nada. "Mom, you aren't on Facebook. What are you on, some alternate site? Facelook? BookFace? What?"

Mom rolled off the bed and stood up straight. "I have an account under an assumed name. Privacy concerns. Do you two not know *anything* about how personal data gets compromised?" She shook her head at us.

"My God. My mother is a social media maven!"

Suze put a hand on her forehead. "Meg! Who have you been consorting with online? Mark Zuckerberg? How do you know all this stuff about data, private groups, and social media aliases? Shit! Pardon my French..."

Mom smiled enigmatically. "You two. You have no idea the breadth of my knowledge. Why, I will bet a Bitcoin that you have never even been on the Dark Web!"

And with that, she chortled like a crone and left the room.

Suze looked as if someone had just punched her in the stomach.

I put my hands together. "Thank you, God, for bringing back her sense of humor."

Then I lay back on the bed and Suze and I both began tapping and scrolling on our phones like mad. "OK. I got it. Bitcoin is some sort of alternative currency. It says something here about block chains. I have no idea what any of this means."

Suze held out her phone screen so that I could see it. "I just Googled The Dark Web. I am afraid to read what it says."

Π

"Wake up! Wake up! It's a blizzard out there!" Mom opened my blinds to capacity, and the glare was shocking. I pulled the covers over my head. December 10. We had been holed up now for just months, but it seemed like a year already. A new season: winter. Christmas. The first one without Mommy. I wondered how on earth we were going to pull it off without major gloom.

Mom pulled the covers away from my face with a yank. "Sit up! Look out there. It's beautiful." She put her hand on the window as if to feel the snow falling. "We can go out in the backyard and make a snowman later! Or we can have a snowball fight! Rules—schmools!"

I looked at her, her hand on the window, her hair in disarray, her robe cinched tightly around her tiny waist. She seemed so fragile. And yet, here she stood, cheering at the first snowfall, encouraging me to play with her in the backyard. I pulled my knees up and rested my face against them. Maybe Mom was recovering just fine, and it was me who needed to concentrate on perking up.

"Is Suze still asleep? If you want to go out there and make snowballs, we need her. I am not going out there with you by myself. Your aim is too good."

Mom turned and smiled at me. It looked pretty authentic, but I detected just a wisp of sadness at the corners of her eyes. She wiped at the corner of one of them. A stray tear, I bet. I threw the covers off and leaped out of bed. "Come on, woman! We have to greet winter the right way! You get dressed. I'll roust Suze and we'll get the dogs and meet you out there in fifteen minutes. Do we have cocoa? We'll need it!"

The snow was a little too dry to make good snowballs, but we managed a few. Herkie and Saylor snooted around in the accumulating powder, sending cascades of it into the air over their heads. They rolled in it. They leaped onto us as we tried to hurl snowballs at them. Mom gave up on the snowman, but she gathered enough pinecones from under the big blue spruce at the end of the yard to make a wreath for the front door. She did that every year for the holidays. We whooped and hollered like kids. Suddenly, my fingers felt numb, and Suze's nose looked like a beacon. Mom's lips looked a little blue. We called it a morning and trooped inside for cocoa.

The three of us sat in front of the roaring gas logs in the fireplace, cradling our mugs. It was cozy inside, with the smell of wet dog, the crackling fake fire, and the snow still falling outside.

"This means Christmas is coming right up, you know," Mom looked into her mug, not at us. "We have to celebrate, not mourn. So can we make a plan? Today is a good day to think about it."

Suze glanced at me, her eyebrows raised.

"Yes. Well. Some old traditions will have to go by the wayside. No going downtown to see the Christmas windows, of course." I took a ragged breath. "And thank heavens we have an artificial tree. No going out to pick one at some freezing cold lot. That's a plus."

Suze set her mug down. "I, for one, am thrilled to be here with you this year. I usually have to spend Christmas with the assorted strays and orphans who are left in Columbus when everybody else goes home to family. It sucks. Having dead parents really takes the oomph out of the holidays." It took about a second for her to realize what she had just said. "Oh, I am *so sorry*. I am an idiot."

Mom blew on her cocoa and took a small sip. "Oh, honey. It's OK. We are just a bunch of misfits, aren't we?"

The fire crackled and Herkie passed gas. I put down my mug to wave both hands around her posterior to disperse the aroma. "We aren't misfits. Not exactly. We are three wonderful people who are moving through some emotional issues together. And we are going to have a wonderful holiday. Nothing can stop us. We will have a big Christmas Eve party." I stopped waving my hands and pointed at Mom. "Can't we? You know, with Rob, and Dana, and Trudy. We can cook elegant food. I'll order Christmas Crackers on Amazon, and we can wear the crowns and sing carols. It will be fun and festive, and we won't miss Mommy." As soon as I said that, I put a hand over my mouth.

Mom pulled out a Kleenex from her pocket and blew her nose. "Oh, I will miss Sam. We will miss her. But Tommy, you are right. We will be as festive as we can." She paused and bit her lip. "Because it is the first one. The first Christmas will be hard." Mom stared at the Kleenex wadded in her fist. "The first one."

I looked out the window. It had stopped snowing, and the sun was glinting off the powder in the front yard. It looked like diamonds. I tried to smile, but it came out more like a grimace.

Chapter Seventeen

Π

"Oh, look at this!" Mom held up a tattered Santa, made out of red construction paper. First grade, Mr. Ponfrit's class. Every kid was scared shitless of him. When he got mad, his voice went to a whisper, and one of his eyes twitched.

"Did you know that Mr. Ponfrit was actually a serial killer?" I put the Santa towards the back of the tree, where I wouldn't have to look at it.

"For God's sake, Tommy. He was just a little unusual, that's all." Mom shifted the Santa to the front of the tree. "I think he had a lazy eye. It made him seem a little creepy, that's all. Well, that and the whispering."

Suze opened a box and pulled out a garland made of gold and silver tinsel. "OK. Subject change. Let's forget Mr. Ponfrit, shall we?" She shook out the garland, untangling the snarls. "I love these. But they never look the way they do in magazines." She wound it around the tree. "See? It looks all clumpy and saggy. Why is real life not like the magazines?"

Mom ran a hand through her now longer, silky hair. Her spikes were a thing of the past – we forgot that staying in meant no hair salons. "Photoshop. Everything is photoshopped. But I prefer real life. Here." She adjusted the garland so that it was a little tighter. "That looks better, doesn't it?"

"What about all the rainbow ornaments? We should distribute them evenly." I held a rainbow angel. One of my favorites. "Mommy got one for us every year. I guess that is a tradition that has ended."

"Nope." Mom walked into the front hall and pulled out an envelope from one of the cubbyholes in the desk. She strode back in and handed it to me. "I ordered this one. The tradition continues."

It was a flat cardboard envelope. I opened it gingerly. Wrapped in tissue paper was a golden dog. Around its neck was a bright enamel neckerchief – a rainbow. "It's so cute! Mom, this is great." I got a lump in my throat.

"It's a pit bull. Look on the back." I turned the ornament over, and saw that it was engraved. *Herkie.* "Oh, I just love it!" I put an arm around Mom, blinking at a tear in my eye.

"I ordered it before Saylor came. Maybe next year I'll do an ornament for her. If she and Suze come back."

Suze laughed. "So everyone knows that I am going to turn out to be a 'foster fail'? Huh. It is that obvious? Hey, where are those vicious dogs?"

Mom pointed through the French doors to the den, where a dog snored on each of the two sofas. "They think decorating is boring. It doesn't involve food."

I turned the ornament over in my hand. "Oh, Mom. I love this. Thank you. It needs to go front and center." I moved a red ball and put Herkie where we would all see it.

Suze fiddled with her garland, tugging on it until it hung sort of symmetrically. Then she stood back to study her work. "It looks lame, but sort of homey. Not Instagram worthy. Those people and their perfect lives. The rest of us live with our pitiful attempts to imitate them."

"I agree. Hey. Do you think it will snow on Christmas Eve? Wouldn't that be the best? We could all go out with the dogs, lick snow from our faces, and sing carols. It would be so Christmassy!"

Mom chuckled and pointed towards the side window. "We could go over to Percy Warner's house and serenade him. With the dogs. Is there a carol that we could train them to howl to?"

"Mom. You are a genius. Not about the howling part. We *totally should* go over to Percy's house late on Christmas Eve and serenade him. Really. This might be just what it takes to soften his crispy, nasty heart." I jumped up and down, grabbed Suze and made her jump with me. "A PLAN! A PLAN! WE HAVE JUST MADE A PLAN!"

Mom put her hands on her hips and frowned. "Are you serious, Tommy? This could backfire. What if he thinks we are goading him? This isn't a Hallmark holiday movie. He'll slam the door in our faces."

Suze stopped jumping, let go of me, and held up a finger. "Maybe he will. But what if we bring him *my world famous brownies with extra Hershey Bar bits inside?* How could he slam the door on those?"

Mom snapped her fingers. "Easy. He will grab the brownies first."

We all laughed as we walked over to the window to look out at Percy Warner's house. All the shutters were drawn. There was no smoke coming out of the chimney. The bare branches of the Black Walnut tree tapped his window in the wind. "Just looking over there gives me the willies," Mom said. "Even his house looks mean."

"Willies or not. We are going to go over there on Christmas Eve. All of us. We'll sing, we'll give him brownies, we'll wish him a Merry Christmas, and we'll see what he does. It can't get any worse than it is right now. He hates us anyway." I tapped my fingernail on the pane, as if that might bring Percy to the window. I shivered at the thought of his face suddenly appearing there.

Suze heaved a sigh. "OK, then. We'll have a wonderful Christmas Eve dinner with standing rib roast, garlic mashed potatoes, green beans almandine, and that recipe for sticky toffee pudding that you said Sam always made at Christmas. We'll be happy and festive, Dana and Trudy will come, and Rob will bring way too many presents. Then we will top it off by going next door and having curses hurled in our faces. Sounds like a great holiday tradition in the making."

I pursed my lips and nodded. "Sounds like a plan."

Π

That night, after I brushed my teeth, I noticed that the edges of the Post-it note were beginning to curl. I was lonely. I rubbed the back of my neck, opened my eyes, and looked at my reflection in the mirror. "Oh, honey. You have always been lonely, haven't you?" I smoothed the edges of the Post-it. Secrets.

In the mirror, the creases at either side of my mouth looked deeper. I had the beginnings of under-eye bags. I touched one of them with my index finger, trying to smooth it out. As soon as I removed my finger, the eye bag returned. "Tommy. Face it. You have anxiety." I smiled ruefully at myself. I wasn't ready to face what was at the root of my unease. Not yet.

Π

Christmas Eve morning. Bright, low thirties. The temps had warmed, melting all the early December snow. Not a speck left on the ground to make us feel festive.

First one up, no surprise, was Mom. I heard the clattering of pans and soon after, the fabulous aroma of bacon and coffee. I threw the covers off, and as I did, Herkie looked up from the pillow on her side of the bed reproachfully. "Herk! Get up, kid! It's Christmas Eve, and I bet Mom fried you and Saylor some bacon!" I had her at "bacon." She trundled off the bed and headed into Suze's bedroom to rouse Saylor. I followed on her heels, noting how adorable her pit bull potbelly looked from the rear.

Suze was snoring. Saylor's head popped up from under the covers. Herkie jumped up on the bed, plunking herself directly on Suze's abdomen, knocking the air out of her with a *pfffffff.* "My God, you are killing me!" Saylor scrambled up and stood over Suze, licking Herkie's face and grunting. It was epic.

"Girl and dogs! It's Christmas Eve! We have bacon! Then we have house cleaning and present wrapping! It's a big day! Get up, you pitiful wench!"

Suze pushed Herkie aside and sat up, rubbing her eyes. "Will there be croissants?"

I snapped my fingers. "DOWN." The dogs jumped off the bed. "Damn, that Dana is the dog whisperer, isn't she? These dogs are so damned well behaved these days. And there may be croissants. Or pancakes, even. Get your robe on and let's go down and make a plan. You have those brownies to make."

Mom poured us coffee, set the creamer on the table, and opened the waffle iron. "Suze, you're first, because you look so much like one of the orphans from *Oliver* this morning."

Suze beamed. "This is so much better than croissants."

I opened the back door to let the dogs out to do their business. "Geez, I guess I had better scoop the poop today." I crumbled some bacon over their kibble. "But at least going out in the backyard is, you know, *going out."* It had occurred to us that the lawn service went on hiatus in the winter months.

Mom poured batter in the machine for my waffle. "Yes. We can all go out there and do some jumping jacks. Or run around for some exercise. After the poop is clear, of course. I wonder how much time Emily Dickinson spent in her backyard, or courtyard, or whatever surrounded her house. She did go out of the house sometimes, didn't she?"

I put nearly an entire piece of bacon in my mouth at once. It was so crunchilicious. "I am not a Dickinson scholar, but just a sec." I Googled her. "She had a conservatory and loved plants. So I guess she didn't. But thank goodness we can go in the backyard. And just think. If it weren't for the night time outings, we would never have met Dana and Trudy."

Mom plopped my waffle on my plate and pushed the butter dish towards me. "And thank God for social media. Without that, I think I would have been overcome with depression and grief. Without my Facebook group, it would have been so much worse. Marjory has been such a good friend to me. She really understands."

Suze poured another puddle of syrup onto her waffle. "Where does she live?"

"Oh, I don't know. I am not sure if Marjory is even her real name. We respect our privacy online. Facebook can be so invasive. All I know is that she is from the Midwest, and is in her fifties. She has two cats, and her daughter visits her infrequently. I think they might be estranged."

"Why don't you private message her and ask her more about herself?"

Mom looked up from her waffle, a startled expression on her face. "Private message? What's that?"

Suze smiled. "Meg, how can you be on Facebook and not know about private messaging? You seem to know so many other social media things! After breakfast, before we get started on the events of the day, I can show you on your laptop. You can message her and lots of the other members of your grief group and get to know them better. Totally private. And did you know that you can do Facetime via Facebook messaging also? You can actually have conversations with Marjory face to face. In real time."

Mom dropped her fork and squealed. "Oh, Suzanne! This is about the best Christmas gift you could ever give me!" She put a hand on each cheek. "It's a window to the world! The only world I want to be a part of right now—with my grief group. Oh, thank you, honey!"

"Mom. This is so wonderful. Is there enough batter for another waffle?"

Chapter Eighteen

ח

Brownies made. Mormon Tabernacle choir on Pandora. Standing rib giving off the most incredible aromas. Potatoes mashed and ready to pop in the oven. Sticky Toffee Pudding a done deal. Nothing left but green beans, so Mom, Suze and I took naps. The dogs do nothing but nap, so they were amenable.

At five o'clock, my cell played the theme from *Downton Abbey*. Rob's ringtone. I struggled to reach it on my bedside table. "Hello, Rob. What is wrong? You are supposed to be coming over in an hour."

He cleared his throat. "Is there enough food for me to bring a guest? It's a woman." Silence. I was in shock, and I supposed Rob was a little shocky as well. It being Christmas Eve, him being single for so long, and none of us expecting him to ever use the term "guest and woman" in the same sentence.

"Well, of course you can. Is this a woman as in *date*? Or woman as in 'pal,' or woman as in 'just someone you know?" Pause. "Rob?"

I heard him take a breath. "It's woman as in 'sort of a date;' I just met her a month ago when she joined the firm; I really like her; she is a specialist in LGBTQ discrimination cases; and here's the thing: she's transgender." He let his breath out in a whoosh. "Tommy. Are you in shock or anything?"

My smile nearly cracked my cheeks. "Are you joking? Rob, this day just keeps getting better and better! Of course you can bring her. And if you 'like slash love' her, we will too. What is her name?"

"Her name is Esme Stills. She is beautiful, three inches taller than I am, and smart. She loves dogs, so that is a relief; she won't freak out at the Pits. I was first attracted to her when she called me 'Shorty' and told me my fly was unzipped. A breath of fresh air, if you know what I mean."

I giggled. "I love the name Esme. She will fit right in with this crowd. She apparently has no respect for you, which is also a huge point in her favor. I hope she isn't a vegetarian or anything weird like that. Roast beef."

Rob sighed – my guess in relief. "She eats anything that moves. And she offered to bring something, so we are bringing four bottles of Shiraz."

Rob, my darling man, this will be so very stupendous. We'll see you both soon. Love you."

"Goes without saying, kid." He disconnected and my heart sang.

I put my cell in my pocket and gazed out at the ice crystals clinging to the grass in the front yard. Sparkled like diamonds. I rubbed my finger along the cold windowpane and thought about Rob. Of course, he would be attracted to an outsider. Our family was atypical from the get-go. All of us, awkward. We didn't fit into "the norm." Rob, who dated women, but never formed any real attachments. The only one he stayed with was Clarice Nettles, and she was as close to "normal" as Rob could seem to get: she was an artist, she was blind in one eye due to a horseback riding accident in which a twig pierced her eye while she was trail riding. So Clarice wore an eye patch and looked totally dashing. She had a pet parrot named Hector who called Rob "honeydew." However, this particular parrot was a hypocrite and tried to bite Rob at every opportunity. Rob and Clarice lasted about a year, and then Clarice and Hector drifted away. I think they moved to Seattle.

In any other family, this proclamation *would* be a huge shock. In ours, no way. We were the outliers, the iconoclasts, the gender benders. We embraced all people, no matter who they were or how they loved. It was second nature.

So for Rob to be attracted to a trans woman? Not a surprise.

Π

The lights on the tree glowed, the garlands Suze draped looked sparkly amidst the mass of ornaments. The wreath on the inside of the front door (because if it were on the outside, we would not be able to look at it, duh) made the whole hall smell like evergreen. This, of course was due to the "natural pine aroma" room spray Mom ordered on Amazon. The food aromas were awesome.

The doorbell rang, and Suze and I sprang to answer, excited dogs at our heels. The dogs dashed to the door, wagging and woofing. I swept the door open, and there stood dearest Dana, wrapped in a gigantic red scarf and topped by a beanie with a startling red and green pom pom. Behind her stood Trudy, also bundled within an inch of her life, holding what looked like a huge ham.

"Merry Christmas, you two!" I motioned them in. "Trudy, what is that?"

"It's a huge ham. I know you are serving food, but what is Christmas Eve without at least two entrees, I always say?" She grinned and held out the platter. "Honey Baked. You just can't go wrong. Serve cold or warm."

I took the platter from her and set it on the hall table temporarily, out of reach of dog tongues. "This smells delicious. And what could be better than ham sandwiches?

Here—let me take your coats and hats and whatever else you are wrapped up in."

Trudy began to shrug off her coat. "Oh, wait!" She dug into her pocket and produced a jar of fancy Dijon mustard. "To go with." She leaned over to pet Herkie, who was nudging Trudy's shin with her nose.

Mom emerged from the kitchen, covered with a large apron, smudges of flour on her cheeks, and a delighted look on her face. "Welcome, you two! Merry Christmas! Oh, I am so happy you are here!" There was an enthusiastic round of hugs.

No sooner had we put the ham in a safe place, poured everyone some eggnog, and settled in by the fire to admire the tree, than the doorbell chimed once more.

Mom leaped to her feet. "That'll be Robert and his friend. Oh, I hope she likes us."

The dogs clamored to the door, barking another welcome chorus. We had to shove them out of the way to open it.

"I hope she likes us, too." I turned to the pit bulls. "SIT, demon dogs!" They got the message and plunked down, tails thumping the floor. "She might think we are way too tame. Or maybe too weird, as we are voluntary hermits. My God, this could be so awkward…" I tried to smooth down my hair and checked under my arms to see if I had sweat stains. Not yet, anyway.

We all stood behind Mom as she swung the door open. Rob looked nervous. His right eye twitched, but he smiled and raised his arm to put it around the most stunning woman's shoulders. "Merry Christmas, everyone. This is Esme Stills." He paused and looked at her. "My g—friend."

This woman was a vision. Six foot three, according to Rob, but she looked even taller than that. Of course—four inch heels. Steel gray eyes. Flawless fair skin and perfect eyeliner. Hair falling in thick and lustrous curls to her shoulders, a shade of platinum/taupe that looked like those expensive suede sofas on HGTV. She wore a *cape.* A burgundy cashmere *cape* trimmed in what I hoped was *faux* chinchilla. Black ankle length skirt with sequins down the sides. Black booties, with the *heels.* Black leather gloves. I looked down at my gray leggings, noticed a small hole over my left kneecap, and felt like a slug. She held a pot of white poinsettias, which she held out to us with a gracious smile. Her voice sounded the way single malt Scotch tastes – like pepper and caramel.

"Hello all. You can shut your mouths. I only look like a super model. But inside here is just the former Eddie Stills of White Sulphur Springs, West Virginia. I grew up eating ramps and singing Dolly Parton. I said 'ain't' until I went to law school. And I am not afraid of these little dogs." She took three steps, stooped over elegantly, and stroked the dogs. They looked entranced.

Suze took the plant, Rob erupted in relieved snorts of laughter, Mom pulled Esme in and reached way up to put her arms around her, and I nearly melted with relief.

After everyone had coats off, drinks in hand, and comfortable seats around the fire, dogs settled in, Herkie lying on top of my feet and Saylor resting her head on Mom's lap, we looked at one another. Nobody seemed to know what to say until Herkie passed gas.

"Now that is an icebreaker!" Esme waved her hand delicately in front of her face. "I have always loved pit bulls. I identify with the underdog."

Trudy pushed her hair behind her ear, revealing her scars. "I am so glad to hear this, because I am an underdog from *way back.*" She pointed to Dana. "This child? My champion." Dana blushed. I don't think I had ever witnessed that.

Esme took a sip of her eggnog. "Tell me. What's life like here at the hermitage?"

Mom scratched her head. "We have figured out a rhythm. You know, Tommy and Suzanne have jobs. They work here from home. Suzanne is a curriculum specialist for the entire state of Ohio public school system. Tommy makes people famous online."

I laughed, but Mom held her hand up and continued. "I am the housekeeper, the cook, and I spend a lot of time on that. I am also collating all of my old photos, mementos, and things into scrapbooks. I do some yoga. I grieve. This is why Tommy and Suzanne are here. To make sure that I survive this year of grief without doing anything stupid. Of course, I wouldn't do that. But they are here anyway." Mom shot us both an accusing look. "Then I have my grief group online. It's a tremendous help, because all the people in it are gay, and they have losses, and they understand."

Rob shifted in his seat. "Meg, none of us think or thought you would do something stupid. It's just that we didn't want you to be holed up over here alone for so long. You needed support, and thank God Tommy saw that. Then Suze. I, for one, am very thankful, and I would like to propose a toast." He held up his cup of eggnog. "To family. To underdogs. To Tommy and Suze. Merry Christmas, and thank heaven for this family," he reached over and patted Esme's elegant fingers, "and these wonderful friends."

We all clinked cups and sipped. Mom set hers down, gently removed Saylor's head from her lap, and stood with a sparkly smile. "Now then! Let's have some roast beef. Just stuff ourselves, all right? But be sure to save room for dessert."

Π

After dinner, we all helped clean up, groaning from the state of our stomachs. Trudy and Dana cleared the table. Esme could reach all the high shelves, and so she put away the platters and serving bowls after Rob and I washed them. Mom and Suze loaded the dishwasher, the dogs cleaned up all the crumbs off the floor, and then we trooped into the living room and collapsed.

"This has been such a thrilling night. I feel like I have found my own kind." Esme wiped an imaginary tear. "You are all such dears."

Dana looked up from her phone screen. "Do people ask you embarrassing questions all the time?"

Esme ran a hand through her hair, and then pointed at Dana's cell. "Oh, honey. Put down that phone. Don't bother Googling. The answers to your questions are: Yes. Top surgery. No, the rest is none of your business. Yes, I am female all the time. No, it wasn't a *decision.* I was just born with the wrong genitals. And no, you may not ask me anything else that you wouldn't ask any other cis woman. OK, girl?"

Dana shoved her cell into her pocket. "I am out of line. I am sorry for that. I have never met a trans person. I don't know what I was thinking. I get mad any time people look cross eyed at Trudy. So I should have known better. Jesus."

"Mary, and Joseph. Yes, they are all involved with this holiday, aren't they? Girl, don't worry your head about it. I have to clear the air just about every time I meet someone new."

Dana frowned. "That doesn't make sense, because you are prettier and more feminine than just about any women I know. How would anybody know you were transgender unless...?"

"I tell them?" Esme crossed her arms over her chest. "Because I tell them. People need to know that this world isn't just two-sided. Hell, the binary world is a thing of the past."

Dana nodded, blue eyes wide. She ran her palm over the scars on her forearm. Esme's eyes widened, and she looked from Dana's arm and met Trudy's eyes. Trudy nodded her head slightly, and then smiled. "Well, Esme, I for one, am so glad to meet you. In my job at the store, I see all sorts of people. One of our checkers is gender queer. Uses the pronoun *they.* And as far as I'm concerned," she ran a hand over her worst scar, "it's such a welcome thing. There is room for all of us 'unusuals' in the world. I think *normal* is boring. At least what the world thinks is *normal*."

Mom applauded. "It's about time, isn't it? Thank God we were not all born in the last century. We would have probably all been accused of being witches or something."

Suze looked at her watch. "As wonderful as this discussion is, and as much as we all need to bond, we have a more pressing deadline."

I uncrossed my legs and moaned. "My God. It's Percy time."

Esme raised her eyebrows. "And that would be...?"

Rob cut in. "Are we really doing this?" He turned to Esme. "Percy Warner is the asshole who lives next door. He harasses Meg and the girls all the time about the vicious pit bulls they are harboring over here." He pointed at Herkie, who was at that moment thumping her tail on the floor and looking adoringly at me.

Esme laughed. "And so we are going over there to TP his house, or what?"

Suze chimed in. "Great idea, but no. I made my special brownies, and we are going over there now to present them to him as a peace offering, and maybe throw in a couple of verses of *Good King Wenceslas.*"

Dana threw herself back on the sofa cushions, hooting. "Whose idea was this? This guy is going to throw the brownies in our faces! Wait. Are they weed brownies? 'Cause that might actually work."

Mom gasped. "Of course not! They are just regular brownies, and we are going to go over there and try to make peace. On Christmas Eve. Like good neighbors."

Esme looked around at the group. "Just a bunch of good neighbors. One gay woman, one tranny, two spinsters, a gothy teenager, and a burn victim. Oh, and a man. This sounds like so much fun. Let me go in and check to see if my mascara is on straight. Where might I find the Ladies'?"

Mom pointed. "Just down the front hall to your left. The door under the stairs.

"No Harry Potter in there?" Esme stood, the muscles in her thighs flexing.

"Nope. Just a toilet and a sink. And my Christmas hand towels, which *you can use.* They are not just there for effect."

While Esme freshened up, Mom gathered our coats and we assembled in the front hall. Esme emerged from the powder room, looking ravishing and so very, very tall.

Suze pulled the leashes off the hall tree. "Are we taking the pups?"

Mom waved her arms in alarm. "No! My God! He might try to shoot them. No, this is on us. Everybody, get your charm on, and let's go over there and *win this man over!"*

We put on our coats, Esme swirled into her cape, we did a group high five, opened the door, and stepped out into the night.

Π

"Look his door knocker looks just like the one in *Scrooge."*

"Shh, Dana! We can't be laughing when he opens the door!" Suze put her hand over Dana's mouth.

We were lined up thus: Mom and I in front, followed by Suze and Dana. Trudy, Rob and Esme took up the rear, Esme towering over all of us, I am sure. I wondered if Percy would think we were some sort of new age gang.

I thonked the knocker three times. Mom took a deep breath and held it. My hands were shaking. Suddenly, Suze whispered: "Look over at our house, MY GOD."

We swiveled to look at the living room window that faced Percy's house. Outlined by the lights of our Christmas tree were two 'meatball' heads, side by side, staring at us.

Wondering, I was sure, what the hell we were doing out here without them.

The door swung open, and we all snapped to attention. Mom nearly dropped the pan of brownies. Percy stood before us, swaddled in a mint green terry bathrobe, riotous paisley pajamas underneath, and fuzzy white slippers. He sneered at us. "What do you want at this hour? How dare you come over here at this time of night!"

Mom held out the brownies. "Percy, I don't know what I have done to offend you. We have lived side by side for years. You knew Sam, and you and she always were cordial. It's Christmas Eve, and we brought you these brownies and we all wish you a Merry Christmas."

Mom's arms wobbled. She kept them outstretched.

Percy's eyebrows shot upwards, nearly disappearing into his toupee, which he had evidently applied hastily when he heard the knocking at his door. It was listing decidedly towards his left ear. "I had nothing against the two of you, even though you *are* lesbians. You minded your own business. But now you have all kinds of people coming and going over there, and then you bring in these vicious dogs! It's a menace! Property values will go down! Nobody will want to live in a neighborhood with dogs like this roaming around!"

Dana pushed me aside and stepped forward. The barbed wire on her neck expanded with her bulging muscles. "Mister, you are nuts." She started ticking off on her fingers. "ONE, they never *roam*, as you call it. They are always on the leash. TWO, they go out on the leash only late at night. Have you ever seen them anywhere but in their own, *fenced-in* yard during the day? NO. THREE, these are the sweetest, friendliest, and most docile dogs you will ever meet. But of course, you *will never meet them, because you are not a good neighbor, and you have never come next door to see for yourself.*" She took a step forward, and before she could punch him or kick him or worse, I grabbed Dana's arm and pulled her back.

"Dana—this is Dana Stryker, my dear friend, by the way..." I stepped aside and indicated Trudy. "And this is her foster mom, Trudy Owens. And this, as you know, is my Uncle Rob." I pointed to Suze. "This is my best friend, Suzanne Lampley, who is one of the 'all kinds of people' you mentioned. Suze is living with us for a while." I tilted my head backwards towards Esme. "And this gorgeous, tall woman is Esme Stills, who is keeping company with my Uncle Rob. Esme is a member of Rob's *law firm,* so I am sure she and my uncle are familiar with local dog ordinances. None of which apply to my dogs."

I stopped to catch my breath, and Mom took a step forward, still brandishing the brownies. "Percy, we are just being neighborly. We want to wish you happy holidays and give you these."

Percy continued to glare at us. "Well, you had *better not* let me catch one of those damn dogs running free. And if they shit in my yard, you will live to regret it!" And with a snarl, Percy snatched the pan of brownies out of Mom's grasp, stepped back into his hallway, and slammed the door in our faces.

"So much for *Good King Wenceslas.*" I put my arm around Mom's shoulders. "Yet he TOOK THE FREAKING BROWNIES!"

"I guess I just kissed that nice Pyrex brownie pan goodbye." Mom started to giggle.

"Oh no, Tommy. This isn't over until the tall lady sings!" With that, Esme began to warble the first verse of *Good King*. After "deep and crisp and even," she faltered. We continued by filling in with "something something something—brightly shone the moon that night, something something something."

We 'somethinged' until the end of the carol, at the top of our voices. The porch light went out. We took the hint and went back home, where the dogs greeted us enthusiastically.

Presents. We opened them, laughing at the pit bull pajamas that Suze gave me, and admiring the beautiful hammered silver necklace that Rob got Mom. Suze nearly died when she opened her gift to discover that it was also pit bull pajamas, in a different pattern. Suze and I gave Dana and Trudy each a set of bath bombs and a pair of smart wool knee socks. Dana and Trudy gave everyone luscious smelling potpourri that they made themselves. Esme had brought sugared almonds for everybody. Mom wept when she opened the scrapbook of old photos, notes, and sayings from Mommy that I made her. We stayed up until way too late. It was happy and cozy.

As we got bundled up to walk Dana and Trudy home, Esme picked up her capacious Coach purse and exclaimed, "Well, lookie what I found in my bag!" She pulled out leather leashes and collars with brass plates engraved *Herkimer* and *Saylor*. "I guess Santa put these in here."

"Oh, these are absolutely elegant!" I put Herkie's collar on, and Suze affixed Saylor's. We clipped on the leashes. "Won't Percy be furious to see these dogs attired in the latest fashion?"

We began the trek to Trudy's house, our breath like smoke. Mom stamped her feet in the cold. "Look up at all the stars!" Trudy said.

"Just glorious. What a night to remember—the fab dinner, Mommy's sticky toffee deliciousness, the fantastic company, topped off by hideousness next door," I said.

Suze clapped her mittens together. "Wait, guys! Did you notice Percy's paisley pajamas?"

Esme put her hands on her hips. "He may be a Scrooge, but nobody, and I mean nobody, can fault paisley pajamas."

"Paisley pajamas. And fuzzy slippers. Perhaps he is hard and pissy on the outside, but gooey and sweet on the inside?" Dana pushed her hands into her stomach. "All marshmallow goodness in there? We just have to find it? With brownies and maybe a thousand good deeds?"

Suze put a finger in her mouth and pretended to gag.

"Knock it off, people. It's Christmas." Rob looked at his watch. "It is seventeen minutes in. Merry Christmas to every single one of you. Now let's all get Trudy and Dana home before somebody gets frostbite."

When we reached Dana's, Trudy invited all of us in for a nightcap. As we trooped up the steps, Dana held me back. "Just a second. Let them go ahead. I have something for you. Just another small gift. Like, not a gift exactly. A talisman." She held out a business envelope, on which she had written THOMAS FROM YOUR TRIBE.

I took it and studied Dana's elaborate printing. Black Sharpie. A simple, straightforward font. Straightforward, just like Dana.

"Go on. Open it." Dana bounced up and down on the balls of her feet.

I carefully tore the end off the envelope, so I wouldn't rip into the lettering. I shook out two puzzle pieces into my palm. One was green, and it looked like a piece of a leaf. The other was bright red. I carefully slid the envelope into my jacket pocket and then tried to fit the puzzle pieces together. They didn't fit. I looked up into Dana's eyes.

"They don't fit. Get it? They are 'misfits.' Just like us."

"This is a 'talisman'? I don't understand." I tried one more time to fit them together.

"Thomas. We are all outsiders. You, me, Trude, your mom, your uncle and his girlfriend. Suze, the Pitties. We are all in this together. We have each other's backs." Dana straightened her spine, looked directly into my eyes and blinked slowly. Her eyes looked blurry for a second. "Merry Christmas, Thomas."

I clutched the puzzle pieces and my nose got runny all of a sudden.

"How did you feel after your Mommy died? I mean, I know it was horrible. How did you cope?" Dana played with a strand of her hair and pierced me with her eyes.

My stomach went sour. "I felt as if a piece of me was missing. There was, I can't describe it very well—like a gaping hole where my guts were supposed to be. And when they say stuff like 'heartache,' that's literally how it feels. I didn't cope, not at first. I cried every day for weeks, until I was dried out. Then I just sort of gathered myself together and went through the motions. I still am doing that. Being home with Mom helps. But it never goes away." I paused. "And you know, not all of my memories are happy ones."

Dana ran her fingers over her razor wire necklace. "I get that. Nobody in their right mind thinks love is all hugs and kisses, all flowery all the time. But at least you have a lot of memories. I don't have any. I only remember their faces from a photo. I have three things of my mom's: Eloise, her wedding ring," Dana pulled a chain from her shirt. It held a slim, gold band. "I wear this all the time. And I have the baby blanket that she knitted for me. I sleep with it every night. I wish it smelled like her, but it just smells like me. I am afraid to wash it. Because then her fingerprints would be gone from it." She sniffed and shook her head. "And I don't have anything of my father's. Nothing." She covered her eyes with her hand for a second, rubbing her eyes. But then, of course, she pulled her hand away and shook her head as if to dislodge all of that emotion and send it out into the atmosphere. "I would give anything for more memories, even sour ones."

I looked at this child who was so very tough on the outside. The stick-straight, glossy hair. The stubby, black polished nails. The stiff, straight shoulders. It was a front for the swirling mess of loneliness and vulnerability inside. She was steel and marshmallow, both. I reached out and stroked her cheek.

"Oh, Dana. I am so sorry you lost your mom and dad. So very sorry. It's a club, but none of us wants to be in it, right?"

Dana let out a ragged breath. "You are done crying? I want to be done crying."

I reached for her hand and twined my fingers with hers. "No. I lied. I did the mega crying during the first weeks. But at night, when I lie in the bedroom I grew up in, I can't help remembering Mommy—the times she held me in her lap. The nights of nightmares when I slept in their bed and she rubbed my forehead until I fell asleep. Her face. Her hands—I loved her hands. She had arthritis, and her knuckles were swollen. I thought that was from all the times she stitched up animals after surgery, and I thought God's hands probably looked that way, too. And I weep. I still weep for her. Dana, I don't think we are ever finished with the crying. Or the loss."

Dana raised our hands to her face and gently kissed the back of my hand. "Thank you for being my friend."

We sat, hand-in-hand, for a few minutes, until the front door opened, and Trudy said, "You two will get pneumonia out there! Come in and have something to warm you up! We are going to play Christmas Carols!"

∏

When I got home that night, I rubbed the puzzle pieces between my fingers. Misfits. Huh. What a kid this Dana was. She seemed to know things, see things, that most people twice her age didn't realize. Her experiences must have made her wise. I clutched the puzzle pieces, and as they poked into my palm, I felt a little lift. My soul expanded just slightly. This girl. Mom. Pit bulls. Suze. Mommy. The house. I looked around at the walls of my room. I wondered if any other children had slept here, feeling lost and somehow on the outside. I hoped they had friends who were wise.

I padded over to my dresser and lifted off the Post-it. I lay sideways on my bed, the Post-it crumpled in my fist.

Poor Dana. She was so tough on the outside, with the razor wire and the attitude. But there was pain inside. She was lonely. She wanted her mother. Her father.

A mom and a dad. Or in my case, a mom and a mommy. Happily ever after. The bogus fantasy. Did Dana's mom and dad really have an all-encompassing love? I lifted my head and smoothed the note under my nose and stared at it. *Secrets.*

Yeah. Maybe it was a good thing that Dana had no real memories of her parents. Perhaps it was a blessing that they died before she was old enough to know exactly what their marriage was like. Because marriage—relationships—they have tiers. The surface might seem straightforward, but underneath are the layers of conflict, betrayal, and lies. I fell back on the quilt Mom had pieced together for me out of flowered chintz. She and Mommy gave it to me for my fifth birthday. I ran my hand over the soft squares and shut my eyes.

Ten years old. Life wasn't all that complicated. Just the assorted "sticks and stones" situations; name calling: "queer," "lezzie." Nothing Mom and Mommy didn't help me handle. I had a really cool bike. Mom made chocolate chip cookies once a week. Mommy clapped and cheered louder than any other parent at my soccer games.

But this was the day that would slice my life apart. Mom was in Indianapolis, at a "girlfriends" weekend with two of her college roommates. Mommy was holding down the fort. I chose that particular weekend to get strep throat, and so I was loaded up with antibiotics, exhausted, and spent most of that Saturday sound asleep in my room.

I awoke to voices. Murmurs and laughter downstairs. For a second, I was disoriented, but the giggles got louder, and joy spread through my chest like a balm. Mom had heard how sick I was, and she came home! I struggled out of bed, holding my stuffed zebra over my mouth to suppress any coughs, and I started to go downstairs.

I took three steps and peered over the banister. Standing in the front hall like Satan incarnate was Leah Nash, her fleshy arms around Mommy. They giggled and nuzzled, then French kissed goodbye. Mommy stroked her cheek. Leah put her hand over Mommy's. She whispered something into Mommy's ear. Mommy inched even closer to Leah, and their foreheads touched. Leah, that fat worm, oozed all over Mommy.

The entire contents of my stomach began to rise into my throat. I backed silently upstairs. Luckily, I made it to the bathroom before losing the ginger ale and toast I had managed to consume for breakfast. The front door slammed. My retching continued even after my stomach was empty.

Mommy must have heard me. She hurtled upstairs.

She rushed into the bathroom, clucking with concern. As I struggled to stand, to try to push past her, she took my head in her hands, stroking my hair away from the bile on my cheeks. As she wiped my forehead, her hazel eyes overflowing with kindness, the voice inside my head began to talk me out of what I had just seen. It couldn't have been. Mommy and Mom loved each other. They loved me.

Mommy settled me back into bed. Her face seemed lit from within—her cheeks glowing. She smiled to herself as she folded the flowers of my quilt under my chin.

After she closed the door softly behind her, the voices in my ears buzzed. This time, they were not reassuring. What if she loves Leah? What if she wants to go live with her and leave us? What if she wasn't really smiling at me? Maybe she was smiling because she was thinking of Leah.

I was unable to stop shaking as I realized that the future was up to me. What if Mommy left? What if she loved Leah more than me and Mom? I wiped my forehead and tried to ignore the heat of my fever—to think clearly. Mom didn't know about this. I couldn't tell her, because if I did, she might get so mad that she would send Mommy away. To Leah. I had to keep this to myself.

My ten-year-old soul became very heavy. I knew what had to be done. I dug very deep inside myself and buried the whole incident. I blotted out what I had seen. I would keep it locked away tight. And I would try to make Mommy love me so much that she wouldn't be able to go away.

I sat up. *Bloody* secrets. I loved Mommy. But my adoration had, from that day, been laced with anxiety, anger, and reproach. This snake of unwanted knowledge I had carried with me for so long. Mom, my innocent, loving parent. Mommy, the cherished one, the deceiver. How could Mommy do this to her? How did Mom not ferret out her partner's infidelity?

And me. The one who watched from the staircase. The one who was never able to face what I saw, talk about it with anybody. The person who walked through life sans emotional attachments, out of what, fear? Lack of trust? Eyes burning, I crushed the square of paper into a ball and threw it. I wished that I could run downstairs and ask Mom for a hug, a kiss, and an explanation.

But I couldn't do that. Mom was mourning the loss of the person she loved and trusted. I was here to help her heal, not tear her apart. I pressed my fingers into the place above my heart where the pain was most acute. Then I lay back on my flowery quilt and slammed the door on my memories. As I had been doing for so long. Secrets.

Chapter Nineteen

П

December morphed into January. The weather was bleak, the days dark, and our moods darkened right along with them. We plummeted into the slough of despond.

Despite my two new clients and their multiple ridiculous demands, I was literally 'phoning it in.' On this particular morning, I sat at my desk, staring at my computer screen and moving the cursor up and around, making figure eights.

Suze wandered into my bedroom, attired in her Christmas pit bull pajamas, a tatty yellow crocheted shawl of Mom's over her shoulders, and her old-lady Dearfoam slippers with roses on them. She gripped her coffee mug with both hands. Her expression was alarming: her eyebrows looked like fighting caterpillars. "I cannot concentrate. I have cabin fever that is threatening to make me homicidal. Tommy, I am going to have to leave this house."

That took a few seconds to soak in. I shut my laptop and rubbed my forehead. "I get it. I would love to go to Starbucks right now and involve every single person there in a deep and meaningful conversation. But I am committed to doing this for the entire lonely and claustrophobic year. For my mother's sake. But you, dear Suzanne, are free to go as you please. You are here at your own pleasure."

Suze took a long sip of her coffee. It must have been less than hot. She leaned against the wall and crossed her ankles.

"I have been watching you and Meg try to deny how totally deflated you both feel. As a matter of fact, I came right out and asked her last night when we came home from dog walking if she thought she ought to go out with us every night. You know, breath of fresh air and all that. Out."

"What did she say?"

Suze scooted down the wall until she sat cross-legged on the floor. She set her mug down beside her and rubbed her palms together. "She said that she might. But she said it halfheartedly. Then I asked her why it was so important that she remain in—wasn't a few months enough?"

I straightened up and stared at Suze. "And?"

Suze continued to rub her palms. She did not meet my gaze. "She didn't answer right away. She teared up. I gave her a used Kleenex from my pocket, and she rubbed it all over her face. Then she said that until her grief 'wasn't so damn heavy,' she could not go out. She said these exact words, Meg: 'When I go out, I want my shoulders to feel light again. Right now, I feel like I am balancing an anvil. When I can drop it, I will go out.' My God, she is carrying around an anvil, Tommy. What about you? Are you lugging around a boulder?"

I closed my eyes. The insides of my eyelids looked like raw meat. "It's a good analogy. Actually, I feel pretty much numb. Empty. When I was making the scrapbook for Mom, it drained the last drops of life right out of me. Since Christmas, I just feel nothingness inside. But this is where I have to be, somehow."

Suze straightened her legs and bumped her head against the wall. "I remember that feeling. When my Dad and Mom died. I felt like all the oxygen left my blood. I could barely move for weeks. It took all my strength to go through the motions."

"So you understand why I am rooted here. But Suze, you need to go out. You can be our lifeline to the world of daylight. The one beyond the backyard."

Suze nodded. "I can. I will. But you know that these last months of winter are brutal. No holidays to brighten things up. Not much sun. It is going to be a rough go for you and Meg."

"Right. So your assignment, should you choose to accept it, is to go out there and bring us back some sunshine. News. Gossip. Citrus fruit. You will be our bringer of good tidings."

"Are you sure you two won't mind my leaving once in awhile? It's not like I am going to start running all over town—I still have my job. If I can just get out a couple of times during the week, I think my outlook will improve."

"Do you want to go back to Columbus? You are totally free to do that, you know. You are here due to the goodness of your heart. There is no legally binding contract or anything."

Suze picked up her mug and looked into it, then put it down again. "I am here for you, kiddo. There is absolutely nothing for me back in Columbus. So you are stuck with me. I want to be with you and Meg when you divest yourselves of the anvil and the boulder or whatever, and step outside into the light of day. Free at last." She put her hands together. "Namaste. Now I have to go and make sure that all the Power Points for Algebra II in Madison County are up and running."

She got up, grabbed her empty mug, blew me a kiss and left the room. I looked over at the sky outside my window. Gray clouds. Tree limbs clacking like black skeletons in the wind. It was a horrid, dank day. I thought about all the people sitting at Starbucks, chatting and laughing. I felt a surge of what? Envy? Jealousy? Resentment?

Then I thought about Mom and her anvil. Me and my boulder. I reopened my laptop and Googled *surviving loss.* Then I Googled *forgiveness.* The first few articles stressed the importance of avoiding isolation. So much for that. One blog talked about forgiveness being like water falling on a desert. I wasn't ready for that kind of hydration, not just yet. But then I found the phrase *tincture of time.* That sounded a bit more reassuring. Time. That is what we were wading through. The time that it was going to take for Mom and me to shore up our hearts and begin to lighten. Time for me to understand things.

Then I had another idea. I went onto Reddit and scrolled around for a few minutes, just wandering through SubReddits for loss, mourning, and just for the heck of it, dating. Nothing interesting to me. I ran my fingers over the keys, looking at all of the threads about absurdities like "gingerheads." I licked my lips, and suddenly, an idea came to me. I typed "growing up with gay parents" in the search bar, and my God; it was a veritable gold mine of threads.

My heart began to beat a bit faster. I scrolled down until I found a thread that looked promising. Called "Gay parents, straight kids." I typed my first comment: *I am a cisgender woman, straight, and my mothers were lesbians. Hi.*

I didn't really expect much. But good God, there was an immediate response.

Hi. Me, too. Are you sure you are straight?

I ignored that one. Geez. There were about fifteen more like that, and I nearly decided to write this off as dumb, when a comment came in that caught my attention. So I joined the group. My Reddit user name was "Media Girl."

Hi, Media Girl, right back. I am a cisgender, straight man whose parents were gay men. I had my share of problems growing up. Are you looking for some sort of support, here?

I leaned back in my seat and stared at the screen. Was I looking for support? Why did I suddenly hop on to Reddit? I shut my eyes for a few seconds, just to get my bearings. A tiny, hopeful voice in my head said, "Go ahead. You might as well strip your soul naked. These folks have no idea who you are, and this guy sounds credible.

I might be looking for support. Or just solidarity.

Well, you are in the right place.

His user name was "Cissy." Weird.

If you are straight, why the name "Cissy"?

Ha. Play on words. "Cis"gender. Gay dads: "Sissies." Get it?

Oh, right! Duh.

So. What is bothering you? You need solidarity? In what way?

I am not sure I want to just blab everything to a complete stranger. How do I know you are legit?

Legit? All right, I can tell you this. My childhood was filled with love; my fathers were devoted. I grew up in New York, where no one bothered the three of us. We had a cadre of great friends, including gay and straight people. My father, Ben, was an artist. He was on his way to becoming known. Really known. His work was featured in the Hathaway Gallery, and he had started selling and making money. Good fortune seemed assured. We were happy. I was twelve, and just starting sixth grade. I got my own cell phone! My father, Sean, was hoping that he could stop driving a cab and go to grad school to get his Master's in Social Work. Then my dad Ben got sick. Nope, not AIDS. He had Stage Four Diffuse Large B Cell (DLBCL) Non-Hodgkin's lymphoma. He died four months later. It was hell.

When Ben died, we hung on for a year, but Sean (I called them Pa and Dad, but will use their first names to avoid confusion) didn't seem to be able to get over it. He had suicidal ideation. I was really scared. My grandma Sue (Sean's mom; Ben's parents were both deceased) encouraged Sean and me to move back home to Charleston, West Virginia, where she and her second husband,

Wes, lived. We did. It was a mistake. Small, fucking towns. To make a long story short, the kids at the middle school were not cosmopolitan. They caught wind of my situation, and from that day forward, I was stigmatized and bullied. You probably know how that goes. It was assumed I was gay. I joined the wrestling team, and as I was agile, strategic, and soon quite strong, I got respect. Life was never really free of crap—I always looked over my shoulder. Is this legit enough for you? Oh, and Sean? He is still here. He still drives a cab. He has had serial partners. It isn't pretty, but he has not talked about killing himself again. Grandma is a force to be dealt with. She's now 92. When she dies, I hope Sean will be OK. I don't live in Charleston any more. When she goes, I may have to go back. LEGIT?? What's your story?

I rotated my neck back and forth—the muscles supporting my head had gone all tight and they stung. I reread Cissy's comment. I felt like jumping into cyberspace and running right up to Cissy, pulling him into a secluded corner where nobody else in the www could hear us, and spilling my guts. But I knew better than that. The cyber world was a maelstrom of danger. People who hung out there were often not what they seemed to be.

I put a hand on the back of my neck and massaged the knots as I considered my options. My fingers hovered over the keyboard, and I found myself typing.

My story? My mothers are Meg (Mom) and Sam (Mommy). Sam died of pancreatic cancer last year. Her death was not a surprise, but it still came as a tremendous shock to Mom. About a month and a half after the funeral, I got a message from a neighbor that Mom had not been seen in the neighborhood for weeks, and that the blinds were all down in the house. Mom did answer the phone and reassured all of us that she was fine.

I didn't buy that. I came home to check on her. She was in bad shape. To make a long story short, she had decided that she just couldn't face the world, and that she was going to shut herself away until she could. I took one look around at the unwashed dishes, the dust on all the surfaces, the wadded Kleenex stuffed between the sofa cushions and realized that I couldn't leave her alone. So we are both now official recluses. I set a hermit "time limit" of one year. After that, we will both be healed over, fine and dandy, and ready to go out there to face the world. Ha.

I am a little stir crazy. I do get out. I have a dog, and I have to take her on walks. We go out late at night. So I see the world, but it is veiled in dimness. So that is my story. I am not sure why I found my way here. I guess I just felt a little alone.

I hesitated before hitting "send." Did I really want to get into anything with this person? Was it really a man? Maybe it was a weird woman. Could it be a lunatic, looking for someone to terrorize? I stared at his comments. I asked my gut what it thought; as we all know that "listening to one's gut" is the cardinal rule for just about everything. Despite what I knew about the reality of online menace, my gut gave the all clear. So I hit "send," heaved a sigh, and shut my laptop.

My back was as stiff, my spine cracked as I moved. My scalp felt tight. The pain from my neck seemed to lodge behind my ears. I rubbed my temples, a sharp twinge lodging behind my eyeballs. Good grief. I scrubbed my scalp with my fingertips, trying to loosen the tightness. It didn't really help. I needed more. Flexing my fingers and swinging my arms to lubricate my joints, I went looking for Mom.

"Hey, Meg Poole! Where are you, and what are you doing this very second? I need at least ten hugs!"

I found her in the living room, sitting on the floor in front of the window, a dog on either side, an arm around each one. They were gazing out at the children skipping and shouting on the sidewalk as they passed on their way home for lunch. A little girl in a red down coat caught sight of them in the window, and she jumped up and down, excitedly waving—her mittens dangling and bobbing from her mitten strings. The dogs "arfed" in response, and Mom waved back, laughing.

Mom heard my steps. She turned and smiled at me. "The kids. We watch for them."

"Mom, are you sure you don't just want to pop outside?"

Her grip tightened around the pups at her side. "No. Not yet. But this suits me, for now."

I turned to go back upstairs, but stopped and went back into the living room. "Well, things will get more exciting around here, anyway. Because Suze is going to start going out on a couple of reconnaissance missions per week—she needs to get out. So who knows what sorts of information, gossip, neighborhood news, and stuff she will bring back? This might be just the shot in the arm we both need."

Mom let go of the dogs, swiveled around to look at me and put her hands over her heart. "Bless her. She shouldn't just waste away here. This will be good for all of us. Oh, honey. Are you sure you don't want to get out along with her? For your own well being? You have been down lately. Don't think I haven't noticed."

I hurried over to her, poking Herkie out of the way, and sank down beside her on the floor. I rested my forehead against hers. We breathed one another's breath for a moment. Mom's smelled like Peppermint Life Savers. "I am fine right here with you."

"Promise you will leave the house if you need to?" Mom's breathing quickened.

"Yes. I promise."

We sat there, head to head, for a few more seconds. I felt my heartbeat slow down, every single muscle loosen. My Mom and I, two temporarily lost souls, blending our breath and our love while the sun shone on us and the dogs surrounded us, licking us until we had to laugh.

Π

Two days later, Suze went out on her first foray. She came downstairs wearing black fleece lined leggings, Uggs, and her Ohio State sweatshirt, topped off with her puffy red down jacket.

I got sweaty just looking at her. "Are you sure you aren't overdressed? This is Ohio, not Siberia."

"My God, Tommy. It is January. The outside temperature is 29. There is a wind chill. I have to bundle up. People who don't go out much are very vulnerable."

I exhaled. It was more like a hiss, I guess. "Suzanne Lampley, you go outside every single night with me and the dogs—when, I might add, it is *colder* than it is during the day. What the hell?"

Suze looked hot. "OK, then." She removed the down coat and wrested the sweatshirt off over her head, huffing as she removed it. "I was wearing the sweatshirt for luck. It reminds me of the fun I had at college. I was carefree and had more than one boyfriend simultaneously. But you are right. I would boil." She put her coat back on. "OK. I am ready to go out and scout for exciting tidbits to bring back here. Oh, and tell Meg not to make lunch. I'll bring that back, too."

"Sounds like a great plan. Nothing with mustard for me."

Suze turned to go. I opened the front door wide, and a stripe of sunlight blasted in and made us both squint. "Have a great time, kid. And listen in on as many conversations as you can!"

Suze strode out into the brightness, but not before giving me a tight hug. As she strode down the front walk, she put her hands over her face and sneezed three times. Direct sunlight and winter air tends to do that to people.

I stood in the open doorway for a few minutes, sun washing over me, watching Suze disappear down the street, hoping that the sun in my face would make me sneeze, too.

It didn't. I shut the door and went upstairs to confront a client about his use of the F word on social media. The hours before Suze returned loomed in front of me like an eternity.

I logged on to Reddit. Cissy wasn't online. He hadn't responded to my comment. Maybe I scared him off. Nobody else in the group looked remotely promising. I logged off and stared at my reflection in my laptop. My eyes looked like dark, ragged buttonholes.

Π

Suze burst back in at 12:30. The dogs went crazy. Mom and I had been trying to act nonchalant, but we had both been trolling the front window since noon. Suze's rusty curls were mussed from the wind, her cheeks were ruddy, and her knuckles gripping the bags of food were white.

"Here, Meg! Take these sandwiches. I got you a tuna on rye, and Tommy a turkey with chipotle mayo on five grain. I got the turkey club. Panera had a special on—you got a free cookie with each sandwich. I got a selection: a shortbread, a brownie with caramel icing, and a giant chocolate chip cookie. We can share. Oh, and chips. Here, pups—I got you each a snickerdoodle."

Suze flung off her coat and tossed it toward the newel post, where it lodged briefly before sliding to the floor. "Come into the kitchen! I have good news and bad news!"

We settled into chairs around the table, and Mom got us each a glass of ice water. We rummaged around in the bags until we each had the correct lunch, and before we could even take a bite, Suze started in.

"Good or bad news first? Never mind. I'll start with the good news." She clapped her hands. "Guess who I met at Panera? Having lunch and *holding hands?*"

I looked at my sandwich, which smelled divine. "George and Amal Clooney?"

Suze's smile disappeared. "How did you know?"

Mom choked on a sip of water. I pounded her on the back. She recovered and wiped her eyes with her napkin. "Really? Are they here filming something?"

Suze rolled her eyes. "My God. Just kidding. No. But this is just as good. I saw Rob and Esme! They are in love! They didn't even see me until I went right up to them and said hi." She paused. "Of course, they wouldn't have noticed me, because they know we don't go outside." She took a bite of her sandwich.

"So what did they say? Were they so surprised to see you?"

Suze held up her hand, chewed her bite, and swallowed. "This is absolutely delicious."

"SUZE! What did they say?"

"They looked behind me to see if you two were with me. They seemed very disappointed when you weren't. But they said they were glad that at least *one* of us is getting out."

At this point, even Mom was becoming agitated. "Suzanne. We aren't interested in that. Tell us what they said about, you know, their relationship? Rob has not shared anything with me. Did they actually say they are dating?"

I went ahead and took a huge chomp out of my tuna. It was good. So foreign. From the outside world—exotically delicious.

Mom waved her hands at Suze to continue.

"Well, I didn't actually confront them on their status. That would have been rude. But I did sit down with them for a few minutes. They asked how things were going. Apologized for not coming over lately—they both are working on big cases and stuff is crazy at work, you know. That sort of thing."

Suze took a sip of water and continued. "But get this. They did not unlock hands the entire time we were chatting! And they both looked sort of mushy around the edges—the starry eyes, the blushing. It was so damn obvious."

Mom looked at me and we both grinned.

Suze set her sandwich down, suddenly serious. "Are you ready for the bad news? It is disgustingly bad."

I stiffened in my seat. "What is it?"

Suze took a deep breath. "There are leaflet/poster things being put up all over the place downtown. They have a photo of a dog that looks a lot like Herkie, and they say FRAMINGTON NEEDS BREED LEGISLATION AGAINST VICIOUS DOGS. PITBULLS ARE DANGEROUS. GET THEM OUT OF OUR NEIGHBORHOODS."

All the color drained from Mom's face. My heart stopped.

Suze nodded slowly. "It's what you are thinking. Percy Warner is campaigning to get pit bulls outlawed. Underneath the bold print it says *contact Percy Warner for more information* and it has his phone number."

She reached into her pocket and pulled up a wadded up poster. Sure enough. The dog could have been Herkie. And there was Percy's information.

Mom stood up, knocking her chair off balance to the floor. "That man needs to go to hell."

Suze got up and righted Mom's chair, and guided her back into it. "Ladies, this isn't the end of the world. We have time to make a plan. Breed legislation is not something one grumpy man can accomplish over night. Plus, we have two lawyers we can consult, and I am sure they will work for us *pro bono*. That means 'for free,' right?"

"Jesus, Mary and Joseph. How a man can call two dogs that only leave the house after ten at night, ON LEASHES, vicious, I do not know. Is he insane?"

Mom looked at us both, her brows furrowed. "He may be. He may be sick. Or he may be just a mean old snake. But girls, I am going to find OUT."

None of us finished our lunch.

Chapter Twenty

П

Rob and Esme sat on the sofa. Esme smiled reassuringly. Rob looked angry, his eyes glinting. Mom, Suze and I sat crowded together on the other sofa, facing them. We ignored the bowl of chips Mom had set out on the coffee table.

"First off, although I am not an expert in this kind of community law, it is my understanding that breed specific legislation is being overturned these days, not implemented." Esme turned to Rob. "Right?"

The muscle just above Rob's left temple pulsed. "Right. Right. This guy's chances of stirring up any kind of support are pretty slim. What kind of a bastard is he, anyway?"

Mom's legs were crossed, and she jiggled her foot until I had to put out my hand to stop her. "Mom has decided to lift her ban on going outside during the day. She is intent on visiting Percy. Interrogating him, maybe?" Mom tried to disengage my hand, but I held onto her leg firmly.

Rob raised his brows. "Meg. No. If you inflame this guy, who knows what he will do? He lives right next door. He knows you are here all the time. He could do something awful to you."

Suze interrupted. "Or to the dogs. Like throwing poisoned meat over the fence."

I put my hands out to shush everybody. "Whoa! Whoa. First off, I think we might be able to spot pieces of random meat in the backyard. Second, we can take the dogs out on leashes back there and make sure they don't ingest anything. But yes, Mom, I don't think you should break house rules and go over there. For God's sake, if you are going to break house rules, let's all go to a movie."

Rob took a turn at interrupting. "People. Hold on. This whole thing is bound to blow over. I think the best thing we can do is ignore this guy."

Esme shook her head. "What if ignoring him doesn't work, then what?" She laughed. "Sic the dogs on him? Show him just how right he is?" When she saw the looks on our faces, Esme leaned forward and flapped her hands at us. "No, no! I am just kidding! This whole situation is ridiculous. I could crush that despicable little bald man between my two fingers." She demonstrated.

Rob continued. "Ignore. If that doesn't work, then I can send him a reminder on our letterhead that he is asking for legal trouble if he continues with this campaign."

"Is there some sort of legal trouble he can get into?" Mom asked.

"Harassment, certainly. I can ask one of the civil attorneys. There must be something. And often, a letter from a law firm is all it takes to shut someone up."

My stomach churned. "How can three women staying at home all day with their harmless dogs cause all this trouble?"

Nobody had an answer. We sat there, me fuming, Mom starting up again with the leg jiggling, Suze whimpering a little, Esme smiling insincerely, and Rob making fists. We must have sent out intense vibrations of negativity, because just then, Herkie and Saylor charged into the room, barreled up onto the sofa, and sat on the three of us.

Rob and Esme both roared.

We shoved the dogs off our laps, and they thumped onto the floor and proceeded to try to jump up onto Esme and Rob's sofa. Rob and Esme managed to fend them off.

"Well, Percy may have a point. These dogs can probably crush you just by being friendly." Rob rubbed Herkie's head firmly.

Esme stood up. Probably to avoid getting dog hair on her pashmina. "I say we forget this whole thing and order Chinese food. There must be something soothing we can watch on Netflix. Or, we can play board games."

I was appalled. "Board games? What is this, 1950?"

We got pot stickers, lo mein with shrimp, mu shu pork, fried rice, and our fortune cookies were all more like aphorisms than fortunes. Then we played Monopoly for three solid hours.

I slept in the next morning. It must have been a monosodium glutamate hangover. I sat up in bed and grabbed my cell. Yikes. It was 10:30. I threw off the covers and grabbed my robe and thrust my feet into my slippers. Herkie and I rumbled down the stairs. Nobody was in the living room. The dining room was empty. The TV wasn't on, either, and that room was uninhabited. Herk and I wandered into the kitchen, where Mom sat, drinking coffee.

In front of her in the center of the table was the Pyrex brownie pan.

Π

After I screamed my head off at the bottom of the stairs for her to "Get your ass down here!" Suze and Saylor stumped downstairs, Suze holding a file folder and looking confused. "I thought we weren't supposed to fraternize during working hours. What the hell? Are all the house rules just being thrown out the window?"

I grabbed her arm and yanked her into the kitchen, where Mom still remained, calmly sipping her coffee.

"LOOK."

Suze glanced at Mom and then back at me. "What? Meg is having coffee. That is normal. It is still morning."

I shook Suze's arm. "LOOK WHAT'S ON THE TABLE!"

It took a few seconds for it to register, but then it clicked in. "Holy hell, is that THE brownie pan?"

Mom set her coffee mug down with a decided clunk. "The very one."

We both pulled up chairs. "Spill it, Mom. What the hell happened?"

"I listened to what you all had to say last night. But I couldn't sleep. I kept thinking about how we had been neighbors for years with no issues. Not that Percy Warner was the friendliest man in the world, but he seemed to live and let live. Sam always spoke to him when she saw him out in his yard, and whenever I waved to him, he nodded. So it had to be something."

Suze pounded her hand on the table. "He was attacked by a dog when he was little! No – his wife was killed by a dog!"

Mom put a finger to her lips. Suze shushed. "Girls. This isn't a TV movie. Nothing is that simple."

I felt as if I might be on the verge of having a stroke. "Mom! For God's sake, what happened?"

Mom got up and poured herself more coffee. She held up the pot. "Any for either of you?"

"Mom, you are killing me here! NO COFFEE!"

Suze poked me. "Actually, I would love some coffee. And milk, please."

Mom took her time getting out a mug for Suze, pouring the coffee slowly into it, and then opening the fridge and rummaging around for the creamer. During that time,

I think I had the beginnings of an aneurysm. "Mom! What the hell happened! Tell me before I have some sort of stress induced medical emergency!"

Mom sat down and began. "I just decided to go over there and ask him for my pan back. It was perfectly legitimate." She looked smug. "When Percy answered the door, he looked apoplectic immediately, so I just brushed past him and walked into his front hall. By the way, he has gorgeous, gold and red flocked wallpaper."

Suze spluttered a bit of her coffee onto the table.

Mom patted her on the back, handed Suze a napkin, and continued. "So we stood there, face-to-face, and I just asked him for my pan."

I groaned.

"Then I said something like 'Percy, if there is something you want to get off your chest, I want to hear it. You and I have lived side by side for years without incident. I need to know why you are so upset all of a sudden. About these innocent dogs, whom you have never even met!' He didn't say anything, but he still looked very red in the face." She stopped and looked towards Percy's house.

"Mom! You are drifting! What happened next?"

Mom turned back to look at us. I swear, there might have been a halo floating above her. "I just put my foot down. I told him that whether he liked it or not, he was coming over here tonight for dinner. And when he started to stutter out an answer, I literally stomped my foot. Really! Then he looked startled long enough for me to tell him that we would lock the dogs in my bedroom, and he would not have to even look at them. He had no choice, really. He just nodded. Then I told him to be her no later than 6:00. Then I said he better go get my brownie pan and be quick about it." She pointed to the Pyrex. "And the rest is history. Or it will be."

I put a hand on my chest to keep my heart from exploding through my ribcage. "So Percy Warner, the nasty little man, is coming over here for *dinner?* Tonight??"

Suze put her fist under her chin. "I have worked with kids with all sorts of problems for my entire career. I see everything from outright cruelty to isolation and depression. For kids, there are all sorts of reasons for acting out. Divorce. Chemical imbalances like bipolar. ADD, ADHD, and a rash of other alphabetical mashups. Maybe this Percy has some sort of mental illness or disorder that is getting worse. Maybe it is the onset of dementia. I think that no matter how much we dislike the man, we need to give him the benefit of the doubt."

That took me aback. I felt a rush of guilt, followed by dismay. "Oh, no. How on earth are we going to handle this?"

Mom squared her shoulders. "I think the first thing to do is to figure out what to have for dinner."

Π

After a debate about comfort food vs. food to impress, we compromised on fried chicken with mashed potatoes and gravy, but served with Suze's aunt's cranberry chutney. Mom would quickly poach some pears, which we got this time of year from Harry and David, and frankly, poaching was gilding the lily.

It was also lucky that Suze was no longer on 'house arrest,' because she went to the grocery in person to pick out organic hens that the butcher quartered for us. She also chose really nice Yukon Golds for the mashing. We had white wine and cinnamon sticks for poaching the pears, according to Mom, the poacher.

My assignment was to create a friendly and unassuming tabletop. This involved a speckled green ceramic pitcher, which looked sort of pudgy around the middle. I thought it might make Percy feel at home. I went into the pantry and rooted around among the seemingly endless varieties of silk flowers that Mom and Mommy never threw away. I managed to arrange a grouping of orange gerbera daisies, intermingled with some tiny white flowers that I thought were probably straight out of the imagination of some floral catalog—no such flowers existed, I was sure. But they looked cheerful together. Next, I hauled out the orange and pink plaid placemats. The evening was developing a springtime theme.

The good silver. Ugh. But when I opened the silver chest, it all looked shiny enough. Shiny enough for a Scroogey neighbor, I thought. So I set the table, using the silver and the Fiesta Ware. Color, color, color! By the time I was finished, the room was so bright and cheery, I wanted to strangle it. But Mom strolled in and clapped her hands like a five year old. "Beautiful and so happy! This will be so nice."

"Mom. Remember who is coming."

She deflated, but only slightly. "I keep telling myself that this evening will work out somehow. You and Suze promise to be on your best behavior. Yes? If he goes at you, you can't react in anger. Remember what Suzanne said about his condition."

"She said he *might* have some sort of condition. But I believe being a horrible, mean person is also a condition. What if his condition is just plain 'ornery old coot?'hat if he is coming over to insult and offend us, while enjoying his delicious, home cooked meal? Huh?"

Mom looked me over from head to toe. "Thomasina, do you perhaps have any Valium or anti-anxiety medication? You or Suzanne? Because right now, I think that would be a very wise road to go down."

I made a face at her. "I don't, but Doc Amblyn gave you some to get you through Sam's final days and the funeral, don't you remember? So yes, I think taking some of your meds might just be the thing for Suze and me this evening. Thank you."

"Oh, you are so right! You know, Tommy, I am going to go upstairs and find them. We can each have a cocktail and a little pill before Percy arrives." I started to say something, but Mom waved me off dismissively. "I know what you are going to say: don't mix drink and drugs. But we both know that having a little gin and one of these pills will mellow us out, correct?"

I nodded, nonplussed.

"OK then. I have chicken to soak and coat with my special crumb mixture. And you, my girl, need to peel potatoes." She looked at the ceiling. "And tell Suzanne I am going to need her to gently peel the pears. ALL HANDS ON DECK."

And so the afternoon passed, pleasantly enough. And by golly, by the time it was 5:00, all three of us sank into kitchen chairs, a pill in one hand, and a gin and tonic in the other. By 5:30, we were mellow and buttery. We each had a second drink, 'for courage,' and then we all went upstairs to change into what Suze called 'upscale casual.' For me that was clean jeans and a black turtleneck with a black and white harlequin print scarf wrapped around my neck. For Mom, it was a silk blouse with teal blue velvet pants that made her look like an elder Audrey Hepburn. For Suze, it was a flowing navy and purple striped gypsy skirt, silver hoop earrings the size of bracelets, a purple boat necked jersey, and of course, ginger curls. She looked edible herself.

Π

One thing you can say about Percy Warner: he is punctual. The doorbell chimed at exactly 5:58. I opened the door, hands and knees shaking. There stood our nefarious neighbor.

Percy Warner is not a small man. Not tall—I would say about five foot eleven. He looks as if he was athletic at one time, many years ago. Broad shoulders, wide neck—perhaps the vestiges of a former football career. A paunch, but the sort that looks hard, like a watermelon, under his shirts, not soft and spongy. Ruddy face, slightly bulbous nose. Dark brown toupee, very obvious—like Barbie hair. His eyes are the only thing about him that radiate energy. Blue, as dark as sapphires. The sort of eyes that look black most of the time.

Percy stood, stiff, a cellophane bag of what looked like licorice all-sorts in his clutches. He wore a ragged Burberry muffler over his camel coat. I hadn't seen a camel coat in ages. Under the coat were dark brown corduroy trousers. As I looked him over, my eyes fell on his black and brown saddle shoes. I nearly choked on my own saliva.

"Well, are you going to let me in, or just stand there staring?" He took a step forward, spluttering.

I felt the vibration of footsteps behind me, as Mom and Suze emerged. My feet seemed glued to the floor. Luckily, Mom shoved me backwards and motioned for Percy to come in. As he advanced into the foyer, still gripping the candies, Suze tried to muffle her gasp. I took it she had noticed the saddle shoes.

"Welcome, Percy. Here, let me get your coat. Do you want to keep the muffler on? It is a chilly evening." Mom helped Percy off with his coat, managing to work around the bag of candy. She ran her hand over the sleeve as she draped it over the banister. "Beautiful wool. I'll just leave it here for you."

She reached out a hand for his muffler, but Percy put a hand on his throat. "I'll keep it on."

Awkward silence. We three women stood like statues in the hall. Then we heard faint woofing coming from upstairs. Percy's entire body jolted as if he had been hit by lightning. "Those dogs! Where are those dogs?"

Mom took Percy's right arm and I took his left, and we escorted him into the living room. It took a bit of force, but we were able to get him to bend his legs and sit on the sofa. He sat, rigid, looking upward, as if he could see through the ceiling. "They are up above us. I can hear their feet! Are they locked in a room? What if they get out? They can break down doors, you know!" He still had a death grip on the candy.

Suze stood in the doorway. "Mr. Warner, you look like you need a drink. Can I get you some wine? A beer? We also have the hard stuff."

Percy did not take his eyes off the ceiling. "I am not usually one to drink."

Suze tried to smile, but it didn't materialize. She looked like she had just tasted liver. "How about a Coke, then?"

Percy nodded.

Mom and I, sitting uncomfortably on the sofa across from Percy, our thighs touching, were both at a total loss. She cleared her throat twice. I couldn't take my eyes off the saddle shoes. Finally, Mom came up with something. "Oh, are those candies? For us?"

Percy looked at the bag in his hand as if he had never seen it before. Then he set it on the coffee table. "It's licorice. My minister sent it over. I hate licorice."

Bingo. That's exactly why he or she sends it to you, you ass. I stifled the thought and said, "Really? Have you ever told the pastor that you don't like licorice? Oh, and thanks for bringing it over *here*." I probably put too much emphasis on the word "here," because Mom stepped on my toe deliberately just then.

Suze entered with a tray. On it was a Coke and three glasses of wine, so full that they sloshed out of the glasses as she walked. Fortification. She offered the Coke to Percy, who took it, stared at it, and then set it down beside the licorice. Mom and I couldn't grab our glasses fast enough. Suze set the tray down on the coffee table, picked up her glass and swigged a good third of the wine before she squeezed onto the sofa beside us. There we were. Three against one. It seemed a bit unfair, so I poked Suze until she understood that she needed to get up and go sit on Percy's side. She did. She took her wine and sat on his sofa, setting the wine down in front of her. She shrunk as far away from him as possible, but at least the configuration of humans in our living room was even.

Mom began the deprogramming session. "Percy, can you tell us why you are so afraid of dogs? Is it just this particular breed? Were you ever bitten by a dog?"

Percy looked at Mom and me as if we had asked him if he were a cannibal. "What are you talking about? I am not afraid of dogs." He humphed. Then humphed again for emphasis.

Suze made a choking sound, reached for her wine, and downed the rest of it in one go. She gasped, fanned her mouth with one hand, then turned to Percy. "What did you say?"

"I said I am not afraid of dogs. But those curs you have aren't dogs. They are for fighting. Everybody knows that." He shot a challenging look in our direction. "Fighters."

Suze's cheeks blazed the way they do in redheads. Two round circles of crimson with a freckled background. She whirled around to face him. "You are a victim of fake news, my friend." She opened her mouth to say more, but I interrupted her.

"Mr. Warner, that is a factual statement. But here is another fact: pit bulls are willing to fight, yes. But do you know why? It is because they are such devoted and loyal animals that they will do whatever is asked of them, despite how much pain and suffering is inflicted upon them. They are the ultimate dogs. They will give you their lives."

Mom took up where I left off. "Percy, if only you could meet them. You would see how sweet and friendly they are."

Percy flung out an arm and pointed at Mom. "Your dogs. YOUR dogs. What about all those other fighting dogs out there? They kill people. They maul people. You see it in the papers all the time!"

Suze was ready for this. She pulled a piece of paper out of her pocket. "Mr. Warner, this is a chart of the number of dog bites in the US by breed in the past ten years. It lists *Dachshunds and Chihuahuas* as more likely to bite than any other breed. Here. See for yourself." She slid the paper on the coffee table so that it was in front of Percy. He didn't look at it.

Percy rubbed his ear with the palm of his hand. "There are vicious dogs. They are spraying poison on crops. The climate is changing. The government is full of crooks." He stopped rubbing his ear and covered his eyes with his hand. "Things are out of control."

Mom pursed her lips and took a deep breath. "Oh, Percy. I know exactly what you mean. I am so worried about how terrible the news is. All the wars in the Mideast. Terrorism. And what kind of environment will be left for the next generation? And of course loneliness. All of it. It weighs so heavily on my shoulders."

I pictured Mom's anvil. She was playing the empathy card. Good for her.

Percy looked at us and seemed to actually see us. He blinked. Then he reached out for his Coke and took a sip. He twirled the glass in his hand and studied the bubbles. "I don't have any friends."

We were, all three of us, temporarily at a loss for words. Then Suze, God love her, thought of something to say. "Mr. Warner, I just love your shoes. You are a hipster, did you know that? So cool."

Percy lifted a foot. "I have had these for forty years."

I had to laugh. "But the socks. Those are emojis? Those can't be forty years old."

Percy peered at them. "Is that what they are? I thought they were little faces. The saleswoman at Elder Beerman told me they were popular." He pointed to the poop emoji. "See? Chocolate chips."

Suze coughed.

"Yes. I believe that is a chocolate chip." I glared at Suze.

Mom guided the conversation back to our problem. "Percy, it sounds as if you and I have similar situations. When I lost Sam, I became so overwhelmed by grief that I couldn't—and still can't—seem to leave the house. I just wanted to bury myself. And you—things in the world are so out of whack that you are also overwhelmed. Do you agree?"

Percy's fierceness seemed to slip, just a notch. "I worry."

Suze scooted a bit closer to Percy on the couch. "Do you go over and over things in your head at night? Is it hard to sleep?"

He nodded.

"Mr. Warner, I was a high school teacher for many years, and I met tons of students with all sorts of problems. Many of them had depression and anxiety. One of the things that people overwhelmed with these things feel is a lack of control. They feel as if they are swirling down a huge drain. Have you ever felt that way?"

Percy immediately stiffened. "What is this? Are you all trying to say I am crazy?" He scrambled to his feet. "Well, I won't have it! You are all trying to gang up on me to prove that I am nuts! You can just go to hell! And take those killer dogs with you!"

Percy marched into the hall, snatched his coat off the newel post, and headed for the door. He made a sudden stop right in front of it, did an about-face, and stomped into the living room, grabbed the licorice from the table, and turned, his coat knocking his glass of Coke onto the floor. He sashayed back into the hall, flung the door open, and slammed it behind him as he left.

A blast of cold air hit us as we remained in our seats, mouths open.

Suze closed her mouth. "He took umbrage."

Mom puffed out her cheeks and released the air. "Actually, tonight is what I would classify as a minor success."

I looked at her, incredulous. "What on earth do you mean?"

Suze tapped her feet in a little floor dance. "Chink in the armor! Chink in the armor! He let his guard down! I am willing to be that all he will think about as he lays in his little cold bed tonight will be that we know he is vulnerable!"

"Yeah, so he will now redouble his efforts at being nasty? In self-defense?"

Mom chafed her hands together. "Suze, you are the expert. Is this what will happen? He will just get meaner?"

Suze smiled reassuringly. "I am not an expert, no. But I will say this. No, he won't get meaner, because WE—the three of us, are going to smother him in kindness."

Mom jumped up and held out both arms heavenward. "Of course we will!"

I felt I had to be the voice of reason. "Guys. We don't leave the house. At least Mom and I don't. How in God's name are we going to smother him in kindness?"

Mom sat back down. "I am not sure. You have a point. But remember what Suze said about throwing things over the back fence? Tommy—stop it. I don't mean *meat.* We don't even need to throw. We can push things, little nice things, through the slats in his iron fence. And there is the postal service. Cards. Suze can go over there." Mom glanced at Suze's face. "Right. We can't ask Suzanne to be our emissary. Not fair to her." She paused, her hand on her forehead in concentration. "But for heaven's sake, I can call him on the phone!"

I held up my hand like a cop. "Slats in fence. No ma'am. There will be no throwing things through slats. Not gonna happen."

Suze said, "What if he is on Facebook?"

I whooped at that. "I will personally bet ten bucks that a man like Percy Warner is not on any kind of social media. And I am just the person to find out, as I am a social media expert. Don't move." I went into the kitchen and pulled my cell out of my purse, and hurried back into the living room. I sat down and began to tap my screen.

Three minutes later, I swallowed, hard. "Well, Mom. It looks like you might want to invite a new member into your grief group. Percy Warner, graduate of Framington High, class of 1956, retired florist, divorced, but still mourning for his dead ex-wife, Frannie. She died fifteen years ago, *yesterday*. He posted this on Facebook."

I held out my phone screen. It was a picture of a sweet-faced woman, her dark hair a cloud of waves around her head. She sat on the front porch of the house next door, her arms full of peonies. Her smile was wide and her eyes were soft. "I owe you ten dollars."

Mom shook her head. "No you don't. Tommy, *everybody* is on Facebook. I can't invite him into my grief group. It's for gay people."

"Do I smell something burning?" Suze sniffed.

Mom jumped up. "I put the chicken in the oven to keep it warm! Come on girls, dinner may be ruined!"

It was only partially ruined. The chicken was a bit dryer than we like it, but the mashed potatoes were perfect, and as we were short one guest, we each had a huge mound of them. When it came time for the pears, Suze looked at them skeptically.

"I like my pears cold and raw. These look sort of slimy and mushy."

Mom took a spoon and sampled one of the pears as they floated in the syrup. "Too sweet. A little mushy. I agree, Suzanne. These are going straight into the trash."

Suddenly, we heard noises coming from upstairs. It sounded like the sort of desperate scratching and stifled moans that hostages might make. "My God! The dogs!"

I rushed upstairs and opened Mom's bedroom door. There, wagging their entire bodies with relief, were Saylor and Herkie, covered with what looked like white froth, and what turned out at closer inspection to be the feathery insides of the three throw pillows from Mom's bed. I knelt down and let them both kiss me. The three of us ignored the mess. I swiped the feathers off them, and the dogs rushed downstairs.

Herkie and Saylor didn't mind the dryness of the chicken one bit.

Exhausted after the ordeal, the three of us went to bed early. Herkie and I shuffled upstairs behind Mom, Suze and Saylor right behind us.

"Goodnight, girls. Keep your chins up." Mom kissed me on the cheek and patted Suze's shoulder. "I am going to take some Tylenol and crash."

"Me, too. But for me, it's Nyquil. Always knocks me out. Come on, Saylor. We need to go to dreamland and dream about sex." She flashed us a guilty grin. "Or dessert. One or the other." Suze and Saylor disappeared into her room.

After I got Herk all settled among the covers, her brown nose all that was visible, I changed into my cozies and grabbed my laptop. There was barely enough room for me on the bed, but I managed to commandeer a spot by gently straightening Herk's spine so that she was no longer sprawled diagonally. I put my feet under the covers and opened up Reddit. There it was:

Sorry for the delayed response. I caught the norovirus God knows how, and I was on what I actually hoped was my deathbed for about a week, and then topped it off with pneumonia. I was too weak and full of self-pity to go online.

I am better now, back to work, and in my right mind. Blown away by your story. You are actually staying in the house? Not going out? This is unbelievable. Let me be frank, because why not? You can shut down this convo if you want to, with no ramifications. So here goes:

Something else must be going on in your head to cause this extreme reaction to a loss. I can understand your mother—she may need this time to mourn, and though her choice is very unusual, I get it.

But you? Giving up an entire year to move home and never leave the house? That makes very little sense. Are you running away from something? Did something happen to you that you can't face? You can tell me about it, because I won't share, I don't know you or your name, so you are completely anonymous. Let's start having our convos via Private Message. Confidential.

Or, if you want to stop talking, we can do that as well. I am going to message you now.

I noticed the "message" icon. There it was. Despite the fact that I could right then hear my pulse thrumming in my ears, and my saliva glands had stopped producing, I clicked on the message icon.

Hey. First names OK? My name is Jack. Let me tell you a little more about myself. I am 39. I am six feet tall. I have brown hair, but Rogaine is definitely an option. Blue eyes. Single now; I was divorced after two years of a misguided attempt at marriage.

I both love and hate my job. I am an attorney—tax law. It doesn't make for much interesting small talk at parties. I also do volunteer work teaching reading and math to at-risk youth at a shelter here in Omaha. I guess it's OK to tell you where I live.

I have never met a person online or off with a story like yours. You sound pretty glib. There is a "story behind the story," for certain. If you would like to share, I am all ears. I am in this Reddit group for the same reason you logged in—Facebook is well and good for sharing lunch photos and baby pictures, but for those of us who have a history of pain or trauma, we need more. Social media provides an entire world of outreach that we feel lucky to tap in to. Life is short, so this group allows us all to just cut to the chase and share our stories. Help when we need it, at the touch of a keyboard.

Let me start. I have a story, too. You might be just the right sounding board.

The reason I volunteer is a personal one. When I was twelve, soon after we moved to Charleston, my Scoutmaster sexually abused me. He was charismatic, fun, he seemed to be totally understanding about my family situation, and I really looked up to him. He took special pains to oversee my projects, and he included me in all sorts of activities: he took me and two other boys on camping trips. He had "private lessons" for knot tying and forestry. He said I was a really gifted Scout, and that I was definitely Eagle Scout material. I trusted and loved him.

I won't go into detail. He groomed me. Then he began subtly to invade my person, but it was so gradual, I didn't realize what was going on until it had gone over the line. He convinced me that all of this was "normal," and I bought it, despite my emotional tur-

moil. My father had just died, I was grieving, I had not made any real friends in Charleston yet, and this man seized the opportunity to prey on that.

When I finally told Sean, he pressed charges against the guy. He was convicted and went to jail. I had to testify in his trial. Sean put me in therapy, and it took years for me to come to terms with all of it. I have put all of that behind me (as much as one can). But this is why I work with at risk kids. So many of them have stories like mine.

And this is why I know when there is something just under the surface. My own history, and my work with kids have given me a nose for this stuff.

There you have it. I hope I haven't scared you off. If you want to keep things light, that is just fine, too. But like I said, life is short. If you don't answer this, I totally get it. Jack

I shut the lid on my laptop. It slid to the edge of the bed and fell to the floor. I hardly noticed. I shut my eyes and tried to do the deep breathing exercises that I learned in yoga, but my lungs just refused to expand much further than ragged gasps. I wrung my hands, massaging the joints in my fingers, the thoughts tossing around inside my brain. This guy just jumped out of the ether and intuited my angst? Was this an opportunity for me? Was it a threat? Should I trust this person? Would he be able to understand? Or should I keep quiet?

I pictured Mom, lying in her bed, probably still feeling the emptiness of the space beside her, sleepless and alone. Imagining Mommy there, lying beside her, holding her hand as they both drifted off to sleep.

Or was she lying there cursing Mommy for betraying her? Was she taking a year at home to try to come to grips with her anger? Was she having fantasies of going after

Leah and assaulting her? Was she wondering why in the Hell I came home to be with her?

I lifted the blankets and uncovered Herkie's face. She opened her eyes slowly and lifted her head to lick my hands. "Oh, Herk. What should I do?"

Herkie laid her face in my lap and sighed. Her eyes closed, and she began to snore softly.

I scooted down until I was lying flat. With my hand on Herkie's soft forehead, I decided to go for it. Jack, his name was. OK then. Let the conversations begin. But first, I had to rest.

Chapter Twenty-One

Π

March in Ohio is a toss-up. It is either even more wintery and miserable than January and February, or it warms up, all the flowering trees get duped and put out buds and then the buds are brutally murdered when it goes down into the twenties again. This was one murderous March.

Suze and I had ordered really cute coats for the dogs. Amazon had quite a selection. Saylor wore her pink and white polka dotted number, and Herkie sported a bright red jacket with turquoise stripes. They trotted along in front of us, not noticing that Suze and I were blue with the cold.

"My God. Why didn't we wear earmuffs? My ears may fall off." Suze traded the leash back and forth in her hands, holding her free one over an ear.

I tried to ignore the searing pain in my own ears, along with the fact that my nose was dripping. "Step it up, then! Dana and Trudy's is only two blocks away." We walked faster, but that only made the wind hit us with greater velocity, it seemed. We trundled along as best we could.

Dana was looking for us through her front window, and as soon as she saw us, she disappeared and the front door burst open. "Come in, guys! You look like you have frozen your asses off! Hi, dog people." She shut the door behind us and bent down to kiss both dog snouts.

"You girls come right in and sit by the fire. I made cocoa." Trudy took our coats and chafed first my hands, then Suze's, to warm them.

"Trudy, you are our honorary mom. We love and adore you." I put my hands on Trudy's cheeks, but she pulled them off. "Tommy, your hands are still like ice cubes. Go in there and sit down, both of you!"

I burrowed into the chair closest to the fire, and Suze stood with her back to it, warming her ass. "I think my buns are frozen solid."

Dana patted the sofa, and both dogs jumped on. They wiggled and twisted until they were both curled up like one large pretzel. They closed their eyes and were soon snoring.

Trudy passed around the cocoa, which did the trick to warm our hands. "I put extra marshmallows on."

I took one out of my mug and ate it. "Here's the thing: Mom doesn't even put *one* marshmallow on hot chocolate. What the hell is wrong with her?"

"Maybe she didn't grow up having it that way. It tastes fine plain." Trudy studied her drink.

"All right, then. Enough boring cocoa observations. I have some news. I may have a BFF." Dana held up her cup. "Shall we have a toast?"

We dutifully clinked mugs, and then Suze asked, "Who is it? Tell us. This is great!"

Dana held out a hand. "Not so fast. She may be a dud. But I think she shows promise. She moved to Framington a few weeks ago, because her dad got a job here. Her name, by the way, is Angie Baker. She is a genius at math. I am, shall we say, a mathematical underachiever. So she has been helping me with Geometry."

Dana looked like she was trying to smile and frown simultaneously. She bit down on her bottom lip. Suze nudged her. "Why do you think she might be a dud, exactly?"

Dana ran a finger under her nose. "Because she is quiet and hardly ever says anything in class. The only reason anybody knows she is a math savant is because Mr. Fleming nearly trips all over himself to praise her whenever he hands back the quizzes. She might be a sort of non-person."

I wrinkled my nose. "Huh? What are you talking about, a 'non-person'?"

"She has, well *had*, a cleft palate. Repaired. But it's obvious. People like that tend to live inside themselves." She looked at Trudy. "You know."

Trudy nodded. "Yes. She probably wants to attract as little attention to herself as possible. To sort of disappear." Trudy pulled her hair that normally hung over her scars away from her face and tucked it behind her ear. "That is a hard habit to break." She cleared her throat.

I looked at Trudy and smiled. Then I turned back to Dana. "How are the other kids treating her?"

Dana drew her fingers into a fist and then released it. "So far, they are just acting as if she doesn't exist. So that's a plus."

Trudy asked, "So are you going out of your way to include her?"

Dana shifted her weight and leaned over to kiss Saylor. "Mother Figure. Of course. We are on the same lunch shift, so we sit together in the cafeteria. We discuss Tolstoy and Feminism." Trudy looked confused.

She snorted. "In reality, we sit beside one another and discuss whether or not the pizza they have is from Pizza Hut or Dominos. Guys. I am doing my best here, but this girl is going to take a lot of encouragement. I am sticking with it because she actually knows what Pythagorean triplets are. People like that are valuable to have as friends."

We all laughed, and that woke the dogs, who jumped off the sofa and began to chase one another around the living room.

Dana continued. "I am giving her another week to loosen up. If she manages to crack a joke or make at least one sarcastic remark about Mr. Fleming, she's in."

"Is Mr. Fleming worthy of sarcasm or jokes?" I wondered.

"He clenches and unclenches his butt cheeks when he is writing on the board. Need I say more?" Dana arched her brows.

"Nope. The butt cheeks have it." Suze plunked her mug down on the coffee table. "My geometry teacher in high school was twenty five, he had guns like you wouldn't believe, and his butt cheeks were mesmerizing. We didn't joke about him; we fantasized."

I held up my hands and waved them at Suze. "Go no further! We do NOT need to hear about your freshman fantasies!" I stuck my tongue out.

Trudy put her hands in the vicinity of her crotch and cackled. "Suzanne, you and I need to have a private talk."

Dana cringed. "Enough. Old ladies talking about sex is a NOPE." She shook her head. "Truly a nope."

I glanced at my watch. "My God, it's almost one. Tomorrow is a school day, and we are keeping you two up. We have to go." I stood and beckoned to the dogs.

Suze hugged Trudy and mussed Dana's hair. "Keep us posted on the friend thing, OK?"

We snapped the leashes on, wormed our way back into our coats, and made for the icy blasts that awaited us.

As we walked towards home, I looked back. Trudy and Dana stood in the window, arms entwined. Dana lifted a hand and waved to us. I waved back.

Suze saw me waving and exhaled loudly. "A girl with a genius brain and a cleft palate. It may be just me and my experience with high school students, but that combination? It sounds like a recipe for disaster."

I tripped over my own feet and nearly crashed onto the pavement.

Π

"Suzanne! Tommy! Come downstairs right now!" Mom's voice was squeaky with alarm. We knew something was up, because it was only 3:00 in the afternoon—working hours were still in effect. We figured this must be an emergency.

I quickly shut down my computer, after telling my client that she needed to start posting more live videos on her YouTube channel. I also closed down the private message window with Jack. We were conversing almost every day. It was a welcome distraction, but I had yet to spill my guts about anything. I was getting close. So far, Jack and I talked mostly about him.

I hustled out of my room and onto the landing, as Suze charged out of hers.

We nearly fell over one another on the way down. We dashed into the sunroom, where Mom stood at the window facing Percy Warner's backyard, peering out.

"Look!"

Mom had apparently let the dogs out. They were both sitting right up against the iron fence line, tails beating the ground furiously. On the other side of the fence stood a tiny girl in a pink coat. Her dark brown hair was put up in lopsided pigtails that stuck straight out like little hyphens. Her cheeks matched the color of her coat, and she laughed as she tore pieces off the sandwich she was holding and extended them to the pups through the fence. They took each piece gently and wagged for more. We watched as she carefully fed what was probably her lunch to the two dogs. When it was gone, she sat down abruptly in the cold grass and extended her chubby arms through the fence. The dogs lay down and the toddler petted their heads and seemed to carry on a conversation with them. They remained that way until Percy appeared from his kitchen door.

The three of us gasped in unison.

Percy jolted into action and ran towards the child, hollering what sounded to us like "STOP! STOP!"

We braced ourselves. As he hurtled towards the child, she stood, looking dignified despite her tinyness. She took a few staggering steps towards Percy, and held up her arms for him to pick her up. When he did, clutching her to his chest, she pushed away, turned towards the dogs and pointed excitedly. Then she turned back to Percy, placing both of her small hands on either side of his face. They stood like that, Percy looking back and forth between the angel child and the dogs, for a minute or so. Then she once again gestured toward the dogs.

We held our collective breath, but then the miracle occurred. Percy carried the miniscule person over to the fence. The dogs stood, still wagging. The little girl twisted backwards in Percy's arms so that she could lean to pat Saylor on the head.

Percy smiled and looked around to see if anyone was watching. Then he set the little one down. She reached through the fence and took Herkie's snout in both of her hands and pulled it through the fence so she could kiss her on the nose. She laughed.

Percy bent down and wrapped his arms around the child, and lifted her up to carry her inside. Then he changed direction, walked back to the fence. He said something to the dogs, who responded by woofing and jumping excitedly.

I looked at Suze, whose eyes were as round as hockey pucks. Mom stood behind both of us and patted me on the back. "That must be Percy's little granddaughter. He must have reconciled with his daughter, Phoebe. They fell out after Percy and his wife divorced. You remember when Frannie Warner left, don't you, Tommy?"

All that came to mind was the photo of his dead ex-wife that Percy had posted on Facebook. "Not really. I just have a vague memory of a woman being over there, but I don't recall anything specific." But I couldn't think about ancient history. Not when witnessing the dogs perhaps turning their worst enemy into a friend. "Yeah, but *did you see what just happened?* Percy Warner, the arch enemy of all vilified dog breeds, just sort of *smiled* at two PITBULLS?"

"I know! Astounding!" Suze rubbed her eyes. "Or did we just all hallucinate?"

There was no sense remaining by the window, looking out at Saylor and Herkie, who had forgotten their new friend and had begun to search for sticks to chew on. So I turned my attention back to Mom. "Wait. When did the Warners divorce? How come?"

Suze and I flopped down on one sofa and Mom, after taking one more look out at Percy's yard and seeing nothing, sat down on the other. "It was the summer that you went off to sleepover camp and lasted two nights. What were you, eight? Sam and I had to drive up there to Michigan to get you. You told us that the cabins were too cold at night, and none of the other girls liked you."

"Oh, God. It was because Mickey Grisham saw you and Mommy holding hands, and she told all the 'Rainbow Trout' campers that I had queers for parents."

Mom grabbed her chest with both hands.

"I guess I never told you that."

"No. You never did. If we had known that, we would have raised hell with those idiots running the camp, for heaven's sake!"

I waved my hands to stop Mom from going any further. "I shouldn't have told you now! It's water under the bridge. Really. Let's get back to the Percy Warner story. So was he a grumper before ol' Frannie left him? Or did the divorce turn him all sour and pissy?"

Mom didn't seem to want to let go of the Camp Rainbow Trout revelation quite yet. "Did they bully you? Hurt you? What happened, Tommy?"

I shut my eyes and time traveled. Lots of green. Mosquitoes, the smell of bacon, pond scum, and campfires that never gave off much more than smoke. Feral girls, screaming and shoving one another on the hiking trails. The whispers after lights out: "Tommy's moms are queer! Tommy must be queer! Tommy is probably really a boy!" The biting laughter. The side eyes of the counselors. I shuddered and opened my eyes. "They were just like every other 'normal' kid in the universe. They banded together to torment the kid who was weak. I should have stayed and kicked all of their asses. Mom. Ancient history. I bet those girls in my cabin are all drug addicts, they have horrible husbands, or they are divorced and living on welfare."

Suze snorted. "Meg, every camping experience is like *Lord of the Flies.* It's common knowledge. At my camp, the girls tried to give me a tattoo with a sewing needle and grape juice. Against my will. We survive."

Mom put her face in her hands for a few seconds, shaking her head back and forth.

"Mom. Focus. The Percy situation. Did his divorce turn him into Ebenezer Scrooge?"

She put her hands in her lap and rubbed her lips together. That smeared her lipstick, but Suze and I didn't mention it. "Frannie Warner was a doer. She was the kind of woman who couldn't sit still. She was a member of all the women's clubs, she sewed, she loved to garden, and she just bustled around all the time. Phoebe was their only child, and Frannie and Percy just worshipped the ground Phoebe walked on. Nothing was too good for Phoebe. Riding lessons. Ballet. Violin. They just invested themselves in that girl."

Mom paused.

"Go on, Meg. We are hanging on your every word!"

Mom rubbed her hands against her thighs, back and forth, back and forth. I could almost hear the wheels turning in her head. "I think they were so in love with that child that they sort of forgot about one another. And when Phoebe was thirteen, the Warners hired a man to do some landscaping in their yard. He was handsome—strapping, you know. And after a few weeks, Frannie left Percy. She and this man moved in together. Of course, Phoebe went with her mother. Percy and Frannie divorced. I think Frannie and this man moved to another state—somewhere out west, maybe Denver? Anyway, Percy was never the same after that. He just shriveled, if you know what I mean. Life without his wife, he may have survived. But that girl leaving just did him in. And now we know that Frannie died fifteen years ago."

Suze held up a finger. "Wait. You mean she ran away with a *landscaper?* Irony of ironies—didn't you tell us before that Percy was a retired florist? Wow. Just Wow."

"Back to the subject at hand, girls. So we just witnessed some sort of transformation, right? The saltiest man in the universe, the enemy of all 'aggressive' dog breeds, just smiled and nearly petted our dogs? Should we rejoice? Bake him a cake?" I could hardly sit still; this was so exciting.

Mom, the voice of reason and maturity, put a finger to her lips. "Shhh. Tommy. Don't get ahead of yourself. Just because the man smiled at our dogs one time doesn't mean he is now going become a dog lover. Especially pit bulls. We have to see what happens, for heaven's sake! We aren't living in a Norman Rockwell painting, you know."

Suze stood up and started to head for the kitchen. "Righto, Meg. We have to see what happens. But that doesn't mean we can't let the dogs have some string cheese, just to let them know 'who's the good girl?' If you catch my drift?"

"I could go for some string cheese right about now. How about you, Mom?"

Between the five of us, we ate an entire package of Sargento.

Chapter Twenty-Two

Π

A few days passed, and we had almost forgotten the scene by the back fence. Almost. I admit I had played out a few fantasies in my head involving Percy, a little brown puppy, and a doghouse in his backyard. Other than that, life had gone on.

At about five o'clock in the evening on a Thursday, the doorbell bonged. I happened to be lounging on the sofa, eating Swedish fish and pushing back my cuticles, so I got up and answered the door. The dogs, naturally, had thundered down the stairs and were barking madly and jumping against the backs of my thighs.

There stood a woman about my age, her shiny brown hair in a messy short cut, blonde streaks snaking through it. She wore gold hoop earrings, knee length black leggings, and a loose, turquoise paisley top. Her smile was wide and friendly. Holding her hand was the little girl who had kissed the dogs through the fence. This little sprite had on her own teensy leggings: pink with white polka dots. Her sweatshirt was gray with a large white daisy in the center. Her baby fine, maple syrup colored hair was in a topknot fountain, sprouting from the top of her head. She held a bag of dog biscuits.

"Hello. My name is Phoebe Warner Browning. This is my daughter, Birdie. Birdie, say hi."

First she looked up at her mother, and then she knit her eyebrows and looked at me and held out the bag. "Hi. These are special biscuits for dogs. They're 'ganic. I want to kiss the doggies." With that, she let go of her mother's hand and marched right in to the front hall, brandishing the biscuits in front of her. "Doggies!" They both stopped jumping and barking and stood, staring at this tiny bearer of edibles.

Birdie said, "Sit down, doggies." They sat. She rustled around in the bag, drew out two biscuits, and set the bag down. "Now stay and be good." My God, they *did.* The little dog whisperer then held out a biscuit in each hand, and the dogs took them gently and began to crunch.

"Oh, I am so sorry. She is brash." Ms. Browning smiled indulgently at the trio, the dogs licking their chops and wagging, Birdie on her haunches, giggling with delight.

The smile never left her face. Her head was at the same level as the dogs' eyes. The three of them stared at one another.

Birdie plunked herself down between them, put a hand on each dog's head, and said, "Mommy, you go talk now. I am here with the doggies."

Phoebe looked at me with raised eyebrows. "Well that settles that. May I come in and chat for a few minutes, though? She would love to spend some time with those two."

I tried not to act confused as I ushered this woman into the living room. I looked back at the gang in the hall, and they all seemed delighted with one another. I motioned towards the sofa, and we both sat down. "Oh, would you like some Swedish Fish?" *Oh my God, lame.* "I was just having some myself." *Getting worse.* "Or a drink? A Coke? Or we have tea, I think."

Luckily for me, she broke in. "Oh, thank you, but no. I just came over to chat for a few minutes. Is your mother home, by any chance?"

I stood up so fast I got a little dizzy. "Of course. I think she is upstairs, ironing. And our roommate, Suzanne, is here, too. Just a sec, I will get them."

I maneuvered my way around the clutch of child and dogs and jogged up the stairs. Mom was indeed ironing. She looked up as I rushed in. "Who was at the door?"

"Oh my God, it's Percy's daughter. That little girl with the dogs is his granddaughter. They brought treats." I was out of breath. "You know, for the dogs. I have to get Suze. Come down. She wants to chat."

I didn't wait for her reaction. I just rushed into Suze's room, where she was eating an apple and reading *Edgar Sawtelle.* "Put that book down. The baby from next door is here. They want to talk."

Suze shut the book. She normally doesn't speak with her mouth full, but this apparently shocked the good manners right out of her. "There is a baby here that wants to talk? What on earth are you saying?" She spit out a tiny piece of apple, and it fell from her lips onto the front of her shirt.

"Not a baby. I mean that little girl who petted the dogs. You know, in Percy's yard! She is here with her mother. Her mother wants to talk to us. Just come down—I left her sitting all by herself in the living room."

The baby is all alone in the living room? Where is her mother?"

I realized how I had mushed the information. "The baby, who is probably three, not really a baby, is sitting at the bottom of the stairs, adoring the dogs. Her MOM is alone in the living room, probably eating all of my Swedish fish. Come ON."

Suze set the half-eaten apple on top of the book, got up, picked the chunk she had spit on herself and popped that into her mouth. She wiped her lips with the back of her hand and stood up. "You have lost your mind. I am coming."

The three of us started down the stairs. Birdie twisted around and watched us approach. The dogs' tails thumped madly. "Hello. I am Birdie. These are good doggies."

As we stepped around her and the dogs, Mom leaned down and stroked the little girl's tiny head. "I know. These are very, very good dogs."

She rose as we entered the room and shook hands with Mom and Suze. "Mrs. Poole, I remember you so well. I am Phoebe Warner. Well, now Warner-Browning. I am Percy's daughter. Mrs. Poole, you haven't aged one bit."

Mom beamed. "Oh, yes. I remember you well. You were such a talented little girl. I was sorry when you moved away. You have met my daughter, Tommy. And this is our dear friend, Suzanne. Now let's all sit down. Phoebe, can I get you something to drink?"

Phoebe shook her head. "No thank you. Tommy already offered."

It was only slightly awkward. Mom cleared her throat, and Suze crossed her legs, her foot ticking back and forth like a metronome. Phoebe glanced out into the front hall towards her daughter, looked at us soberly, and began. "I am here to try to explain—apologize, really, for my Dad."

"No need, really." Mom jumped in.

I shot Mom an incredulous look and nodded at Phoebe. "Let her tell us why she came over, Mom. Go on, Ms. Warner. Browning. Warner-Browning." I bit the inside of my lip.

Phoebe waved her hands. "No, just call me Phoebe. Do you want the long version or the short one?"

I, of course, wanted her to cut to the chase, but my ever-gracious mother said, "The long version, of course. We are happy to listen to whatever you want to tell us."

Murmurs of adoration from the front hall, where Birdie continued to entrance the dogs.

"All right. My father and mother were married for a long time before they had me. They had given up on having a family when I was born. Mother was 43. Dad was 50. They were devoted to me, but also set in their ways. Dad was a lot more strict than Mother thought he should be. So there were constant battles about rules and regulations. I felt like I was the cause of so much friction!" Phoebe looked away from us for a second, shut her eyes, composed herself, and continued. "Finally, when I was in eighth grade, Mother left my Dad. They divorced, and she took custody of me. We were both angry at my father, and although he had visitation rights, I didn't really want to see much of him."

No mention of the gardener. Of course, I wasn't surprised. We didn't know this woman. I was surprised she had even told us this much. I looked over at Suze, whose expression was confused. Mom, however, looked as if having complete strangers share their life stories out of the blue happened all the time.

Phoebe continued, "Dad was never what I would call 'convivial,' but he got less and less outgoing after their divorce. Mother got word from local friends that Dad had turned into a curmudgeon. He had confrontations with all sorts of people."

Phoebe's face, which was covered with an assortment of freckles, flushed. She pushed a strand of amber colored hair off her forehead. "Our relationship was strained until Mother died fifteen years ago, and then I reached out to Dad. We reconnected, sort of." She licked her lips and took a deep breath.

"Then Birdie came along. Dad, of course, was happy. My husband and I were excited for Birdie to meet her Grandfather. He has come a long way, really." She paused and studied our faces. "He told me about the fracas concerning your dogs. I tried to explain to him that he was being completely unreasonable. He got defensive, but at least I convinced him to let go of that ridiculous breed-ban idea."

Mom heaved a sigh of relief. "Oh, Ms—Phoebe. That is so good to hear!"

Phoebe pursed her lips. "Dad is complicated. He is a jumble of mixed up feelings about things. The world. He is all alone over there, and I know he hates it, but he brings it all upon himself. I think if you give him time and try to understand how lonely and mad at the world he is, he will come around." She pulled at her bangs. "I think so, anyway. I just came over to tell you how sorry I am for his behavior. Birdie and I will be here for a couple more days, and I will keep trying to soften him up. Maybe if you go over there and try to talk to him or something..."

Suze stopped fidgeting. "We are all alone over here, you know. The three of us. We don't go out. Of the house."

Phoebe's face clouded in confusion.

"Meg lost her wife, Sam. I am sure you remember her, when you were a kid next door—she was a veterinarian? They were married for a long time, and after Sam died, Meg just couldn't face the world. So then Tommy, who *also couldn't face the world,* (Suze shot me a knowing look) decided to join her. One year of solitude. To heal. To introspect. I know *introspect* isn't a verb. Anyway, Tommy seemed to be at very loose ends, so I decided to join the two of them. As ballast. You know, to help them figure out why in the hell they are doing this. So far, I haven't had much luck."

I was taken aback. I didn't think I was at 'loose ends.' For heaven's sake. I was here to support my mom.

"You three don't go out *at all?"* Phoebe looked stunned.

I cut in. "Just for one year." As soon as I heard the words coming out of my mouth, I realized how ridiculous that sounded. So I pressed on. "One year, to grieve for our loss. To think about where we fit into the scheme of things. To assess where we want to go from here. You know, why we don't have that many friends. Why we feel like outsiders. Well, we are outsiders, really."

Mom looked at me with what I can only describe as a "steely gaze." "Tommy, speak for yourself."

I thought of Jack. I looked at Mom and Suze, who both seemed fixed on what I would say next. I wiped my conversations with Jack out of my head for the moment.

"Phoebe, your father must feel so isolated over there. No wonder he lashes out. The world seems like one big Venn diagram. Little circles of isolation that intersect just barely. You and Birdie just changed your father's life by visiting, didn't you? His Venn diagram just changed for the better, right?"

Mom and Phoebe looked confused, but Suze, who knew Venn diagrams like the back of her hand from all of her teaching background, put an arm around me and grinned. "Forget the Venn diagrams. What she is saying is that we are glad you came over, we will continue to send goodwill in your father's direction, and you have the cutest little girl who has ever been born, I wager."

Things improved from there, and Birdie left the dogs long enough to sit on Mom's lap and allow Mom to stroke her head. Phoebe hugged the three of us and promised to keep in touch. We exchanged cell numbers. Then Suze insisted on taking a picture of Birdie standing between the two dogs, all three of them with huge grins. It was Instagram worthy.

When Birdie and her mom left, I went upstairs, opened the bedside drawer, and took out a Post-it. I wrote *Venn Diagram: expand my circle—outsider? on* it. Underneath that, I made a list:

Me
Mom
Mommy
Rob
Dana
Trudy
Pit bulls
Percy
Jack

I looked at the list for a long time. Then I logged onto Reddit.

How do you deal with anxiety? Betrayal?

My God. What is it?

A long story. Do you have time to hear it?

Of course.

So I told Jack. As soon as I hit "send," the boulder I had been balancing on my shoulders seemed a tad lighter.

Π

After Phoebe and the tiny Bird left, we had no expectations of détente from next door. Life went on, and although Mom mentioned how much she wished that Phoebe and Birdie lived with Percy, we thought we had forgotten all about the grumper next door. The weather was looking a bit more encouraging, and we were looking forward to changing seasons—March was waning, and what with the icy winds, bone-soaking sleet, and gray days, we had had it with winter.

The dogs, however, loved cold weather. The raw winds were apparently invigorating, as both Herkie and Saylor took to dashing and skidding around the backyard whenever one of us let them out. "Zoomies," I think they call those times when dogs seem to lose their minds and need to exhaust themselves by running in circles.

I had just let them out and was making myself a cup of tea when I looked out the kitchen window to watch Herkie nearly capsize Saylor by crashing into her while zooming at full speed. They righted themselves and kept on going, and I caught a flash of blue out of the corner of my eye.

Standing on his back steps, wearing a bright blue muffler and matching earmuffs, was Percy Warner. He seemed very intent on studying the dogs at play. I watched him look around his yard, then walk purposely toward the tree at the end of his property. There, he bent down and picked up a stick about the size and breadth of a rolling pin and moved toward the fence separating our yards.

I braced myself and prepared to run outside if he so much as TRIED to hit one of the dogs. I felt steam seeping out of my ears, and I hurried to the back door.

Before I could throw the door open and fly outside, Percy had lifted his arm and flung the stick into a high arc over his head. It landed in just about the center of our yard, tumbling over itself a few times. Both dogs took off after it, but Herkie got there first. She grabbed the stick with gusto and dashed up to the fence where Percy stood.

My mouth fell open. Herkie dropped the stick. Percy reached carefully through the fence, finagled the stick back through the bars, took a few steps backward, and threw the stick again. This time, Saylor got it, trotted back to Percy, and dropped the stick. The game continued as I stood in shock, watching it transpire.

After a few more tosses, the cold must have gotten to our neighbor. Percy blew on his uncovered hands, rubbed them together, and the next time the dogs returned the stick, he pulled it through the fence, tucked it under his arm, put his hands in his pockets, and went back inside.

I forgot all about making tea. The gravity of what I had just seen pushed all thoughts of hydration out of my head. I opened the back door, called for the dogs, who rushed in, their tails wagging and their fur icy as they twisted around me, expecting treats. I rummaged around in the cupboard, located the Milk-Bones, and dropped a couple of them on the floor. I didn't even wait to make sure that Herkie didn't eat Saylor's bone.

I just tore upstairs, stood in the center of the hall, and shrieked, "MY GOD, PERCY WALKER HAS FORGIVEN THE DOGS! FOR REAL THIS TIME!"

Π

Suze stopped by to say goodnight, and I shut my laptop with a snap.

"What on earth? Are you on Tinder or something?"

I wiped the top of my MacBook, trying to look nonchalant, but my shaking fingers probably betrayed me. "Nope. Not Tinder. In order to set up a date, *you have to be able to leave the house."*

She scratched her elbow and laughed. "Right! So what are you ashamed of that you slapped that thing closed so fast? Porn? Of course. That makes sense. Nothing to be ashamed of, you know. Everybody watches porn these days." She plunked herself down on my bed and raised her eyebrows. "Well?"

My emotions began arguing with my sense of self-protection. I stuck a finger in my ear and rubbed vigorously, hoping to dislodge something inside my brain. Then I blinked, trying to settle things down. What the hell. "OK, OK. It's Reddit. I joined a group convo—sort of like Mom's Facebook grief group. Only this one is for straight people who were raised by gay parents. It's been very...um...interesting."

Suze leaned against the footboard and crossed her legs, campfire style. "So. What are you all discussing?"

"All the stuff we had to deal with, growing up. Bullying. Being ashamed of our families not being 'normal.' Anxiety. All the usual baggage."

She picked at a loose thread on the hem of her sweatshirt. "Right. But for some reason, you acted as if you were looking at dick pics? Is there more to this? You look as guilty as hell."

I pushed the laptop off my lap and drew my knees up. I wrapped my arms around them and held on tight. "Geez, Suze, you are more like a pit bull than your own dog! If you must know, I met a guy on there. He seems really smart. He seems to understand me. We talk regularly."

Suze squinted. "AND?"

"He has told me some very personal things. And I have shared some of my own shit with him. It's just good to have a sounding board, that's all."

Suze put a hand on her chest and thumped it like a heartbeat. "Love, maybe? Soul mates?" She giggled.

"For God's sake, Suze. It's *an online thing*. An outlet. We don't know one another's last names, even. It's an anonymous way for both of us to, you know, vent. We have so much in common."

Suze reached over and patted me on the leg. "I totally get it. Anonymous. Of course, some day, you will tell your grandchildren all about how you met. Anonymously. HA HA!" And with that, she got up, stuck her tongue out at me, and toddled off to bed.

I watched her disappear and amble down the hall. I grabbed my laptop and sent one more PM.

Hey. You won't tell anybody what we have been talking about, will you? I would never share any of your secrets. I hope you will respect my privacy as well. His reply came back almost instantly.

I would never share anything we talk about here. Let me say this, though. My story isn't a secret. Yours is. Secrets like that have a way of destroying you. Maybe you have been holding on to yours for too long. There is only one way for you to work out your feelings about what your Mommy did. Talk to your Mom about it.

His words slammed into me like a tsunami. My heart ramped up like a drumroll. I shut my computer and thrust it under the covers where I wouldn't have to look at it.

I sat there, my insides roiling, until Herkie loped in for a goodnight snuggle.

Chapter Twenty-Three

Π

When we approached Dana's house, there were two girls sitting on her front steps. As soon as they caught sight of us, they stood. Dana waved, but the other girl stepped back and stood warily behind her. "Oh, my God. Dana has a friend over who is scared of the dogs. Let's do heeling." I shortened Herkie's leash and put her in heel. Suze did the same with Saylor.

"Oh, no, guys! You can release the curs!" Dana waved us up onto her porch. "This is my new friend, Angie Baker. She likes dogs. She's just shy." Dana gently but firmly thrust Angie's arm towards the dogs. Herkie immediately held up her paw for a shake. Angie broke out into a grin that almost lit up the entire block.

"Hello, puppy." Angie looked up. "What's her name?"

Suze could not hold Saylor back any longer. She wanted to get in on the action, so she nosed Herk out of the way and jumped up on Angie. Suze was mortified. "Saylor! NO!" Saylor sat down. "I am humiliated. Dana taught these dogs how to behave, but sometimes I am simply overruled. The dogs know a potential BFF when they see one."

The night wasn't as cold as previous ones, but Dana invited all of us in. Trudy had made snickerdoodles, and we settled down in the comfy living room to stuff ourselves with sugar and cinnamon goodness.

"Angie is a genius at math. She is my lifeline in Geometry." Dana pointed to Angie with her cookie and smiled.

"So, do you know the Pythagorean triplets personally? Like, are they your locker mates or something?" Suze—always droll.

Angie paused chewing her cookie and looked nonplussed. Dana cut in. "That must be an academic in-joke. Suze is some sort of online guru for the Ohio schools."

Angie looked at Suze with interest. She swallowed and said, "Actually, I do know the triplets very well. That's funny! Are you a teacher?"

"I was. But now I oversee online learning for high schools across the state. I am sort of a consultant. I work from home." Suze looked over at me. "Well, from Tommy's home. I am living with her and her mom, temporarily."

I studied the contrast between Dana and her friend. Dana—bold, her sea blue eyes flashing, always rimmed in black. Tattoos brandished like armament. Dana never slouched or wilted. A defender. Angie, on the other hand, with her wispy vanilla hair and hazel eyes, freckles dusting her pale cheeks, seemed to want to disappear into the upholstery. She burrowed her spine into the cushions of the sofa and appeared to shrink into herself. It wasn't a surprise. The scar on her lip that ran up into her left nostril stood out from the rest of her complexion, a salmon slash. It had been repaired well, but the cleft palate scar still stood out from all the other features on Angie's small face.

I picked up a second cookie and held out the plate. "Does anybody want another one? Nothing to be ashamed about. We all consume Trudy's baked goods in vast quantities. Angie? Another?"

She held up the cookie she was nibbling on and shook her head. "No thanks. This one will be plenty."

Dana took another, however, and chomped on it with relish. It went down in a flash. Dana turned to Angie to explain our situation. "These are interesting people." She cocked her head in our direction. "They decided not to go out of their house for a whole year. Hermits."

Angie, I noticed, had a nervous tic. She blinked rapidly a few times, then squeezed her eyes closed, as if to shut it off. "I see. Are you doing some sort of research or something? Or are you sort of like Thoreau?"

"It's a long story. No. We aren't like Thoreau. We are in mourning, my mom and I. Sam, my other mother, died recently. Mom decided she couldn't face the world, and so I am staying with her inside for the year. Suze is watching over both of us." This sounded more ridiculous the more I explained it. But Angie just nodded and smiled, as if many of her friends were recluses.

Suze stood up and walked over to the fireplace and stuck out her hands. She rubbed them together and turned to look at Angie. "How are things at school? Are you making any friends?"

Angie did not meet Suze's gaze. "Sort of. Well, Dana. And there is a boy named Ethan in my history class that saves me a seat in the third row. But not really. It's OK, though. I am an introvert."

Yeah, out of necessity. I flashed a look at Suze, *don't pursue this line of inquiry,* but she ignored it and went on. "Nobody is teasing you, or being rude, are they?"

Angie brightened. "Actually, there is a girl in my gym class who seems nice. Her name is Jill. She invited me to go to Starbucks with her and some of her friends on Friday after school. So I am looking forward to that." I noticed Dana stiffen.

My armpits dripped all of a sudden. "Dana, did you tell her about the time Jill invited you to Starbucks?"

Dana jolted out of her seat and turned to face Angie and Trudy, who sat, looking alarmed. "Do *not* go. They won't be there. Or if they are there, they will do something cruel. Stay away from those girls; they're toxic."

What little color there was in Angie's face drained out of it. Her scar stood out in livid contrast to the whiteness of her skin. "I thought things might be different in a smaller town." She lifted her forefinger to swipe at her eye. "But things never really change."

Trudy scooted over and encircled Angie in her arms. "Oh, honey. I know exactly what you mean. People like you and me have to be on our guard all the time, don't we? But sweetheart, you do have friends. We are sitting right here with you." She stroked Angie's hair. "Don't ever underestimate the friends you have."

I looked at the steel blue barbed wire surrounding Dana's throat. "Angie, Trudy is right. Does Dana look like a pushover to you?" Angie shook her head in a 'no.'

Dana laughed. "I am no Arnold Schwarzenegger. I *may* be a little bit like John Cena. Ha! But you have a friend in me."

Suze, the smooth operator that she is, changed the subject. "Hey, how come everyone thinks of Thoreau when the subject of reclusiveness comes up? What about J. D. Salinger?"

Π

April Fool's Day. I was prepared not to believe a thing that Mom said all day. She was such a great liar on April 1. I vowed the year that she convinced me that she had been chosen as "Mother of the Year" by the Framington Sentinel that I would not be taken in again.

We heard sirens in the distance at around noon, but paid them no heed. As the sound got closer, I wondered if someone nearby had had a heart attack or something, but I was engrossed in the Google analytics of a particularly bad website that a client had created, and so I put the noise out of my mind.

Mom didn't even knock on my bedroom/office door. She threw the door open and rushed to my desk, panting. "Oh, my God, there is a fire at Percy Warners'!"

This was one of her better efforts, I thought. I didn't even shut my laptop. I swiveled in my chair to look at her. Her face was red—even the tips of her ears looked like they had a sunburn. Her eyes were wild, and she grabbed me by the shoulder and yanked me out of my chair.

"Mom. Take it easy. April Fool. You got me. Now I have to get back to work."

"No, no! Come downstairs! Look out the window! There is a FIRE!" Before I could react, Mom turned and headed into Suze's room, where she continued to sound the alarm.

Holy mother of God. By the time we crowded around the side window in the living room, we could see smoke pouring out of Percy's house. The bitter smell seeped into the room. One of us coughed.

A fire hose snaked from a huge fire truck up Percy's walk and through the open front door. There were at least four fire fighters in full regalia milling around outside, where Percy stood, oven mitts on both hands, a chef's apron hanging from his neck, ties undone, and a look of sheer terror on his face.

We clutched at one another. Suze said, "House rules be damned. Let's go!"

It was hard to keep the dogs from following us, but we managed to get outside and shut the door, pushing Saylor and Herkie's noses out of the way. Mom ran up to the fire truck, where one of the fire fighters leaned against the side, sweating and frowning. "What happened? Is everything going to be all right? I live next door."

He grunted and smiled at Mom. There was a dab of soot on one cheek. His smile was dazzling. I assumed he used those whitening strips. I made a mental note to order some for myself. He pointed to the house. "Fire in the kitchen. The occupant (he pointed to Percy, who still stood, oven mitts clutched to his heart) was frying bacon. The frying pan caught on fire, and he did exactly the wrong thing and poured water on it. There was a chemical reaction, and a pretty significant explosion. It's under control now, but there is quite a bit of damage to the kitchen. Ladies, remember this: *Never pour water on a grease fire.*" The look on his face as he said this indicated that he had probably said this a million times before, but not one person had actually listened.

"Yes, we know about that. How is Percy?" Mom didn't wait for the answer. She hurried over to where Percy stood, gently pulled the mitts off his hands, dropped them, and put a hand on either side of Percy's face, murmuring to him. That seemed to calm him down a bit. By this time, the fire hose was being dragged towards the truck, the firemen were walking around the house to make sure there was nothing more amiss, and a police car pulled up. Two officers got out of the car. They conferred briefly with the fire guys. A lot of head shaking.

One of the officers, her hand on her holster, ambled up to us. "Hello. I am Sergeant Alberts. Which one of you is the resident?"

Percy, who seemed to be shocky and unable to speak, held up his hand.

"Yes. This is Mr. Warner. I am Tommy Poole. This is my mother, Meg. And this is Suzanne Lampley. We live next door."

Sgt. Alberts shot me a look as if to say she could not care less that we lived next door, and she moved between us and Percy, putting a hand on his elbow to lead him away where they could talk without the three of us horning in. At least that is how it looked to me.

Suze shrugged. "I think we are extraneous here. Let's go home."

We turned and started to walk back through Percy's lawn, up the slight rise and over to ours, when Mom said, "Wait. Just a second."

She trotted back over to Percy's, where he and the Sergeant were still deep in conversation as the last of the firefighters loaded up in their engine and drove away. Mom leaned over and picked up the oven mitts off the front walk and carried them over to where we stood watching her. When she caught up to us, she held them out. "These may be all that's left of the kitchen. They are nice ones. I like the red gingham. They look brand new. He'll want these back."

Mom hung them on a hook by the oven in our kitchen. They looked pretty cheery; I have to admit. I wondered when and if we would ever be able to give them back to Percy. After all, we had violated house rules *out the wazoo* that afternoon.

I mentioned this at dinner.

"Should we throw the mitts over the back fence? We really can't go over there and ring his doorbell."

Suze looked confused. "How come?"

"For one, we have violated house rules big time by going over there. Well, Mom and I have. You are off the hook."

"Exactly. I can take them back."

Mom took a bite of her wedge salad (Roquefort dressing—divine), chewed slowly, and picked up her knife and waved it around at the two of us. "Yes. Suze. You take them back, and invite him over here for dinner. We can try one more time. He can't cook over there. It's the neighborly thing."

"Mom. The dogs."

"You said he forgave them. So it will be fine."

And the rest, they say, is history.

Chapter Twenty-Four

Π

We watched Suze trudge over to Percy's house clutching the oven mitts, her shoulders hunched. She knocked the knocker, the front door opened, and she entered. I looked at Mom with eyebrows raised high. "Do you think he will clobber her or anything?" Mom socked me in the ribs. We continued to watch. Five minutes. Thirteen minutes.

Suze came back home, shaking her head. "Guys. He looked at me with the saddest eyes and said, 'You are the only person to show any concern. Nobody cares about me.' I said I didn't know that, but of course, I wasn't at all surprised. He showed me the disaster in his kitchen. Pretty bad. A complete gut job. He said he would come, though. I told him it was this coming Saturday at 6:30."

A sorrowful expression on her face, Mom replied, "The poor man. Well, this can be a new start. We'll invite everybody."

"Let's sit down, then, and make a plan. I have my phone with The Food Network app. Come on, into the kitchen." The two of them dutifully followed me into the kitchen, where we sat down at the table as Mom got out three glasses and poured us all some Diet Coke.

I scrolled. We sipped in silence. Mom drummed her fingers on the tabletop, then looked around and said, "It would be nice to have an excuse to redo this kitchen. Bacon, anybody?"

It took a few seconds for us to get it, but we both guffawed. Suze poured herself some more Diet Coke from her can. I was considering reading them the ingredients to "Basil Pesto Lasagna" but Suze interrupted. "What if Percy is now fine with the pit bulls but has an aversion to tattoos, people with scars, and transgender women?"

I spit a little Diet Coke onto my phone screen. Mom harrumphed. "Girls. He lived next door to a lesbian couple for decades. He knows that we are not mainstream types over here. For heaven's sake, we haven't left the house in months. He is totally aware of our situation."

I had never thought of me and my mother and our lives as a "situation." I let that sink in.

Mom ran her tongue over her teeth, as if there was spinach lodged somewhere. "Dump cake. Have you ever had that?"

Suze spewed soda all over herself. Brushing ineffectively at her chest, she said, "Dump Cake. Appropriate." Suddenly, Suze turned into Queen Elizabeth. "I say, Percy, would you take a Dump Cake?"

We died.

П

How are things?

We are plodding along. Beginning an easing of tension with the neighbor I told you about: the bellicose guy who hates pit bulls. His kitchen caught on fire, so we are having him over for dinner. Rob and Esme are coming, too. I'll let you know how THAT goes. He might have a coronary...

How about you and your mom? Any news?

Jack, give me time.

П

Saturday was a very fine example of early April in the Midwest: Cool but not cold. The trees displayed those tender, chartreuse buds that gladden the hearts of the winter-weary. The sun shone like a boss, and there were daffodils budding out in the front beds. The three of us got up early to get things ready.

The menu: Roasted pork loin. Gravy. Applesauce. Mashed potatoes with chives—the chives that had just begun to sprout outside the kitchen door. Sautéed julienned carrot strips with honey and a dash of curry powder. These were delish but a pain in the ass to julienne—of course, I was elected to do the julienning. Salad with Green Goddess dressing. Another Mom specialty. And, naturally, the Suze enhanced brownies. She decided to add Hershey's Rolos to the batter this time, for extra sinfulness. We had ice cream to top it off. Epic.

I Swiffered the hell out of the downstairs. Mom cleaned the powder room, and Suze vacuumed. The dogs had been bathed earlier in the week, so all we needed to do was spritz them with a little Bath & Body Warm Vanilla Sugar from Suze's arsenal, and tie clean bandannas around their necks. Suze used Febreeze on all of the upholstery. We felt very HGTV.

By the time the food was simmering, or whatever food does when Mom fixes it, the smells wafting around the house were irresistible. We had plenty of ice, soft drinks, and bowls of nuts. Rob was in charge of the wine. Esme was in charge of being completely gorgeous and charming. Dana would probably be her usual outrageous self, and Trudy of course, could be depended on to be kind, demure, and the one to keep Dana in check. Suze would ask all the right questions. I wasn't sure what my role was. Of course, that is nothing new.

Percy, his toupee on straight, arrived first with a beautiful bouquet of mixed blooms, all pink and white. Of course, he was a florist. As soon as I opened the front door, he held them up in front of his chest like a shield and looked frantically around the front hall. "The dogs! Are they protective about visitors?"

I took the flowers out of his hands, sniffing them. They smelled like worn out sachets. Percy's look of alarm increased with his then empty arms. "Percy, the dogs are in the backyard. I promise you, they will be OK. But let me put these in a vase, and I will give you dog biscuits to hand them. They will love you forever after that."

Mom and Suze swished in, looking a smidge nervous. Suze took Percy by one arm and Mom by the other, and we escorted him into the living room. "Sit down, Percy. Here, do you care for a nut? These are the deluxe kind." Mom sat beside him on the couch and slid the nut bowl towards him. Suze remained standing. I lingered for a second, still clutching the flowers.

We heard the dogs barking to come in. They knew it was a party; they are no dummies. Percy sat up very straight, all of a sudden, the handful of nuts he had taken slipping out of his fingers onto the rug at his feet.

"It's OK! Suze and I will get them, and we won't let anything happen. They will remember you from playing with Birdie, and the stick-throwing, won't they, Suze?" I gestured to her with the bouquet.

"Of course. We will be right back. Things will be fine and dandy." Suze raised her eyebrows as if she had never heard the words "fine and dandy" issue from her lips, and we escaped to the kitchen. I grabbed a vase out of the pantry and stuffed the flowers into it. I totally forgot to add water.

"What if the dogs decide to take a bite out of him?"

"For God's sake, Tommy. These are household pets, not wolves. They are not going to attack Percy. They might slobber all over him, but that will be their way of saying 'hiya.' Calm down." She opened the oven and sniffed. "This pork roast smells scrumptious."

I set the vase down on the counter, took a deep breath, and walked like a robot over to the kitchen door. I looked through the window to see the dogs, front paws on the top step, wagging their rumps as if their lives depended on it.

That gave me a bit of confidence. I swung the door open, and they bolted in with smiles on their faces.

Suze, the ever prepared, stood behind me with their leashes in hand. She grabbed first Herkie, then Saylor, and clipped them to their leads, handing Herkie's lead to me. She stood, Saylor at her side, and saluted me. "Let's do this. Keep the leashes high and tight, and don't lose control. *Operation Meet the pit bulls* is now underway!"

I felt droplets of sweat roll down the back of my neck as we passed through the front hall and into the living room. Mom had one hand on Percy's arm, as if to hold him in place in case he tried to bolt. As soon as the dogs saw him, they naturally made a beeline right for him. Percy gasped as if he had been shot in the chest.

"The treats! You said you would give me treats!" Percy held out his free arm as if to ward off an attack.

Mom kept a firm hold on him; and quick thinker that she is, grabbed the bowl of nuts with her free hand and shoved them into Percy's lap. "NUTS. Percy! The nuts! Dogs like nuts! Hand them each a peanut!"

Percy didn't sort through the nuts looking for a couple of peanuts. He just held the bowl out to the dogs, who shoved their noses into it and began to snarf up every single nut, including the Brazil nuts, which we all know nobody likes, except for pit bulls, apparently.

That did the trick. The dogs ate half the nuts before I could wrench the bowl away. They sat on either side of Percy, jammed between the couch and the coffee table, slobbering lovingly in his direction. Percy slumped in relief and reached out a hand and patted each dog carefully on the head. They sank down into a puddle at his feet. We all smiled, despite the fact that Mom, Suze and I knew there would be dog diarrhea to deal with later.

The tension in the air dissipated. Percy smoothed his "hair," laid one arm on the armrest, and I swear he tried to look casual. He crossed one leg over the other, nearly missing Herkie's snout, let out a sigh, and said, "I am very sorry that I set myself against you and your dogs." He cleared his throat. "I don't guess that you will forget what I did."

There was an uncomfortable silence until the doorbell rang, just in time to put an end to Percy's atonement, thankfully.

Rob and Esme arrived in a cloud of Chanel No. 5 and the aroma of one of Rob's favorite cigars. Esme, her hair a cloud of soft, loose waves, held a bouquet of white roses and pink stock. As she handed me the flowers, she whispered, "Oh, Tommy. I am so happy to be here." She kissed me on both cheeks; her own flushed with either happiness or the chill outside. April evenings in Ohio held onto the whisper of winter. She reached down to pet the dogs, who surrounded her with their tails rotating like propellers.

Rob removed Esme's faux leopard jacket, then took off his own. He handed them over to me, and as I draped them over the newel post, I heard the two of them whispering. Cheesy.

Next, Dana and Trudy arrived. Mom and Suze sat on the extra chairs they pulled in from the dining room. Dana sat cross-legged on the floor. I plopped down next to Percy. Rob and Esme lowered themselves onto the sofa across from us. Esme fidgeted, adjusting the collar of her crisp white blouse, which she pulled up around her ears, a la Katherine Hepburn. The look suited her.

"I certainly hope that April continues to warm up. This better not be another cold spring." I wondered what sort of threat Mom could hold out against Mother Nature.

Mom stood and announced, "It's cocktail time. Of course, I am not a drinker, usually. Although I promise to drink a sip or two of champagne later. Can I get anyone a beer? Some wine? A Coca Cola?"

Rob raised his hand like a student. "Wait. Champagne? How did you know?"

Mom looked confused. "Know? What do you mean? We are celebrating the détente between us and our new dear friend, Percy here. You know that. That is why you were invited. To celebrate."

Rob stood up and walked over to Percy, took his hand and shook it vigorously. "Of course, of course! But you know, I think we should just go ahead and toast everything now rather than later. Don't you agree, Es?"

Esme blushed and ran her left hand through her hair. "I do. No pun intended." She tucked her hair behind her left ear, but her left hand remained at the side of her face. She waggled her fingers. Attached to one of them was a twinkling emerald cut diamond nearly the size of a playing card. I don't know how we had managed to miss it.

I leaped to my feet and nearly trampled Herkie as I rushed over to hug Esme. "THIS IS EPIC! Rob, you lucky man! No wonder you waited so long to get married! You were waiting for the perfect woman!" I hugged Esme so hard she nearly suffocated.

Happy sobbing. Mom and Rob were wrapped in one another's arms. Mom blubbered into his shoulder, and Rob kissed her hair. Trudy clapped her hands. "Suze, Percy, let's go get the champagne."

The dogs circled us, wagging and nuzzling. Dana and Trudy applauded. Glasses clinked in the kitchen, and before the living room chaos subsided, Suze and Percy arrived with a tray with two bottles of Veuve Clicquot and nine glasses.

Percy poured each of us a generous glassful. For Dana, he was more cautious – just a sip in her glass. He poured himself a bit more. We all stood, glasses held high.

Mom stepped forward. "To my loving and generous brother, who has been by my side through happiness and grief. Robert, I owe you everything. You gave me my family." Mom paused to sniff and wipe a tear from her eye.

"To Esme. How on earth you are going to be able to put up with my brother's idiosyncrasies, I will never know, but bless you for loving him. And welcome to this family." She turned her gaze to Percy. "And to Percy Warner, who finally let his guard down and joined our circle of friends. You are a welcome guest." She held her glass high.

"Cheers, everybody!" Honestly, it took a good fifteen seconds for all of us to clink. I took a sip of the delicious bubbly, and it glided down my throat, warm, buzzy, and golden. Suze downed her glass in one long gulp. Dana tasted hers and spluttered. Esme and Rob crossed their arms in that pretzel lover thing and drank theirs. We all sat down, but Percy remained standing.

"I need to apologize. I have not been a good neighbor. I have not been a good citizen." His eyes clouded, and the hand holding his glass of champagne began to tremble.

Suze interrupted. "You have already apologized. Enough said. It's is all behind us. Right? We have other, happier things to celebrate tonight."

Dana surprised me. She got up and went to Percy, hand outstretched. "I heard you were just a nasty old fart." She took his hand and shook it. "Not that they talked trash about you. Just factual." Percy looked at once offended, confused, and abashed, if all those emotions are possible in one person's face.

Dana continued. "But you are a good person, deep down inside." She let go of his hand and sat back down.

Percy lowered himself onto the sofa, his eyes glistening a little. Hands shaking, he took a sip of his champagne, and tried to set the glass carefully down on the coffee table, but a few drops sloshed out. Looking stricken, Percy tried to wipe them away with his palm. My heart, full of equal parts guilt and friendship, skipped a beat. I stared at Percy for a second, and then something in me said *what the Hell* and I leaned over and planted a loud kiss on his left cheek. Without turning, he reached out and grasped my hand and squeezed it.

"This may be way too much happiness for one evening," Dana pronounced. "I am not sure that I can handle it."

Suze giggled. "It might get even better. Maybe Santa Claus will show up or something!" Everybody laughed.

Mom sniffed. "My God! I have to check the pork! Percy, will you help me by mashing the potatoes?"

Percy, looking relieved, sprang up. Mom and Percy disappeared into the kitchen, accompanied by two tidbit-hopeful pit bulls, Percy glancing behind with only a touch of fear remaining in his eyes. The rest of us sat, smiling and sipping, Esme holding out her hand so that we could all admire the glory of her engagement ring.

"Have you set a date?" Trudy beamed. "Will it be a big wedding?"

Esme shook her hair over her shoulders and leaned against Rob. "We haven't even thought about that. For now, I am getting prepared for what might happen if anyone tries to challenge the legality of the union." She squeezed Rob's arm. "Gay marriage is legal in Ohio. Also in Ohio is the statute that a transgender person may not legally change their gender on their birth certificate, so legally, Rob and I are two gay men getting married. But I need to be ready for the sorts of legal challenges that may arise."

Rob nodded in quick agreement. "Luckily, as an LGBTQ legal expert, Es is up to the task."

Jesus, Mary and Joseph. Once again, our family teetered at the abyss of social rejection. Same old, same old.

Π

Suze and I lay on her bed, ruminating. "Do you suppose we will get to be bridesmaids?"

I rolled over on my side and looked at her. She had that dreamy 'what if' gaze. "Maybe. But we are old." I sighed.

Suze whacked a heel against the mattress. "The *bride and groom* are old. Thus, we are legitimate considerations for the bridal party." She clapped. "Eureka! The pups can be bridesmaids!"

Although my heart warmed at the suggestion, I had to be the voice of reason. "May I remind you that this is not your wedding to plan? That privilege resides with the bride? And more likely, her mother?"

Suze wrinkled her nose. "I know, I know. But a girl can dream. Because neither of us has any suitors waiting in the wings, you catch my drift?"

"Hey, what do you think Mom meant earlier when she said something about Percy and the neighbors knowing about our 'situation'? What situation? Is there town gossip, do you think?" *What if everybody knew about Leah and Mommy?* My bowels churned.

Suze put a hand on her forehead. "Your family is not exactly like, what—Leave It To Beaver? That old show. You know, from the fifties, when all families were white, the moms wore high heels to clean the bathrooms, and the word 'gay' meant happy?"

She turned her head and stared at me as if I were an idiot. "Tommy. You grew up in a family with two mothers. Yes, all of Framington knew that. You are a person who is so out of touch with your own self that you were willing to give up a year to live here in isolation. OK, I am too, but let's focus on your issues for the moment. You have not had a real relationship with a man; you only go out on a series of pointless dates. You have no circle of friends. Just me and what, Audrey, who moved away months ago?"

I opened my mouth to answer, but Suze stuck out a finger in warning. "I am not finished. Your name is *Tommy.* You love stray dogs and stray people, as in Dana Stryker! Your Mom is totally aware that she lives her life outside of the mainstream, but she is OK with that. She seems to be blossoming as a result of this year. I think she is letting go of her grief. But you seem to be stalled out. Staying right where you have always been. Throwing up walls around yourself to stay safe. Embracing semi-agoraphobia." She wagged her finger again. "You act chipper and crack jokes all the time, but you also look blank and stare into space quite often around here when you think I'm not watching. Catch my drift?"

I caught it. I dropped it like a hot potato. I put my hands on my abdomen and pressed hard. "Let's change the subject, OK? I always thought Rob would remain single. Now Rob and Esme are getting married? I am so happy for them."

Suze snapped her fingers. "One more piece of evidence. Rob's choice of a mate. Non-traditional. Face it, Tommy. You come from a long line of unusuals. They seem to have come to terms with it. Have you?"

I stood up, guts still roiling, and ran for the bathroom.

Suze shouted after me, "Tom, are you all right?"

I flushed the toilet, washed my hands, and returned to Suze, still sitting on the bed, a look of concern on her face.

"Nothing. Just a little diarrhea. It must have been that tuna salad at lunch."

Suze shook her head.

Chapter Twenty-Five

Π

We took out the storm windows and put in the screens. Spring breezes wafted in and lifted our spirits. The dogs took to standing, paws in the windowsills, woofing at passers-by. The star magnolia outside the dining room began to bud, and things on the home front were calm.

Mom and Percy had discovered a mutual liking for card games, and while Suze and I embarked on our nightly forays into the neighborhood with the dogs, Mom and Percy played Pinochle. They tried to teach us. It was a half-hearted effort. Both Suze and I got the message that the two of them preferred their own twice-weekly competition.

This night was no different. As we slipped the collars on the dogs and attached the leashes, Mom waved us off blithely. "Have a nice walk, and tell Trudy and Dana hello. Say I will be texting them a dinner invitation as soon as I can come up with a suitable menu!"

We said goodbye and exited the building amidst much wagging and leaping. The dogs did that. Suze and I merely skipped.

April had finally turned the corner. Evenings were just cool enough to be restorative. The cool air filtered the winter sediment out of our lungs, replacing it with pollen and leaf mold. We had no allergies, so we felt glorious. We strolled down streets, looking into lit windows, making up stories about what might be going on inside.

"See that man sitting at his dining room table? He is staring at his laptop. Do you think he's looking at porn?" Suze took a step closer to the house. I grabbed her and pulled her back.

"Would you watch porn at your dining room table? For God's sake. He is probably shopping for electronics on Amazon." I dragged her down the block. "Look over there. A family, a big screen TV, and CNN. I bet they are all depressed as Hell."

We crossed the street and headed down towards Trudy's. I stopped short in front of the brick colonial. "There's that woman in the window. The one who always seems to look out at night? I wonder what she is looking for. Let's see if she sees us." I waved, and she waved back. "She looks lonely. I wonder if she's some sort of shut-in."

As we watched, the woman seemed to dissolve into the soft glow of the light behind her. "There's a story there, for sure."

It was a short jog to Dana's, and the dogs' tails began to wag the moment Trudy's house came iinto view.

Trudy served lemonade. Very quenching. We sipped, both of us relaxing into the softness of the upholstery. Dana hardly touched her drink. She fidgeted, staring at her hands, chewing at her cuticles.

"What is going on, kiddo? I can almost see steam coming out of your ears."

Dana took her thumb out of her mouth and laughed. The sort of laugh that doesn't indicate glee. "The fuckers at school have decided to make Angie's life miserable, that's all." She made a fist with one hand and ground it into the palm of her other hand. "They have started to call her 'Harry.' Get it? Harry, for harelip?"

Trudy gasped. Suze and I froze.

"Yup. Jill and the crew of bitches."

Suze leaned forward. "Dana, have you reported this to the principal? There is zero tolerance for bullying in schools now."

Dana snorted. "Oh, yes. I reported it. And you know what happened? *Absolutely nothing.* Mr. Stewart said that they would 'look into' it. That meant a generic 'be nice to others; bullying is not tolerated at Framington High School' announcement over the PA system. Over and out."

We sat, the three of us, in silence. Trudy rubbed her temples. I fumed. Suze tried again. "Do you want me to step in? I can email your principal and inquire."

Dana made a face. "You? A total outsider? And how would you say you knew anything about any of this?" Dana rolled her eyes. "Come on, Suzanne. That's ridiculous."

I gave it a whirl. "Does Angie know to just ignore it? That if she ignores them, the bullies will move on?"

Dana jumped up and jeered at us. "Just ignore them! Who in God's name came up with that line? Because it is fucking misguided, naïve, and just plain idiotic! Just ignoring bullying INTENSIFIES IT. Bullies get off on bullying! They don't get discouraged when their target tries to pretend they don't notice! Because anyone with even a reptilian brain realizes that OF COURSE TARGETS OF ABUSE NOTICE IT." With that, Dana ran out of the room and up the stairs. Trudy hustled after her.

My stomach was in knots. Five minutes ticked by, as Suze and I stared at one another, at a loss for words. Trudy returned and sat on the edge of the couch. She reached out to rearrange the magazine stack on the coffee table, decking them up like cards, ticking them on the wood, again and again, setting them down only to pick them up and repeat.

Suze stood. "Should I go up there? I could share some of the sorts of coping skills we use in schools. I am not an expert or a counselor, but I do know something about how to deal with school bullies."

Trudy ran two fingers over the scar closest to her ear. "She won't talk any further. She asked me this evening to tell you not to come over for a while. I don't know what to do."

Suze whispered "come!" and the dogs slunk over to her, ears back. Even they seemed to be worried. Herkie nuzzled Suze's hand. Saylor whined. "Oh, you two. This is a real bitch, isn't it?" She dropped to her knees to hug the girls. They licked her face, which brought a tiny smile to Suze's lips.

I reached for my nearly empty glass of lemonade and gulped down the last inch or so. The sugary sediment nearly choked me. So I sucked on an ice cube, hoping that it would melt the grittiness away. None of us spoke. Trudy's lights were apparently on timers; the floor lamp by the front window clicked off.

"We have to go. Trudy, I am so sorry about all this. Maybe things will settle down at school tomorrow or in the next few days. They made their little bully joke, and they will be satisfied, you know what I mean?"

Trudy arched her eyebrows. "I doubt it. But you know what? This isn't your problem, is it?"

I felt as if cold water had just been thrown at me. "Oh, Trudy..."

She put a finger to her lips. "Sshhh. Honey, I am not scolding you. What I mean is this: you can't solve this for Dana. None of us can. Look at me—my face. I have had to walk around with this face virtually my entire life. The looks, the taunts, the outright humiliation. It was and is my burden. I have to deal with it. No matter how much my parents or anybody else tried to help me, it was just me who has had to deal with it. Angie knows this. Dana will have to learn it, too."

Trudy gathered the glasses and put them on the tray. She stood by the door, tray in hand, as we leashed the dogs, threw on our windbreakers, and opened the door. The glow from the porch light blurred her scars. Her eyes shone with kindness. "Goodnight, girls. We will get through this, won't we?"

The night had gotten cooler. The dogs pulled against our hands, as if they just couldn't wait to get home and get cozy on our beds. The stars were out. I looked up at them, hanging there, twinkling at us.

"Damn it, Suze! Look up! Which one of those suckers are you supposed to wish on?"

Π

We had been taking the dogs on a different route for the past couple of weeks, in deference to Dana's wishes. At first, it was hard to turn the dogs left instead of right. Corners were a challenge, as the dogs tried to reverse us at every intersection, as if we had lost our way to Dana's. It was exhausting.

"My God, I think they have radar." Suze tugged on Saylor's leash while pivoting. "How much longer do you think we will have to do this?"

"I texted Dana today. I asked her how things were going, and if she might want to come over, like after school or something."

"What did she say?"

"She just texted back a thumbs up emoji and the word *soon*. So your guess is as good as mine."

Suze yanked again on Saylor, who remained intent on her mission to change our route. "It is her life. Trudy was right. We just have to give her time."

We cut the walk short, as being dragged by sixty pound dogs is not much fun. As we rounded the corner to our house, we saw Rob's car parked outside. It was midnight.

"What the hell?"

Rob and Mom's heads were together, but they jerked up as we entered the living room. Rob's hair stood up all over. He had been raking it. Mom waved us into the room with a fierceness that was unusual.

"What's up?" I kissed Rob's cheek while trying to smooth down his hair.

Rob looked at me, despair in his eyes. "It's Esme's mother Phyllis. She is trying to kill me."

"Sit down. Both of you." Mom pointed to the empty sofa.

We settled in and looked at the two of them, thigh to thigh, furrowed brows and restless hands. "Spill it," I said.

Rob raked his hair with both hands, undoing my efforts. "She wants us to get married in White Sulphur. She wants one of those epic weddings that will be touted on the Instagram and Facebook accounts of all of her friends. She wants a sit-down rehearsal dinner for two hundred."

"What does Esme think? Does she want an epic wedding?"

Mom leaned towards us. "That's just it. No. First of all, Esme left White Sulphur Springs when she went off to college. None of her friends live there any more. After Esme's parents divorce, her Dad moved to Boston. He couldn't deal with Eddie becoming Esme. They're estranged. Phyllis, however, is Esme's biggest fan. Esme says her mother, although ditzy and annoying, is the one who gave her the courage to admit she was transgender. So Esme understands that Phyllis just wants to give Esme a storybook wedding. A wedding that Esme most decidedly *doesn't want.*"

Suze whistled. "So. This is a predicament."

"No shit. When I left, Esme was on the phone with her mother, ranting."

Mom took a Kleenex out of the box on the table and blew her nose loudly. "So. The wedding will not be in West Virginia, it will be here. Esme's mother may not choose to come, but we will cross that bridge when we come to it."

I interrupted. "Am I missing something? Had you set a date and I didn't get the memo?"

Rob shut his eyes and wrinkled his nose. "NO. It's Phyllis who is jumping the gun, forcing the issue, and insisting on all of this. We haven't decided when to have the wedding. But Phyllis thinks Christmas in White Sulphur will be magical. One of us is going to have a stroke, and I doubt that it will by Phyllis."

"OK. OK. Here's the thing. Don't set a date!" Suze smiled as if she had just invented the wheel.

Mom pressed her lips together. Rob continued, "We have to get married in Ohio. Es is very confident that legally speaking, we'll be fine here. But she is prepared to fight it out in the courts if we're challenged. Her specialty, you know that. So no, West Virginia is out. But how are we going to get Phyllis off our backs? She'll want to have an extravaganza in Framington, too."

"Look, Rob. There are all kinds of extravaganzas. We can probably have a mini-extravaganza here. But Suze is right—certainly you can come up with some sort of stalling tactic for setting a date. Say you have a big court case coming up. Say that Mom has to get a hip replacement and needs time to rehab. Lie. You can put her off!"

Rob straightened out his legs so that his feet were under the coffee table, flung out his arms, and lay back as if he had just had the stroke he referred to. Just then, we heard a car door slam, footsteps pounding up the walk, and the front door burst open. Esme flew in, cheeks flushed, holding shut a lime green silk robe over a gauzy white nightgown, her hair in a chopstick bun on the top of her head. She draped herself on the arm of the sofa, kissed the top of Rob's head, and exclaimed, "I have put out a contract on my mother."

Rob put his head in Esme's silky lap. "How much? I'll go in halfies. Who'd you call? The mob?"

Mom stomped a foot. "Stop it right now! Esme, what did you do?"

"I lied. I told her that Rob and I have not been getting along lately, and so we have decided on a trial separation."

Rob lifted his head, took both of Esme's hands, and kissed her fingers. "Es, you are a genius and I love you."

There was a universal heaving of sighs of relief. Suze got up and headed out of the room. "I'm getting snacks! Fritos and beer?"

We all got a buzz on. Mom waxed ecstatic about all the weddings she had been to and how often she cried. Esme kept checking her phone for texts from Phyllis. Suze fed Fritos to the dogs. And I wondered if Dana was planning to murder anyone.

Π

My favorite time of the day. The wee hours, after dog walking. Lying in bed with a tuckered-out pit bull, chatting with Jack. It was now a habit. We were becoming very close. As close as you can be with a person you have never met. We had exchanged photos and our entire names. Jack Duncan. I liked the sound of that.

I am having a little anxiety about the engagement. What if somebody does or says something horrible about Esme? Or makes a threat? This is such a small town, and who knows how people will handle a transgender person marrying Rob? I am scared.

It's understandable. But remember that Rob and Esme are not kids. They are both attorneys, and Esme specializes in LGBTQ issues. She is no stranger

to threats. They are not, either of them, unready for what might happen. Question for you: are you projecting onto them your own uneasiness? It strikes me that maybe you haven't come to terms with your own feelings about your mothers. Have you talked with your mom yet about your discovery that they weren't in a monogamous relationship? You have told me about your feelings that you were always an "outsider" growing up with lesbian parents. God knows, I get that. I am no psychologist, but Tommy. Have a conversation with your mom about things. Don't think you can hide your anxiety about the past from her. She knows you better than anyone. This wedding is bringing out all sorts of fear and uneasiness that you have been tamping down.

Yeah. You aren't a psychologist. So please stop trying to be one where I am concerned, OK?

I wished I hadn't hit "send" on my comment, but it was too late. I shut my computer and vowed to keep my thoughts and feelings to myself. Jack wasn't Dr. Phil. I snorted, and Herkie opened one eye to peer at me. "It's OK, Herk. I am not going to ruin the wedding by spilling my guts. It won't accomplish anything; it will just hurt Mom. Jack is dead wrong on this one." A frisson of doubt vibrated through my gut. I ran my hand over Herkie's velvet forehead and took a deep breath. "Do you think Jack will ever speak to me again?"

Herkie didn't answer. So I cracked my laptop back open. A "bing," and there was Jack's reply:

Got it. Happy to take a "time out." If you want to resume our chats any time, just send me a DM. I hope you work through things.

Shit. What had I done?

Chapter Twenty-Six

April drew to an end, continuing to be glorious. The daffodils were blooming—their scent floating in through the open windows. It was the kind of weather that beckoned us to shut down the entire recluse operation and run wild. So we spent a lot of time sunning ourselves in the backyard, throwing tennis balls for the dogs and hoping to get a little bit of tan on our winter white skin.

The late afternoon sun glinted off my computer screen; I had two clients who were thrilled that my efforts had resulted in over five thousand new social media followers each. I had done a successful vlog with another client, who needed a script to sound "spontaneous" in her segments. She loved all the "ad-libs" I had written for her. I shut my laptop and stretched. I felt three vertebrae in my lower back pop. "Hey, Suze! Quitting time!"

Suze and I wandered downstairs, looking for snacks. Mom was in the dining room, finishing up her sixth and last scrapbook. Photos were strewn around her on the table. I picked one up and held it out to show Suze. "Me. Senior in high school. Did you have that many pimples?"

Suze took the picture and laughed. "My complexion was flawless. I did have braces, though. I suffered through my entire high school career encased in wire. I didn't get them off until the summer after graduation. No wonder I didn't have dates."

I shuffled through a few more shots, looking for more evidence of my awkward stage that wouldn't quit. Just as I discovered a photo of Mom, Mommy and me standing in front of the house holding ice cream cones—no wonder I had pimples—someone began to bang on the front door.

"Hold on! I am coming!" I opened the door, and there stood Dana, her face ferocious, bent over with the weight of what looked like all of her earthly goods in her backpack. Before I could open my mouth, Dana thrust her way into the house. She wrested the backpack from her shoulders, slammed it down on the floor, and looked wildly around. "Where are the dogs? I need the dogs. I have been suspended from school."

My heart dropped into my stomach. Suze rushed in from the dining room, Mom on her heels. "Wait. What?"

"You heard me. Two weeks. No make up work allowed. Further punishment to be determined. Those fuckers!"

Suze took charge. "You go in there and sit down. I'll go get the dogs; they are in the backyard. Tommy, get Dana some Coke, maybe." Dana continued to writhe. "Go ON. Settle down and then tell us the whole story."

She rushed into the kitchen, flung open the back door and shouted, "Herkimer! Saylor! Come! Come this instant! You are needed!"

We heard the paws hit the linoleum, and the tap of their paws as they galloped in. We shepherded Dana into the living room and Suze forced her down onto the sofa. The dogs jumped up on either side of her, licking and wriggling. Dana reached out blindly and put an arm around each dog.

"Now just a second. I will bring the caffeine. Oh, shit. Maybe we don't need stimulants. I'll just bring ice water. Hold on; I will be right back. Take cleansing breaths!" Suze zoomed once more into the kitchen. We heard her crashing around in there, and it only took her about one minute to return with a tray of tumblers filled with water. She forced one into Dana's grasp. "Take a few sips, kid."

Dana's hands shook as she lifted the water to her lips. She took a long gulp, then held the glass to her forehead and ran it across her brow. Her breathing was jagged. She rubbed a tear away as it escaped from her lower lid. Her face was white and waxy.

Mom tried to draw Dana out of herself. "Honey, what happened?"

Dana set her glass on the coffee table. "The shit came down all over. That's what happened."

My heart, still down there in my stomach, throbbed. "Go on."

Dana rubbed the dogs. The barbed wire on her neck bulged. "Hell. Every year, one lucky nerdhead is awarded the Framington Engineers' Club Excellence Prize. It goes to the student who 'shows promise in the areas of math and science.' It usually goes to a graduating senior. A stupid trophy and $500." She paused and shot us a look. "Of course, you can see where this is going. Angie got the award on Monday."

Dana picked up her water glass, took another sip, and set it back down with such force that water sloshed onto the table. Dana ran a finger through the puddle. "Angie was so excited. She couldn't wait to tell her parents about it. It was such a good day." Dana put her finger to her mouth and licked off the water.

The three of us held our breath, perhaps because we were so tightly packed on the sofa across from Dana, but I think it was out of the fear of what was coming next.

"Yeah. Well. Tuesday, Jill Bolton and her gang of shithole girlfriends walked into the cafeteria at lunch, stood at the front, and peeled up their T-shirts to reveal identical homemade tees underneath that said CONGRATS ON THE MATH THING, HARRY—TO BAD ABOUT YOUR

FACE! They screamed and clapped, and everybody but Angie and I laughed. It was all over so fast. They pulled their shirts down and left by the back entrance, still laughing and cheering.

"But of course, someone took a photo on their phone and texted it around to the whole school. Everybody saw it. Angie was so upset she left after fifth period without a pass. She just got the hell out of there, and I don't blame her."

Dana pulled her cell phone out of her pocket and flashed a photo at us. She didn't give us a chance to actually look at it closely before she stuffed it back into her pocket.

Mom gasped.

The dogs sensed the situation and began to whimper. Dana didn't even seem to notice. I looked around for someone to take control of things and make it all go away. That person was not in the room.

"This is all terrible. I get that. But I don't get the connection between the scenario in the cafeteria and your getting suspended, Dana." Suze took the words right out of my mouth.

Dana let out a gush of air and made a fist. "Because I called them OUT on it. I shared their vulgar selfies all over my social media framework. Every nerd, gamer, brainiac, outcast, and wimp in Framington high who hadn't heard about the fiasco saw my post. They were outraged, and they spread the post around. It got shared and retweeted like wildfire. We pariahs have a huge social network." Dana tossed her head. "Jill and her gang of bitches were outed, and the wrath of social media rained down upon them. The posts went viral, and by today, the school had been called, emailed, and the Framington High website was flooded with complaints from as far away as Portugal. It was astronomic."

Suze sighed. "So the result was suspension. What happened to Jill? How is Angie doing?"

Dana unclenched her fist and rubbed her hand on her jeans. "Angie is OK, I guess. She hasn't been back to school. We have been texting, but right now, she says her mom won't let me come over. Jill, as luck would have it, was also suspended."

I felt a sharp pain in my frontal lobe. I tried rubbing my temples. "What will happen in two weeks? The two of you just go back to school as if nothing occurred?"

Before Dana could answer, Suze cut in. "No. There will be other consequences, I guarantee you. Am I correct, Dana—you said further consequences to be determined?"

Dana pulled on the ring that pierced her eyebrow. "Yeah. There is going to be a meeting. The parents, the principal, the school counselor, and me, Angie, and Jill." Dana got up, turned and reached out to Suze and touched her on the shoulder. "Since I have only one parent, and she isn't really my mother, can you come to the meeting, too? It won't be fair if Jill gets to have two people there to back her up, and all I have is Trudy." Dana closed her fingers around Suze's shoulder. "Please? You know how schools work. You'll know what to say. Trudy is too meek. Suzanne, I could be expelled." Suze held out both arms and Dana sank into them, her face crumpling.

Suze pulled away to look into Dana's face. Dana shuddered, her tears flowing freely at this point. She looked like a frightened little kid, despite the tattoo and piercings.

"When is this meeting, hon?"

"In two weeks. Monday after next, at four-thirty, when all the kids have left the building. Ms. Flood, the superintendent, will be there, too." Dana hiccupped. "I am so scared."

"Does Trudy know about this yet?" Suze glanced down at her watch.

"No. I came straight here."

Suze slapped her thighs. "All right, then." Wipe your tears. Go get your stuff. Let me put some shoes on, and we'll go over to your house together. I hate to tell you this, Dana, but you are in a crapload of trouble."

As soon as the door shut behind them, Mom began to hyperventilate. I pushed her head down between her knees and rushed to the powder room for a cold cloth. I handed it, still dripping, to Mom, who pressed it to the back of her neck. That seemed to bring her around. She sat up, some of the color returned to her cheeks. "What should we do, Tommy? Is there anything we can do?"

Mom looked at me, lost for words. I had to take it from there. "I don't know. But don't forget that Suze is a trained professional. Her entire career has been dealing with high school shit like this. Let's just chill out for now and see what she says when she gets back. I bet she'll have a plan."

I didn't believe a word that I had just said. But it seemed to perk up my mother. She removed the wet cloth, ran it over her face, and put it on top of the fruit bowl on the coffee table. She stood up and rooted around in her pockets until she located her cell. "Do you know Angie Baker's number?"

I nodded. Thank heaven for group texts.

"Tell me what it is."

I pulled my cell phone out of my bra and looked up Angie in my contact list. As I recited the number, Mom punched it into her phone.

Before the world turned completely upside down, I heard her say, "Angie? Honey? Is this Angie? Oh, yes. Of course. Mrs. Baker. You don't know me, but this is Meg Poole. I am a dear friend of Dana Stryker and her mother—foster mother—Trudy Owens. Is there anything I can do?"

Chapter Twenty-Seven

Π

We got the story when Suze returned. Trudy was understandably horrified, also understandably in complete sympathy with Angie and Dana. The coming meeting at the school terrified her, but with Suze accompanying them, she felt able to face the administrators and the Boltons. They agreed that Suze would go over there to strategize a few times before the meeting.

Mom's conversation with Sheryl Baker, Angie's mom, was not at all surprising. Mrs. Baker was angry, gratified that Dana had supported her daughter, and worried about the upcoming meeting. Mom said that Mrs. Baker must have referred to Dana as an "angel" at least five times during the conversation. Mom, naturally, invited the Bakers over for breakfast, lunch, or dinner, whichever they preferred. Meanwhile, Angie would remain at home until after the meeting at the school.

Our evenings were altered. Suze spent the days before the meeting with the "school firing squad," as she dubbed them, over at Trudy's. They were rehearsing as if preparing for a trial. The biggest challenges were keeping Dana quiet and encouraging Trudy to speak. Suze did this by peppering Dana with accusatory questions and rehearsing reactions from Dana that didn't include the F word or yelling. For Trudy, Suze prepared note cards with logical arguments and critical aspects of Dana's history of abuse.

Suze also scheduled a hair appointment for Trudy for the morning of the meeting at school. An upsweep. So that her scars were completely revealed.

Π

Percy and Mom found it hard to concentrate on Pinochle. They suspended their games for a time, and on this evening, Percy came over "just for a few minutes, to settle his nerves." Mom had gone to bed already, claiming a headache.

We sat at the dining room table, drinking Coke. Percy scratched the scalp just under the crown of his toupee. "I can't stop thinking about the bullying situation." He pushed his wig back a tiny bit and continued to rake his brow. "I was a bully of a father. I just took Frannie and Phoebe's love for granted. But I drove them both away." He readjusted his toupee.

I watched him do it. He looked so vulnerable. My heart swelled up with sympathy. "Percy, you aren't the only one. I take Mom for granted all the time."

"Yes, and stop that." A thin smile. "That's not the half of it. I nagged at Phoebe all the time, too. Her grades weren't good enough. She didn't stand up straight. She wore wrinkled blouses. Sometimes I wonder how she turned out so well, with such a grouch for a father."

"Oh, Percy. I am so sorry." I reached out and put my palm over his. "We all make mistakes. We are all in a constant state of trying to be the masters of our own lives. And most of us suck at it. This year has been full of growth and development for Mom and me. Actually, mostly for Mom. I am sort of floundering. But Mom seems to be working through her loss. She has found a lot of support in her Facebook grief group."

"She told me about her new friend in that group. Marjory Steiner."

I looked at Percy. " How do you know about this Marjory person? How do you know her last name? Mom said they don't share names or locations. Privacy reasons."

"Oh, I don't think Meg knows her last name. I figured all of that out myself from what Meg has told me about her. How many Marjory's with amputations and partners named Corrine could there possibly be? It has to be Marjory Steiner. Wheelchair. Doesn't go out. There's a regular caregiver. She lives over on Lemon Street. You know that big brick colonial with the fanlight? Black shutters? That's Marjory's."

I felt as if I had stuck my finger in a light socket. "Percy! My God! Why haven't you told Mom this? This Marjory is right here in Framington?"

He put his finger into his ear and rooted around. I wanted to snatch it out and wallop it, but *earwax.* "Percy, this is an outrage! Marjory could be Mom's new best friend, for heaven's sake!"

Percy held up his finger, and I tried not to look at it, because *earwax.* "First of all, your mother has vowed not to leave the house until August." He held out another finger, one that I could look at. "Second, Marjory is a shut-in, herself. She is in fragile health, with the diabetes and her leg. She depends on her caregiver for everything. I used to deliver flowers to her at the hospital."

It hit me like a ton of bricks. "Oh my God. Marjory is the woman in the window!"

Percy used that same finger, ugh, to rub his nose. "What are you talking about?"

"Suze and I see her. At night, when we take walks. She seems to float into view, watching for us. She waves to us sometimes, and we wave at her. Then she seems to dissolve away. Of course! It's the wheelchair. She rolls."

I sat back and thought about the times we had seen Marjory. I marveled that she was right here in Framington.

I looked out the windows that surrounded us in our TV room—a screened porch converted into a sunroom. The lights of neighboring homes glinted in the darkness. The Jones' house—doors opening and shutting at all hours of the day: teenage children. The Hathaways: lights flicking on and off at predictable hours, because they spent winters in Florida and used timers year round. The house directly behind us: a kitchen light on, nothing else except for the beam of one bare bulb in the attic dormer. I didn't even know those people's names, and they had moved into the house over a year ago.

So many stories in so many houses around us. Sickness and health. Divorce and family breakups. Births, miscarriages. And entire world of humanity, looking out of windows, speculating about one another. Mom, locked in this prison of her own choosing, reaching out to others via the vastness of the internet only to connect with another grieving woman, also locked in, right here in our own insular little suburb. My mind was blown.

We chatted for a while longer, until I noticed the bags under Percy's eyes. He looked tired. Having his kitchen torn up, arguing (I wagered) with all the workmen, worrying about Dana and Angie. I knew he regretted his past, missed Frannie. I was thankful that Phoebe and Birdie had appeared to ease his miseries. If only they lived close by.

I stood up and kissed Percy on the top of his head. His "hair" felt coarse and grainy on my lips. "Goodnight, you old grump. Thank you for telling me about Marjory. I am going to go up and tell Mom. I think she will be thrilled."

Percy waved me off, but not before having the final word. "My bet is that you will be leaving a pan of those world famous brownies on Marjory's doorstep before long."

"I am not wagering on that one, Percy."

He stood, carefully pushing his chair back underneath the table. At the front door, he gave me a halfhearted smile.

"Good night, Tommy." I watched him as he plodded home, his wrinkled shirt tucked into his belt, his baggy trousers billowing. I thought he looked so lonely. I wished that he had a parrot, or at least a hamster to keep him company.

Π

Mom looked up from her computer at my knock. To my surprise, she was playing poker, not sleeping.

"Wait. I thought you were too tired. Percy came over. I would have asked you to come down. What are you doing? Are you *betting*?" I tried to disguise my displeasure.

"Only a dollar a game. I gave myself a ten-dollar limit. Honey, it's a distraction. I have to focus on the game, not everything else that is going haywire right now. So far tonight, I have won five dollars." She shut her laptop and turned to smile at me. "Come on in and sit down. You look like you are bursting."

I hopped up onto her bed and tried not to seem as excited as I was. "You will never guess what!"

She scooted the desk chair around to face me, stretched out her legs, scratched her knee, and said, "What?"

I could hardly contain myself. "You know Marjory? As in Marjory and Corrinne? You told Percy about her? Well guess what? SHE LIVES IN OUR NEIGHBORHOOD."

Mom clasped her hands together like a child on Christmas morning. "What? My Marjory from Facebook? She lives here? How could you possibly know that?"

I felt so smug. "Ha! You told Percy about her. Percy, the retired local florist who knows everybody from weddings, funerals, and the *hospital.* He put two and two together. After all, how many possible Marjory's are there out there whose partner was named Corrinne? Who have diabetes and only one leg? Percy used to deliver flowers to her. When she was in the hospital for her amputation. When

Corinne died. Her name is Marjory Steiner, and she can't go out. Just like you!"

Mom beamed. "This is incredible! She is nearby, my word. Wait till we talk about this coincidence!"

I shook my finger at her. "No, no, you can't. You told me that none of you in the group have shared information. If you blurted out that you know her and where she lives, even if you did it via private message, it would alarm her. She would think you are some kind of stalker."

Mom tapped her foot and wiggled around in her chair. She drew her lips together and nodded. "Of course, of course. And it's not like I could just go over to her house for a visit."

"I know. But maybe someday, after our hiatus from life is over."

Mom tipped her chair back and roared. "I swear, there is more action in my life since Sam died than there ever was. Good grief, my life before was dull and boring. Becoming solitary just hasn't been what I expected it to be."

"So is it ridiculous to continue? Should we just open the door, walk out, and call it a day, so to speak?"

Mom tipped her chair back down and sat straight in it, her hands on her thighs, elbows akimbo. "I started this in good faith as not only a time to heal, but as sort of a tribute to Samantha. I intend to make good on my vow to her and to myself." She paused and stared at her lap. "Tommy, grief is like a chronic disease. You try to fight it off, and some days, you think you are getting over it—you know, healing. And then, you open a drawer to put away your underpants, and there is one of her old bras, and you pick it up, hold it to your heart, and nearly fall down in pain." She raised her head and smiled, but only with her lips. The rest of her didn't take part. "So although I seem to be doing great, making progress, there is backsliding. A lot of it."

Every single organ in my body ached.

"You know, sweetheart, I am getting so much out of this experience. From all of the things that have occurred in these few months to turn all of us upside down. But also from what has happened to me. In here." She touched her heart and then her temple. "I am going through a metamorphosis." She grinned, and this time, it looked sincere.

Despite feeling like worms were crawling inside my veins, I hugged Mom. "I am going to turn in." A voice inside my head called me a chicken, and I heard an echo of Jack, encouraging me to confront Mom with my story. I ignored all of that, and skulked off to bed.

Π

I was kidding myself. The nights were getting worse. Not talking to Jack. I hadn't realized how important our conversations had become. Walking the dogs didn't make me tired enough to fall asleep, so the tossing and sweating and turning increased. I really needed my friend.

Hey, are you online by any chance? I am sorry I cut you off like that. Can we talk again? I need your straight thinking.

Nothing. Par for the course. I had cut him off. Oh, well.

I was just about to shut my laptop and take some melatonin, when I heard the "bing."

Not a problem. No need to apologize. Life sucks, doesn't it?

OK, then. Here goes:

You keep encouraging—no—pushing me—to have a heart to heart with my mother. If I tell Mom what I saw, what if she gets defensive? What if she denies it? Calls me a liar or worse?

This is your mother. She knows you. She won't think you are lying, because you don't lie, plus why on earth would anyone make up a story like this about a person they love? She might get defensive, you are right there. So give her the room to do that,

and don't get all in her face about this. Just try to have a calm discussion. Try.

Thanks. You are such a great friend, Jack. I will keep you posted if I have the guts to tell her. Talk soon.

No better time than the present.

I sat up and felt the sweat drops roll from my armpits down my sides to the waistband of my boxers.

Tea. Chamomile. That might help. I rolled off the bed and walked over to the window to look out at the sky. Two lonely stars. Or planets. They looked the same to me. I put my palms on the smooth glass and wished on them (please help me get this off my chest, please, please). I motioned for Herkie to get up and come down with me, but no luck. So I tiptoed down the stairs.

There was a light on in the kitchen. When I entered, Mom looked up at me. Her hair stood up in back like porcupine quills, her eyes droopy. There were mascara tracks down her cheeks. The veins on her hands looked inky and swollen. Nevertheless, she smiled at me. "Couldn't sleep, either?"

"Nope. It's getting humid—summer is coming, all right. I am all sticky. We should get an AC unit for the attic, before it really gets hot out there." I reached for a mug, opened the tea caddy, and pulled out a chamomile tea bag.

"There is hot water in the kettle. I just boiled some for myself." She held up her mug. "Mint. It settles my stomach."

I poured the scalding water over my tea bag and watched as the tea leaves swelled and steeped. "Chamomile. Maybe it will help me go to sleep. It never does. I think chamomile is overrated, but I keep giving it one more chance."

Mom sipped her tea. The purple of her eyelids looked like makeup. Mom never wore eye shadow. "Honey, what's keeping you up? I can't sleep for thinking about the wedding. Imagining how it might be. It takes my mind off missing Sam, but I am not getting enough sleep." She slid a notepad towards me. "Lists. I am making lists—you know, suggestions for when we start planning in earnest." She ran her index finger over the cuticle of her thumb. "I just wish Sam were here to share this with me. She would have loved all of it. I miss her so much."

I glanced at her latest list. "Right. Planning a wedding. 'To love, honor and cherish.' Right up her alley."

Mom looked up at me, her eyes wide. "What?"

I felt something inside of my head let go. The words gushed out like the air from a pricked balloon. "What does marriage mean to gay women? Is it different for you? I know marriage wasn't an option for a long time. So gay couples—do you all just make up your own rules about relationships?"

She nearly dropped her tea, but managed to set it down on the table without spilling any. "Tommy, what is your point? You seem upset. Don't think I haven't noticed that something has been bothering you for weeks. I see you staring off into space and frowning. Brooding when you think I won't see it. What have I done? What are you driving at? What do you mean about 'rules'?I hate having you like this."

This was it. IT. **No better time than the present.** I felt as if my heart would explode out of my chest. I put my hand over it to hold it in. "Mom. Fidelity. Monogamy. You know, the idea that if you are 'married,' or 'partners' with somebody, you don't go outside of that relationship for sex?"

Her eyes left my face, and she looked beyond me, staring at the wall as if to forget I was sitting beside her, uneasiness seeping out of my pores. Her nose began to run and a single droplet hung on her nostril. She ignored it.

I had gone over this in my mind. I explored it in my heart. I recited it in my head. It flayed my nerves. But Jack was right. This heaviness had been bearing down on my soul for twenty-three years. It had woven its way into my veins, pulsing with every heartbeat. I had to rip it out and wave it in the air.

The dogs must have heard us down there. They danced into the kitchen, grinning and shambling. When they saw Mom at the table, they thought it was party time, and began to wag, jump, and whine for treats.

"SIT. For heaven's sakes, sit DOWN!" I waved my arms at them. They stopped wriggling, ducked their heads, and slunk out of the kitchen, for the first time looking fearful in their submission.

A look of alarm crossed her face. "Tommy, what is it? You never speak to the dogs that way. Are you all right?"

I reached over, pulled out a chair and sank into it heavily, me and my damn emotional boulder. "Mom. I want to talk about something."

She nodded, her eyebrows in a knot of concern. "Honey." She reached out to touch my arm, but I pulled back.

My breathing became difficult. It took me a good ten seconds or so to get it under control. I put my palm on my chest to steady myself and began. "I saw them. Sam and Leah. I have known about Mommy all along."

She bit her lip. "What do you mean? Tommy. What on earth are you saying?"

I licked my lips. They were so dry. "Leah Nash. I have always hated her."

Mom's cheeks lost their color. She wrapped her arms around her chest as if in a cold wind.

"I was ten years old. Do you remember when I had strep when you were out of town? It doesn't matter if you do or not. Because that Saturday has been smothering me ever since. *I saw them.*"

Mom shut her eyes.

She looked sick. I wanted to shake her. "Why? Why did Mommy do it? How could she betray us? How did you live with it, with the fact that she was screwing this woman? My God, she came to the funeral!"

She opened her eyes and turned to me. She put both hands on her thighs and straightened her spine. There was spittle in the corners of her mouth as she spoke. "I need to know what you saw. Tell me, Tommy!"

"I came downstairs because I heard voices. I thought you were home, and I was so happy. They didn't see me, because they were so absorbed in each other. They were kissing. They were *slobbering* all over one another at the door. Kissing goodbye after having sex, with me in the house. They had been *fucking*."

It was as if I had slapped her. She recoiled, a look of agony on her face. "Oh, Tommy! Why didn't you speak up? How did you live with this? I am so sorry. Oh, Tommy. This has been eating away at you, and if only you had said something..."

"And what? You would have told me that it is OK for Mommy to have sex with others? That you had an open marriage? Do you think that would have helped? Do you know that after that my biggest fear was that Mommy would leave us? That the two of us would be alone? Do you know how hard I tried to make Mommy love me more than Leah, so that she wouldn't abandon us?" I tried to keep from screaming, but my voice echoed in my ears.

She thrust her hands out in front of her chest. "Stop! Tommy. Stop! Shut up and listen to me!"

I covered my mouth and gasped into my hand, my tears warm against my cheeks.

"Let me remind you of something you may have forgotten. Dr. Creighton—Joanna Creighton. She was a partner in Sam's practice. Specialized in exotics. She fought depression, apparently her entire life. Sam didn't know this—Joanna masked it well at the clinic. But Tommy, that was the year she committed suicide. It was horrendous. She injected herself with Pentobarbitol, the drug kept there for euthanasia. Tommy, Sam discovered Joanna's body."

I moved a little closer to Mom. She tried to smile but failed; she winced.

"Sam blamed herself. She 'should have noticed.' She 'should have reached out.' It didn't matter that there was nothing she could have done—she and Joanna weren't friends. They were simply co-workers. Joanna had only been with the practice for a year, and you may remember that there were four veterinarians, it was a busy practice, and they didn't all work the same hours. There was no way Sam could have prevented this. But she took personal blame for it because she owned the practice—it was 'her responsibility' she said. Patients started leaving the practice in droves. You know – it was creepy to them, having their vet do such a thing. Sam had to hire a new vet and do all sorts of PR to calm down all the remaining clients, to reassure them that her doctors were not a bunch of mentally unstable people. She worried about losing the practice. Tommy, she had a breakdown. Do you remember the nights she would come home and just go to bed? The weekends she spent just sitting with a book in her lap, not reading but just staring?"

"Yes." It was a whisper.

"I tried everything to help her. She resisted going to a therapist, but when she did go, it wasn't effective. Our friends were a Godsend. They sent food, had parties. You probably don't remember any of this. A little kid wouldn't. You had your own life, your childhood to experience. We tried to shield you from all of it. She pretended in front of you. She thought she could spare you from the trauma she had experienced. We thought it worked. We thought we could keep all of it away from our little girl. Obviously, we were wrong."

She paused and took a breath. "But one of our friends took it upon herself to 'take care of Sam' in her own, immoral way. Leah had always had a crush on Sam; that was obvious to all of us. She used this harrowing time to swoop in and 'comfort' Sam. Sam was so vulnerable, and all of the platitudes I threw her way were not having an effect on her psyche. Sam was withering away. So Leah used her body to make Sam forget herself."

I shuddered. "Bitch."

Mom put out her hand to touch my cheek. "Oh, Tommy. If only I had known what you saw. If only I could have explained things to you." She stroked my face. It felt like feathers on my skin. "You tried to make Sam love you more. Oh, honey, she couldn't possibly have loved you any more than she did."

"But why did she do it? She betrayed us. She tore my soul to bits. That never went away." I slammed my hand over my heart.

"Tommy, if only I could go back in time. But Sam and I didn't know what you saw! We thought we had a problem between the two of us. We never even dreamed that it had sifted down to your level; that it affected our child. We worked so hard to put on a 'good face' for you at home. I said that, didn't I? Sam and I had a hard time after that; although Leah was just a passing thing; I wouldn't even classify it as an 'affair.' She was a temporary salve for Sam's grief and guilt. Sam regretted that; she and I worked through it. We thought we were home free—that our tight little family was unsullied by all of this. I was able to forgive Leah in my own way. Oh, Tommy. You knew. You *knew*."

Mom had curled her fingers into her palms so hard that they left white crescents. "You have suffered so much and so long, and for no real reason. You were wounded. The adults in your life failed you completely. I am so sorry."

I rubbed my temples, thrumming like harp strings. "I thought it was my fault. That the reason Mommy was with Leah was that we weren't good enough. That *I* wasn't lovable enough, or maybe a disappointment as a daughter." I slumped into the revelation. "I thought when I told you this, you would get furious. Maybe tell me I was a liar. I thought you would hate me for tattling on Mommy. This is why I have never said anything. I was terrified inside that you would leave, too. I didn't know what would happen to me – where I would end up."

Mom wiped her nose. Her head dropped to her chest for a second, then she regained herself with a deep breath.

She opened her arms, and I folded myself into them. "Tommy, I love you. I don't blame you for anything." She kissed my eyelids, her lips against my tears. "You and I, we are both survivors of this thing. And you know what? We will get over it together. This is why you are here with me; this is why you came to stay—now it all makes sense. You had to garner the strength to tell me this, finally. This is our year to heal."

"You aren't furious with me? That I just vomited this whole story out? No warning? You still love me as much as before?"

"Oh, my darling girl. You think telling a truth would cause me to stop loving you? To be angry at that little, defenseless ten-year old child? Never. Never!"

I believed her. We sat, wrapped around one another, mother and daughter. For the first time since I was a sick and terrified ten year old, my heart, my guts, my brain, my blood, and my nerves let go, and I relaxed into the loving arms of my dearest remaining parent.

I padded up the stairs an hour later, my eyes finally dry. My muscles sagging in relief. My computer, still open on my bed, beckoned. I had one more thing to do before sinking into what I hoped would be a blissful, healing sleep. I balanced on the edge of the bed, the laptop on my knees.

Hi. I can't thank you enough. Long story. There was a death by suicide. I was only dimly aware of it...

Chapter Twenty-Eight

Π

The tension in the air was like electricity. Suze left the house, a sheaf of notes in her purse, at three o'clock. She was going over to Trudy's early enough to go over, one final time, the notes for the meeting and the last entreaty for Dana to refrain from losing control.

As soon as she left, Percy showed up, wondering if it was OK to wait with us to see what happened. I waved him in. None of us could sit still. Percy fidgeted, running his fingers up and down his thighs, walking from one living room window to the next. Mom couldn't seem to relax either, as she sorted and resorted the magazines on the coffee table. I wanted to jump out of my skin.

"Guys. The meeting is at four. God knows how long it will last. If we keep up with this pacing and twitching, we'll drop from exhaustion before Suze gets back. Let's try to settle down, shall we?"

Percy grunted and plopped down in the nearest chair. Mom stood up, looking at her watch. "Tommy, you're right. Come on, Percy. Let's keep busy. We can make some chocolate chip cookies. Suzanne will probably need some carbohydrates after the ordeal."

As Percy and Mom rustled around in the kitchen, I tried to imagine all the possible outcomes of the meeting. Would Dana be expelled? Would Jill? Or would they have to do some sort of penance project, like cleaning the restrooms with toothbrushes? Would this go on their permanent records? Do permanent records really exist? And do colleges like Harvard or even Ohio State look at them?

The more I imagined outcomes, the more apprehensive I became. At four fifteen, the living room darkened suddenly. I looked out of the window—the sky had turned slate gray, and a stiff breeze had kicked up. The lilac bushes at the corner of the house swayed in the gusts. Of course. An omen. A spring storm was brewing. After all, tornado season in Ohio begins in May. This might just be an early one. I felt the vibration of distant thunder, followed by a boom that sounded very close by.

I smelled cookies and followed the scent into the kitchen, just as a bolt of lightning lit up the sky. "Do you think this is an omen?"

Percy took off his oven mitt and peered out the window. Another crack of thunder.

Mom rattled dishes in the sink. "Let's not be superstitious. It's the usual spring storm. It was predicted. We are just Nervous Nellies! Only three more minutes, and we can each have a cookie to steady our nerves."

"Mom, that's a good idea. Here, I'll start a pot of coffee to go with them."

The cookies were meltingly warm and delicious. We each had two. The coffee may not have been a good idea, what with the caffeine. My nerves jangled at a slightly higher frequency after I finished my mug. I set it down on the table, and stared at Mom and Percy, drumming my fingers on the tabletop. They stared right back.

Mom got up. "This is ridiculous. Let's go in and see what's on TV. Isn't The Price is Right on, or maybe Let's Make a Deal? Or maybe Ellen?"

We trooped into the sunroom and sure enough, there was a woman trying to roll some dice two times to add up to six in order to win a Mazda. She lost. The big deal of the day was a trip to Australia. Mom remarked that she wished we were all down under right about now. Ellen came on, and she danced through the audience. Her guest was Timberlake or Justin Bieber; you know, one of the Justins; I wasn't paying close attention. Ellen was pretty funny, but I only laughed once. Percy bit his nails during the entire show, and Mom stared into space. Grueling.

At five-thirty, the front door opened. The three of us jumped up and jostled one another like Keystone Cops as we tried to get through the archway into the front hall. The dogs clamored down the steps to greet Suze, licking the raindrops off her ankles. We were all out of breath.

She stood there, umbrella dripping, hair plastered to her head. Her expression was unreadable.

Mom clucked at her. "Suzanne! Put your umbrella in the rack and come into the kitchen. I have towels in there—you look soaked. Oh, and we made cookies. Come on, we want to hear all about it."

We herded into the kitchen. Mom pulled some tea towels out. Suze rubbed her face and hair with them. Percy poured more coffee, and we crowded around Suze at the table. It was like an interrogation, but with Martha Stewart overtones.

"Here. This one has lots of chocolate chips. Do you want milk or cream in your coffee? So what was it like? Did Dana behave herself?" Mom started the onslaught.

"Did they raise their voices at Dana? Was that Jill girl remorseful? What about her parents? Were they sorry for what their daughter did? What did the superintendent do?" Percy hammered out his queries like a TV cop.

I spoke over both Percy and Mom. "What's the punishment? Will they get expelled or anything? What about the other girls who wore the shirts? Are they going to be punished, too? How come they didn't have to show up for this meeting?"

It was too much for Suze. She put her thumb and forefinger between her lips and issued an ear-splitting whistle. It shut us up. Sidebar: I want to learn how to do that.

As soon as we shut up, Suze began. "It is a long story, and I will attempt to answer all of your questions, as long as you don't interrupt me. There will be a question and answer session at the end of my remarks. Do we understand?"

The three of us nodded. The dogs ate cookie crumbs off the floor.

"Attending the meeting were Trudy, Dana, and me. Jill. Angie Baker's mom, Sheryl. I didn't know this, but there is no Mr. Baker; they separated pretty recently, I guess. The principal, Mr. what's his face, was there, along with Superintendent Judy Flood, whom I now want to nominate for the Nobel Peace Prize. The guidance counselor put her face into the doorway, but was waved off. Also there was Dee Dee Bolton. Mr. Bolton was a no-show." Suze put her hands under her boobs and lifted them up and out. "Dee Dee is just what I expected: Fiftyish, stuffed like a sausage into her Lululemons, and enough makeup to sink a ship. Blond hair, black roots." Percy reached up and touched his toupee.

"She kept a protective hand on her daughter's arm during almost the entire meeting. Blood red fingernails. Fake."

Percy massaged his temples. I slid another cookie over to him. "Go on."

"It all started out predictably. The principal, what's his name; I don't even care—pontificated for the first five minutes about the 'zero tolerance for bullying' policy, the 'fine reputation of this school,' and the need for 'more discipline.' Then, Judy Flood—I want to be her new best friend—took over. She shut the principal up with one wave of her hand. Then she asked Jill to tell her side of the story."

I put a finger in my mouth and pretended to gag.

"Jill, often interrupted by her mother, basically said the whole thing was 'just a joke,' and nobody meant anything by it. The girls made the T-shirts at the Bolton's house under the supervision of Real Housewife Dee Dee, who offered up her opinion that this whole thing was just an innocent prank that got blown way out of proportion." Suze put her hand over Percy's. "She also stated that 'these kids,' and she was referring to Angie, 'need to get a thicker skin, because the real world is a cruel place.' I wanted to grab the letter opener off the desk and stab her with it, but I managed not to."

Suze took a break to sip her coffee. "Judy Flood cut Dee Dee and Jill off and asked Dana for her side of the story. This is where things got interesting. I had my fingers crossed that she wouldn't react to Jill and her mom and just blast us, but you would be so proud of Dana Stryker."

Mom clapped her hands. "What did she say?"

"First of all, Dana stood up. This immediately gave her the advantage. It was a brilliant strategy, and I didn't come up with it. Dana just knew what she was doing."

Suze stood to demonstrate. "Dana walked over to the principal and pulled up the sleeve of her T-shirt." Suze used Percy as a model and held her forearm out to him. 'Do you see these scars? These are burns. From a cigarette. They were bestowed upon me by my aunt. She was 'taking care' of me after my parents were killed. She decorated me with these whenever I fussed too much. I was three years old.' I am paraphrasing here, of course. To his credit, principal Mish-mash gasped. Dee Dee—by the way, I bet her middle name is Krystal – and Jill just sat there, looking defensive."

Suze sat back down. "Dana told the group her story. About being removed from her aunt's custody, only to be shuffled around from foster home to foster home, some of them more horrific than the others, but all of them losing patience with Dana because she was 'too strong willed.' She defended herself, and that didn't go down with these fosters. Dana told us how she finally ended up with Trudy. This was the best part. Dana asked everyone to look at Trudy's face. 'See those scars? Can't miss them. Burns from a pot of scalding water that she pulled off the stove when she was just a toddler. And guess what? People have been calling her things like Frankenstein her whole life. Out there,' and Dana pointed a finger right in Dee Dee's face—'in the real world.' It was *awesome,* you all."

Suze paused to take a breath. "Dee Dee interrupted Dana and asked what this had to do with her daughter, and Dana crucified her. She said something like 'it has everything to do with your daughter and her gang of bitches, because it is people like them who make life for people like us Hell on earth."

Suze pounded the table. "She crushed them like a fly."

I started to say something, but Suze knew where I was going. "I know. Judy Flood asked Dana to sit down. Then she asked the obvious question. 'Why, then, did you use your social media influence to make life miserable for Jill and her group?' Apparently, they received death threats."

It was Mom's turn to gasp. "Death threats? I didn't know this!"

Suze nodded. "So. There we were. Two bullies. One who is just a terrible bitch, who was egged on by her mother; and the other a defender of the oppressed, who went too far."

Percy, at this point, was pale. Beads of sweat ringed his toupee. I wondered if he might be having a medical emergency. He patted his temples with a napkin, then blew his nose with it. "Tell us what the punishment is. I can't take much more of this."

Suze's face softened. "Percy, I am so sorry. I'll get to the point. As I said before, that Judy Flood is a genius. Principal Googah began to bluster around about having a school wide assembly with formal apologies. Flood put a stop to that. She had such a good take on all this. She told us that the only way for bullying to end was for all of the parties involved to come together. She then came up with the absolutely most creative solution. She said that she would give them until the end of the school year to come up with a project to work on together during the summer. A project that would focus on helping others—those who are misunderstood. The end of the school year is what, May 25? This gives them about a month. Oh, yeah. The three of them are to work on this project together: Dana, Jill, and Angie. They are to write a report about what they did and what they learned to turn in at the beginning of the school year."

"And the other T-shirt girls, too?" I asked.

"No. Since they were 'manipulated' by Jill, they get off with just the two-week suspension. The project is just for the two perps and Angie."

I was confused. "Why Angie?"

Suze lifted her brows, eyes wide. "That's the wonder of it all. Bullies and victims. They work together, and those distinctions disappear."

Mom twirled her coffee mug. "But do you think poor Angie will want to do this? It seems like they should leave her out of this."

"I know what you mean. But just think about it. Angie has spent her whole life thinking of herself as a helpless victim. Dana thinks of herself as a victim, too, but she took on the mantle of a superhero. They are all just people. Judy Flood has given them the opportunity to see themselves differently. I just can't get over it."

"Neither can I. I just hope we survive the summer."

Suze smiled. "Oh yeah. I forgot. Dana asked me to tell you that she is sorry, and it's OK for us and the dogs to come over. She says she needs a posse."

I looked around the room. "Mom, where did you put my cowboy hat?"

Π

"I have been emailing Judy Flood. It is her suggestion that the meeting about the summer project be on neutral territory. No parentals. So it's going to be here, naturally." We sat at the kitchen table, watching Mom chop vegetables for stir-fry.

Mom paused, ginsu knife pointing at the ceiling. "Here?" She gulped.

"Mom. Do you have any other suggestions?"

Suze, who was busy looking at her cell phone, glanced first at me, then at Mom. "I will keep the confrontational horror to a minimum. I promise."

Mom put down her knife and wiped her hands on her apron. "I have to admit that I would like to meet this Jill character. If nothing else, so I can give her a piece of my mind."

"HA! Me, too." I gave the airspace in front of me a one-two punch.

I thought Suze might reach over and rip one of my ears off or something. "So the people I will have to control in this 'confrontational' environment are you and Meg? Holy Hell."

Mom held her hands out in supplication. "I promise to be on my best behavior. Honestly. And what about you, Tommy? Do you think we can handle this?"

I raised my hands over my head like a detainee about to be frisked. "I promise. I will put three sticks of Juicy Fruit into my mouth right before the meeting. That will make it hard for me to speak clearly. And I was just pretending about punching Jill. Now Dee Dee, that could be another story."

Suze shut off her phone, stood up and grabbed a carrot from the cutting board, crunching it as she left the room. She seemed in quite a hurry to leave the two of us behind.

"Oh, boy. Maybe this isn't such a good idea. What if we end up with some sort of free for all at this meeting? What if Dana does something else to Jill? Tommy, what shall we do about this?" Mom put her knife down and leaned against the counter.

I stood my ground, figuratively, as I was seated at the table measuring out hoisin sauce. "Listen. It is meant to happen. And you, Suze, and I will be at this meeting. I think between all of us, we can hold Dana down if she tries to attack anybody. Suze knows we were kidding about yelling and hitting people. Maybe it is fate, bringing this whole group of people together. Everything happens for a reason. Kismet? Karma?"

"Honestly, Tommy. You sound like Oprah." Mom turned back and chopped some celery with way too much ferocity. The dogs looked up from the floor where they had sprawled, sensed that food was being prepared, and scrambled over to Mom, who gave them each a piece of carrot. Saylor ate hers, and when Herkie refused to even try hers, Saylor ate that piece, too.

I took a carrot and left the three of them to commiserate.

Chapter Twenty-Nine

Π

The first one to show up to the meeting was Dana. "My knees are knocking, and I might throw up. I wish parents were invited. I need Trudy." Mom brought her two Tums and I pushed her down onto the sofa. "Take deep breaths, kiddo. And remember your inside voice." Dana looked wildly around for the dogs.

"They are banished to the yard. We can't have any distractions." Dana heaved a sigh.

Angie arrived next, her timid knock on the door almost inaudible. Suze ushered her into the living room, where she sat as close to Dana as she could. She was so pale that every freckle on her face was magnified, her scar livid.

A car door slammed. Suze glanced out the window. "Here she comes. Cleansing breaths, everybody."

I opened the door. There stood a sturdy blonde girl, about five foot seven, shoulder length hair pulled back in a narrow, royal blue headband. Long, French manicured nails. Enough mascara to sink a ship. She wore skin-tight torn jeans, a black tank top, and silver hoops the size of extra large onion rings. She swayed back and forth to whatever music that emanated out of her earbuds. I took an instant dislike to just about everything about her. I motioned for her to come in.

Jill breezed into the living room and flung her ass into a seat beside Mom on the sofa. She rolled her eyes, pushed the earbuds deeper into her ears, and crossed her legs, her flip-flops flapping.

Suze, Dana, and Angie sat across from them. I perched on the edge of the ottoman Mom had pulled up to the grouping, wishing Suze hadn't put the kibosh on violence.

Suze cleared her throat and began. "Everybody. Before we get started, let me make sure we know who is who." She pointed to me. This is Tommy Poole. She is my good friend." She indicated Mom. "This is Meg Poole. This is her house." Suze took a huge breath. "My God. JILL! TAKE OUT YOUR EARBUDS!"

Jill, startled by the shout-out, grabbed her ear buds and yanked them out of her ears. She cocked her head and blew a bubble.

I watched as Suze clasped her hands tightly, her face turning shades of first pink, then a sort of ruddy plum, and finally purple. I wondered if her declaration of confrontation control would go up in flames along with her complexion. She took a few cleansing breaths, unclasped her hands to run her fingers through her curls, and having regained control, began. "So, we are assembled to discuss potential summer projects. We all want to hear what you have come up with. Which one of you wants to go first?"

Dana raised her hand. "What about something to do with pit bulls? You know, something to help undo the stereotype that they are mean?"

Jill yawned. "I hate dogs."

I was relieved that we had decided to keep the dogs out back for the duration of the meeting.

Suze shifted in her seat. Mom cut in. "Does anyone want a cookie? Chocolate chip walnut. I made them this morning." Jill looked at them on the plate and wrinkled her nose.

"I am allergic to walnuts."

Angie reached out and took a cookie. Her voice wavered. "I love walnuts." She took a small bite and twirled the cookie between her fingers as if her life depended on it.

Suze kept the pressure up. "So, Jill. You hate dogs. What did you have in mind, then, for the project?"

Jill stared back at Suzanne, blankly. "I didn't think of anything. I thought you were going to tell us what to do. Like all adults."

Dana began to jerk out of her seat, but Angie dropped her cookie into her lap and held out her arm to stop her. Dana retreated. I sighed.

"Angie? Do you have any ideas?"

Angie picked the cookie out of her lap and set it on the table. She wiped nonexistent crumbs off her thighs. An apparent stall tactic. She blinked rapidly. "I talked with my mom about this. We like the idea of volunteering in a soup kitchen. But the nearest one of those is in Columbus. I guess there aren't that many hungry people in Framington, because it's so small. Then we looked into the blood bank, but to work there, you have to be at least sixteen, because of liability. We thought about Goodwill, but they have the same rule about being sixteen."

There was an awkward silence. "Dana?" Suze asked.

"Nada. I was so sure that the dog thing was a good idea, I didn't come up with anything else."

Suze glowered. "This meeting was a waste of everybody's time. We will reconvene one week from today. And if none of you can come up with something that you three can agree on, I WILL. Four thirty, next Wednesday. No earbuds."

Jill smirked and took out her phone. She pushed a button and barked into the phone, "Come back and pick me up. This whole thing was a disaster!"

"Angie, do you need transportation?" I asked.

"Oh, no. My mom is waiting for me at Starbucks. I can walk there."

The girls filed out, Dana tossing a beseeching look in our direction before shutting the door behind her. We sat in stunned silence. I passed around the plate of cookies. "I assume none of you are *allergic* to walnuts?"

Mom took a cookie, but sat, staring at it.

Suze laid herself out on the sofa and closed her eyes. "Jesus, Mary and Joseph. Someone call me an ambulance."

I grabbed two cookies and headed upstairs. "I need to take a long, restorative bath. Call me if you hear that Dana has murdered anybody."

Eating cookies in hot bath water is not only calming, it encourages introspection. I watched the chocolate chip I had dropped into the water slowly dissolve, and I wondered what I would have done if I were Dana. I shut my eyes and drifted back into middle school. Gym class. Volleyball. Tilly Lewis. Tilly the Hun, as I liked to think of her. She had caramel colored hair and blue eyes with long eyelashes. Boys followed her around like puppies. She had a devastating smile. And she was cruel.

It was her turn to serve the ball, and instead of sending it over the net, she spiked it onto the back of my head, sending me crashing to the boards. The skin on my kneecap split open, and blood smeared all around me, and I slipped in it trying to get up. The other girls swarmed around me, but Tilly just stood back, smiling, one hand over her left eye. "It was an accident. I got something in my eye, all of a sudden." She flashed her smile at Mr. Davenport, the gym teacher. Of course, he absolved her of any evil intent.

In the locker room after class, as we went into the showers, Tilly leaned over and whispered to me, "Sorry, not sorry, *Butch.*"

As soon as I got out of the tub and dried off, I threw on a robe, padded into my room, and logged onto Reddit.

Hey. Are you online?

What's up?

Traumas. We just carry them with us all the time, don't we? Even when we think we are over them?

Yes and no. In my case, the trauma was much diluted with therapy and maturity. But it's PTSD. Things trigger it. I told you I don't go inside churches any more. God isn't in those buildings. But this isn't about me. What is activating your anxiety right now?

Remember Dana, the girl I told you about?

An hour later, my head cleared, I logged off. Thank God for this man. This understanding, brilliant friend, out there in the ether.

Π

Esme and Rob dropped in unexpectedly. Esme with a bottle of wine in each hand, Rob holding two extra large pepperonis with extra cheese from Rinaldo's. The best pizza in town. This was an incredible treat because Rinaldo doesn't deliver. The three of us were so glad to see them, as were the dogs, who licked everyone and then retired to the sunroom to resume their naps.

All the windows in the dining room were open. The cross ventilation was divine. "Let's use paper plates!" Mom suggested. This was another incredible thing, as Mom is a slave to proper table settings.

Rob sat at the head of the table. Mom sat at the other end. I sat alone on one side, feeling a bit at a loose end, and Suze and Es sat across from me. I burned my mouth on my first bite of pizza, and cheese stuck to my chin, but I didn't even care. My soul and my nerves needed cheese, tomato sauce, and grease. After a couple of slices of pizza and as many glasses of wine, we were all pretty mellow.

"So, beautiful people, have you set a date yet?" I pulled one more slice out of the box and removed the pepperoni. I always eat the pepperoni first. Yes, I also bisect the Oreos and lick the icing before crunching the wafers. I am a true American.

Es sipped her wine. The refractions from her diamond were blinding. "Not really. But we have an idea. This is why we came over." She looked at Rob for encouragement. He gave her the go signal with a grin. "Meg, we thought that this might be the perfect way to celebrate both our nuptials and the anniversary of the 'recluse project.' August 27 falls on a Saturday this year. What do you think of having the wedding that day?"

Mom held up her wine. "I think it is the most perfect ending to our year of solitude, ever! I would like to propose a toast to happy endings."

Suze picked up her glass, and then set it down again. "I think we might be jinxing things to toast to happy endings. We don't know how the whole Dana/Jill/Angie bully thing will end, and we are smack dab in the middle of that one."

"Pick up your glass, Suze. We'll toast to good luck, then." When Suze didn't react fast enough, I picked up her glass and forced it into her hand. "Come on, sport! TO GOOD LUCK. TO WEDDINGS. TO THE BULLIES, THE DEFENDERS, AND US—THE SUPPOSED GROWNUPS."

"Speaking of those girls, did they come up with an appropriate punishment?" Rob asked.

Suze folded the cover over the pizza box. Rob stood and refilled everyone's wine glass. Suze swirled the wine in her glass like a pro. "Rob, not a punishment. The suspension is the punishment. They have to come up with a project that the three of them can work on."

Es pushed her paper plate away. "If I eat one more slice, I will bloat. Sorry, so what is the project?"

Suze looked disgusted. "They came up with nothing. Dana wanted to do something with pit bulls..." as she spoke, Suze snuck a crust to Saylor, who sat at Suze's feet underneath the table. "But darling Jill 'hates dogs.' So that was a veto. Each girl gets one veto, so Jill is stuck with whatever they come up with next. Angie, the only one who put any thought into it at all, researched working with homeless people or Goodwill, but all the jobs, even the volunteer ones, have an age requirement, and none of the girls are sixteen."

I jumped in. "We set up another meeting, and emphasized the importance of each of them actually coming up with viable ideas. I am not holding my breath on that one."

Mom began to collect the plates to clear up. "Let's all go sit in more comfortable chairs, shall we? I'll just put the leftover pizza in the fridge, and leave the rest for later. Go on!'

It was the gloaming. That magical dusk when streetlights begin to switch on, the shadows gather around the trees like soft blankets, and the birds chitter in the branches as they settle down for the night. I switched on the lamp in the corner. The soft glow made us all look at least five years younger. We were full, buzzing a little from the wine. I looked at the group and my heart swelled with benevolence. "Rob and Es, this is so exciting. I know it will be a fantastic wedding. We can help you with it, of course. Right, guys? Do you have a venue?"

Esme's face clouded. She set her glass down and scowled. "This is the issue. If we want to have the wedding on the 27th, which we are determined to do, for you all," she drew her brows together, "we are stymied on a venue, because if you want to get married, the thing to do is *plan ahead.* The venues that we want all book up about a year in advance."

My darling and magnanimous mother held up her glass once again. "Then let's have it here. Lord knows, we three have nothing better to do than plan a wedding. It's not like we are going anywhere. We can do it in the backyard. Tents! And if it rains, we'll just move it inside." She looked at me and Suze for affirmation. We raised our glasses in sync.

Esme took a sip, squealed, and nearly knocked Rob over climbing over to us in order to squeeze us one by one in fierce hugs. Suze's smile gleamed. Mom tutted. Esme sat back down and surveyed the three of us. "Are you sure about this? It is not as if any of you have wedding planning experience."

My fingers actually tingled. Every single gear in my brain turned, and a few of them jammed. I tried to picture a crowd of people, all of them raising the inside temperature with their collective body heat, standing shoulder to shoulder in our living room, smiling and perspiring. I thought about how much rumaki we would have to make, and how in God's name we'd fit a DJ and all of his equipment in here if it rained. I pasted on a brave smile and said, "Nothing I like more than a challenge. We are totally up to this." I was, of course, lying.

Esme turned to Rob with a radiant smile. "Robbie, doesn't that sound like a perfect solution?" She kissed him on the ear and turned back to us. "We don't want a big wedding. About fifty people. Is your house big enough? Are you sure?"

Mom did a quick neck roll, and I heard her vertebrae crack. So she was also feeling a titch stressed. But she held out her arms as if to embrace the world and said, "Fifty would be comfortable, inside. Certainly plenty of room for that many out in the backyard. So we will just hope for a dry day. August is known for being droughty in late August, so we just won't worry."

Esme and Rob seemed a little overwhelmed by the offer, but they both looked glowy. Rob's eyes glistened. "Es and I will think about it and let you know. It is so generous of you, Meg. What about your mom?"

Es waved an arm in a dismissive arc. "I will take care of Phyllis. No worries."

I rubbed my palms together. "I am going to order every single Bride magazine on Amazon. Hey, are there any HGTV shows about weddings? Is there an app for that?"

Suze grabbed for her cell. "I will download every wedding app I can find!"

"Let's just take our glasses into the sunroom and turn on the TV!" Mom stood and we followed her in. We had to shoo the dogs off the couches, and they got down reluctantly. Rob pulled a piece of beef jerky out of his pocket where he carried it at all times for protein purposes. He tore it in half and offered it to the dogs. They heartily appreciated it.

There were no wedding shows, but that didn't matter, as I reminded them about the forthcoming Bride magazines and all the apps that we would soon carry around on our phones. We spent the rest of the evening crowded around the television in the sunroom, watching House Hunters, followed by a few episodes of Love It Or List It. None of us could understand why granite countertops and stainless steel appliances are so necessary. If Mom said it once, she said it twenty times: "Two sinks in the bathroom? Hasn't anyone ever heard of getting ready one person at a time?"

Good times.

Chapter Thirty

Π

"Are we all ready for this meeting? Our emotions under control? Remembering that we are the adults?" Suze stood in front of us with a clipboard, her sleeveless white cotton blouse buttoned all the way up to her neck, Old Navy khakis crisply pressed, and black Danskos. She wore her black-rimmed half-glasses low on her nose. The entire effect was both professional and a bit intimidating. Mom and I nodded.

"Then let's have a group high-five."

Suitably pumped up, we awaited the girls' arrival. First to ring the bell was Angie. She entered, shoulders bowed, head down. Suze grabbed Angie and pulled her shoulders up. "Straight and confident, kid! Face 'em like a contender!"

Angie broke out into a meek smile, but marched into the living room, back straight as a ramrod. She took a seat on the sofa and crossed her hands in her lap. She sat totally still. I thought she resembled a mouse.

A loud thump on the door and Dana entered, a black bandanna around her forehead, in camo pants and black high top Chucks. We bumped fists, and she sat beside Angie.

We twiddled our thumbs for another ten minutes. Suze's complexion began to burn. Mom, standing sentinel at the window, finally announced, "There's a Jeep pulling up. Yes! It's Jill. Finally."

She swept in, the scent of Vera Wang Princess nearly knocking me down. No earbuds, but she was texting as she walked through the hall. Suze snatched the phone out of Jill's hands the second Jill stepped into the living room. "I'll return this after the meeting. Sit down." Suze sat and patted the empty space next to her.

Jill flipped her hair over her shoulder, made a nasty face at all of us, then sat down beside Suze with a simpering smile. "I am ready, dear leader."

Suze crossed her legs. "Ten minutes late. Not the best way to impress us with your sincerity." She cleared her throat. This is your last chance to come up with a plan for the summer. I sincerely hope that you have done your homework."

Jill smirked and whispered "What*ever*" under her breath.

Dana nearly exploded. "Shut the *fuck* up, you bitch! You don't care about any of this, you and your slutty mom. You are both scum!" She started to get up. Luckily, Angie was possessed of quick reflexes, and she put both arms out and grabbed her friend by her shoulders and pushed Dana back down into the cushions.

I felt a heart attack coming on.

Jill jumped up and put her hands out as if to ward off a punch. "Shut up! That's a big lie! And I don't have to stay here and listen to lies!" She turned to run out of the room, but Suze was faster. She followed Jill like a bullet and intercepted her in the doorway. "Nope! This is a mandatory meeting. Just sit down, Miss Bolton. And Dana, keep a civil tongue in your head, for God's sake."

Suze let us all sit in silence long enough for it to get awkward. She looked at us each in turn, as if to challenge us to dare to start anything. "Let's get started, shall we?" She pointed to Angie. "Angela, you may go first. What other ideas have you come up with?"

Angie took a strand of her baby fine hair and twirled it around her finger. She looked down at her lap as she said, "We could have a lemonade and cookie stand to raise money for a charitable cause. I love to bake."

Jill hooted. "That is about the lamest idea I have ever heard! How old did you say you were again, *five*?"

I thought the top of Dana's head might just blow off. "Shut the Hell up!" Angie put out a hand again and placed it firmly on Dana's thigh. "It's OK, Dana. Just ignore her."

A vein stood out on Angie's temple, and she gritted her teeth.

Jill continued, tossing her head. "I suppose we could go around and collect money for some charity. Like for retarded kids or something. I could see myself doing that."

Suze took off her glasses and glowered at Jill. "Do you know what you sound like, using a term like 'retarded'? You sound like a privileged brat. While collecting money for a charity for people who are *disabled* is worthwhile, I think it is too easy. I want the three of you to actually have to work together on something. To collaborate. To learn. This isn't something that you can just throw money at."

"So I am a brat. Who cares? This whole thing is stupid. The tees were a joke. You all are way too PC. Nobody cares about this but you and the dumbasses who run the school." She muttered, "just a bunch of pussies," under her breath, but we all heard it.

By this time, Angie was visibly trembling, Dana looked as if she had swallowed a rat, and the rest of us were paralyzed. Jill had one parting shot:

"Just pick a fucking project. I don't give a shit what it is. I'll do it because I have to. But don't expect me to be all goody-goody. And don't expect me or Mom to be like 'Oh, we are so sorry. Forgive us.' *Because nobody gives a shit about this but you.*"

Jill leaped off the sofa, sneered at us, held up her middle finger, and simply left. She stomped out, snatched her cell phone off the desk where Suze had put it, threw open the door, and slammed it behind her. We watched through the window as she threw herself down in the tree lawn, punched her phone, and sat waiting for her ride.

Angie remained planted in her seat, a glazed expression on her face. Dana, I swear, had steam issuing from her pores. Mom and I moaned in unison.

Suze sighed. "This is turning out well, isn't it?"

Π

Microwave popcorn is best eaten after a long dog walk, at one o'clock in the morning, sitting on the bed with your best friend, worrying.

"What about volunteering with the city, weeding flower beds or doing craft projects with the kids in the park?" Suze threw a kernel up in the air and caught it in her mouth, a trick I have never been able to master.

"Nope. They most likely would be separated to do different jobs. They have to work together." I gave it one more try, but the kernel missed my mouth by a mile, and Herkie caught it.

"Jesus, Mary, and Joseph." Suze finished the last unpopped kernel—those are the most delectable, by the way. She crumpled the popcorn bag and lobbed it into the wastebasket, where the dogs knocked it over and tore the bag into shreds. Suze shrugged. "I have Googled myself into a state of exhaustion over this, and I cannot come up with one blessed idea. The meeting, in which I announce the project to the 'three amigos,' is in two days. What in the world am I going to tell Judy Flood?"

We lay back on the bed and stared at the marks up there where I knelt on my top bunk (I loved those Daniel Tiger bunk beds) and wrote the F word a dozen times on the ceiling. Mommy dismantled the bunks, bought me a queen-sized bed, and called in a handyman to repaint the ceiling. But those red Sharpies were not to be vanquished, and a few months later, faint traces of my handiwork reappeared. "How about cooking classes?"

Suze twisted her cameo ring. A sure sign of frustration. "That won't work! How does learning how to make pound cake improve the lives of others? Who is helped by that?"

"We would be. Pound cake with strawberries and Cool Whip is my most favorite dessert."

Suze pounded her pillow. "Tommy, be serious. The girls are not going to harmoniously unify with a humdrum project. Jill is mutinous." She pounded her pillow again, this time sending it onto the floor with such velocity that both dogs left the room in a huff.

Time passed in complete silence, despite the wheels in my head turning so fast I thought they must certainly be audible.

Suze yawned.

Something exploded in my brain.

"OH MY FREAKING GOD. I have the solution!"

Suze twisted her ring some more. "Don't make jokes."

I sat up and tried not to shout. I was unsuccessful. "JUST CALL ME JUDY FLOOD, BECAUSE I AM A GENIUS! WE WILL HAVE THE GIRLS PLAN ROB AND ESME'S WEDDING."

Suze got off the bed and spun to look at me, a stunned expression on her face. Then she began to pump her arms like a cheerleader. "Go Tommy! Go Dana! Go Angie!" Then she stopped, mid cheer. I have never seen Suzanne Lampley smile like that. "Shitballs, Tommy! Do you realize what you just did? You came up with not only the perfect summer project, *but also you figured out how on earth we can produce this wedding! We don't have to do it alone! Helpers. There will be helpers!*" She paused and crossed her fingers. "Well, we can hope about Jill actually helping. That may be a stretch. But still. It's a great plan!" Suze began to shake imaginary pom-poms. "Tommy, Tommy, she's my man! If she can't do it, no one can!"

I got down off the bed. I put my hands on top of my head, to make sure it wasn't blown off with my stroke of Judy Flood genius. "We need some beer, we need Mom, and we need to have a strategy meeting, NOW."

"You realize it is almost two in the morning. I think this can wait until tomorrow."

I nodded.

Then Suze and I went into her bedroom and woke Mom up.

Chapter Thirty-One

Π

Bleary eyed, Mom sat on the edge of her bed, the few wisps of hair sticking up like straw. She rubbed her eyes. "Slow down, Tommy. What are you saying about the wedding?"

Suze and I sat on the loveseat tucked into the bay window. I could hardly contain my excitement, but I forced myself to slow down. "We need a project that the girls can work on together. Something that will 'help others and involve kindness.' This ticks both those boxes. The girls can plan the wedding. Since we are having the wedding here, the whole thing falls smack dab into our jurisdiction. The bride is transgender. Esme is also an LGBTQ litigator. If anyone is both misunderstood and represents misunderstood people, it's Es." I paused to catch a breath.

"By planning this wedding, Jill gets an opportunity to learn about gender discrimination, she learns why bullying is so destructive. And she will be right under our noses in case she needs to be brought into line. Of course, my dearest hope is that Jill, Dana, and Angie will magically reconcile. Not holding my breath there. But what could play into the hearts and minds of fifteen year old girls more effectively than planning a wedding? My God, the wedding dress alone!" I stopped and looked at Mom, who crinkled her nose and frowned.

"Tommy, have you even consulted Rob and Esme? Aren't you being awfully presumptuous?"

I had not even gone there. "Geez, Mom. You do have a point. But as you recall, Esme does not want her mom Phyllis involved, and we both know that Rob and Esme are workaholics. When will Es have the time or the inclination to plan her wedding? This seems like the perfect solution to me."

Suze hopped off the loveseat and began to pad around the room. "Flowers! My God. Percy can be in charge of the flowers, and Jill can work with him. Who better to reform a bully than a former bully?" She poked the air with a finger. "We can assign other areas of responsibility later, but the flowers thing—genius, no?"

I clapped.

Mom patted the bed, and the dogs jumped up beside her, circled twice as they do, and curled up into tight balls. As she stroked Herkie's ears, Mom continued. "Of course, we can't call Rob or Esme now. But before you get any more excited about all this, you have to get their approval. Their permission."

I nodded eagerly. "I will call them first thing in the morning."

Suze laughed and pointed out the window, where faint rosy light had started to appear over the horizon. "I do believe it is first thing in the morning in about ten minutes."

Mom fell back onto her sheets, tucking them around her shoulders. "Wait at least until seven to call them. I am going back to sleep, for heaven's sakes. Now shoo, all of you! Girls, you need to go lie down as well. None of us are young enough for all of this middle of the night nonsense!" And with that, Mom waved us out.

Suze and I returned to her room. I felt too excited to rest, but the popcorn and excitement had gotten to her. She opened the drawer of the nightstand, pulled out a bottle of Rolaids, and crunched on a few. "Ick, I hate how chalky these are."

Suze crawled onto the bed and closed her eyes. "Get out of here. Come and get me at seven. I want to listen to your end of the call."

Alone in the hall, I argued with myself. Should I go back to bed? Should I go down and see what was on TV? Should I take a shower?

Another brainstorm. I dashed into my room, grabbed my phone, and sent Rob and Esme each a text:

As soon as you wake up, call me. This is the first day of the rest of your lives, kids!

I sat on the top of the stairs and waited. I stared at my phone. I thrummed my fingers on the floor. I twitched.

Π

My cell beeped ten long minutes later. "Hello, Es?"

Esme sounded rushed. "Hey, girl, what is it? I have a deposition at eight this morning, and I need to go over some things. Why the crack of dawn text?"

I bounced up and down on the step. "Es. You know the saga of Dana, Jill and the bullying of the girl with the cleft palate, right?"

"Yeah, why?"

"Because they have until close of the school year, which is in two weeks, to come up with a mutual project to work on over the summer. One that will get them involved in helping others, focusing on a person or people who might be misunderstood. Like Angie, the one with the cleft palate."

"And? You want them to intern in my office? Sorry hon. No can do. They are just kids. They would be underfoot."

"No, no, Es. Better than that. I thought they could plan your wedding."

Silence.

"Wait. What? You want Rob and me to put the most important day of our lives in the hands of three renegade fifteen year olds with bullying issues?"

The phone shook in my hand. "Well, yes. But don't forget. The wedding is right here. Suze is the project overlord. There is a lot riding on this. This is an opportunity for you to get out from under all the pressure of planning this thing, which I know you don't have time for. It gets your mother off your neck. Really, Es. This is a win-win."

I heard a sharp intake of breath on Esme's end. "You are starting to convince me. Especially where it comes to Phyllis. Let me think about this. Don't call Rob."

"Why not? He needs to be in on the decision!"

Es chuckled. "Exactly. And as soon as he is done brushing his teeth, I will ask him."

Chapter Thirty-Two

Π

We thought it would be a good idea for all of us to get together to talk about my genius idea. Mom wasn't sure that Rob and Esme took in the full implications of having a trio of fifteen year olds plan such a huge milestone in their lives. The specter of Judy Flood and the Framington High School administration sat on Suze's shoulders like a yoke.

We invited Percy over as well, in hopes that as soon as he heard the flowers idea, he would be on board. It was a huge gamble—the flowers sort of make the wedding, if you know what I mean. And the prospect of pairing Percy and Jill was fraught, but Suze stood by that idea.

I felt I needed to do a sales pitch to win them over, so we assembled in the living room after a light dinner, wine glasses in hand. Rob looked relaxed, his dark swirls of hair untamed, a light stubble on his cheeks. He seemed carefree—at the moment. Es was her usual stunning self, in black leggings, a loose tangerine tank top tied at her waist, four-inch heels, and no makeup except for mascara. Her eyelashes were a mile long, my God. Percy's hair was on straight, but he had an uncharacteristic stain on the collar of his sport shirt, and he licked his lips nervously.

I started. "We have had a brainstorm which I think you all will agree is totally first-rate." The audience was rapt. "We are having the wedding here at the house, which we are all agreed will be beautiful." They continued staring at me.

"You are also all aware that our dear Dana has gotten herself into a bind by defending her friend, Angie Baker, from the bullying at school perpetrated by this Jill Bolton girl and her gang of thugs." Nods all around. "And you also know that they are required to come up with a project to work on together that will raise their awareness of why bullying is wrong, as well as hopefully bring the three of them together?" More nods, but this time I sensed a bit of skepticism, even on Rob and Esme's faces.

"Here is the idea. We think that the three girls should be in charge of planning the wedding." No more nods. Instead, resigned looks by Rob and Es, and a coughing fit on Percy's part. I waited for Percy to simmer down and continued.

"Nominally. In charge nominally. Of course, Mom, Suze and I will be the ultimate arbiters. And of course, Rob and Es make all the final choices. The girls will be right under our noses. And weddings are such girly things. How can they not get swept up?" I turned to Percy. "And Percy, we would be honored if you would consent to do the flowers for the wedding. We trust your good taste and talents. We would be thrilled, wouldn't we, Rob and Es, if you would consent to do them."

Percy's blush reached all the way to the edges of his ears. His Adam's apple bobbed as he swallowed, overcome with emotion. It took him a few seconds to get control, and then he exclaimed, "Oh, I would love to do the flowers. I am bowled over..." he swallowed again and put a hand over his heart, "it will be my privilege."

I knew I had him, so I launched in with the one potential deal breaker, while I had Percy overwhelmed. "Percy. As you know, the perpetrator of the original bullying incident in the cafeteria is Jill Bolton. She is sort of a problem child. We wanted to make sure that she is in good hands at all times as we go forward. So we thought that we would make her your assistant. Floral assistant." The ruddiness drained quickly out of his face. Oh, no. "Because, Percy, you will know exactly how to talk to her about her behavior and be a good role model." I cleared my throat. "Because you had such a turnaround yourself with us and the dogs." I looked around the room for support.

Mom sensed that I was starting to panic. She added, "Percy, you have gone from being our opponent to being our dear friend. Won't you see your way clear to help us on this?"

He pursed his lips and took a breath. Just one spot of red remained in the center of each of his cheeks. The rest of his complexion was waxy. He seemed to be torn; we could almost see the conflicting thoughts roiling around inside his head. He blinked a few times, rubbed his thighs with his palms, and then licked his lips. "I am not sure if I can do anything with that awful girl. I will try. But if she gives me any trouble, I will not be responsible. She will have to go. The flowers come first. But Rob, Esme. Do you approve of this arrangement?"

Rob took Esme's hand and put his finger over her diamond. "This Jill kid. Tommy says she has an attitude you can cut with a knife. Es, are you sure you want to deal with that sort of brattiness all summer?"

Esme uncrossed her legs and stood up. All six foot three of her, plus four inches of high heels. "Look at me, people." She ran her hands down her sides, just like those models on quiz shows. "This. Do you think for one minute that any fifteen year old tyrant stands a chance against *this?"* Es smiled beatifically as she slapped her palms together. Then she sat back down and kissed Rob's cheek.

"All right, then. Here is what I thought we would present to the girls. I want to make Dana the project manager—you know. A clipboard, a spreadsheet, and all the boxes to tick—working on the guest list, invitations, caterers, etc. I also think that Dana would not really enjoy shopping for a wedding dress with Es, so I want to give her that as a specific chore—we need to provide her with something that is out of her comfort zone, as a learning experience." I looked over at Esme, who raised one eyebrow and cocked her head. "If that is OK with you, Es." She shrugged. I took that as compliance. So I went on.

"As we just decided, Percy and Jill will be in charge of all the flowers and bouquets. Calm down, Percy. It will work out, because it *has* to. Since Angie is really the innocent victim in this whole situation, we want to give her a responsibility that she will really like. I talked with her mother, Sheryl Baker, on the phone earlier today, and she said that Angie loves doing things in the kitchen. Mom has volunteered to make the wedding cake, so it's a natural that she and Angie can do that together."

Suze raised her hand. "To reassure you, Rob and Es, we will be riding herd on the girls to make sure all of the loose ends do get tied. There will be continuous quality control meetings. Every decision has to be first of all, of course, approved by the two of you, but more importantly to the process, unanimously agreed upon by the girls. They have to not only work with the adults on this, but also make all decisions together. A TEAM."

I surveyed the group. The furrows had smoothed out on Mom's forehead, and she looked somewhat relaxed. She had stopped wadding the Kleenex in her hand. Rob, although his shoulders had crept up around his ears, seemed agreeable to the idea. Es looked thoughtful. Percy adjusted his hair and sat back. Suze seemed to be her old self again—cool as a cucumber.

Suze took over from me. "All right, then. I am going to call a meeting with the girls for as soon as they can all make it, keeping the deadline from Judy Flood in mind. I would like for you and Rob to be here for that, Es. OK?"

Rob nodded blindly. Esme put out a manicured hand for attention. "There is one more thing. This Jill girl. She is quick to ridicule 'freaks,' right? This T-shirt thing was her idea? I want to make sure I have the events in the correct order of occurrence. This Jill girl and her gang flashed the cruel T-shirts in front of everyone in the cafeteria? A kid took a shot of it and shared it all around school, right? On Snapchat or something? Followed up by Dana, who used the same social media techniques to punish Jill, but she used her outcast friends and Twitter, Instagram, Reddit and Facebook as well, so all of her callouts went viral. This then resulted in Jill getting pushback, including nasty threats, correct? Along with the school being inundated with emails, texts, and phone calls. Is this accurate?"

Suze and I nodded simultaneously.

"OK then. I have one more addition I would like for you to insert into the plan. I would like for Dana and Jill to spend one day with me at my office. I have a sheaf of documentation, including news stories and YouTube videos, which I would like for the two of them to witness. After they read about how bullying, both in person and online, can affect victims and their families, I think they might both have their eyes opened wide. I am sure. If I can locate the documentary, *Bully,* about the suicides of Tyler Long and Ty Smalley, I want them to watch it. Can I insist on that, as the transgender bride?"

"That is an absolutely stellar idea. Genius."

"Wait. Es is not entitled to that title! That is reserved for Judy Flood and for me!" I poured two more fingers of wine into my glass and chugged it down. "Now we just have to gird our loins for the meeting with the girls."

Percy raised his glass of wine. His hand swayed. The wine sloshed. Percy was definitely a lightweight in the alcohol department. "To the wedding! May it be beautiful and full of happiness."

We all toasted. It was so joyful that we toasted at least two more times. Percy began to slur his words, and Suze and I got an excellent buzz on. Rob and Es, apparently used to cocktail hours and long, martini-filled date nights, looked amused.

I did notice, however, that on the way to their car, Esme giggled and fell off one of her stilettos.

Π

"Angie, I promise that this whole summer will be fine. We will make sure that you are not in any way bullied, teased, or made uncomfortable. You will be surrounded by adults. You do not need to fear Jill in any way."

Angie, the first to arrive for the meeting, sat trembling on the couch, her arms crossed around her midsection. "Why do I have to be involved?"

Suze had developed a tic. Her upper eyelid twitched. I felt proud that she was spearheading all of this, despite the incredible stress. She pulled on her earlobe before answering Angie. "Because, sweetheart, Dana and Jill both need to come to grips with the consequences of their behavior." More eyelid twitches.. Suze pushed her eyelid down with her forefinger and continued. "Humanity. It is all about humanity. Dana and Jill need to realize that we are all the same under the skin. And, sweetie," Suze put her hand out and smoothed Angie's hair, "you do, too. The three of you. You need to come together."

Angie's cheeks flushed. She unclasped her arms and sat up a little bit straighter. A look of determination washed over her. "I get it, Suzanne. We all have a lesson to learn. I am scared. I'll be OK. I am pretty sure I will be OK."

I died a little inside. No time to worry, though, because there was a bang on the door, and Dana arrived, her eyes snapping. "Hi, all. I am loaded for bear. Where are my dogs?"

"They are in the backyard. We didn't want any distractions." Mom gave Dana a gentle shove in the direction of the living room as we heard the characteristic slam of the Boltons' Jeep, followed by the slap of Jill's sandals as she came up the walk.

"Let's get this whole charade over with," Jill announced, as she sashayed into the house, gum popping, a cloud of perfume surrounding her. "I have a date in an hour."

At that moment, if I had a gun in my possession, I would have shot this kid, but unfortunately, she sailed into the living room unscathed.

There were cookies and lemonade on the table. I had entreated Mom not to serve refreshments, but she insisted. Percy and Suze sat on the sofa across from Dana and Jill. Angie, Rob and Esme sat at the edges in dining room chairs. As soon as Mom sat down next to Jill, Suze began.

"I would like to introduce Robert Carruthers. He is Meg's brother and Tommy's uncle. And this is Esme Stills, his fiancée."

Jill immediately piped up. "Is she a drag queen or something?"

Dana leapt to her feet and lunged at Jill. Luckily, Esme is not only tall, she is powerful. She grabbed Dana by the arm and swung her around before she could connect with Jill. Dana struggled briefly in Es' arms, but Esme overpowered her and shoved Dana back into her seat.

Then Esme walked around the rear of the couch and gently eased Mom out of her seat next to Jill. Es lowered herself onto the sofa and leaned toward Jill, their faces a mere inch apart. "I am a woman, little girl. Guess what, though? *I used to be a man.* And I still have the strength, the muscles, and the power of a man. If I were you, I would keep my mouth shut, because when I am angry, I can do a lot of damage."

Esme snapped her fingers. Jill jumped.

"Exactly." She stood and motioned for Mom to retake her seat beside Jill. "Now, Suzanne, may we continue?" Esme sat down beside her fiancé gracefully, folding her flowery sundress underneath her, the picture of elegance and grace.

Suze spent a good half hour laying out the project. When it came to the individual assignments, Angie squeaked with delight at the prospect of the wedding cake. "May we do cupcakes? I love cupcakes, and we can do a bunch of different kinds!" Her face lit up with excitement.

Esme beamed. "Cupcakes. Such a great idea! I don't want to cut a cake and do the cake shoving routine. My makeup, for heaven's sake!"

Mom seemed just as excited. "Oh, yes! Cupcakes! It will be so much fun to decorate them!"

Dana was underwhelmed at her assignment, but she perked up when Suze told her that her title was "Project Manager." From that point on, Dana was all rapt attention.

Jill reacted as predicted. A bored look on her face, she seemed not to be paying attention to anything being discussed. But when Suze pointed to Jill and said that all flowers would be ordered, arranged, and placed by Percy, with Jill's close assistance, Jill hissed, "This isn't fair. Why do I have to work with the old fart?"

Mom, who is ordinarily the non-confrontational type, twisted to look at Jill full in the face. She pointed her finger, bringing it to within an inch of Jill's nose. "Listen here, Jill Bolton. We are all sitting here in this room, having this meeting, because of what *you* did. We all have better things we could be doing. But because you have committed an act of extreme unkindness, we are all involved in trying to help *all three of you* learn something from it. Especially you. So shut up and cooperate. *Do you understand me?"*

I had never heard Mom tell anyone to shut up. Suze sat up a little straighter in her seat, and both Rob and Esme muffled gasps. Percy looked at Mom as if she had just dropped down from heaven or something.

Jill stopped chewing her gum and her eyes widened. "OK, OK." She rolled her eyes. "I'll do as I am told. But don't expect me to be happy about it."

The rest of the meeting was uneventful, with Angie looking elated, the gears in Dana's head obviously turning as she muttered under her breath, and Jill sitting straight but looking none of us in the eye.

Suze began to sum up, but Es stood, her skirt floating around her ankles. "There is one additional requirement to the project that has nothing to do with our wedding." Es clicked her fingers in Jill's direction. "Look at me, please. That's better."

Esme smiled at Angie. "Freaks. Outsiders. Monsters. Angie has heard all of that, all of her life. Fag. Dyke. Tranny. Fairy. Pansy. I have heard much worse, but I won't share. Terms like this and the sort of actions they incur cause incredible damage to those on the receiving end. I want to make very sure that you, Dana, and Jill understand this. Yes, Dana, you thought that what you did was in defense of your friend, Angie. But your actions brought about the same sort of threats and potential violence that can result from bullying—no matter what the intent. Jill bullied Angie. Dana, you bullied Jill."

Dana and Jill sat, still as statues.

"So. The two of you, at a date mutually agreed upon, will spend a day with me at my law office, doing a little research on just how far reaching bullying is. You will look at videos and documentation about the end results of bullying behavior in the time of social media. I think it will be most unsettling." With a sweep of her hand, Esme sat back down.

"Does anyone want a cookie? Lemonade?"

Dana, mute, reached out for a cookie. Jill jumped out of her seat, flung a last look of disgust at all of us, and rushed out of the room, into the hall, and out the door. She left it wide open.

Esme switched seats with Rob so that she could sit next to Angie. She held out a hand, and Angie put her hand in Es' palm. Es rubbed it between her hands. "Sweetheart, are you going to be all right?"

Angie broke into a smile as a tear collected on her lower lashes. "Oh, Ms. Stills. I am so very happy to meet you. I just know I will be fine."

Rob rubbed his eyes. "Allergies. Really."

Esme winked at Angie. "He's a liar. He's crying. Oh, and by the way: my name is Esme. None of that Ms. nonsense."

Chapter Thirty-Three

Π

My eyes were just closing. Visions of wedding dresses and cupcakes swam in my head. I made a mental note to ask Mom and Angie to include carrot cake in the assortment, my mouth watered. Just then my bedroom door opened and Mom switched on the overhead light. Herkie jerked awake and jumped off the bed to leave the room. She curled up in the darkness of the hall, probably feeling resentful for the disturbance.

I struggled upright, unable to open my eyes all the way, due to the blinding fluorescence above. "Mom. My God! Turn that off!" I switched on the light on my bedside table.

There were dark circles under her eyes. I motioned for her to join me in bed. She plumped a pillow and lay down beside me, neither one of us looking at the other.

"Honey, are you sure you and Suze want to go through with all of this wedding stuff?" She worried her wedding ring with her finger. "I am doing fine. I can do the wedding. You don't need to stay here any more. You should go. Start your life up again. Forget about the trials and traumas you experienced growing up here. Honestly, sweetheart."

I was shocked to find tears welling up in my eyes. "Traumas do follow you around. But they get diluted. Talking about them. Facing them helps. Having a friend to talk to helps." I blinked as I rubbed the wetness off my cheeks.

Mom turned and surrounded me with her arms. "Tommy. Don't be afraid to be furious. With Sam, with me—with the world. You need to get it all out, purge yourself of all of that anger and feelings of betrayal. Only then will you be able to navigate your future. You must deal with this—you have stifled it all for too long." She kissed my soaking cheeks.

"Oh, Mom," I hiccupped. "You sound like Jack."

"Jack?"

I blew my nose on my sleeve, and Mom didn't even flinch.

"Didn't I tell you that I joined a Reddit group of children raised by gay parents? Jack is in the group. He has his own sordid tale, but mostly, he has tried to support me. I told him about Mommy and Leah."

Mom smoothed the hair back from my hot forehead. "What was his advice?"

I hiccupped again. "This. What we have been doing. Being honest. Facing up to things."

Mom rubbed her eyes. "Oh, sweetie, this is just the start of coming to grips with this for you. Me? I have made my peace with Sam and Leah. Don't think I didn't spend many a session with a therapist, in addition to fights with myself, tears, sleepless nights, and all the times I packed my bags to leave. It was wrong not to share that with you. It kept you in the dark, and that made your discovery about Mommy so much worse. I should have helped you to understand."

"You know what, Mom? The more Jack and I talk, the more he helps me to see that what happened, even though it was terrible for me—it shaped me. I am me. Here. Now. The past is the past." I thumped my forehead with my palm. "Jesus. I can't put this into words."

I tried to organize the clutch of ideas swirling around in my head. "You, Mommy, Rob, and the whole lifestyle. Being 'different.' It made us US. Then what I saw – Mommy and Leah. It colored my life; it bloodied me. I thought I was the only one in the world weighed down by such a burden. But I wasn't. I have finally realized this. My friend Jack was abused. Dana was, too. Trudy, her scorched face. You, disowned by your parents. Rob, trying his best to make up for them. And having a daughter he could never claim. Mommy and Dr. Creighton. Leah and Mommy. We all have our own shit to deal with."

She took a long breath, sat up, and took my face in her hands. "I love you more than anything in the world. All I can say is that you owe that Jack person a debt of gratitude for helping you realize that you have to face your trauma head on. You have to work through it somehow. We do, both of us. Together."

She rubbed her cool thumbs over my eyelids. The muscles behind my eyes relaxed.

"Spend time by yourself. Think. Worry. Gnash your teeth. Pretend to hit Sam with a hammer. Hell, scream out loud! Suze and I won't care, and the dogs will know you aren't angry with them. Don't think you have to snap your fingers and things will just sort out and calm down inside you. Take your time. But do the work. I am here to help you if I can. And your friend Jack. Or you may need to do this alone. Don't forget that we are all fallible, and nobody is either perfect or even well adjusted. We are all just walking around inside our skins, hoping for the best, and doing what we think we have to do."

I clutched at her for dear life, and we sat, Mom cooing and stroking me, until I lifted my head, looked into her eyes, and said, "You are a gift to me. I hope some day to deserve you."

She kissed the top of my head, leaned her cheek against my forehead, and got up. "Now go to sleep and rest your psyche. It has a lot of growing to do." She shut off the lamp and tiptoed over Herkie snoring in the hall, stooping to stroke her head as she passed.

I woke my dog as I stepped over her to go to the bathroom. She padded in behind me, her rear end wiggling with happiness. Dogs. They have such simple, clear souls.

I squeezed some Crest onto my toothbrush. I caught sight of myself in the mirror as I swished the toothbrush against my gums.

I leaned in closer and studied the surface of my face. Pores enlarged. Frown lines beginning to etch themselves like parenthesis around my mouth. An age spot (how could that be?) on the right side of my nose. Two spider veins running across my nostril. *My God. I am turning into a crone.* I reared back, looked at myself again, but the results were the same. I rinsed and spat, splashed some cold water over my face and turned out the bathroom light. All that remained in the mirror was my shadow. Much better. I got the hell out of there and tumbled into the softness of my mattress.

It came to me like an electric shock. I jolted upright in bed. I scrambled to my feet. Herkie looked up at me from her spot on the rug. "Don't worry, girl. I'll be right back."

I used the flashlight on my cell to see my way downstairs. I did not want to wake Mom or Suze, or God forbid, Saylor.

I snapped on the little lamp Mommy bought when she redecorated the kitchen. "Atmospheric," she called it, because it gave off such a weak glow that it was useless as a source of illumination. But Mommy thought it looked like something out of a kitchen in House Beautiful. Just enough light for me at that moment. I pulled open the junk drawer and rooted around, extracting a steno pad and a pair of scissors..

I sat at the table and propped up my phone so that I could see what I was about to do.

I carefully tore out and folded two sheets of paper, and cut out outlines of two people. They looked sort of like gingerbread men. No matter. I folded another sheet and cut out a smaller figure. These were Mom, Mommy, and me.

I folded four sheets together. Cutting through them was a little harder, but I was able to produce a total of twelve small figures. That didn't seem like enough, so I did twelve more. Good. I was ready.

I set Mom, Mommy and me on the table, and arranged all the little people around us in a circle. I put my chin in my hands and stared at them. It was us, as I always thought of our family: the three figures, isolated on our tiny little family island, with everybody in Framington surrounding us. We were cut off from the rest of the world. I took a deep breath.

Leah. The disruptor. I grabbed one of the figures from the outside circle, moved her next to Mommy. I pounded Leah with my fist. Then I picked her up, shredded her, and dropped the pieces on the floor. Poof. She didn't even matter.

Cancer. I took Mommy, kissed her five times, folded her carefully, and put her in the pocket of my robe. Mom and I stood, still surrounded. Alone.

I moved one of the little figures into the circle and set it next to me and Mom. Dana. It looked a little less solitary, there in the center. I took a deep breath. Then I slid another tiny figure into the center. Suze. Now the circle outside of us was broken. Air could rush in to the center. My shoulder muscles dropped. I massaged my neck.

I pulled one more paper doll into the center with us. Trudy. It was starting to look like a party in the middle! I slid another figure in. Percy. It was starting to get crowded in there, the wall around the edges breaking up even more.

I pulled in Jill, then Angie. Rob, Esme. Hell, I even invited Marjory Steiner inside. Gosh, not to forget Judy

Flood. At this point, the group in the center was starting to push the remaining figures around the edges away. The wall would just have to go.

I didn't even notice the tears rolling down my cheeks as I swept all of the remaining paper dolls off the edges off the table, so that standing in the center was the world that had grown up around me during this year of solitude, this year in which Mom and I had decided to withdraw. But instead, our world grew in ways that I had not expected and thought I didn't even want.

I was not alone. Not an outsider. That wall around me was as flimsy as the dolls scattered over the floor at my feet. And the crowd of people surrounding me were loving people. Accepting people.

I swiped at my eyes, sniffed, and then laughed out loud. I pulled two more sheets of paper and did my best to cut out two paper dolls that looked sort of like dogs. I set one of them next to the Suze paper doll and one of them next to me. Then I took Mommy out of my pocket and slid her back into the group. She was always with us! Every cell in my body sang a little song. I smiled at the group on the table, blessing each of them with a small prayer to the universe.

Then I picked up each doll, kissed them one-by-one, and put them all in the pocket of my robe. I floated up the stairs into my room.

I turned the light back on, reached on the floor for my laptop, and logged in to Reddit. I typed a quick DM to Jack:

You are very kind and wise. Are you sure you aren't related to Wayne Dyer or Ram Dass? It's late, and I am exhausted. Mom and I are talking more and more. My corporeal and spiritual bodies both feel lighter. I will be in touch.

An answer binged as I was closing the lid of my computer.

I have been waiting all my life for a message like this. I am sending you all my best wishes. Courage! You can untangle this. I am here if you need me.

I thumped the bed. "Herkie, come up here!" After she made three circles and curled up by my stomach, I kissed her on her dear doggy head. I fell asleep with my face against Herkie's.

In my dream, I was running down the street, following my dog into the sunshine. People lined the street as I ran, waving and smiling. I waved and smiled back. I ran so fast, my feet nearly left the ground. I was free.

Π

The day of reckoning at the law firm was set. Suze wanted to go too, but Esme nixed that idea. She wanted to have that day under her control. The girls were to be dropped off at the office at eight in the morning, to be released at Esme's discretion.

The day dawned cloudy and humid. School let out the week before. Wednesday, June 1, 2016. The beginning of wedding season. Suze and I vowed to work that day, paying no mind to what might be coming down with Esme and the girls, but neither of us could concentrate. Percy, luckily, had consultations with the flooring people and some plasterers, so he was not underfoot. Mom, on the other hand, went up and down stairs and into our respective rooms to 'check on us' so often, we finally gave up. At two o'clock, we shut our computers and went downstairs.

Mom had all of her recipe cards strewn on the kitchen table, as well as The Joy of Cooking and her laptop, open to the Food Network website. She wound a hank of her hair around her finger as she flipped through the cards. "Hi, you two. Giving up for the day?"

"Mom. Between worrying about Esme's indoctrination of the girls and your constant interruptions, we had no choice. What are you doing?"

Mom held up a card, waving at her cheeks like a fan. "I apologize for bothering you girls, but I just can't settle down. I decided to look at cake recipes. So far, I thought I would show these to Angie and Esme: classic white cake, chocolate fudge, coconut, lemon, carrot, and maybe spice?"

Suze picked up a card. "Oh, this sounds good. White chocolate."

Mom took the card and looked at it. "I'll add it to the pile. We can't take on too many varieties. Angie can prepare a tasting, and the girls can try to convince Es of their favorite. Then Es can choose."

I opened the fridge and pulled out the orange juice, got a glass and poured some. Suze got out a glass, too, and filled it with juice. We both sat down with Mom. Suze picked at her cuticles. I glanced at the time on my cell. Every five minutes.

The afternoon stretched on for what seemed like an eternity, but at four, Suze's cell binged. "Hello? My God, Esme, how did it go?"

We watched Suze's head, bobbing and nodding. Every few seconds, she said, "Right," or "OK," and finally, "Budweiser." She punched the red button and set her phone down.

"Well?"

Suze grimaced. "Es said it was good, bad, and awful. She and Rob are coming over at six. She said to order pizza and they will bring wine. She asked what kind of beer Percy likes, and I said Bud, but since he has probably had a grand total of three beers in his entire life, two of them being the other night, my guess is that it doesn't matter."

Mom scratched her nose with a recipe card. "This sounds ominous to me. Why do you suppose they have to come over to tell us about it?"

Suze tapped her juice glass on the table. "If Es told me over the phone, I would have to translate all of it to you all.

Certainly there will be questions. It makes sense that Rob and Es want to tell us in person, so that we can all get the message at once. I have to admit, though, I wonder about the 'bad' and 'awful' part." She twirled her glass. "We had better invite Percy; he needs to know what is going on with his 'partner' in the wedding planning."

By six o'clock, we had three large pizzas, plates, napkins, and headaches. Rob and Esme arrived with wine, beer, and a bouquet of daisies. "Couldn't resist; they are so cheerful," Esme said.

After we each had a couple of bites, Percy held his cool beer glass to his cheek and demanded a full accounting.

Esme finished her first glass of wine and refilled it halfway. "Do you want the good, the bad, or the awful?"

Mom groaned. "You might as well start with the awful."

Esme took a large sip. "Right. As soon as they arrived, it occurred to me that I should have mentioned a dress code."

Suze rolled her eyes.

Esme nodded at her. "Right? I mean, who did I think I was dealing with? Dana was on the cusp of acceptable. She arrived wearing torn jeans, a white T-shirt, and an orange bandanna, but at least she or Trudy had thought about it, and the bandanna was tied around her neck. The barbed wire wasn't visible."

I felt a distinct throbbing in my temples. "So what was Jill wearing?"

"You mean when she finally arrived? A half hour late? Let me see. How to describe it. Jill was decked out in short shorts. SHORT shorts. Her lower buttocks were on full display. Her tank top was bright pink, and there was no bra visible. Nipple extravaganza. She had a wad of chewing gum and blew bubbles until I nearly ripped the gum out of her mouth." Esme held up a finger. "Restraint, people. I exercised restraint and told her to spit it in a napkin."

Mom's mouth was wide open in shock. Percy drained his beer. Suze asked, "This was the awful, correct? Can we move on to the bad?"

Esme grimaced at Rob, who picked up another slice of pizza, folded it, and pointed it at Es. "Go on, hon. This part is sort of funny, actually."

Esme set her wine glass down, looked longingly at the bottle, but pushed it away. "I need to stay sober for this. I took them into my office and told them to have a seat while I got the folders of clippings and documents that I wanted them to read. I realized that I had left one of the file folders on my secretary's desk. I called Loretta and asked her to bring them in. In case you aren't aware, Loretta is 24, African American, a dead ringer for Jennifer Hudson. She brought in the folder, and I swear, Jill's eyes nearly popped out of her head. As soon as Loretta left, Jill pointed at the door and *get this,* asked if Loretta was a man or a woman."

Esme leaned back, eyebrows in two arcs, waiting for our reactions. Percy was first.

"I'm confused."

"So was I, until Jill began to giggle. She said, 'I was just joking.' I swear, at that point, I wanted to murder her."

Rob swallowed his bite of pizza with an audible gulp. "But tell the rest, Es."

"Dana – and by the way, she is worth her weight in gold – said nothing. She just untied the bandanna from around her neck, got up, and tied it around Jill's mouth like a gag. Then she just sat back down and looked at me. I nearly died."

We all started to laugh. "What did Jill do?" Mom asked.

Esme gave in, leaned over to grab the wine bottle, and poured herself another glass. "She pulled the bandanna off, but she shut the hell up."

The good part, as it turned out, was really good. Esme told us that the clippings she showed them concerned suicides that occurred as a result of bullying. She also shared with them articles about gays and non-whites who suffered beatings and murder at the hands of local vigilantes. After that, she introduced them to Arthur, one of the attorneys in the firm, who represented a young man who killed his neighbor. This neighbor had tormented the young man for years about being gay. The guy finally broke. He shot the neighbor six times, once through the heart.

"By the time we stopped for lunch, Jill had wiped the smirk off her face. She seemed to be just a bit more humble. Dana, by the way, was openly devastated by the stories. She could not eat her lunch. She spent the large part of lunch hour in the rest room."

Esme continued. "After lunch, I sat them in a conference room with a big screen TV. I played the documentary, *Bully,* and the three of us watched it." Esme stopped, her lips trembling. By the end of it, Dana was crying. Jill, although I could see that it had affected her, remained defensive. When I turned the lights on, she wouldn't look at either of us. I asked her what she thought." Es sighed. "She said, and I quote, 'It seemed fake to me.' I wanted to throttle her. Guys. This kid is a tough nut."

Suze looked resigned. She put her hands together and thumped them into her lap. "Not surprising. Tearing down her wall of defiance will take time. We just have to keep at it." She looked around at all of us. "I can see that you are wondering if this girl is salvageable. I don't know if she is. But this is our only option. It's my job on the line here—I jumped into this situation with both feet. So are you all still with me on this? Yay or nay?"

We "yayed." It wasn't with a lot of conviction, but we "yayed," nonetheless.

Chapter Thirty-Four

ח

We were relieved that Judy Flood and the powers that be at the school gave their seal of approval to the whole wedding planning scheme. As a matter of fact, Judy Flood told Suze that it was truly an "outside the box" solution, and that she admired us for coming up with it.

We waited until school was out to begin planning in earnest. All the girls had been told to clear their schedules for the summer: no camps, no vacations, no anything until after the wedding. Of course, the only complaints came from Jill's mother, who said that cancelling their trip to Cabo would "cost them a lot of money." Judy Flood's reply, something to the effect that "Jill's having to repeat a year of high school might also be costly," seemed to quell that objection.

Our first meeting was at four o'clock on a Saturday afternoon in mid-June. We had less than three months to plan, so Suze and I had a full agenda for the meeting. Mom prepared from-scratch lemonade, and Suze made *the brownies.* Percy brought a few flower catalogs over. We were ready.

Dana and Angie came together—they walked over from Dana's. I could see their friendship blossoming. I grinned when I opened the door. They were out of breath and slightly sweaty. Dana's hair was pulled up into two short pigtails, which stood out straight from behind her ears. Sweat gleamed on her forehead, and she had her arm around Angie's waist. Angie also gleamed with sweat. But on her pale face, it looked as if she had been crying—but her giggles belied that. She wore a yellow headband and a matching top. They both bobbed up and down on their tennis shoes.

"Come in, you two. We have brownies!" They hopped in, arms still entwined. As soon as they saw Mom, Angie squealed, "Oh, Mrs. Poole, I just LOVE brownies!" And of course she kissed the dogs, who clamored for attention.

Mom hugged them both. They sat down and Dana drank her entire glass of lemonade down, smacked her lips, and smiled. "We skipped the whole way here. I was in a state of complete dehydration." She laughed and grabbed a brownie.

Suze and her clipboard were ready. Percy leafed through his catalogs, ignoring the refreshments. I thought he seemed apprehensive. I didn't blame him. I was apprehensive, too. We didn't know what to expect from Jill, after all.

There was plenty of time for us to eat every single brownie on the platter and have a couple of glasses of lemonade each, because naturally, Jill Bolton was late. The black Jeep pulled up at four twenty, screeched to a halt, and Jill alighted. We watched through the front window as she got out of the car, then leaned over and conducted a five-minute long conversation with her mother before finally turning and swishing towards the front door, a smirk on her face.

We let her ring the bell and stand waiting for a good minute. We agreed that she needed to wait, just as we had. As soon as I opened the door, Jill pushed past me into the living room, shot us all a condescending look, and sat down, nearly squashing Angie. And so it began.

Suze went over her list of all of the things that needed to be accomplished and in what order. There were so many. Invitations. Catering. The dress. Bridesmaids. Officiant. Rehearsal dinner, or no? Music. On and on. About halfway through her dissertation, it became obvious that Jill wasn't listening. As a matter of fact, she seemed to be falling asleep.

Dana, who sat beside Mom on the couch, was intent on Suze, and didn't notice Jill. But Dana caught the expression on my face as I watched Jill's eyes roll back into her head. Dana snapped to attention. She jumped up, shot over to Jill, and shook her by the shoulders. "Wake up, bitch! How dare you be so rude?"

Jill pushed Dana away, stood up and yawned. "God. This whole thing is *borrring."* Dana looked ready to pounce. Suze set her clipboard down on the table. She stood, swelling up into her full, educator/referee posture, and commanded, "Dana Stryker, SIT DOWN. Jill Bolton, YOU MAY TAKE YOUR SEAT AS WELL. We will not have any rudeness, physical expressions of anger, or any other sort of negativity. Understood? Dana?"

Dana nodded.

That wasn't enough for Suze. "Dana, I need you to answer. Yes or No?"

"Yes. I understand."

Suze pointed to Jill. "And you? Do you understand?"

They both sat back down. My heart resumed beating. Suze continued her lecture.

Jill shut her eyes and leaned her head back on the sofa. She waved a hand in our direction. "What ev."

That was the last straw for Dana. She leaped to her feet again. The anger surged from every pore. None of us could have stopped her. She made for Jill, grabbed her by the hands and pulled Jill to her feet. They stood, face-to-face. Dana began speaking, her words like bullets aimed at Jill's face.

"Do you understand what all of this is about?" Jill's look of defiance left her; she stood in front of Dana, eyes wide. She didn't answer.

"Let me explain this to you, OK? Humiliation. It's a horrible feeling, right? I know you have felt humiliated, because I was in Math class that day when you were wearing white jeans and *you got your period.* Everybody saw it! Kevin Hardway pointed it out when you went to the board. The guys *laughed.*" Dana smiled. "Remember that, Jill?"

Jill sat back down on the sofa, hard. She nodded, but still didn't speak. She balled her hands in her lap and stared at them.

"So, Jill. Wasn't that awful? So mortifying, right? You had to be excused to go home and change. Everybody talked about it for the rest of the day. Yeah. Pity and shame. And entertainment. Your embarrassment was entertainment for the rest of the school." She sneered. "Look at me, Jill."

Jill looked up, her eyes blank, then she dropped her head down once again to study her fists. You could have heard the proverbial pin drop. I don't think the rest of us were even breathing.

Dana continued. "So. Everybody got over it. Stuff happens all the time, so your little humiliation was forgotten. The kids moved on. But for us? The ones who are the constant focus of bullying? The humiliation never ends." Dana pointed her finger at Jill. "Magnify how you felt that day when you stained your jeans. Magnify it by a thousand. That is how we feel, all the time. Humiliated. Embarrassed. Shamed. Laughed at. Hurt. We want to stay home and never go out—it's that bad. But we can't. We have to live in this world. No one can protect us. So we learn to wall ourselves off. To try to pretend we don't care."

Jill continued to look at her hands. She didn't move.

"Jill. Do you hear me?" Dana's voice cracked.

It was a whisper, but Jill replied. "Yes."

"This is why we are here. You and your friends set out to embarrass and degrade Angie because of the way she looks. She looks like that every day. No going home to change. No 'getting over it.' You used Angie's face as a way to shame her and make yourselves feel, what? Better than she is? You used Angie as entertainment. You hurt her. And I tried to hurt you. To pay you back for all of the shitty things you and your stupid girlfriends do. Get it? You acted like monsters. I wanted to make you feel the way Angie and I do, *every single day of our lives.* Understand? Can you begin to *understand?*"

Dana pivoted, slumped onto the sofa and put her head in her hands. Mom put her arms around her and rocked her back and forth. Suze looked stunned. Tears ran down Angie's face. Percy and I were momentarily paralyzed.

A few moments passed in silence. Then Jill looked up. There was almost no color in her face, and her lips trembled. She grabbed the hem of her T-shirt and used it to wipe her nose. Then she said in a soft but distinct voice, "I'm sorry."

Nobody seemed able to move. We remained rooted in our seats, overcome with the scene we had just witnessed. Finally, Percy got up and leaned over the coffee table, his sheaf of catalogs extended to Jill. She stared at them, unseeing. Percy waved them at her. "Miss Jill. Take these. We have a lot of decisions to make. Look at these at home, and then maybe you can come over to my house and we can discuss table decorations, the aisle way outside, and most importantly, the bouquets."

Jill reached out and took the catalogs, and set them in her lap. Percy sat back down. Jill stroked the cover of the top catalog. Then a funny thing happened. Angie put her hand on Jill's forearm and said, "I just love daisies. Do you?"

Jill turned her head and looked Angie square in the eyes. She seemed both relieved and worn out at the same time. She nodded at Angie. "I do, too. I love carnations, but everybody says they're so *generic.* What do you think?"

The wind generated by our collected sighs of relief could have knocked down a skyscraper.

Π

Preparations began in earnest. Rob and Esme provided a guest list. It would be a small wedding, forty people—we still planned to have the wedding in the back, with tents and tables. The rain plan was to have it inside. We felt confident that either way, we could handle forty people.

Dana swung into gear, going online to a wedding planning site and creating www.ROBANDESMESTILLS/CARRUTHERSWEDDING. These kids today! Within a few hours, there were pictures of Rob and Es standing in front of a fountain, Rob and Es kissing beneath a rose arbor, and some of them in front of our Christmas tree. There was an online invitation (of course, this whole affair would be coordinated online!), and some wedding gift suggestions 'no kitchenware or home goods—these two are grownups'—instead, Dana installed a click icon for donations to the honeymoon, location yet to be determined.

We had weekly planning meetings in which the girls shared their progress and hassled over everything. But decisions were made. Everything was emailed to Rob and Esme, who basically "carte blanched" everything.

Jill still caused blood pressures to rise. She pronounced Angie's idea of having someone sing at the wedding "cretinous, and straight out of the 50's." We had to restrain Dana from strangling her. She was also late to every single planning meeting, so we began to call them for an hour earlier, telling everyone else the actual time to arrive. It worked pretty well.

By the third planning meeting, when Jill snapped her gum all through Dana's presentation of schedules and the catering options, Suze finally had enough. She banished all of us except for Jill from the room and shut the door. We heard her muffled voice for about ten minutes. Not a peep out of Jill.

When they came out, Jill looked chastened, apologized, and promised to behave from that day forward. Her face was wreathed in fear. We managed to work through the rest of the meeting without a hitch. Everyone but Jill left smiling.

Π

I confronted Suze later that night as she was brushing her teeth. "What on earth did you do to settle Jill down?"

Suze spit, rinsed, and gargled. Then she smirked at me. "I used the nuclear option. Only for severe emergencies as documented in the Ohio Board of Education Rules and Regs, Classroom and Student Management, Section 3, Paragraph Four. If I told you, I would have to kill you."

"OK, then. I hope you never have to use that on me."

"Do you EVER."

I shuffled back to bed and pulled the covers over my head. Just for protection.

Π

Jill and Percy immersed themselves in ordering floral wire, oasis floral foam, shears, and ribbons. Esme had decided upon white roses and "something pink and green" for her bouquet. Percy and Jill drove to Columbus to a huge floral warehouse and spent the day surrounded by blooms. The centerpieces were to be pink, green and white also. Percy wanted to do garlands along the stairs, just in case the weather caused us to hold the wedding inside. He wanted to do something spectacular for the mantel. Jill threw herself into the process, and her suggestion of a mantel array of white roses, baby's breath, pink hydrangeas, and *glitter* was met with applause. Angie also suggested pink ribbon curlicues. Jill actually *smiled and clapped her hands* at the concept. Angie beamed.

They had similar spectacular plans for outside. Fairy lights under the tent ceilings. Centerpieces of pink lilies, green carnations, and white roses. Baby's breath out the wazoo. Green, pink and white ribbons on the backs of all the chairs.

Esme declared that the three girls would be her bridesmaids. She thrilled them by telling them that they could wear whatever they wanted, as long as it was below the knee, and either pink or green. They decided between the three of them that Dana and Jill would wear green, and that Angie should be the maid of honor in pink. Other than that, their outfits would be a surprise. If Mom told us once that 'don't worry, we can trust them,' she told us a hundred times. Dee Dee took them shopping. I feared the worst, but kept quiet.

Dana suggested that Herkie and Saylor should be the flower girls. Percy offered to make them collars with white and pink roses. This whole wedding was destined to be a smash hit.

I had done online research, as I was the media maven. I set Mom and I up with Stitch Fix. Glorious company. They set you up with a personal shopper, who quizzes you about your personal style, sizes, and even has you evaluate about a hundred garments and shoes. Then they send you a package of clothes that you can keep or send back for free. Yippee! When the packages of dresses arrived, Suze sat on the bed to view the outfits that Stitch Fix included. First off, I emerged from my room wearing a melon orange strapless dress, gathered under the bodice with small daisies. It flowed into a full skirt. "Scratch that on off the list; it makes your hips look big. Plus, cantaloupe? What were they thinking? This isn't the 60's." I took that one off.

Mom floated into the room in a crisp lavender linen pantsuit, a cream shell underneath the jacket. The jacket flared out around her hips, fastened by one rhinestone encrusted button. "I love that—the way it flares out."

Mom twirled, studying the effect in the full-length mirror. "That's called a peplum." She held out the edges of the jacket. "I do like it. But after about an hour, it will look as if I have slept in this. Linen."

"Exactly. Strike that one. Next?" I thought Suze was enjoying this just a little too much. I chose outfit number two: a floor length dress made out of something silky. Maybe silk. It was sleeveless, deeply curving from the bodice up to a mock turtle neckline. It fell like a dream, straight down from the bodice, but swirled around me like a breeze when I took a step. I absolutely adored it. It was the color of the leaves as they first come out in the spring. It came with gold spike heels, which would most likely give me bunions, but they looked stunning with the dress.

"Go no further, Tommy. That's the one."

Mom, who just then entered the room, enveloped in dusty pink, agreed. "Oh, Tommy! You look like a super model!"

That was enough for me. "Done. Mom, what is that getup?"

I was beginning to lose faith in Mom's personal shopper. This outfit consisted of a full, taffeta skirt. Pink. Underneath, puffing the whole thing out like some sort of nightmarish tutu, were at least ten layers of tulle, alternating between white and pink. The bodice was tight, sleeveless, made out of that same ghastly pink taffeta.

"My God. That would look great on Cyndi Lauper. What was Stitch Fix thinking?"

Mom nodded and hurried out of the room. We heard her rustling around, and then she called out, "I think this one is a winner! Just a minute!"

We held our breath. With a "TA DA!" Mom wafted into the room. She wore a simple, cream-colored sheath with a jewel collar. Over it was the most gorgeously cut coat, the exact length of the dress, dupioni silk. Mandarin collar, buttons all the way down the front. A single, blowsy pink bloom affixed to the left shoulder. Pink kitten heels. Suze and I both gasped.

"Mom, you look like Diane Keaton."

Mom drew the collar up around her face and smiled. "I know. I saved the best for last."

Suze jumped off the bed, shot into her room, and ran back, carrying her laptop. "Give me the URL of that Stitch Fix place! I want to get my outfit from them!"

Π

The cupcake bakers weren't faring so well. So far, Angie and Mom had tried three versions of white cake. One was too dry, the other was too bland, and the third was mushy. The carrot cake recipe was good, but when they made it into cupcakes, each one was so heavy, what with all those carrots, raisins, and cream cheese frosting – that eating one was the equivalent of eating a full meal – so the carrot cake was eliminated from the running.

The rest of us absolutely adored the entire cupcake enterprise at first, smacking our lips at all the varieties, but after a couple of weeks of this, Percy said his gout was kicking up, Suze had gained four pounds, and I was so high on sugar that I had trouble sitting still. Thank goodness, the girls and Esme finally settled on three kinds of cupcake: simple chocolate, Trudy's mother's lemon cake recipe, and under the threat of death if it were to be revealed, white cupcakes from Costco. The decorations were simple: edible glitter and multicolored sprinkles. One more problem solved.

As the date grew closer, Jill and Percy swung into full gear, Percy arriving at our house for the weekly card games with punctures from floral wire, a rash on his forearms from the ferns ("the damn things scratch like the devil"), and a gigantic appetite. He and Jill put in long hours, and all of that arranging had to be taxing. We ate a lot of delivery food, and I wondered if I might be developing some bloating from MSG.

Jill flitted in and out, her arms sometimes full of flowers for us, "Rejects. Percy said you might like to have them," other times to try a cupcake or grab a sandwich, "Mom forgot to pack me a lunch today, and Percy eats *sardine sandwiches. His breathe REEKS.*"

We chugged along, getting more and more excited. Rob and Esme had dinner with us at least once a week. Esme discussed bridal hairstyles with us, and we all agreed that she should wear her hair in a chignon, with a pearl tiara holding her finger tip veil. She and Dana had chosen a dress, but it was a secret. All Esme would tell us is that she felt like a princess the moment she tried it on.

Three weeks before the big day, while I was trying in vain to satisfy a client that his 45,000 Twitter followers adored his every tweet, and Suze had gone down for a nap, there was a pounding on the door. I heard it swing open, followed by a loud squeal from my mother. Suze, the dogs, and I nearly collided as we rushed out of our rooms to run down to see if someone had tried to stab her.

Dana stood in the front hall, holding a wiggling ball of brown and white fur. Mom stroked it, giggling. She took it out of Dana's arms and held it up to us, a la The Lion King. "Look! Look! It's a puppy!"

The pup squeaked as Herk and Saylor could not contain their excitement, nearly knocking Mom and Dana down in their attempts to lick the puppy. They wagged themselves nearly to death, and as soon as Mom set the puppy down, they surrounded and nearly nuzzled the life right out of it.

"Meet Sabine." Dana looked at the waggling mass adoringly. "She's a gift from my mom, because I have been such a trouper this summer. Her mom is a pit bull, and her dad is a mutt. She's ten weeks old, from the shelter. I picked her because she stuck her little paw out of the cage and tapped my ankle as I walked by. I just loved her right off."

I don't know what shocked me more: the puppy, or the words "my mom" coming out of Dana's mouth. I think the same thing occurred to Suze and Mom simultaneously, because they both stopped petting Sabine at the same instant and straightened up to peer at Dana.

"Mom. You said *mom?*"

She beamed at us. "I know. It's a shocker. But this has been the summer to end all summers. You know what they say—like, it's been a 'rite of passage.' I grew up, you know what I mean? So I decided that it would be a good thing to let Trudy adopt me. She has been wanting to all along, but I thought since I already had a mom and dad – I didn't want to forget them, you know." There was a catch in her voice. "Then I realized with all of these…" she gestured in a circle, taking in all of us and the rest of the world, "…goings on, that I need to take care of Trudy for the long haul." Dana looked down at Sabine as she writhed around with the big dogs. "And I guess I need her to take care of me."

Mom wrapped her arms around Dana and hugged her within an inch of her life. Suze and I grabbed one another's hands and held on tight. The puppy peed on my tennis shoe.

Dana lifted Sabine up in the air, still dribbling, and hustled her out into the front yard to finish. Then she praised the hell out of her, I took off my tennis shoes, and we all went into the kitchen for a cupcake.

Later on that night, after a rousing walk with the dogs during which they discovered a Labradoodle behind a fence that was apparently a complete stud—we could hardly tear them away—we repaired to our bedrooms to cool off. Suze took a box of Triscuits to bed to share with Saylor, murmuring sweet nothings to her dog as she shut the door behind them.

I was just logging off Reddit after telling Jack about the puppy, the adoption, and how wonderful life was, when Mom poked her head around the door frame. She looked hopeful, happy, the light in the hall surrounding her with an aura of gold.

"Tommy, are you going to be all right?"

"Mom, I am going to be just fine."

Chapter Thirty-Five

π

August can be brutal in Ohio. Humidity like fog. Highs in the 90's. We had decided to have the wedding inside, and the reception in the back, after things had cooled down. We rented huge fans. I hoped they wouldn't blow anyone away. The wedding was the next day. Callooh, callay.

The house was as clean as a whistle. Why whistles have such a reputation for cleanliness was a mystery. We had moved a lot of furniture out of the living room into the dining room. Forty chairs were being delivered in the morning. The tents would go up at noon. Percy was coming over at the crack of dawn to do the flowers. He had told Jill she could sleep in until eight, and then come over. She didn't even whine about it.

I looked over Mom's shoulder as she and Percy played their final round of Pinochle for the evening. "Why are you holding on to that Jack?"

Percy looked aggrieved, and Mom poked me in the stomach with her elbow. "You just gave things away!"

I slunk into the TV room to see what was on. I watched Mom and Percy through the French doors, bobbing and nodding at one another. They looked pretty cozy in there. Mom slapped a card down on the table and Percy groaned. Wonderful.

I tuned in to a rerun of Seinfeld. It never gets old. Suze came down a half hour later. She made some microwave popcorn, and we discussed how tomorrow would go. The wedding was to take place at four, with the reception at six—photos in between.

The caterers, hired by the girls with Esme's input, were serving 'heavy hors d oeuvres' for the reception, and they had a mobile kitchen that would be set up in the corner of the yard. They also had two bars, one at either end, with the full compliment of alcohol. Angie's cousin played violin in a string quartet, so Dana and Esme hired them. No DJs for this couple!

Suze flipped a kernel to each of the dogs. "Can you believe it? We pulled it off!"

I grabbed a handful of corn and stuck my tongue out at Suze. "Judy Flood has nothing on us."

"I did not think there would be a happy ending to any of this. I thought both Jill and Dana were too stubborn, too immature, and in Jill's case, too nasty to ever come together. I really thought, in my heart of hearts, that you were no Judy Flood."

I threw a handful of popcorn at Suze's face, but she ducked. "Ha! By the way, did Judy Flood RSVP? Is she coming to the reception?"

"Yes. So you will be able to gloat with her over champagne."

There was an exclamation from the living room as Mom threw her cards down on the table. "Percy, you are the devil incarnate! I think you cheated!" They both started to laugh.

"Look at the time! It's nearly eleven! Percy, I need to get my beauty sleep."

Suze threw another kernel of corn to the dogs. "We might as well stay up a while longer. Sleep is definitely not going to help either one of us, beauty-wise."

I agreed. I knew I wouldn't get one wink of sleep, anyway.

Chapter Thirty-Six

Π

My alarm binged at five a.m. At first, I felt resentful. But then the realization hit. Today was THE WEDDING. I sprang up. Sort of. My knees locked as I sprang, so it was more like a scrabble, but I got myself out of bed in record time. A few vertebrae in my spine popped as I stretched. I heard a whoop from Suze's bedroom.

We met in the hall. Suze's curls were smashed on one side, and she had sleep creases in her left cheek, but her eyes flashed. "Wedding, wedding, wedding! Are we ready to rock and ROLL?"

We joined hands and did a little dance. The dogs joined in for a few moments of lighthearted chaos. The noise must have alerted Mom. She yoo hooed from her bedroom. We frolicked into her room.

There she sat, covers askew, knees drawn up, a list in her hand.

"So. You are full of last minute nerves?"

Mom nodded. "Come in. I couldn't sleep."

We snuggled next to her. The dogs curled up on the floor at the foot of the bed. I patted Mom's hand and ran my fingers over her wedding band. "Have you thought about the date? That today is the last day of our year of 'solitude' that was anything but solitary? I wonder if Emily Dickinson had this many people flowing in and out of her house. How do you feel?"

Mom set the list down on the duvet and tilted her head back and forth until her neck cracked. "It went fast. I made all of my scrapbooks, and I worked out a lot of things in my own head." She smiled and extended her legs in a long stretch. "If you hadn't stumbled across darling Dana, who knows how boring and claustrophobic the year might have been? Maybe we would have both needed to escape. I am glad we didn't."

I looked at Mom, her hair no longer spiky, her face relaxed, the deep furrows on her forehead now mere wrinkles. I remembered how frail and breakable she seemed last August. Now, she lamented the 'pot belly' that developed after all of the cupcake experimentation, but she looked beautiful and so much less spindly, her cheeks full, and her arms softly rounder. To me, she looked robust and healthy once again.

"Are you ready to take the world by storm?" I asked her.

"I think so. But what about you, honey? Will you and Herkie go back to Columbus?"

I fanned my face with the list. "Suze and I like it here. The dogs have bonded. We both feel like Dana is our little sister. We are thinking about looking around for an apartment here in Framington. We certainly proved that we can do our jobs remotely. Oh, and did I tell you? Judy Flood has nominated Suze for some sort of Teacher of the Year kind of award. I forget what it's called. I am sure Suze is a shoe-in." My smile nearly cracked my cheeks. "And Mom. I have been doing the work. Sorting myself. Healing. You don't need to worry about me."

Mom turned to look at me with shining eyes. "That makes me the happiest person in this universe."

I put my head on her shoulder. "Let's just all take a few minutes to meditate. How about it?"

Suze got up, blew us both a kiss, and turned to leave. "I have a lot to do, and I want to be the first one in the shower. You two rest up. It is going to be such a big day."

Mom lifted the sheet, and I slid my legs under it. We lay back, watching the blades of the ceiling fan as they circled slowly, lulling us like a hypnotist's amulet.

We fell asleep, arms entwined. It was the most restful fifteen-minute nap I ever had.

Π

Suze's knock on the doorframe woke us. She stood, wrapped up in a towel, and giggled. "You two had your beauty rest; now it's time to get a move on!"

We barely had time to collect our thoughts before the front door banged open, and we heard Percy bellowing in the hall. "Meg! Tommy! Suzanne! Girls, come down here! I am having an emergency!"

We hurtled down the stairs to see Percy, standing there in his robe, every one of the seventeen strands of his actual hair standing on end. He wrung his hands as we surrounded him, teetering back and forth on his heels. "My hair! I sent my hair out to be refreshed, and they guaranteed that it would be here by noon today. I just checked the tracking number, and it was sent to FRAMINGHAM MASSACHUSETTS. I won't have my hair in time for the wedding!" He moaned and reached out blindly for Mom.

I swear Suze snickered, but she insists it was Herkie who yipped.

I used my most soothing tones. "Percy, what have we told you time and time again? You are a bald man, but you are a handsome bald man! You have a lovely, round head. Here, feel this!" I took Percy's hand and placed it on the top of my head and forced him to rub it. "Feel that divot? If I were bald, people would think somebody had hit me with a shovel!" Percy shuddered and snatched his hand away.

Mom shot a withering glance in my direction. The divot strategy was apparently a poor one. "Try to ignore Tommy, Percy. It's so early, her brain is still scrambled. Probably from the divot. Come in and sit down for a minute. Suze, can you make some coffee? I think we could all use some."

Suze disappeared into the kitchen, and Mom sat Percy down on the sofa. She took his hands between hers, rubbing them gently. "You know, toupees are not really the style, these days. Have you seen The Rock?" Percy looked confused. I could just see the wheels turning in Mom's head.

She brightened. "How about Yul Brynner? Now there was a handsome man. Not a hair on his head." She watched for Percy's reaction. When he dipped his chin in a sort of a mini-nod, she went on. "All you have to do is turn on the TV, Percy. So many men are going bald. The ones with hair shave their heads, did you know that? It's considered to be very sexy." She jerked her head in my direction. "RIGHT, Tommy?"

I licked my lips. "Oh, right! Right!" I wracked my brains for a name that Percy might recognize. "Yeah, yeah. Vin Diesel!" Percy looked blank. "Bruce Willis—heard of him?" Nothing. Then I hit the bull's eye. "Sean Connery! James Bond! He is bald in real life! He stopped wearing a toupee years ago!"

Percy immediately perked up. He pulled his hands out from between Mom's and ran them over the top of his head. "Really? James Bond?"

"Absolutely. You will look 'studly,' as Dana says. Won't he, Suze?"

Suze set a tray with three mugs of coffee down on the table. "Huh?"

"Percy without his hair. At the ceremony today. He will look like Sean Connery, right?"

Suze studied Percy for a few seconds, frowning. "No."

I gasped.

"He will look better than that. He'll look like Patrick Stewart. Captain Jean-Luc Picard? Star Trek?"

Percy squinted at Suze. "You mean the bald one?"

That caused a group chuckle. "Yes! Yes! The bald one! And today, you will be the star of the wedding, especially if you shave off those few remaining hairs. Really, Percy. If you go bald, you have to go all the way." Suze clinched it. Percy rose, squaring his shoulders. Mom handed him his mug of coffee to take with him, and he scuffed into the front hall. "I will see you girls soon. I have to start decorating, and as soon as Jill arrives, we have to tie up all the bouquets with ribbons and place all the centerpieces. I will send her over with the dogs' collars as soon as we wire on the roses. So much left to do!" He exited in a flourish, running a hand over his head.

I clutched at my chest. "Geez. Problem one solved. How many more crises will crop up in the next eight or so hours?"

Chapter Thirty-Seven

Π

It was two o'clock. Mom, Suze, and I had dealt with the following: the caterers had no vegetarian options, so there had to be some last minute creations involving celery. Phyllis Stills had a hissy fit when she realized she had forgotten her shoes—the ones that had been specially dyed to match her apple green suit. Luckily, she and Mom wore the same size, and Mom lent Phyllis a pair of cream-colored heels, which everyone agreed would look just fine, thank you. The Unitarian minister we were so thrilled to find called in sick. Laryngitis. My God. After a round of hysterical phone calls, it was discovered that Rob and Esme's law partner, Allison Delaney, had one of those certificates that allowed her to marry people, and since she was invited to the reception anyway, she was available to do the service.

The three of us were exhausted. But still to come, as a matter of fact, in fifteen minutes, was the wedding party. Esme, Jill, Dana, Angie, Suze, Mom and I were going to have our hair and makeup done by the staff of Salon Jolie. There would be hot rollers, false eyelashes, and plucking involved. There was nothing to do but pound down some Coke for the caffeine and sugar boost, and soldier on.

My stylist was named Zoe, and she had purple hair and a pierced nose. Zoe talked a blue streak as she pulled on strands of my hair and held them up to the light. "You should have come in earlier in the week for color. I can give you a good cut, but I can't do anything about this...muddy brown. You should have gotten some highlights. Too late."

Zoe managed to work wonders with my muddy hair, and by the time she was finished, I looked like Natalie Portman. Well, Natalie Portman's hair. Zoe then went to work on my face, and *my God.* Concealer. Sculpting. Foundation. False eyelashes. Eyeliner, eye shadow, and eyebrow enhancement (all that plucking was excruciating). Lip liner and lipstick. Powder, followed by some sort of spray that Zoe assured me would keep my makeup looking dewy until at least three in the morning.

When she held up the hand mirror for me to see myself, I nearly died. I was stunningly beautiful. My skin was flawless; my eyes were huge, framed by eyelashes that looked like velvet spikes. I had lips like Angelina Jolie. I reached for my phone and asked Zoe to take my picture, so that someday, when I am old and wrinkly, I can show my children that their mother was once magnificent.

The other stylists from Salon Jolie worked their magic on the rest of us as well. We congregated in the upstairs hall to admire one another. Suze looked like a curly-haired version of Jessica Chastain, I swear. Mom was Diane Keaton from head to toe. The girls looked like whatever pop stars are now in vogue—I couldn't tell you any of their names. Suffice it to say, we were knockouts.

But then, Esme swept out of Mom's bedroom. The breath was just sucked out of all of us. Her hair, pulled up in a tight chignon, gleamed like antique silver. Esme had gone in for highlights, of course. I had not noticed how high her cheekbones were before now, and how aquiline her nose. Her golden eyebrows were perfect arcs above those deep blue eyes, framed by eyelashes that curled up into the sooty gray of the shadow on her lids. She smiled at us, and suddenly I wished that I had ordered those whitening strips on Amazon.

We were ready.

π

I could write an entire book about the wedding, but a few highlights will have to do.

Esme, along with Dana and the girls, chose a very simple wedding gown. Lace. All lace over a strapless sheath. Long sleeves, her skin glowing beneath. Jewel neckline. Wide satin sash. A pearl choker. Her tiara, of pearls and crystals, holding back her veil, also trimmed with a band of lace, that flowed down to the tips of her fingers.

Esme was not the first one to descend the staircase that Percy and Jill had draped in roses, hibiscus, and ferns. First came Dana, her pear green dress loose to her knees, with narrow satin straps. She wore a cream velvet ribbon around her neck, covering the barbed wire. Her glossy black hair shot straight to the edge of her chin. She carried a bouquet of pale green roses with tiny violets tucked among them. Violets symbolize peace. Percy made that choice. Dana looked luminous.

Next down the steps floated Jill. Her fair hair was French braided and twisted into a knot at the nape of her neck. Her dress was the color of sea glass. With a slightly scooped neck and cap sleeves, it fit tightly across her chest and was belted in a slightly darker green satin, one small bow off to one side. Jill carried a bouquet of cream-colored roses, with a single purple hyacinth in the center. The flower that means "I am sorry." She and Percy chose her bouquet after much consideration.

The maid of honor was Angie. She tiptoed down the steps in a pale pink sleeveless shift. Embroidered in tiny green flowers and hemmed with sea green ribbon, it enhanced her slight figure. The makeup artists had excelled—Angie's complexion was flawless. She looked like an angel. She carried a bouquet of dusty pink roses with two white gerbera daisies at the center. Again, Jill and Percy had done their homework. The daisies represented strength.

Everybody chuckled as Suze led the flower girls down. Herkie and Saylor, bathed and spritzed with Chanel No. 5, pranced downstairs at the end of bright pink flowered leashes, the roses around their necks not fated to last longer than a few more minutes. The big surprise was the tiny puppy in Suze's free arm: Sabine, a single white daisy affixed somehow to the top of her head. She squirmed like crazy.

Rob cleared his throat nervously as he waited at the foot of the stairs. Then the bride appeared. She was such a vision that Rob's knees gave out, but luckily Percy took hold of Rob's arm in the nick of time, steadying him.

Esme seemed to defy gravity and merely floated down the stairs, her veil like mist around her face. She carried a lush bouquet of white roses, ferns, and lily of the valley. Placed at the center of her bouquet, so subtle as to be almost invisible, was a single dandelion—the symbol for overcoming hardship. Jill and Percy had outdone themselves.

The wedding ceremony was brief. Rob and Esme wrote their own vows, promising simply to love, support, and defend. They exchanged platinum bands; Esme's containing a myriad of tiny diamonds. Rob, against instructions, kissed the bride four times. Mom cried. Percy cried. Suze and I almost cried.

It was the perfect wedding. The guests filtered out, to return later for the reception. Rob and Es had invited all of their friends to the reception. We expected around seventy-five guests. The caterers arrived just in time, and they had begun to set up in the back as soon as the wedding was over.

Suze and I took a break in the kitchen, to sneak a cupcake, which we split. It was one from Costco; we didn't want to eat any of Mom and Angie's creations. Suze licked some frosting off her fingers and sighed with satisfaction. "Wasn't it the most perfect wedding in the world?"

"The epitome of perfection." I swallowed the last crumb. "I think the reception will be so much fun. I am going to dance all night. With Percy."

Π

Ten tables for eight, each with a different centerpiece, all of them in varying degrees of pink, green, and white. The canapés were delicious. I had at least twenty shrimp puffs. Champagne flowed. Percy stood up, his bald pate gleaming proudly, and proposed a toast to "forgiveness, love, family, and friendship." Mom sobbed. Rob and Es fed one another cupcakes, no face smooshing.

The string quartet managed to play not only Vivaldi, but also the Beatles and even a little Coldplay. They were ready for anything; they even took requests. Every single woman took her high heels off and threw them in the corners. There was a tiny dance floor; filled with people. We danced ourselves silly. I was shocked that Percy knew how to do the Macarena, for heaven's sake.

Judy Flood introduced herself to me. I was flabbergasted. I had imagined a tall, raven-haired woman with steely eyes and a fierce smile. Judy Flood was at best five foot two, nearly as wide as she was tall. She had gray hair curled under in a pageboy, bright pink glasses, and bracelets that jangled as she shook my hand. We had a lively conversation in which I decided that Judy Flood was, indeed a genius and a gentlewoman.

At eleven, after a brief hiatus, Rob and Esme reappeared. Rob wore jeans and a blindingly white Ralph Lauren Polo Shirt. Esme wore sequined black leggings, Havaianas, and a vintage orange, purple, and pink Emilio Pucci blouse, which accentuated her narrow hips and flashing eyes. They kissed everyone, drank one more toast, this one to all of us, and left for parts unknown. We showered them with birdseed. Angie said we should forego rice and include the birds in the festivities.

Things wound down after that. We were all tired, and Dana was worried about the puppy in the crate next door. House training was touch and go so far. As the caterers packed up, the band put away their instruments, and we all sat, watching, Dee Dee Bolton picked up her champagne glass and headed in our direction.

She pulled up an empty chair and sat beside Percy. She held up her glass, and looked expectantly at the rest of us. Oh. So we raised our glasses as well.

"I would like to propose a toast." She hesitated, lowering her glass to her lap. She dropped her eyes for a moment. She raised her head, eyes glistening, and held up her glass once more. "I want to thank you for what you all have done. This summer was a learning experience for me. I have watched my daughter learn an important lesson, and she has taught me a lesson, too." A tear rolled down her cheek, along with a trail of mascara. She swiped her face with her free hand and continued.

"We are both so very, very sorry, and I wish that we could take back what we did to Angela and her family. But we can't. Jill, come over here." Dee Dee stood and motioned for Jill.

Jill came to stand beside her mother. They clasped hands.

"So. I would like to propose a toast to the bride, the groom, Angie Baker and her family, and all of you good people. Thank you."

It was the perfect ending to a perfect day.

Chapter Thirty-Eight

ת

We all slept in. I awoke at ten the next morning, my head throbbing. I cursed myself for drinking so much champagne. I bumped into Suze in the bathroom, rooting around in the medicine cabinet for aspirin. "I think you can take four of these without damaging your liver or anything," Suze said, as she shook them out into our palms. She handed me a paper cup out of the dispenser, turned on the tap, and we filled them. "I would like to propose a toast to my very best friend and fellow hermit, Thomasina Carruthers. May you now go outside and prosper." We tapped cups and nearly choked on the pills.

I put on a pair of bike shorts, sandals and a Maroon 5 T-shirt and wandered downstairs. Mom was already frying bacon and buttering toast. She looked none the worse for the wear in an orange sundress and Keds.

"Sit down, honey. You look like something the cat dragged in. Or the dog, I should say. Here, have some coffee. Do you want some eggs with your bacon?"

I held up a hand. "No, no. Just a piece of toast. I am waiting for the aspirin to kick in."

I slurped my coffee as Suze arrived, followed by Saylor and Herk. She opened the back door and they cantered out happily. "Oh, Meg. I need coffee infused directly into my veins. What time does the rental company come to clean up?"

We sat; comparing notes about the day before, marveling at the beauty of the bride, the gorgeousness of the decorations, and the wonder that was Percy's bald head. Suze managed to choke down four pieces of bacon and a fried egg. I managed one piece of toast with a scraping of marmalade.

Suze and I prepared to spend a lazy day, perhaps taking long baths and watching *Friends* reruns before cleaning all the litter from the night before out of the yard, but Mom seemed in a big hurry for us to finish breakfast and get out of her way.

"What is going on, Mom?"

She looked at us as if we had suddenly grown horns. "It's August 28! For heaven's sakes, girls! I am going OUT!"

We followed her as she sped into the hall, fiddled with her hair in the mirror, and picked up one of the centerpieces left over from the reception. She smiled at herself in the mirror while holding the flowers next to her face. Then she flung the front door wide open and stepped out into the sunshine.

We watched my mother turn her face up to the sky briefly, then walk purposely down the walk, taking a sharp right and heading down the block.

I shouted, "Where on earth are you going?"

Mom, already at the end of the block, turned and held the pot of flowers in the air over her head. "TO MARJORY'S HOUSE! SHE'S A SHUT-IN, YOU KNOW!"

I turned back toward the house, but Suze seized me by the arm. "Tommy. You are liberated today, too. Have you forgotten? Your year of isolation is officially over."

She clipped the leash on Herkie, handed it to me, and pushed me out the front door. I stood blinking in the brightness, watching Mom as she made her way toward Marjory Steiner's house. Before she turned the corner, she pivoted and waved at us. "WISH ME LUCK!"

I blew her a kiss. The leash was cool in my hand. Herkie and I hesitated, letting the sun wash over us like a benediction. Then we stepped out together, my dog and I, to walk away from the past and toward our future.

The End

Acknowledgements

Writing a novel is never easy. I want to thank my mentor and spectacular editor, Lou Aronica, for all the help and kind encouragement. Without you, Lou, I would just be a woman, sitting at home, wondering what to do with myself. You made me an author.

Good grief. Trudy Krisher, William Franz, Hazel Dawkins, Dennis Fairchild, Jane and Dave Reeder, Suzanne Kelly-Garrison, David Lee Garrison, Sheryl Kammer, Bryan Sander, Lisa Rosenberg, Ann Imig and Creative Alliance, Alexandra Rosas, Suzy Soro, Amy Sherman, the Erma Bombeck Writer's Workshop. Early encouragers and cheerleaders. Thank you.

All of the book groups and fellow writers on social media are worth millions. To Andrea Katz and Great Thoughts, Kristy Barrett and A Novel Bee, Barbara Khan, The Back Booth, Reader's Coffeehouse, Catherine Ryan-Hyde, Craig Lancaster, and on and on. You are my friends always.

Paul Waller, Oakwood High School Principal, who advised me about all things bullying: thank you. You have a tough job!

Vanessa Lowe and the brilliant podcast Nocturne, which served as an inspiration for the night world in the book—thank you!

To all of the readers of my blog, who started with me and have stayed with me for all these years, it is such a compliment to me that you read my weekly columns.

To Dayton, to fictional Framington, and to Ohio: it is the best place to live and write.

My husband, Charlie, who listens to me drone on about plot lines and my crazy ideas: thank you for everything.

My children. My grandchildren. Suze, the pit bull.

For every author of every book. I admire you, I learn from you, and I thank you.

About the Author

Π

Molly D. Campbell is a two-time Erma Bombeck Writing Award winner and the author of two previous novels, *Keep the Ends Loose* and *Crossing the Street.* Molly blogs at http://mollydcampbell.com. Also an artist, Molly's work can be found at http://www.cafepress.com/notexactlypicasso. She lives in Dayton with her accordionist husband and four cats.